· THE OXFORD SHERLOCK HOLMES ·

General Editor
Owen Dudley Edwards

The Return of
Sherlock Holmes

ARTHUR CONAN DOYLE

The Return of Sherlock Holmes

Edited with an Introduction by
Richard Lancelyn Green

Oxford   New York

OXFORD UNIVERSITY PRESS

1993

Oxford University Press, Walton Street, Oxford OX2 6DP

Oxford New York Toronto
Delhi Bombay Calcutta Madras Karachi
Kuala Lumpur Singapore Hong Kong Tokyo
Nairobi Dar es Salaam Cape Town
Melbourne Auckland Madrid

and associated companies in
Berlin Ibadan

Oxford is a trade mark of Oxford University Press

British Library Cataloguing in Publication Data
Data available

Library of Congress Cataloging in Publication Data
Data available

ISBN 0-19-212317-3
ISBN 0-19-212329-7 (set)

1 3 5 7 9 10 8 6 4 2

Typeset by Pure Tech Corporation, Pondicherry, India
Printed in Great Britain
on acid-free paper by
BPCC Paperbacks Ltd
Aylesbury, Bucks

CONTENTS

THE RETURN OF
SHERLOCK HOLMES

ACKNOWLEDGEMENTS

G RATEFUL thanks and acknowledgements are due for permission to examine and quote from the original MSS in: the Rosenbach Museum and Library, Philadelphia; the Berg Collection, New York Public Library; the Huntington Library and Art Gallery, San Marino, Calif.; the Houghton Library, Harvard University; the British Library; the Harry Ransom Research Center, University of Texas; the Fondation Martin Bodmer (Bibliotheca Bodmeriana) at Cologny-Geneva; the Treasure Room MSS Collection, The Library, Haverford College, Penn.

They are also due for permission to quote from letters and MSS to: HM the Queen; the Arthur Conan Doyle Collection, Metropolitan Toronto Library; the Lilly Library, Bloomington, Ind.; and the Arthur Conan Doyle Foundation, Lausanne.

Particular thanks are due to Cathy Henderson, Research Librarian at the Harry Ransom Humanities Research Center; Sara S. Hodson, Curator of Literary MSS, Huntington Library; Francis O. Mattson, the Curator, and Philip Milito, Technical Assistant, Berg Collection; Leslie A. Morris, Curator of Books and MSS, Rosenbach Museum and Library; and also to Cameron Hollyer, former Curator of the Arthur Conan Doyle Collection in the Metropolitan Toronto Library, and to William S. Cagle of the Lilly Library.

I am personally indebted to Norman S. Nolan, of Middletown, New Jersey (owner of the MS of 'Black Peter'); to James D. Pepper, of Santa Barbara, Calif. (owner of the final part of 'The Solitary Cyclist' MS); to Steven Rothman, of Philadelphia; and to Markus Geisser, of Arbon, Switzerland.

RLG

GENERAL EDITOR'S PREFACE
TO THE SERIES

ARTHUR CONAN DOYLE told his *Strand* editor, Herbert Greenhough Smith (1855–1935), that 'A story always comes to me as an organic thing and I never can recast it without the Life going out of it.'[1]

On the whole, this certainly seems to describe Conan Doyle's method with the Sherlock Holmes stories, long and short. Such manuscript evidence as survives (approximately half the stories) generally bears this out: there is remarkably little revision. Sketches or scenarios are another matter. Conan Doyle was no more bound by these at the end of his literary life than at the beginning, whence scraps of paper survive to tell us of 221B Upper Baker Street where lived Ormond Sacker and J. Sherrinford Holmes. But very little such evidence is currently available for analysis.

Conan Doyle's relationship with his most famous creation was far from the silly label 'The Man Who Hated Sherlock Holmes': equally, there was no indulgence in it. Though the somewhat too liberal Puritan Micah Clarke was perhaps dearer to him than Holmes, Micah proved unable to sustain a sequel to the eponymous novel of 1889. By contrast, 'Sherlock' (as his creator irreverently alluded to him when not creating him) proved his capacity for renewal 59 times (which Conan Doyle called 'a striking example of the patience and loyalty of the British public'). He dropped Holmes in 1893, apparently into the Reichenbach Falls, as a matter of literary integrity: he did not intend to be written off as 'the Holmes man'. But public clamour turned Holmes into an economic asset that could not be ignored. Even so, Conan Doyle could not have continued to write about

---

[1] Undated letter, quoted by Cameron Hollyer, 'Author to Editor', *ACD— The Journal of the Arthur Conan Doyle Society*, 3 (1992), 19–20. Conan Doyle's remark was probably *à propos* 'The Red Circle' (*His Last Bow*).

Holmes without taking some pleasure in the activity, or indeed without becoming quietly proud of him.

Such Sherlock Holmes manuscripts as survive are frequently in private keeping, and very few have remained in Britain. In this series we have made the most of two recent facsimiles, of 'The Dying Detective' and 'The Lion's Mane'. In general, manuscript evidence shows Conan Doyle consistently underpunctuating, and to show the implications of this 'The Dying Detective' (*His Last Bow*) has been printed from the manuscript. 'The Lion's Mane', however, offers the one case known to us of drastic alterations in the surviving manuscript, from which it is clear from deletions that the story was entirely altered, and Holmes's role transformed, in the process of its creation.

Given Conan Doyle's general lack of close supervision of the Holmes texts, it is not always easy to determine his final wishes. In one case, it is clear that 'His Last Bow', as a deliberate contribution to war propaganda, underwent a ruthless revision at proof stage—although (as we note for the first time) this was carried out on the magazine text and lost when published in book form. But nothing comparable exists elsewhere.

In general, American texts of the stories are closer to the magazine texts than British book texts. Textual discrepancies, in many instances, may simply result from the conflicts of sub-editors. Undoubtedly, Conan Doyle did some re-reading, especially when returning to Holmes after an absence; but on the whole he showed little interest in the constitution of his texts. In his correspondence with editors he seldom alluded to proofs, discouraged ideas for revision, and raised few—if any—objections to editorial changes. For instance, we know that the *Strand*'s preference for 'Halloa' was not Conan Doyle's original usage, and in this case we have restored the original orthography. On the other hand, we also know that the *Strand* texts consistently eliminated anything (mostly expletives) of an apparently blasphemous character, but in the absence of manuscript confirmation we have normally been unable to restore what were probably stronger original versions. (In any case, it is perfectly possible that Conan Doyle, the consummate professional, may have come to exercise self-censorship in the certain knowledge that editorial changes would be imposed.)

Throughout the series we have corrected any obvious errors, though these are comparatively few: the instances are at all times noted. (For a medical man, Conan Doyle's handwriting was commendably legible, though his 'o' could look like an 'a'.) Regarding the order of individual stories, internal evidence makes it clear that 'A Case of Identity' (*Adventures*) was written before 'The Red-Headed League' and was intended to be so printed; but the 'League' was the stronger story and the *Strand*, in its own infancy, may have wanted the Holmes stories established as quickly as possible (at this point the future of both the Holmes series and the magazine was uncertain). Surviving letters show that the composition of 'The Solitary Cyclist' (*Return*) preceded that of 'The Dancing Men' (with the exception of the former's first paragraph, which was rewritten later); consequently, the order of these stories has been reversed. Similarly, the stories in *His Last Bow* and *The Case-Book of Sherlock Holmes* have been rearranged in their original order of publication, which—as far as is known—reflects the order of composition. The intention has been to allow readers to follow the fictional evolution of Sherlock Holmes over the forty years of his existence.

The one exception to this principle will be found in *His Last Bow*, where the final and eponymous story was actually written and published after *The Valley of Fear*, which takes its place in the Holmes canon directly after the magazine publication of the other stories in *His Last Bow*; but the removal of the title story to the beginning of the *Case-Book* would have been too radically pedantic and would have made *His Last Bow* ludicrously short. Readers will note that we have already reduced the extent of *His Last Bow* by returning 'The Cardboard Box' to its original location in the *Memoirs of Sherlock Holmes* (after 'Silver Blaze' and before 'The Yellow Face'). The removal of 'The Cardboard Box' from the original sequence led to the inclusion of its introductory passage in 'The Resident Patient': this, too, has been returned to its original position and the proper opening of 'The Resident Patient' restored. Generally, texts have been derived from first book publication collated with magazine texts and, where possible, manuscripts; in the case of 'The Cardboard Box' and 'The Resident Patient', however, we have employed the *Strand* texts, partly because of the restoration of the latter's opening, partly to give readers a flavour of the magazine in which the Holmes stories made their first, vital conquests.

In all textual decisions the overriding desire has been to meet the author's wishes, so far as these can be legitimately ascertained from documentary evidence or application of the rule of reason.

One final plea. If you come to these stories for the first time, proceed now to the texts themselves, putting the introductions and explanatory notes temporarily aside. Our introductions are not meant to introduce: Dr Watson will perform that duty, and no one could do it better. Then, when you have mastered the stories, and they have mastered you, come back to us.

OWEN DUDLEY EDWARDS

University of Edinburgh

INTRODUCTION

I

'THE news of the death of Sherlock Holmes has been received with most widespread regret, and readers have implored us to use our influence with Mr Conan Doyle to prevent the tragedy being consummated', said *Tit-Bits* on 6 January 1894 when replying to 'G. and Very Many Others' in its 'Answers to Correspondents'. 'We can only reply that we pleaded for his life in the most urgent, earnest, and constant manner. Like hundreds of correspondents, we feel as if we had lost an old friend whom we could ill spare. Mr Doyle's feeling was that he did not desire Sherlock to outstay his welcome, and that the public had had enough of him. This is not our opinion, nor is it the opinion of the public; but it is, we regret to say, Mr Doyle's.'

'The Death of Sherlock Holmes' was the title which appeared under the frontispiece for 'The Final Problem' and was used in the announcements for the 1893 Christmas Number of the *Strand Magazine*. It appeared to confirm that Sherlock Holmes was dead. George Newnes (1851–1910), addressing his shareholders, spoke of the 'dreadful event' and the *Sketch* referred to Holmes's 'Tragic Death' (20 December 1893), but others felt there was still hope that he might be found alive. 'There is no proof positive given by any eye witness whose veracity is unimpeachable of the death of the great amateur detective', said *Punch* (30 December 1893). 'His many admirers will cling to the last to the hope that he may be found alive', said *Harper's Weekly* (16 December 1893).

Conan Doyle was at first adamant. 'I hold that it was not murder,' he said in a speech to the Authors' Club on Monday, 29 June 1896, 'but justifiable homicide in self defence, since, if I had not killed him, he would certainly have killed me. For a man who has no particular astuteness to spend his days in inventing problems and building up

xi

chains of inductive reasoning is a trying occupation. Besides it is better not to rely too much upon the patience of the public, and when one has written twenty-six stories about one man one feels that it is time to put it out of one's power to transgress any further' (*Queen*, 4 July 1896). And to David Christie Murray (1847–1907) he said: 'Poor Holmes is dead and damned, I couldn't revive him if I would (at least not for years), for I have had such an overdose of him that I feel towards him as I do towards *pâté de foie gras*, of which I once ate too much, so that the name of it gives me a sickly feeling to this day' (David Christie Murray, *Recollections*, 1908; letter dated 8 May 1896). He even claimed in an interview in 1904 that it 'was merely by accident that I didn't chronicle the finding of his body' (*Daily Mail*, 8 October 1904).

The possibility of a revival was never entirely ruled out, and the publisher using *Tit-Bits* as a mouthpiece stated that Doyle had promised that he would 'at some future date, if opportunity may occur, give us the offer of some posthumous histories of the great detective' (6 January 1894). And when he was in the United States in December 1894 Doyle admitted that though 'Holmes was probably dead' he 'might escape, and be revived' (*New York Daily Tribune*, 13 November 1894).

The first sign of a weakening in his resolve came in 1896 when he wrote 'The Field Bazaar', a short pastiche about Sherlock Holmes, which appeared in the Bazaar Number of the Edinburgh *Student* (20 November 1896). Then at the end of 1897 there was a flutter of interest when it was revealed that he had written a play about Sherlock Holmes in which Herbert Beerbohm Tree (1852–1917) had expressed an interest. Unfortunately the actor wished to make a number of changes. 'I have grave doubts about Holmes on the stage at all—it's drawing attention to my weaker work which has unduly obscured my better,' Doyle told his mother: 'but rather than re-write it on the lines which would make a different Holmes from my Holmes, I would without the slightest pang put it back in the drawer from which it emerged' (Adrian M. Conan Doyle, *The Sherlock Holmes*

Exhibition, Catalogue, 1952). But it was retrieved a year later when William Gillette (1853–1937) came forward as the ideal person to reshape the drama and to impersonate the great detective. Doyle allowed him a free hand, and in 1899 Sherlock Holmes reached the stage.

Doyle's reference to the Sherlock Holmes stories as his 'weaker work' was not the view of Herbert Greenhough Smith (1855–1935), the editor of the *Strand Magazine*, who felt they had qualities which set them apart from all Doyle's other work. If he could not have new stories, he at least hoped to bridge the gap and find a way of repeating their success. Early in 1898 it seemed a possibility when Doyle announced he was at work on a series of stories dealing with crime and mystery. However, he quickly disabused Smith of the idea that they would be Sherlock Holmes stories under another name: ' "Detective Stories" would not fairly characterise them, and I want to give myself a very free hand so that in case any tap runs dry I can turn on another. I should therefore not say anything about Detectives or Holmes in the announcement. To say however that they deal in mystery and adventure would be true, also that they are concerned with the weird and the terrible' (Metropolitan Toronto Library, MSS). Two of the stories in the 'Round the Fire' series printed letters supposedly from the newspapers, one by 'a well-known criminal investigator' ('The Man with the Watches', *Strand*, July 1898), and the other by 'an amateur reasoner of some celebrity' ('The Lost Special', *Strand*, August 1898), and these have since been claimed (by Christopher Morley, *Saturday Review* (New York), 3 March 1934) as 'apocryphal' Sherlock Holmes stories. It may be that the stories were a joke at Holmes's expense, but the theories put forward by the unnamed investigators proved incorrect and the style is only intermittently Holmesian.

Greenhough Smith made a further attempt to turn Doyle's attention back to crime in 1900 when he proposed a series of 'Strange Studies from Life', but the result was far from satisfactory. After three of the twelve had been written, he called a halt and did no more.

The 'inevitable relapse after repentance', as Doyle called it in 1901 in the preface to *The Adventures of Sherlock Holmes* in the Author's Edition, came in March 1901 when Bertram Fletcher Robinson (1872–1907) stimulated him with a plot for *The Hound of the Baskervilles*. Holmes did not return from the dead, but he was revived and the quality of the work and excellence of the plot disarmed criticism. Those who had feared that Holmes would be spoiled were proved wrong, and the way was clear for the corpse to be disinterred.

II

Doyle's attitude towards his detective and towards detective stories in general was given in an interview for the thousandth number of *Tit-Bits* ('Conan Doyle Tells the True Story of Sherlock Holmes', 15 December 1900) and in the preface to the Author's Edition. In the latter he referred to detective stories as an 'elementary' form of fiction cast in a 'primitive and conventional form', and yet said that it was work of which he was not ashamed. 'My own feeling upon the subject is that all forms of literature, however humble, are legitimate if the writer is satisfied that he has done them to the highest of his power.'

He acknowledged a debt to Edgar Allan Poe (1809–49), whom he called the 'father of the detective tale'. Poe had 'covered its limits so completely,' he said, 'that I fail to see how his followers can find any fresh ground which they can confidently call their own. For the secret of the thinness and also of the intensity of the detective story is, that the writer is left with only one quality, that of intellectual acuteness, with which to endow his hero. Everything else is outside the picture and weakens the effect. The problem and its solution must form the theme, and the character-drawing be limited and subordinate. On this narrow path the writer must walk, and he sees the footmarks of Poe always in front of him. He is happy if he ever finds the means of breaking away and striking out on some little side-track of his own.'

The extent of the debt had long been recognized. In 'The Evolution of Sherlock Holmes', written in 1897, Robert

Blatchford (1851–1943) compared Doyle with Poe (and with Gaboriau (1832–73)). 'We have in Doyle the same detective, the same friend, the same police that we have in Poe and Gaboriau . . . There is nothing new in his theory of induction. It is simply Dupin watered down to popular strength. So far as I can ascertain there is not one idea in the philosophy of Sherlock Holmes, or Lecoq, that has not been directly taken from Poe . . . My point is that the character, the theories, the position, and the methods, always; and the incidents and phrases often, which have made Sherlock Holmes a household word, are taken directly from from Dupin and Lecoq' (*Clarion*, 24 July 1897). Blatchford overstated his case, but there are direct echoes and Doyle realized that his work was at times 'unconsciously imitative'. In justification, he pointed out that it was not to be expected 'that a man's style and mode of treatment should spring fully formed from his own brain' (preface, Author's Edition).

Doyle's assessment of his work may be challenged on two counts. The first is his assumption that Sherlock Holmes is typical of other detectives. 'There is no great originality required in devising or constructing such a man,' he said, 'and the only possible originality which one can get into a story about a detective is in giving him original plots and problems to solve, as in his equipment there must be of necessity an alert acuteness of mind to grasp facts and the relation which each of them bears to the other' (*Tit-Bits*, 15 December 1900). This is fair of detectives in general and it is true that Holmes is the direct heir of Dupin, but Doyle's achievement was to place the detective at the centre of the story and to make the character more interesting than the plot. The stories are about a great detective, rather than being great detective stories. The problem or puzzle is less important than the man who solves it.

The second point, which follows from the first, is that Sherlock Holmes is not, as Doyle sometimes declared, the man of reason, the characterless reasoning machine. Doyle did not mind saying that he should be so—'Holmes is as inhuman as a Babbage's Calculating Machine', he told Joseph Bell (1837–1911) on 16 June 1892, 'and just about as likely to fall in love' (*Uncollected Sherlock Holmes*, 23)—but his quirks and the limits of his knowledge meant that Holmes reaches into the realms of the improbable and sets himself apart from those who are bound by the possible. The stories, as they developed, veered off into a realm of fantasy, and became at times a form of escapist literature—deeply satisfying because of the bravura performance of the central character, who is part showman, part conjuror, part witch-doctor. While Poe seldom wrote in a comic vein, the Sherlock Holmes stories are great comic creations. This was partly intentional and partly unintentional. 'Round the centre of deduction and inference and observation which I have heard you inculcate,' he told Bell, 'I have tried to build up a man who pushed the thing as far as it would go—further occasionally' (4 May 1892; *Uncollected Sherlock Holmes*, 18–19). Much of what Doyle wrote and many of the observations seemed valid to him, so the reader becomes a willing accomplice of Dr Watson and the occasional absurdity or improbability becomes apparent only after s/he has accepted the basic premiss.

The defensive tone which Doyle adopted when speaking of the Sherlock Holmes stories as his 'weaker work' may strike a modern reader as odd, but this was because of the low standing of the genre at the time the stories were written. Poe was the exception, as his stories had eminent followers, but the sensational novels of Gaboriau stood at the head of a mass of 'penny dreadfuls' and 'shilling shockers' which, in the eyes of some arbiters of public taste, pandered to the worst instincts and at times seemed to encourage immorality. Thus Doyle went out of his way to stress the lack of crime. 'In dealing with criminal subjects,' he said, 'one's natural endeavour is to keep crime in the background. In nearly half the number of the Sherlock Holmes stories, however, in a strictly legal sense no crime was actually committed at all. One heard a good deal about crime and the criminal, but the reader was completely

bluffed. Of course, I could not bluff him always, so sometimes I had to give him a crime, and occasionally I had to
make it a downright bad one' (*Tit-Bits*, 15 December 1900).
Or as he put it on another occasion: 'One strong objection
to the detective story has always been that it must deal with
crime, and that the idea of crime is not a wholesome one
for the young. It must be admitted that there is some force
in this contention. If no crime were ever committed in these
stories the reader might feel that he was the victim of a
practical joke, but it is a fact (never observed, as far as I
remember, by any critic), that in a considerable number of
these stories the effect is produced by the anticipation of
what might have been, not of what is, and that there has
actually been no grave legal crime whatever' (preface,
Author's Edition).

III

The success of *The Hound of the Baskervilles* achieved a double
purpose. It brought Holmes back before the public without
the author having to explain away the presumed death and
it proved that the skills of the great detective had not
diminished. *The Return of Sherlock Holmes* now appears as an
inevitable consequence of that reappearance. Editors on
both sides of the Atlantic had in the past used all the means
at their disposal to encourage Doyle to revive the detective,
but he had refused. Now in 1903, he had the confidence to
continue and the desire to do so, and at no other time would
the financial rewards have been greater. It was Colliers of
New York, the publishers of what became the *National
Weekly*, who tipped the scale with a generous proposal which
reached Doyle via his literary agent in the early spring.
They offered $4,000 per story (or as much as $9,000 if some
of the newspapers who got wind of the offer are to be
believed)—and this irrespective of length. The number of
stories was at first left open. It was to be no less than six,
preferably eight (to make up a volume), and ideally twelve.
They also hoped, but did not insist, that some of the stories
would have American settings or be of relevance to the

USA. The offer was accepted and a contract for eight stories was drawn up (with an option on twelve).

Several people expressed their fear that the new stories could not match the earlier ones, and one of those who did so was Doyle's mother. But having set to work, he told her: 'I don't think you need to have any fears about Sherlock. I am not conscious of any failing powers, and my work is not less conscientious than of old . . . I have done no short Sherlock Holmes stories for seven or eight years and I don't see why I should not have another go at them. I might add that I have finished the first one, "The Adventure of the Empty House". The plot, by the way, was given to me by Jean; and it is a rare good one. You will find that Holmes was never dead, and that he is now very much alive' (Adrian M. Conan Doyle, *The Sherlock Holmes Exhibition*, Catalogue, 1952).

Had the body of Sherlock Holmes been lifted from the bottom of the Reichenbach Falls at the end of 'The Final Problem', or had Watson watched in horror as the great detective and his arch-enemy fell to their death, the problem of Holmes's resurrection would have required greater ingenuity than it did. But as Doyle said later, 'no coroner had pronounced upon the remains, and so, after a long interval, it was not difficult for me to . . . explain my rash act away' ('Mr Sherlock Holmes to his Readers', *Strand*, March 1927). Holmes had walked away from the Falls, leaving Watson to grieve and Mrs Hudson to keep up the empty apartments in Baker Street while he disported himself in the remotest corners of the earth.

The 'rare good' plot consisted of the lightly sketched murder of Ronald Adair, the dramatic reappearance of Holmes, the explanation of his absence, the attempt upon his life, and the capture of the assassin. The 'Jean' to whom Doyle referred in his letter was Jean Leckie, whom he had met in 1897 and with whom he had fallen in love. Doyle had turned back to 'The Final Problem' (*Memoirs*) in which there was a reference to 'air guns' and was also perhaps influenced by the way in which Raffles had been brought back from the dead.

Watching closely as the stories were written was the editor of the *Strand Magazine* who felt protective towards the character. Doyle's replies suggest that Smith was open in his criticism of the second and third stories. He may have felt that the character had changed (which was the opinion of some of the reviewers: 'He has grown a little careless', said the *Athenaeum* on 1 April 1905, 'his methods have become a little offhand'.) 'The Empty House' had admirably achieved its purpose, but the two which followed used the dramatic set piece in place of the reasoning which had been the hall-mark of the earlier stories.

Doyle admitted (in a letter dated 14 May 1903) that there were weaknesses in 'The Solitary Cyclist'. 'I did not like it so well nor was I satisfied with it, and yet I could make no more of it. It has points but as a whole is not up to the mark' (Metropolitan Toronto Library, MSS). But he refused to accept the strictures directed against 'The Norwood Builder' and said he would place it in the 'very first rank of the whole series for subtlety and depth. Any feeling of disappointment at the end is due to the fact that no crime has been done & so the reader feels bluffed, but it is well for other reasons to have some of the stories crimeless. Take the series of points, Holmes' deductions from the will written in the train, the point of the bloody thumb mark, Holmes' device for frightening the man out of his hiding place &c. I know no Holmes story which has such a succession of bright points.' He ended by saying:

You will appreciate more fully now my intense disinclination to continue these stories which has caused me to resist all entreaty for so many years. It is *impossible* to prevent a certain sameness & want of freshness. The most one can do is to try to produce such stories that if they had come first and the others second, they would then have seemed fresh and good. That I hope to do and I don't think we are much off the rails up to now. Anyhow I'll do my best and no man can do more. The Americans have been asking me to make the series 12, but in view of your letter I will keep it to 8.

The letter was sent from the Hill House Hotel, Happisburgh (in Norfolk), where he was staying while visiting his brother-in-law E. W. Hornung, who had a country cottage at East Ruston. It was while there that he came across the 'dancing men' which provided the idea for the fourth story, and this would mark the half-way point if the series were kept to eight. 'I have got three bull's eyes and an outer', he told his mother. But finding suitable plots remained the greatest challenge. 'The writing is easy,' he told her. 'It is the plots which butcher me; I must talk over the plot with somebody' (Carr, n.d. [May 1903], 202).

There were two people to whom he could turn. One was his brother-in-law E. W. Hornung (1866–1921), who had published two series of stories about Raffles. The first, *The Amateur Cracksman* (1899), was dedicated 'To A.C.D. This form of flattery'. 'I think,' Doyle wrote in his autobigraphy, 'I may claim that his famous character Raffles was a kind of inversion of Sherlock Holmes, Bunny playing Watson. He admits as much in his kindly dedication' (*Memories and Adventures* (1924), 259). But in 1903 the roles were to be reversed. Doyle studied the Raffles stories carefully, talked over his plots with Hornung, and profited by the exchange of ideas. The method of Holmes's return was one example. The plot for 'The Six Napoleons' is another. It has a counterpart in 'The Gift of the Emperor' where Raffles conceals a pearl in a bullet. Or again there are the bicycles in 'The Priory School' which recall 'The Wrong House', and in 'Charles Augustus Milverton' Holmes and Watson act in a way which resembles Raffles and Bunny.

The second person with whom Doyle discussed the plots— and the most obvious person with whom to do so—was Bertram Fletcher Robinson (1871–1907), who had provided the inspiration for *The Hound of the Baskervilles*. It cannot be entirely a coincidence that Robinson and Doyle both produced a series of detective stories with similar plots and that both *The Return of Sherlock Holmes* and *The Chronicles of Addington Peace* were published in book form in 1905.

Robinson's stories were serialized after those of Doyle ('The Chronicles of Addington Peace' began their serial publication in the *Lady's Home Magazine* in August 1904), and they were probably written later, but it does not preclude the possibility that the ideas were reached jointly and that each developed them in his own way. There is no similarity between the Holmes stories and those of Martin Hewitt by Arthur Morrison, yet there are numerous parallels between Doyle and Robinson, for example between 'Black Peter' and 'The Mystery of the Jade Spear' (where a man is skewered by a spear driven in with tremendous force), or between 'The Golden Pince-Nez' and 'The Vanished Millionaire' (where a man is secreted in a priest hole and identified by spreading flour on the floor).

The close relationships between Doyle and Hornung, and Doyle and Robinson, constitute a virtual 'group', and one thing they had in common was cricket. It was of great importance to Hornung, but was also Doyle's main recreation during this period when he played regularly for the Marylebone Cricket Club (MCC), with twenty-six days devoted to it between May and August 1903. Cricketers provided names used in the stories, and the cricket pavilion was the place where he could meet and exchange ideas with fellow-authors. Doyle's youngest sister, 'Dodo' (Bryan Mary Julia Josephine Angell, 1877–1927), could also be included in the group. Her book *The Episodes of Marge*, which she published with her brother's assistance, under the pseudonym 'H. Ripley Cromarsh', appeared in July 1903. 'The episodes, though strung together so as to make a story, stand by themselves', said the Baron de Book-Worms (Sir F. C. Burnand (1836–1917)) in a review in *Punch* on 29 July 1903: 'They suggest to my Baronite a sort of reversal of the adventures of Sherlock Holmes. He saw crime from the outside and, with unfailing success, pursued the criminal. Marge, from the inside, shows how these things are done.' P. G. Wodehouse (1881–1975) also played in the Authors' teams with Doyle and Hornung; he collaborated with Robinson on 'The Progressive's Progress' in the *World* for 1 January 1907; he interviewed Doyle in the summer of 1903 for a magazine called *V. C.* (when Doyle's sporting prowess was the subject); he wrote two Sherlockian parodies inspired

by the publicity for *The Return of Sherlock Holmes*: 'The
Prodigal' in *Punch* on 23 September 1903, and 'The Adven-
ture of the Missing Bee' in *Vanity Fair* (a magazine edited by
Fletcher Robinson) on 1 December 1904; and in Jeeves and
Wooster he created comic characters who are in the same
tradition as Holmes and Watson.

The parody which Wodehouse wrote for *Punch* was inspired by the report 'that Sherlock Holmes, when he re-
appears will figure in a series of stories of American origin'.
News of this had been printed in the USA and was then
picked up by the English papers, and it was more than a
rumour. Doyle had been asked by Collier's to use American
settings and had considered the possibility of spending some
time in the USA. A report from a correspondent for the *New
York Daily Tribune*, from Montauk, Long Island, on 6 June
1903, said:

A letter received here from London from Dr A. Conan Doyle
states that the creator of Sherlock Holmes is about to sail for this
country and will spend the summer at this place. The author has
contracted to bring the detective back to life, and he is coming to
Montauk to do it, principally because in some of the new stories,
Holmes's skill is to be employed in solving mysteries of American
origin, the sand dunes and moors of Montauk furnishing the local
colour. The stories are to appear in *Collier's Weekly* at an early date,
but the author's 'copy' is far from ready.

That he may have absolute seclusion while writing, Dr Doyle
will lease an entire hotel; that is to say, the only house available
for his exclusive use is the historical Third House, an inn used in
winter as a shooting box by New York sportsmen, but closed in
summer.

The letter was an enquiry, and not an absolute statement
of intent, and nothing came of it, other than an unexpected
and flattering response from the White House in Washington, DC. The acting secretary to the President (Theodore
Roosevelt) wrote to S. S. McClure on 27 July 1903 saying:
'The President has heard that Sir Conan Doyle will soon be
in this country, and wishes me to ask if you know when he

will be here and where he can be reached after his arrival.
If you can furnish this information it will be very much
appreciated' (Lausanne: Arthur Conan Doyle Foundation
MSS).

By September 1903 the eighth story had been written, and
the magazines were on the point of beginning the serial
publication. *Collier's Weekly* announced the series on 19
September 1903:

SHERLOCK HOLMES RETURNS!

In next week's issue of *Collier's*, the Household Number for
October, will begin the most notable series of short stories of the
year,—'The Return of Sherlock Holmes,' by Sir A. Conan Doyle.
Those familiar with the previous adventures of the famous detective—and are there any who are not?—will remember that the last
heard of Mr Holmes was the report that he had been hurled
headlong over a precipitous cliff. It was not believed that any
man—either in fact or fiction—could survive such a shock as this,
and even the detective's best friends (even those who most realised
the very good reasons Holmes might have for wishing himself to
be considered dead) began to give up hope of ever again hearing
of his wonderful genius or of witnessing its almost infallible
operation. But Holmes did not die. He survived the deadly peril
through which he passed, and of this and of the ensuing adventures
Sir Conan Doyle tells us in the remarkable series which he has
called 'The Return of Sherlock Holmes.'

The *Strand* also publicized the series with handbills,
printed advertisements, and an announcement on the last
page of the September 1903 issue:

THE RETURN OF SHERLOCK HOLMES

The Readers of the *Strand Magazine* have a vivid recollection of the
time when Sherlock Holmes made his first appearance before the
public, and of the Adventures which made his name a household
word in every quarter of the world. The news of his death was
received with regret as at the loss of a personal friend. Fortunately,
that news, though based on circumstantial evidence which at the
time seemed conclusive, turns out to be erroneous. How he
escaped from his struggle with Moriarty at the Reichenbach Falls,

why he remained in hiding even from his friend Watson, how he made his re-appearance, and the manner he signalled his return by one of the most remarkable of his exploits will be found narrated in the first story of the New Series, beginning in the October number.

At that time it was still not clear whether Doyle intended to continue the series and Collier's were resigned to having a series of eight. 'There are to be eight of them,' announced an editorial 'A Few Words from the Lion's Mouth' on 26 September 1903, and they were able to name the first six: 'The names of the last two stories of the series we are at present unable to state.' Their newspaper advertisements also spoke of eight stories. 'Sherlock Holmes is still alive. He makes his reappearance in this week's (Household) number of Collier's', said the advertisement in the *Philadelphia Inquirer* on 24 September 1903: 'Conan Doyle at last reveals the secret of the famous detective's escape from apparently certain death in the Alps. He has given us in the "Return of Sherlock Holmes" a new series of mysterious adventures. The first story is called "The Adventure of the Empty House," and will be followed by seven others, one in each Household Number of Collier's.'

One of the first to hear of Doyle's future plans was A. S. Watt (the son of A. P. Watt, the literary agent). Writing to his father on 22 September 1903, he said:

Doyle also writes this morning off his own bat re the new 'Sherlock Holmes' stories:—

'I can see no use in hurrying over our decision about further stories. If I give a definite answer by Christmas it leaves them ample time. If I did them I should not promise four, but do one at a time and so lessen the feeling of strain.'

This I take it means that he is certainly going to do the four stories and that he will write to us to that effect within the next two or three months.

This was indeed Doyle's intention. The autumn of 1903 had been set aside for politics, as he had decided to accept the nomination for the Border Burghs constituency and had agreed to give a number of speeches in the towns, but by the new year he again had time on his hands and the remaining four stories were written at monthly intervals. The last, 'The Abbey Grange', was finished on 26 April 1904, and he immediately notified the editor of the *Strand Magazine*: 'Just a line, my dear Smith, to say that the stories are all done—a solid dozen—he ends on his top note, I think. | Requiescat in pace' (University of Virginia Library MSS).

There remained one further story which was independent of the Collier commission and had been promised to Samuel Sidney McClure (1857–1949) with whom Doyle had had a close business relationship since 1891. McClure had acquired the rights for the first of the short Sherlock Holmes stories and syndicated them in the USA. He had then bought other works by Doyle, including *The White Company*, which he sold to the *New York Sun* and the second series of Sherlock Holmes stories which he sold to *Harper's Weekly*. The second series at first consisted of eleven stories, and the last, 'The Final Problem', was an afterthought which McClure retained for use in his own magazine (which he started in June 1893). The association became closer when Doyle visited the USA at the end of 1894 and provided McClure with $5,000 out of the receipts of his lecture tour, and thereafter the link was maintained with McClure syndicating Doyle's novels and stories, and acting as his publisher, as he did for both *The Hound of the Baskervilles* and *The Return of Sherlock Holmes* (for which he also had the second serial rights).

McClure raised the possibility of further stories during a lunch in London on 18 November 1903, and offered $75,000 for a new series of twelve, or $25,000 for 'a novelette of the Sherlock Holmes Type' to run through three or four issues of his magazine. Doyle rejected the first proposal because he felt that he had exhausted the available plots, but he was prepared to write one last story, equivalent to 'The Final Problem', to mark the end of the saga, though he would not be drawn on the length and would not commit himself until he had completed the stories for *Collier's*.

On 20 May 1904 A. P. Watt wrote to McClure reminding him of the offer of a 'single "Sherlock Holmes" story for a special occasion' and telling him that while Doyle would not commit himself until the story was written or mapped out in his mind, he intended to proceed with it. Publication would have to be deferred until January 1905 at the earliest as the contract with Collier's prevented the publication of any new Sherlock Holmes story until their series was complete, and they had made arrangements to hold back the last four stories so as to use them in the October, November, and December issues. Watt's letter continued:

Will you therefore kindly let me know on what date in January or after January next it would be convenient for you to use the story. Sir Arthur informs me that he told you that the price for the American serial rights to the story was £1,000, and I may add that, while in a letter I have just received from him, he tells me he cannot bind himself as to length, he assures me that this will be the very last 'Holmes' story he will do (Lilly Library, Indiana, (S. S. McClure MSS)).

The offer was, however, declined because McClure's partner, John S. Phillips, felt that it would be hard to justify the expense for one short story which would not serve as a 'subscription pulling lever'.

The title of the last adventure was to be 'The Second Stain', which had been mentioned in two of the earlier stories and had particularly intrigued Arthur Bartlett Maurice, the junior editor of the American *Bookman*, who mentioned it to Doyle when they met in the summer of 1903. But however dramatic Doyle made the story, its purpose—which was to send Holmes into retirement—could never arouse the same interest as Holmes's death, and the high price which Doyle and Watt had agreed should be asked acted as a deterrent. Even the *Strand Magazine* had qualms about accepting these terms, and Doyle eventually agreed to have them lowered. In a letter to Greenhough Smith, dated 14 September 1904, he said that buying stories was a form of speculation. 'I could have obtained that price elsewhere, and though I am anxious that my work should appear where it has always appeared it would hardly be fair that I should make actual pecuniary sacrifice for this.' He continued:

On the particular question of this new story, it is a large full-dress story, it is the last, and it is for the Xmas number, all of them points which should add to the value. I am in a difficult position if I interfere after I have once entrusted it to Watt, but I take it that you will not mind my showing him your letter and telling him that I do not desire to make hard terms over this—in view of what has passed.

For *Collier's* the extra story was an unexpected bonus, and it did not matter that they had first announced eight stories, then month after month had informed the readers 'There will be twelve stories in this new Sherlock Holmes series'. When they reached the twelfth, they said: 'The last story of the series, "The Adventure of the Second Stain," and according to the determination of Sir Conan Doyle, the last Sherlock Holmes story ever to be written by him, will be published in the Household Number for February, dated January 28.' Great play was made of it being the 'Last Adventure of Sherlock Holmes' (on the cover), and 'The Last Sherlock Holmes Story ever to be written by A. Conan Doyle' (in the heading), while the note below described it as 'the thirteenth and last story of the new Sherlock Holmes series'.

Word of Holmes's forthcoming retirement to the Sussex Downs appeared in the press some months before the story was published. 'So far as I know there is not the slightest intention of his ever again entering on the work of the detection of crime', Doyle told an interviewer from the *Daily Mail*: 'From what I know Sherlock Holmes's retirement will be final. He will not again emerge' (8 October 1904). But the public was disinclined to believe him. There were a few letters—one from a professional bee-keeper and another from a potential housekeeper—intent on helping Sherlock Holmes during his retirement, but most people expected

Holmes to be tempted back. And they were not disappointed for within three years the following advertisement appeared: 'Mr Sherlock Holmes presents his compliments to the reader, and begs to say he will have much pleasure in renewing a long-standing acquaintance in the *Strand Magazine* for September 1908.'

IV

Doyle was concerned about the reaction of the public and was worried that they might not 'take to Holmes' when he made his reappearance. His fears at first seemed groundless. 'It is extraordinary the interest that is taken in this gentleman,' said *Tit-Bits* on 26 September 1903; 'the advance demand for the October Number is such that it will tax our resources to be able to supply all that are wanted in time.' But the interest was not as great as for *The Hound of the Baskervilles*, and Doyle may have been right in thinking that the public had become so accustomed to the methods of Sherlock Holmes that the stories lost some of their novelty. Where Holmes had once stood alone, he now had many rivals. Doyle joked later that the 'most trenchant criticism' of Sherlock Holmes after his return came from a Cornish boatman, who said 'When Mr Holmes had that fall he may not have been killed, but he was certainly injured, for he was never the same man afterwards' ('Some Personalia about Mr Sherlock Holmes', *Strand*, December 1917). The editor of the American *Bookman* both praised and criticized 'The Second Stain'. It was a good story: 'But it is open to the criticism that unlike the tales of *The Adventures* and *Memoirs*, it does not convince you of Holmes's superior powers of analytical reasoning. In the old stories you were put into possession of the facts. Here you must take them for granted' (*Bookman*, New York, February 1905).

Analytical reasoning had seemed to some commentators the *raison d'être* of the earlier stories. Dr Joseph Bell in his review of *The Adventures* in the December 1892 *Bookman* (which later served as a preface for *A Study in Scarlet*) and Sir Robert Anderson (1841–1918, Late Assistant Commissioner of Police, Registrar of Habitual Criminals, and for many years head of the Criminal Investigation Department), in an article on 'Sherlock Holmes as seen by Scotland Yard' in *T. P.'s Weekly* on 2 October 1903, both made this point. Anderson said that Doyle's 'purpose has been not to give us pattern cases of crime detection in order to instruct police officers in their duties—some of his best stories, indeed, have no relation whatever to crime—but to promote in all of us the habit of thinking; and to teach us, as he himself expresses it, "to think analytically"—"to think backward" '. He thought the stories 'partake of the character of parables; and in a parable the value of the narrative depends on its fitness to exemplify and explain the truth it is designed to teach.'

Much of the criticism was of a satirical nature, either in the form of parodies which ridiculed the character of the great detective, or in mock-serious articles which were addressed to Dr Watson rather than Conan Doyle and treated Holmes as if he were a real person. Frank Sidgwick complained in 'An Open Letter to Dr Watson' in the *Cambridge Review* of 23 January 1902 about the inconsistencies in the dates given in *The Hound of the Baskervilles*; and Andrew Lang in his 'At the Sign of the Ship' column for *Longman's Magazine* in July 1904 suggested that Holmes was a victim of his own complacency. 'I have often thought', he said, 'that Dr Watson overrates the acuteness of his friend and hero, Sherlock Holmes. In some cases Sherlock has blundered egregiously, and been taken in, though he never knew it. Now, in the *Strand* for June, Sherlock is the victim of a college don and an undergraduate, who have "played it rather low" on the world-famed detective.'

The most influential exponent of the satirical mode of criticism was Ronald Knox (1888–1957) whose 'Studies in the Literature of Sherlock Holmes' (*Blue Book*, July 1912; and *Essays in Satire*, 1928) lampooned the 'higher criticism' of the Bible and classical scholarship. He treated the stories as if they were a combination of the classics and Holy Writ, and with citations from imaginary authorities such as Herr

Sauwosch and M. Piff-Pouff, examined the nature and
structure of the stories. In the process he identified certain
weaknesses in *The Return* (and in one or two of the earlier
stories) and was driven to the conclusion that it was spurious, claiming it to be either the invention of Dr Watson or
the work of a second hand, a 'deutero Dr Watson'. The
character and methods of Holmes were different, he said;
the later narratives contained certain impossibilities and
were at times inconsistent with those which had preceded
them. The Holmes of *The Return* was discourteous to a client;
he had a morbid craving for serious crime; he called a client
by her Christian name; he quoted Shakespeare, split infinit-
ives, deliberately abstained from food, and gave way to
'ludicrously bad logic' (in 'The Dancing Men'). The
examination paper in 'The Three Students' and the deductions concerning the direction of the bicycle in 'The Priory
School' were given as examples of impossibilities, while the
inconsistencies included the attempted marriage in 'The
Solitary Cyclist' (where no witness was required—unlike 'A
Scandal in Bohemia' where the marriage could not take
place without one), Moriarty's Christian name (which in
'The Empty House' was the same as that of his brother in
'The Final Problem'), and Holmes's dressing-gown which
had become mouse-coloured. Such arguments were not
intended to be taken seriously. There is no 'deutero Dr
Watson' and there are no spurious stories, but to argue
against Knox is to defend Dr Watson, and to defend Dr
Watson is to deny Conan Doyle—and therein lies the great
power of the stories, for to many readers Holmes and Watson
soon become more real than their creator.

Doyle for his part was flattered by the attention which
Knox paid to the stories and admitted in a letter of 5 July
1912 that they were 'written in a disconnected (and careless)
way, without referring back to what had gone before'. He
agreed that Holmes's character had changed as the stories
progressed. 'In the first one, the *Study in Scarlet*, he was a
mere calculating machine, but I had to make him more of
an educated human being as I went on with him.' 'Another

point', he said '—one of the few in which I feel satisfaction but which I have never seen mentioned—is that Watson never for one instant as chorus and chronicler transcends his own limitations. Never once does a flash of wit or wisdom come from him. All is remorselessly eliminated so that he may be Watson' (Penelope Fitzgerald, *The Knox Brothers* (1977), 106). But he remained convinced that the later stories could produce the same effect as the earlier ones and would have done so had they come first. When he came to select the twelve best Sherlock Holmes stories for a competition in the *Strand* (which excluded those in *The Case-Book*), he chose four from *The Return*: 'The Dancing Men' was placed third on account of the originality of the plot; 'The Empty House' was placed sixth because it explained away the 'alleged death' of Sherlock Holmes and introduced 'such a villain as Colonel Sebastian Moran'; 'The Second Stain' came eighth because it dealt successfully with 'diplomacy and intrigue'; and 'The Priory School' was placed tenth 'if only for the dramatic moment when Holmes points his finger at the Duke' ('How I Made My List', *Strand*, 73 (June 1927), 611–12).

One would not wish to part with any of these stories. The mark of their greatness is that all criticism pales before them. Holmes lives in the pages, as he lives beyond them, and the London of his day, the apartments in Baker Street, the suburbs and the outlying countryside, the cast of villains and clients, shine as brightly as stage jewels. The artifice is the art.

RICHARD LANCELYN GREEN

NOTE ON THE TEXT

The manuscripts for the stories in this collection (twelve of which have been available for comparison) have light punctuation and inconsistencies in spelling. The additional punctuation (inverted commas for spoken words, commas and semi-colons in place of dashes) and correct spelling was provided by the typist (a Miss Neal). Three copies (a top copy and two carbons) were made and though none are known to have survived, it is clear from the uniform punctuation in *Collier's Weekly* and the *Strand Magazine* that both are derived from it. The only error introduced by the typist (or the only one which escaped correction) was a misreading of 'b' for 'h' (giving 'bustled' in place of 'hustled' in 'The Six Napoleons'). The typist did not correct errors in names or inconsistencies within the text, and did not break up long paragraphs. Neither did the editor of *Collier's Weekly* whose text (except for the American spelling) copies the typescript and therefore perpetuates errors found in the manuscript (such as 'convex' for 'concave' in 'The Golden Pince-Nez', or the description of the 'wooden'/'marble' mantelpiece in 'The Abbey Grange').

The text used in the *Strand Magazine* was subjected to greater editorial control and changes were made with the agreement of the author. Minor errors were corrected, long paragraphs were broken up, and ambiguities were removed. This is therefore the preferred text. However, there were further changes which are less easy to justify. A strict policy was imposed by the proprietor, George Newnes, to suppress where possible the use of strong expletives, in particular those referring to God or the devil. Here the author's original expressions (which were retained in *Collier's Weekly*) have been restored, so Black Peter resembles 'a lost soul in hell', rather than 'a lost soul in torment'; he is 'full of the devil', instead of being 'in a vile temper'; and Charles Augustus Milverton is 'as cunning as the Devil', and not 'as

cunning as the Evil One'. 'By God' and 'Damn the beast'
are reinstated in place of the milder 'Good Heavens' and
'Curse the beast'. Other *Strand* usages which have been
dropped are the use of italics for French words and the use
of 'Halloa' where the author wrote 'Hullo'.

The first edition published by George Newnes in 1905 was
set from the *Strand Magazine*. A few minor changes were
made and these are incorporated in the present text. The
text has also been collated with *The Complete Short Stories*,
published by John Murray in 1928.

SELECT BIBLIOGRAPHY

I. A. CONAN DOYLE: PRINCIPAL WORKS

(a) *Fiction*

A Study in Scarlet (Ward, Lock, & Co., 1888)

The Mystery of Cloomber (Ward & Downey, 1888)

Micah Clarke (Longmans, Green, & Co., 1889)

The Captain of the Pole-Star and Other Tales (Longmans, Green, & Co., 1890)

The Sign of the Four (Spencer Blackett, 1890)

The Firm of Girdlestone (Chatto & Windus, 1890)

The White Company (Smith, Elder, & Co., 1891)

The Adventures of Sherlock Holmes (George Newnes, 1892)

The Great Shadow (Arrowsmith, 1892)

The Refugees (Longmans, Green, & Co., 1893)

The Memoirs of Sherlock Holmes (George Newnes, 1893)

Round the Red Lamp (Methuen & Co., 1894)

The Stark Munro Letters (Longmans, Green, & Co., 1895)

The Exploits of Brigadier Gerard (George Newnes, 1896)

Rodney Stone (Smith, Elder, & Co., 1896)

Uncle Bernac (Smith, Elder, & Co., 1897)

The Tragedy of the Korosko (Smith, Elder, & Co., 1898)

A Duet With an Occasional Chorus (Grant Richards, 1899)

The Green Flag and Other Stories of War and Sport (Smith, Elder, & Co., 1900)

The Hound of the Baskervilles (George Newnes, 1902)

Adventures of Gerard (George Newnes, 1903)

The Return of Sherlock Holmes (George Newnes, 1905)

Sir Nigel (Smith, Elder, & Co., 1906)

Round the Fire Stories (Smith, Elder, & Co., 1908)

The Last Galley (Smith, Elder, & Co., 1911)

The Lost World (Hodder & Stoughton, 1912)

The Poison Belt (Hodder & Stoughton, 1913)

The Valley of Fear (Smith, Elder, & Co., 1915)

His Last Bow (John Murray, 1917)

Danger! and Other Stories (John Murray, 1918)

The Land of Mist (Hutchinson & Co., 1926)

The Case-Book of Sherlock Holmes (John Murray, 1927)

The Maracot Deep and Other Stories (John Murray, 1929)

The Complete Sherlock Holmes Short Stories (John Murray, 1928)
The Conan Doyle Stories (John Murray, 1929)
The Complete Sherlock Holmes Long Stories (John Murray, 1929)

(b) *Non-fiction*

The Great Boer War (Smith, Elder, & Co., 1900)
The Story of Mr George Edalji (T. Harrison Roberts, 1907)
Through the Magic Door (Smith, Elder, & Co., 1907)
The Crime of the Congo (Hutchinson & Co., 1909)
The Case of Oscar Slater (Hodder & Stoughton, 1912)
The German War (Hodder & Stoughton, 1914)
The British Campaign in France and Flanders (Hodder & Stoughton, 6
   vols., 1916–20)
The Poems of Arthur Conan Doyle (John Murray, 1922)
Memories and Adventures (Hodder & Stoughton, 1924; revised ed., 1930)
The History of Spiritualism (Cassell & Co., 1926)

2. MISCELLANEOUS

A Bibliography of A. Conan Doyle (Soho Bibliographies 23: Oxford,
1983) by Richard Lancelyn Green and John Michael Gibson, with
a foreword by Graham Greene, is the standard—and indispensable—source of bibliographical information, and of much else
besides. Green and Gibson have also assembled and introduced
The Unknown Conan Doyle, comprising *Uncollected Stories* (those never
previously published in book form); *Essays in Photography* (docu-
menting a little-known enthusiasm of Conan Doyle's during his
time as a student and young doctor), both published in 1982; and
Letters to the Press (1986). Alone, Richard Lancelyn Green has
compiled (1) *The Uncollected Sherlock Holmes* (1983), an impressive
assemblage of Holmesiana, containing almost all Conan Doyle's
writing about his creation (other than the stories themselves)
together with related material by Joseph Bell, J. M. Barrie, and
Beverley Nichols; (2) *The Further Adventures of Sherlock Holmes* (1985),
a selection of eleven apocryphal Holmes adventures by various
authors, all diplomatically introduced; (3) *The Sherlock Holmes Letters*
(1986), a collection of noteworthy public correspondence on Holmes
and Holmesiana and far more valuable than its title suggests; and
(4) *Letters to Sherlock Holmes* (1984), a powerful testimony to the
power of the Holmes stories.

   Though much of Conan Doyle's work is now readily available
there are still gaps. Some of his very earliest fiction now only

survives in rare piracies (apart, that is, from the magazines in which they were first published), including items of intrinsic genre interest such as 'The Gully of Bluemansdyke' (1881) and its sequel 'My Friend the Murderer' (1882), which both turn on the theme of the murderer-informer (handled very differently—and far better— in the Holmes story of 'The Resident Patient' (*Memoirs*)): both of these were used as book-titles for the same pirate collection first issued as *Mysteries and Adventures* (1889). Other stories achieved book publication only after severe pruning—for example, 'The Surgeon of Gaster Fell', reprinted in *Danger!* many years after magazine publication (1890). Some items given initial book publication were not included in the collected edition of *The Conan Doyle Stories*. Particularly deplorable losses were 'John Barrington Cowles' (1884: included subsequently in *Edinburgh Stories of Arthur Conan Doyle* (1981)), 'A Foreign Office Romance' (1894), 'The Club-Footed Grocer' (1898), 'A Shadow Before' (1898), and 'Danger!' (1914). Three of these may have been post-war casualties, as seeming to deal too lightheartedly with the outbreak of other wars; 'John Barrington Cowles' may have been dismissed as juvenile work; but why Conan Doyle discarded a story as good as 'The Club-Footed Grocer' would baffle even Holmes.

At the other end of his life, Conan Doyle's tidying impaired the survival of his most recent work, some of which well merited lasting recognition. *The Maracot Deep and Other Stories* appeared in 1929, a little over a month after *The Conan Doyle Stories*; 'Maracot' itself found a separate paperback life as a short novel; the two Professor Challenger stories, 'The Disintegration Machine' and 'When the World Screamed', were naturally included in John Murray's *The Professor Challenger Stories* (1952); but the fourth item, 'The Story of Spedegue's Dropper', passed beyond the ken of most of Conan Doyle's readers. These three stories show the author, in his seventieth year, still at the height of his powers.

In 1980 Gaslight Publications, of Bloomington, Ind., reprinted *The Mystery of Cloomber*, *The Firm of Girdlestone*, *The Doings of Raffles Haw* (1892), *Beyond the City* (1893), *The Parasite* (1894; also reprinted in *Edinburgh Stories of Arthur Conan Doyle*), *The Stark Munro Letters*, *The Tragedy of the Korosko*, and *A Duet*. *Memories and Adventures*, Conan Doyle's enthralling but impressionistic recollections, are best read in the revised (1930) edition. *Through the Magic Door* remains the best introduction to the literary mind of Conan Doyle, whilst some of his volumes on Spiritualism have autobiographical material of literary significance.

ACD: The Journal of the Arthur Conan Doyle Society (ed. Christopher Roden, David Stuart Davies [to 1991], and Barbara Roden [from 1992]), together with its newsletter, *The Parish Magazine*, is a useful source of critical and biographical material on Conan Doyle. The enormous body of 'Sherlockiana' is best pursued in *The Baker Street Journal*, published by Fordham University Press, or in the *Sherlock Holmes Journal* (Sherlock Holmes Society of London), itemized up to 1974 in the colossal *World Bibliography of Sherlock Holmes and Doctor Watson* (1974) by Ronald Burt De Waal (see also De Waal, *The International Sherlock Holmes* (1980)) and digested in *The Annotated Sherlock Holmes* (2 vols., 1968) by William S. Baring-Gould, whose industry has been invaluable for the Oxford Sherlock Holmes editors. Jack Tracy, *The Encyclopaedia Sherlockiana* (1979) is a very helpful compilation of relevant data. Those who can nerve themselves to consult it despite its title will benefit greatly from Christopher Redmond, *In Bed With Sherlock Holmes* (1984). The classic 'Sherlockian' work is Ronald A. Knox, 'Studies in the Literature of Sherlock Holmes', first published in *The Blue Book* (July 1912) and reprinted in his *Essays in Satire* (1928).

The serious student of Conan Doyle may perhaps deplore the vast extent of 'Sherlockian' literature, even though the size of this output is testimony in itself to the scale and nature of Conan Doyle's achievement. But there is undoubtedly some wheat amongst the chaff. At the head stands Dorothy L. Sayers, *Unpopular Opinions* (1946); also of some interest are T. S. Blakeney, *Sherlock Holmes: Fact or Fiction* (1932), H. W. Bell, *Sherlock Holmes and Dr Watson* (1932), Vincent Starrett, *The Private Life of Sherlock Holmes* (1934), Gavin Brend, *My Dear Holmes* (1951), S. C. Roberts, *Holmes and Watson* (1953) and Roberts's introduction to *Sherlock Holmes: Selected Stories* (Oxford: The World's Classics, 1951), James E. Holroyd, *Baker Street Byways* (1959), Ian McQueen, *Sherlock Holmes Detected* (1974), and Trevor H. Hall, *Sherlock Holmes and his Creator* (1978). One Sherlockian item certainly falls into the category of the genuinely essential: D. Martin Dakin, *A Sherlock Holmes Commentary* (1972), to which all the editors of the present series are indebted.

Michael Pointer, *The Public Life of Sherlock Holmes* (1975) contains invaluable information concerning dramatizations of the Sherlock Holmes stories for radio, stage, and the cinema; of complementary interest are Chris Steinbrunner and Norman Michaels, *The Films of Sherlock Holmes* (1978) and David Stuart Davies, *Holmes of the Movies* (1976), whilst Philip Weller with Christopher Roden, *The Life and Times of Sherlock Holmes* (1992) summarizes a great deal of useful information concerning Conan Doyle's life and Holmes's cases, and in addition is delightfully illustrated. The more concrete products of the Holmes industry are dealt with in Charles Hall, *The Sherlock Holmes Collection* (1987). For a useful retrospective view, Allen Eyles, *Sherlock Holmes: A Centenary Celebration* (1986) rises to the occasion. Both useful and engaging are Peter Haining, *The Sherlock Holmes Scrapbook* (1973) and Charles Viney, *Sherlock Holmes in London* (1989).

Of the many anthologies of Holmesiana, P. A. Shreffler (ed.), *The Baker Street Reader* (1984) is exceptionally useful. D. A. Redmond, *Sherlock Holmes: A Study in Sources* (1982) is similarly indispensable. Michael Hardwick, *The Complete Guide to Sherlock Holmes* (1986) is both reliable and entertaining; Michael Harrison, *In the Footsteps of Sherlock Holmes* (1958) is occasionally helpful.

For more general studies of the detective story, the standard history is Julian Symons, *Bloody Murder* (1972, 1985, 1992). Necessary but a great deal less satisfactory is Howard Haycraft, *Murder for Pleasure* (1942); of more value is Haycraft's critical anthology *The Art of the Mystery Story* (1946), which contains many choice period items. Both R. F. Stewart, *. . . And Always a Detective* (1980) and Colin Watson, *Snobbery with Violence* (1971) are occasionally useful. Dorothy Sayers's pioneering introduction to *Great Short Stories of Detection, Mystery and Horror* (First Series, 1928), despite some inspired howlers, is essential reading; Raymond Chandler's riposte, 'The Simple Art of Murder' (1944), is reprinted in Haycraft, *The Art of the Mystery Story* (see above). Less well known than Sayers's essay but with an equal claim to poineer status is E. M. Wrong's introduction to *Crime and Detection*, First Series (Oxford: The World's Classics, 1926). See also Michael Cox (ed.), *Victorian Tales of Mystery and Detection: An Oxford Anthology* (1992).

Amongst biographical studies of Conan Doyle one of the most distinguished is Jon L. Lellenberg's survey, *The Quest for Sir Arthur Conan Doyle* (1987), with a Foreword by Dame Jean Conan Doyle (much the best piece of writing on ACD by any member of his family). The four earliest biographers—the Revd John Lamond (1931), Hesketh Pearson (1943), John Dickson Carr (1949), and Pierre Nordon (1964)—all had access to the family archives, subsequently closed to researchers following a lawsuit; hence all four biographies contain valuable documentary material, though Nordon handles the evidence best (the French text is fuller than the English version, published in 1966). Of the others, Lamond seems only to have made little use of the material available to him;

Pearson is irreverent and wildly careless with dates; Dickson Carr has a strong fictionalizing element. Both he and Nordon paid a price for their access to the Conan Doyle papers by deferring to the far from impartial editorial demands of Adrian Conan Doyle; Nordon nevertheless remains the best available biography. The best short sketch is Julian Symons, *Conan Doyle* (1979) (and for the late Victorian milieu of the Holmes cycle some of Symons's own fiction, such as *The Blackheath Poisonings* and *The Detling Secret*, can be thoroughly recommended). Harold Orel (ed.), *Critical Essays on Sir Arthur Conan Doyle* (1992) is a good and varied collection, whilst Robin Winks, *The Historian as Detective* (1969) contains many insights and examples applicable to the Holmes corpus; Winks's *Detective Fiction: A Collection of Critical Essays* (1980) is an admirable working handbook, with a useful critical bibliography. Edmund Wilson's famous essay 'Mr Holmes, they were the footprints of a gigantic hound' (1944) may be found in his *Classics and Commercials: A Literary Chronicle of the Forties* (1950).

Specialized biographical areas are covered in Owen Dudley Edwards, *The Quest for Sherlock Holmes: A Biographical Study of Arthur Conan Doyle* (1982) and in Geoffrey Stavert, *A Study in Southsea: The Unrevealed Life of Dr Arthur Conan Doyle* (1987), which respectively assess the significance of the years up to 1882, and from 1882 to 1890. Alvin E. Rodin and Jack D. Key provide a thorough study of Conan Doyle's medical career and its literary implications in *Medical Casebook of Dr Arthur Conan Doyle* (1984). Peter Costello, in *The Real World of Sherlock Holmes: The True Crimes Investigated by Arthur Conan Doyle* (1991) claims too much, but it is useful to be reminded of events that came within Conan Doyle's orbit, even if they are sometimes tangential or even irrelevant. Christopher Redmond, *Welcome to America, Mr Sherlock Holmes* (1987) is a thorough account of Conan Doyle's tour of North America in 1894.

Other than Baring-Gould (see above), the only serious attempt to annotate the nine volumes of the Holmes cycle has been in the Longman Heritage of Literature series (1979–80), to which the present editors are also indebted. Of introductions to individual texts, H. R. F. Keating's to the *Adventures* and *The Hound of the Baskervilles* (published in one volume under the dubious title *The Best of Sherlock Holmes* (1992)) is worthy of particular mention.

A CHRONOLOGY OF ARTHUR CONAN DOYLE

1855   Charles Altamont Doyle, youngest son of the political cartoonist John Doyle ('HB'), and Mary Foley, his Irish landlady's daughter, marry in Edinburgh on 31 July.

1859   Arthur Ignatius Conan Doyle, third child and elder son of ten siblings, born at 11 Picardy Place, Edinburgh, on 22 May and baptized into the Roman Catholic religion of his parents.

1868–75   ACD commences two years' education under the Jesuits at Hodder, followed by five years at its senior sister college, Stonyhurst, both in the Ribble Valley, Lancashire; becomes a popular storyteller amongst his fellow pupils, writes verses, edits a school paper, and makes one close friend, James Ryan of Glasgow and Ceylon. Doyle family resides at 3 Sciennes Hill Place, Edinburgh.

1875–6   ACD passes London Matriculation Examination at Stonyhurst and studies for a year in the Jesuit college at Feldkirch, Austria.

1876–7   ACD becomes a student of medicine at Edinburgh University on the advice of Bryan Charles Waller, now lodging with the Doyle family at 2 Argyle Park Terrace.

1877–80   Waller leases 23 George Square, Edinburgh as a 'consulting pathologist', with all the Doyles as residents. ACD continues medical studies, becoming surgeon's clerk to Joseph Bell at Edinburgh; also takes temporary medical assistantships at Sheffield, Ruyton (Salop), and Birmingham, the last leading to a close friendship with his employer's family, the Hoares. First story published, 'The Mystery of Sasassa Valley', in *Chambers's Journal* (6 Sept. 1879); first non-fiction published—'Gelseminum as a Poison', *British Medical Journal* (20 Sept. 1879). Some time previously ACD sends 'The Haunted Grange of Goresthorpe' to *Blackwood's Edinburgh Magazine*, but it is filed and forgotten.

1880   (Feb.–Sept.) ACD serves as surgeon on the Greenland whaler *Hope* of Peterhead.

1881   ACD graduates MB, CM (Edin.); Waller and the Doyles living at 15 Lonsdale Terrace, Edinburgh.

1881–2 (Oct.–Jan.) ACD serves as surgeon on the steamer *Mayumba* to West Africa, spending three days with US Minister to Liberia, Henry Highland Garnet, black abolitionist leader, then dying. (July–Aug.) Visits Foley relatives in Lismore, Co. Waterford.

1882   Ill-fated partnership with George Turnavine Budd in Plymouth. ACD moves to Southsea, Portsmouth, in June. ACD published in *London Society*, *All the Year Round*, *Lancet*, and *British Journal of Photography*. Over the next eight years ACD becomes an increasingly successful general practitioner at Southsea.

1882–3 Breakup of the Doyle family in Edinburgh. Charles Altamont Doyle henceforth confined because of alcoholism and epilepsy. Mary Foley Doyle resident in Masongill Cottage on the Waller estate at Masongill, Yorkshire. Innes Doyle (b. 1873) resident with ACD as schoolboy and surgery page from Sept. 1882.

1883   'The Captain of the *Pole-Star*' published (*Temple Bar*, Jan.), as well as a steady stream of minor pieces. Works on *The Mystery of Cloomber*.

1884   ACD publishes 'J. Habakuk Jephson's Statement' (*Cornhill Magazine*, Jan.), 'The Heiress of Glenmahowley' (*Temple Bar*, Jan.), 'The Cabman's Story' (*Cassell's Saturday Journal*, May); working on *The Firm of Girdlestone*.

1885   Publishes 'The Man from Archangel' (*London Society*, Jan.). Jack Hawkins, briefly a resident patient with ACD, dies of cerebral meningitis. Louisa Hawkins, his sister, marries ACD. (Aug.) Travels in Ireland for honeymoon. Awarded Edinburgh MD.

1886   Writing *A Study in Scarlet*.

1887   *A Study in Scarlet* published in *Beeton's Christmas Annual*.

1888   (July) First book edition of *A Study in Scarlet* published by Ward, Lock; (Dec.) *The Mystery of Cloomber* published.

1889   (Feb.) *Micah Clarke* (ACD's novel of the Monmouth Rebellion of 1685) published. Mary Louise Conan Doyle, ACD's eldest child, born. Unauthorized publication of *Mysteries and Adventures* (published later as *The*

Gully of Bluemansdyke and *My Friend the Murderer*). *The Sign of the Four* and Oscar Wilde's *The Picture of Dorian Gray* commissioned by Lippincott's.

1890   (Jan.) 'Mr [R. L.] Stevenson's Methods in Fiction' published in the *National Review*. (Feb.) *The Sign of the Four* published in *Lippincott's Monthly Magazine*; (Mar.) First authorized short-story collection, *The Captain of the Pole-Star and Other Tales*, published; (Apr.) *The Firm of Girdlestone* published; (Oct.) First book edition of the *Sign* published by Spencer Blackett.

1891   ACD sets up as an eye specialist in 2 Upper Wimpole Street, off Harley Street, while living at Montague Place. Moves to South Norwood. (July–Dec.) The first six 'Adventures of Sherlock Holmes' published in George Newnes's *Strand Magazine*. (Oct.) *The White Company* published; *Beyond the City* first published in *Good Cheer*, the special Christmas number of *Good Words*.

1892   (Jan.–June) Six more Holmes stories published in the *Strand*, with another in Dec. (Mar.) *The Doings of Raffles Haw* published (first serialized in Alfred Harmsworth's penny paper *Answers*, Dec. 1891–Feb. 1892). (14 Oct.) *The Adventures of Sherlock Holmes* published by Newnes. (31 Oct.) Waterloo story *The Great Shadow* published. Alleyne Kingsley Conan Doyle born. Newnes republishes the *Sign*.

1893   'Adventures of Sherlock Holmes' (second series) continues in the *Strand*, to be published by Newnes as *The Memoirs of Sherlock Holmes* (Dec.), minus 'The Cardboard Box'. Holmes apparently killed in 'The Final Problem' (Dec.) to free ACD for 'more serious literary work'. (May) *The Refugees* published. *Jane Annie: or, the Good Conduct Prize* (musical comedy co-written with J. M. Barrie) fails at the Savoy Theatre. (10 Oct.) Charles Altamont Doyle dies.

1894   (Oct.) *Round the Red Lamp*, a collection of medical short stories, published, several for the first time. *The Stark Munro Letters*, a fictionalized autobiography, begun, to be concluded the following year. ACD on US lecture tour with Innes Doyle. (Dec.) *The Parasite* published; 'The Medal of Brigadier Gerard' published in the *Strand*.

1895   'The Exploits of Brigadier Gerard' published in the *Strand*.

1896   (Feb.) *The Exploits of Brigadier Gerard* published by Newnes. ACD settles at Hindhead, Surrey, to minimize effects of his wife's tuberculosis. (Nov.) *Rodney Stone*, a pre-Regency mystery, published. Self-pastiche, 'The Field Bazaar', appears in the Edinburgh University *Student* (20 Nov.).

1897   (May) Napoleonic novel *Uncle Bernac* published; three 'Captain Sharkey' pirate stories published in *Pearson's Magazine* (Jan., Mar., May). Home at Undershaw, Hindhead.

1898   (Feb.) *The Tragedy of the Korosko* published. (June) Publishes *Songs of Action*, a verse collection. (June–Dec.) Begins to publish 'Round the Fire Stories' in the *Strand*—'The Beetle Hunter', 'The Man with the Watches', 'The Lost Special', 'The Sealed Room', 'The Black Doctor', 'The Club-Footed Grocer', and 'The Brazilian Cat'. Ernest William Hornung (ACD's brother-in-law) creates A. J. Raffles and in 1899 dedicates the first stories to ACD.

1899   (Jan.–May) Concludes 'Round the Fire' series in the *Strand* with 'The Japanned Box', 'The Jew's Breast-Plate', 'B. 24', 'The Latin Tutor', and 'The Brown Hand'. (Mar.) Publishes *A Duet with an Occasional Chorus*, a version of his own romance. (Oct.–Dec.) 'The Croxley Master', a boxing story, published in the *Strand*. William Gillette begins 33 years starring in *Sherlock Holmes*, a play by Gillette and ACD.

1900   Accompanies volunteer-staffed Langman hospital as unofficial supervisor to support British forces in the Boer War. (Mar.) Publishes short-story collection, *The Green Flag and Other Stories of War and Sport*. (Oct.) *The Great Boer War* published. Unsuccessful Liberal Unionist parliamentary candidate for Edinburgh Central.

1901   (Aug.) 'The Hound of the Baskervilles' begins serialization in the *Strand*, subtitled 'Another Adventure of Sherlock Holmes'.

1902   (Jan.) *The War in South Africa: Its Cause and Conduct* published. 'Sherlockian' higher criticism begun by Frank Sidgwick in the *Cambridge Review* (23 Jan.). (Mar.) *The Hound of the Baskervilles* published by Newnes. ACD accepts knighthood with reluctance.

1903   (Sept.) *Adventures of Gerard* published by Newnes (previously serialized in the *Strand*). (Oct.) 'The Return of

Sherlock Holmes' begins in the *Strand*. Author's Edition of ACD's major works published in twelve volumes by Smith, Elder and thirteen by D. Appleton & Co. of New York, with prefaces by ACD; many titles omitted.

1904   'Return of Sherlock Holmes' continues in the *Strand*; series designed to conclude with 'The Abbey Grange' (Sept.), but ACD develops earlier allusions and produces 'The Second Stain' (Dec.).

1905   (Mar.) *The Return of Sherlock Holmes* published by Newnes. (Dec.) Serialization of 'Sir Nigel' begun in the *Strand* (concluded Dec. 1906).

1906   (Nov.) Book publication of *Sir Nigel*. ACD defeated as Unionist candidate for Hawick District in general election. (4 July) Death of Louisa ('Touie'), Lady Conan Doyle. ACD deeply affected.

1907   ACD clears the name of George Edalji (convicted in 1903 of cattle-maiming). (18 Sept.) Marries Jean Leckie. (Nov.) Publishes *Through the Magic Door*, a celebration of his literary mentors (earlier version serialized in *Great Thoughts*, 1894).

1908   Moves to Windlesham, Crowborough, Sussex. (Jan.) Death of Sidney Paget. (Sept.) *Round the Fire Stories* published, including some not in earlier *Strand* series. (Sept.–Oct.) 'The Singular Experience of Mr John Scott Eccles' (later retitled as 'The Adventure of Wisteria Lodge') begins occasional series of Holmes stories in the *Strand*.

1909   ACD becomes President of the Divorce Law Reform Union (until 1919). Denis Percy Stewart Conan Doyle born. Takes up agitation against Belgian oppression in the Congo.

1910   (Sept.) 'The Marriage of the Brigadier', the last Gerard story, published in the *Strand*, and (Dec.) the Holmes story of 'The Devil's Foot'. ACD takes six-month lease on Adelphi Theatre; the play *The Speckled Band* opens there, eventually running to 346 performances. Adrian Malcolm Conan Doyle born.

1911   (Apr.) *The Last Galley* (short stories, mostly historical) published. Two more Holmes stories appear in the *Strand*: 'The Red Circle' (Mar., Apr.) and 'The Disappearance

	of Lady Frances Carfax' (Dec.). ACD declares for Irish Home Rule, under the influence of Sir Roger Casement.
1912	(Apr.–Nov.) The first Professor Challenger story, *The Lost World*, published in the *Strand*, book publication in Oct. Jean Lena Annette Conan Doyle (afterwards Air Commandant Dame Jean Conan Doyle, Lady Bromet) born.
1913	(Feb.) Writes 'Great Britain and the Next War' (*Fortnightly Review*). (Aug.) Second Challenger story, *The Poison Belt*, published. (Dec.) 'The Dying Detective' published in the *Strand*. ACD campaigns for a channel tunnel.
1914	(July) 'Danger!', warning of the dangers of a war-time blockade of Britain, published in the *Strand*. (4 Aug.) Britain declares war on Germany; ACD forms local volunteer force.
1914–15	(Sept.) *The Valley of Fear* begins serialization in the *Strand* (concluding May 1915).
1915	(27 Feb.) *The Valley of Fear* published by George H. Doran in New York. (June) *The Valley of Fear* published in London by Smith, Elder (transferred with rest of ACD stock to John Murray when the firm is sold on the death of Reginald Smith). Five Holmes films released in Germany (ten more during the war).
1916	(Apr., May) First instalments of *The British Campaign in France and Flanders 1914* appear in the *Strand*. (Aug.) *A Visit to Three Fronts* published. Sir Roger Casement convicted of high treason after Dublin Easter Week Rising and executed despite appeals for clemency by ACD and others.
1917	War censor interdicts ACD's history of the 1916 campaigns in the *Strand*. (Sept.) 'His Last Bow' published in the *Strand*. (Oct.) *His Last Bow* published by John Murray (includes 'The Cardboard Box').
1918	(Apr.) ACD publishes *The New Revelation*, proclaiming himself a Spiritualist. (Dec.) *Danger! and Other Stories* published. Permitted to resume accounts of 1916 and 1917 campaigns in the *Strand*, but that for 1918 never serialized. Death of eldest son, Captain Kingsley Conan Doyle, from influenza aggravated by war wounds.
1919	Death of Brigadier-General Innes Doyle, from post-war pneumonia.

1920–30   ACD engaged in world-wide crusade for Spiritualism.

1921–2   ACD's one-act play, *The Crown Diamond*, tours with Dennis Neilson-Terry as Holmes.

1921   (Oct.) 'The Mazarin Stone' (apparently based on *The Crown Diamond*) published in the *Strand*. Death of mother, Mary Foley Doyle.

1922   (Feb.–Mar.) 'The Problem of Thor Bridge' in the *Strand*. (July) John Murray publishes a collected edition of the non-Holmes short stories in six volumes: *Tales of the Ring and the Camp*, *Tales of Pirates and Blue Water*, *Tales of Terror and Mystery*, *Tales of Twilight and the Unseen*, *Tales of Adventure and Medical Life*, and (Nov.) *Tales of Long Ago*. (Sept.) Collected edition of ACD's *Poems* published by Murray.

1923   (Mar.) 'The Creeping Man' published in the *Strand*.

1924   (Jan.) 'The Sussex Vampire' appears in the *Strand*. (June) 'How Watson Learned the Trick', ACD's own Holmes pastiche, appears in *The Book of the Queen's Dolls' House Library*. (Sept.) *Memories and Adventures* published (reprinted with additions and deletions 1930).

1925   (Jan.) 'The Three Garridebs' and (Feb.–Mar.) 'The Illustrious Client' published in the *Strand*. (July) *The Land of Mist*, a Spiritualist novel featuring Challenger, begins serialization in the *Strand*.

1926   (Mar.) *The Land of Mist* published. *Strand* publishes 'The Three Gables' (Oct.), 'The Blanched Soldier' (Nov.), and 'The Lion's Mane' (Dec.).

1927   *Strand* publishes 'The Retired Colourman' (Jan.), 'The Veiled Lodger' (Feb.), and 'Shoscombe Old Place' (Apr.). (June) Murray publishes *The Case-Book of Sherlock Holmes*.

1928   (Oct.) *The Complete Sherlock Holmes Short Stories* published by Murray.

1929   (June) *The Conan Doyle Stories* (containing the six separate volumes issued by Murray in 1922) published. (July) *The Maracot Deep and Other Stories*, ACD's last collection of his fictional work.

1930   (7 July, 8.30 a.m.) Death of Arthur Conan Doyle. 'Education never ends, Watson. It is a series of lessons with the greatest for the last' ('The Red Circle').

The Return of
Sherlock Holmes

The Empty House

IT was in the spring of the year 1894 that all London was interested, and the fashionable world dismayed, by the murder of the Honourable Ronald Adair, under most unusual and inexplicable circumstances. The public has already learned those particulars of the crime which came out in the police investigation; but a good deal was suppressed upon that occasion, since the case for the prosecution was so overwhelmingly strong that it was not necessary to bring forward all the facts. Only now, at the end of nearly ten years, am I allowed to supply those missing links which make up the whole of that remarkable chain. The crime was of interest in itself, but that interest was as nothing to me compared to the inconceivable sequel, which afforded me the greatest shock and surprise of any event in my adventurous life.* Even now, after this long interval, I find myself thrilling as I think of it, and feeling once more that sudden flood of joy, amazement and incredulity which utterly submerged my mind. Let me say to that public which has shown some interest in those glimpses which I have occasionally given them of the thoughts and actions of a very remarkable man that they are not to blame me if I have not shared my knowledge with them, for I should have considered it my first duty to have done so had I not been barred by a positive prohibition from his own lips, which was only withdrawn upon the third of last month.

It can be imagined that my close intimacy with Sherlock Holmes had interested me deeply in crime, and that after his disappearance I never failed to read with care the various problems which came before the public, and I even attempted more than once for my own private satisfaction to employ his methods in their solution, though with indifferent success. There was none, however, which appealed to me like this tragedy of Ronald Adair. As I read the evidence at the inquest which led up to a verdict of wilful murder against some person or persons unknown,* I realized more clearly than I had ever done the loss which the community had sustained by the death of Sherlock Holmes. There were points about this strange business which would, I was sure, have specially appealed to him, and the efforts of the police would have been supplemented, or more probably anticipated, by the trained observation and the alert mind of the first criminal agent in Europe. All day as I drove upon my round I turned over the case in my mind, and found no explanation which appeared to me to be adequate. At the risk of telling a twice-told tale I will recapitulate the facts as they were known to the public at the conclusion of the inquest.

The Honourable Ronald Adair* was the second son of the Earl of Maynooth,* at that time Governor of one of the Australian colonies.* Adair's mother had returned from Australia to undergo an operation for cataract, and she, her son Ronald, and her daughter Hilda were living together at 427 Park Lane.* The youth moved in the best society, had, so far as was known, no enemies and no particular vices. He had been engaged to Miss Edith Woodley, of Carstairs,* but the engagement had been broken off by mutual consent some months before, and there was no sign that it had left any very profound feeling behind it. For the rest, the man's life moved in a narrow and conventional circle, for his habits were quiet and his nature unemotional. Yet it was upon this easy-going young aristocrat that death came in most strange and unexpected form between the hours of ten and eleven-twenty on the night of March 30, 1894.

Ronald Adair was fond of cards, playing continually, but never for such stakes as would hurt him. He was a member of the Baldwin, the Cavendish and the Bagatelle Card Clubs.* It was shown that after dinner on the day of his death he had played a rubber of whist at the latter club. He had also played there in the afternoon. The evidence of those who had played with him—Mr Murray, Sir John Hardy, and Colonel Moran*—showed that the game was

4

whist, and there was a fairly equal fall of the cards. Adair might have lost five pounds, but no more. His fortune was a considerable one, and such a loss could not in any way affect him. He had played nearly every day at one club or other, but he was a cautious player, and usually rose a winner. It came out in evidence that in partnership with Colonel Moran he had actually won as much as £420 in a sitting some weeks before from Godfrey Milner and Lord Balmoral.* So much for his recent history, as it came out at the inquest.

On the evening of the crime he returned from the club exactly at ten. His mother and sister were out spending the evening with a relation. The servant deposed that she heard him enter the front room on the second floor, generally used as his sitting-room. She had lit a fire there, and as it smoked she had opened the window. No sound was heard from the room until eleven-twenty, the hour of the return of Lady Maynooth and her daughter. Desiring to say good night, she had attempted to enter her son's room. The door was locked on the inside, and no answer could be got to their cries and knocking. Help was obtained and the door forced. The unfortunate young man was found lying near the table. His head had been horribly mutilated by an expanded revolver bullet,* but no weapon of any sort was to be found in the room. On the table lay two bank-notes for £10 each and £17 10s. in silver and gold, the money arranged in little piles of varying amount. There were some figures also upon a sheet of paper with the names of some club friends opposite to them, from which it was conjectured that before his death he was endeavouring to make out his losses or winnings at cards.

A minute examination of the circumstances served only to make the case more complex. In the first place, no reason could be given why the young man should have fastened the door upon the inside. There was the possibility that the murderer had done this and had afterwards escaped by the window. The drop was at least twenty feet, however, and a bed of crocuses in full bloom lay beneath. Neither the

5

flowers nor the earth showed any sign of having been disturbed, nor were there any marks upon the narrow strip of grass which separated the house from the road. Apparently, therefore, it was the young man himself who had fastened the door. But how did he come by his death? No one could have climbed up to the window without leaving traces. Suppose a man had fired through the window, it would indeed be a remarkable shot who could with a revolver inflict so deadly a wound. Again, Park Lane is a frequented thoroughfare, and there is a cab-stand within a hundred yards of the house. No one had heard a shot. And yet there was the dead man, and there the revolver bullet, which had mushroomed out, as soft-nosed bullets will, and so inflicted a wound which must have caused instantaneous death. Such were the circumstances of the Park Lane Mystery, which were further complicated by entire absence of motive, since, as I have said, young Adair was not known to have any enemy, and no attempt had been made to remove the money or valuables in the room.

All day I turned these facts over in my mind, endeavouring to hit upon some theory which could reconcile them all, and to find that line of least resistance which my poor friend had declared to be the starting-point of every investigation. I confess that I made little progress. In the evening I strolled across the Park, and found myself about six o'clock at the Oxford Street end of Park Lane. A group of loafers upon the pavements, all staring up at a particular window, directed me to the house which I had come to see. A tall, thin man with coloured glasses, whom I strongly suspected of being a plain-clothes detective, was pointing out some theory of his own, while the others crowded round to listen to what he said. I got as near him* as I could, but his observations seemed to me to be absurd, so I withdrew again in some disgust. As I did so I struck against an elderly deformed man,* who had been behind me, and I knocked down several books which he was carrying. I remember that as I picked them up I observed the title of one of them, *The Origin of Tree Worship*,* and it struck me that the fellow must be some poor bibliophile who, either as a trade or as a hobby, was a collector of obscure volumes. I endeavoured to apologize for the accident, but it was evident that these books which I had so unfortunately maltreated were very precious objects in the eyes of their owner. With a snarl of contempt he turned upon his heel, and I saw his curved back and white side-whiskers disappear among the throng.

My observations of No. 427 Park Lane did little to clear up the problem in which I was interested. The house was separated from the street by a low wall and railing, the whole not more than five feet high. It was perfectly easy, therefore, for anyone to get into the garden; but the window was entirely inaccessible, since there was no water-pipe or anything which could help the most active man to climb it. More puzzled than ever, I retraced my steps to Kensington. I had not been in my study five minutes when the maid entered to say that a person desired to see me. To my astonishment, it was none other than my strange old book-collector, his sharp, wizened face peering out from a frame of white hair, and his precious volumes, a dozen of them at least, wedged under his right arm.

'You're surprised to see me, sir,' said he, in a strange, croaking voice.

I acknowledged that I was.

'Well, I've a conscience, sir, and when I chanced to see you go into this house, as I came hobbling after you, I thought to myself, I'll just step in and see that kind gentleman, and tell him that if I was a bit gruff in my manner there was not any harm meant, and that I am much obliged to him for picking up my books.'

'You make too much of a trifle,' said I. 'May I ask how you knew who I was?'

'Well, sir, if it isn't too great a liberty, I am a neighbour of yours, for you'll find my little bookshop at the corner of Church Street,* and very happy to see you, I am sure. Maybe you collect yourself, sir; here's *British Birds,** and *Catullus,** and *The Holy War*—a bargain every one of them.

7

With five volumes you could just fill that gap on that second shelf. It looks untidy, does it not, sir?'

I moved my head to look at the cabinet behind me. When I turned again Sherlock Holmes was standing smiling at me across my study table. I rose to my feet, stared at him for some seconds in utter amazement, and then it appears that I must have fainted for the first and the last time in my life. Certainly a grey mist swirled before my eyes, and when it cleared I found my collar-ends undone and the tingling after-taste of brandy upon my lips. Holmes was bending over my chair, his flask in his hand.

'My dear Watson,' said the well-remembered voice, 'I owe you a thousand apologies. I had no idea that you would be so affected.'

I gripped him by the arm.

'Holmes!' I cried. 'Is it really you? Can it indeed be that you are alive? Is it possible that you succeeded in climbing out of that awful abyss?'

'Wait a moment!' said he. 'Are you sure that you are really fit to discuss things? I have given you a serious shock by my unnecessarily dramatic appearance.'

'I am all right; but indeed, Holmes, I can hardly believe my eyes. Good heavens, to think that you—you of all men—should be standing in my study!' Again I gripped him by the sleeve and felt the thin, sinewy arm beneath it. 'Well, you're not a spirit, anyhow,'* said I. 'My dear chap, I am overjoyed to see you. Sit down, and tell me how you came alive out of that dreadful chasm.'

He sat opposite to me and lit a cigarette in his old nonchalant manner. He was dressed in the seedy frock-coat of the book merchant, but the rest of that individual lay in a pile of white hair and old books upon the table. Holmes looked even thinner and keener than of old, but there was a dead-white tinge in his aquiline face which told me that his life recently had not been a healthy one.

'I am glad to stretch myself, Watson,' said he. 'It is no joke when a tall man has to take a foot off his stature for several hours on end. Now, my dear fellow, in the matter of these explanations we have, if I may ask for your co-operation, a hard and dangerous night's work in front of us. Perhaps it would be better if I gave you an account of the whole situation when that work is finished.'

'I am full of curiosity. I should much prefer to hear now.'

'You'll come with me tonight?'

'When you like and where you like.'

'This is indeed like the old days. We shall have time for a mouthful of dinner before we need go. Well, then, about that chasm. I had no serious difficulty in getting out of it, for the very simple reason that I never was in it.'

'You never were in it?'

'No, Watson, I never was in it. My note to you was absolutely genuine. I had little doubt that I had come to the end of my career when I perceived the somewhat sinister figure of the late Professor Moriarty standing upon the narrow pathway which led to safety. I read an inexorable purpose in his grey eyes. I exchanged some remarks with him, therefore, and obtained his courteous permission to write the short note which you afterwards received. I left it with my cigarette-box and my stick,* and I walked along the pathway, Moriarty still at my heels. When I reached the end I stood at bay. He drew no weapon, but he rushed at me and threw his long arms around me. He knew that his own game was up, and was only anxious to revenge himself upon me. We tottered together upon the brink of the fall. I have some knowledge, however, of *baritsu*, or the Japanese system of wrestling,* which has more than once been very useful to me. I slipped through his grip, and he with a horrible scream kicked madly for a few seconds and clawed the air with both his hands. But for all his efforts he could not get his balance, and over he went. With my face over the brink I saw him fall for a long way. Then he struck a rock, bounded off, and splashed into the water.'

I listened with amazement to this explanation, which Holmes delivered between the puffs of his cigarette.

'But the tracks!' I cried. 'I saw with my own eyes that two went down the path and none returned.'

'It came about in this way. The instant that the professor had disappeared it struck me what a really extraordinarily lucky chance Fate had placed in my way. I knew that Moriarty was not the only man who had sworn my death. There were at least three others whose desire for vengeance upon me would only be increased by the death of their leader. They were all most dangerous men. One or other would certainly get me. On the other hand, if all the world was convinced that I was dead they would take liberties, these men; they would lay themselves open, and sooner or later I could destroy them. Then it would be time for me to announce that I was still in the land of the living.* So rapidly does the brain act that I believe I had thought this all out before Professor Moriarty had reached the bottom of the Reichenbach Fall.

'I stood up and examined the rocky wall behind me. In your picturesque account of the matter, which I read with great interest some months later,* you assert that the wall was sheer. This was not literally true. A few small footholds presented themselves, and there was some indication of a ledge. The cliff is so high that to climb it all was an obvious impossibility, and it was equally impossible to make my way along the wet path without leaving some tracks. I might, it is true, have reversed my boots,* as I have done on similiar occasions, but the sight of three sets of tracks in one direction would certainly have suggested a deception. On the whole, then, it was best that I should risk the climb. It was not a pleasant business, Watson. The fall roared beneath me. I am not a fanciful person, but I give you my word that I seemed to hear Moriarty's voice screaming at me out of the abyss. A mistake would have been fatal. More than once, as tufts of grass came out in my hand or my foot slipped in the wet notches of the rock, I thought that I was gone. But I struggled upwards, and at last I reached a ledge several feet deep and covered with soft green moss, where I could lie unseen in the most perfect comfort. There I was stretched when you, my dear Watson, and all your following were investigating in the most sympathetic and inefficient manner the circumstances of my death.

'At last, when you had all formed your inevitable and totally erroneous conclusions, you departed for the hotel, and I was left alone. I had imagined that I had reached the end of my adventures, but a very unexpected occurrence showed me that there were surprises still in store for me. A huge rock, falling from above, boomed past me, struck the path and bounded over into the chasm. For an instant I thought that it was an accident; but a moment later, looking up, I saw a man's head against the darkening sky, and another stone struck the very ledge upon which I was stretched, within a foot of my head. Of course, the meaning of this was obvious. Moriarty had not been alone. A confederate—and even that one glance had told me how dangerous a man that confederate was—had kept guard while the professor had attacked me. From a distance, unseen by me, he had been a witness of his friend's death and of my escape. He had waited, and then, making his way round to the top of the cliff, he had endeavoured to succeed where his comrade had failed.

'I did not take long to think about it, Watson. Again I saw that grim face look over the cliff, and I knew that it was the precursor of another stone. I scrambled down on to the path. I don't think I could have done it in cold blood. It was a hundred times more difficult than getting up. But I had no time to think of the danger for another stone sang past me as I hung by my hands from the edge of the ledge. Half-way down I slipped, but by the blessing of God I landed, torn and bleeding, upon the path. I took to my heels, did ten miles over the mountains* in the darkness, and a week later I found myself in Florence,* with the certainty that no one in the world knew what had become of me.

'I had only one confidant—my brother Mycroft. I owe you many apologies, my dear Watson, but it was all-important that it should be thought I was dead, and it is quite certain that you would not have written so convincing an account of my unhappy end had you not yourself thought that it was true. Several times during the last three years I have taken up my pen to write to you, but always I feared lest your affectionate regard for me should tempt you to some indiscretion which would betray my secret. For that reason I turned away from you this evening when you upset my books, for I was in danger at the time, and any show of surprise and emotion upon your part might have drawn attention to my identity and led to the most deplorable and irreparable results. As to Mycroft, I had to confide in him in order to obtain the money which I needed. The course of events in London did not run so well as I had hoped, for the trial of the Moriarty gang left two of its most dangerous members, my own most vindictive enemies, at liberty.* I travelled for two years in Tibet, therefore, and amused myself by visiting Lhasa and spending some days with the head Lama.* You may have read of the remarkable explorations of a Norwegian named Sigerson,* but I am sure that it never occurred to you that you were receiving news of your friend. I then passed through Persia,* looked in at Mecca,* and paid a short but interesting visit to the Khalifa at Khartoum,* the results of which I have communicated to the Foreign Office. Returning to France, I spent some months in a research into the coal-tar derivatives, which I conducted in a laboratory at Montpellier, in the south of France.* Having concluded this to my satisfaction,* and learning that only one of my enemies was now left in London, I was about to return, when my movements were hastened by the news of this remarkable Park Lane Mystery, which not only appealed to me by its own merits, but which seemed to offer some most peculiar personal opportunities. I came over at once to London, called in my own person at Baker Street, threw Mrs Hudson into violent hysterics, and found that Mycroft had preserved my rooms and my papers exactly as they had always been.* So it was, my dear Watson, that at two o'clock to-day* I found myself in my old armchair in my own old room, and only wishing that I could have seen my old friend Watson in the other chair which he has so often adorned.'

Such was the remarkable narrative to which I listened on that April evening*—a narrative which would have been utterly incredible to me had it not been confirmed by the actual sight of the tall, spare figure and the keen, eager face, which I had never thought to see again. In some manner he had learned of my own sad bereavement,* and his sympathy was shown in his manner rather than in his words. 'Work is the best antidote to sorrow,* my dear Watson,' said he, 'and I have a piece of work for us both to-night which, if we can bring it to a successful conclusion, will in itself justify a man's life on this planet.' In vain I begged him to tell me more. 'You will hear and see enough before morning,' he answered. 'We have three years of the past to discuss. Let that suffice until half-past nine,* when we start upon the notable adventure of the empty house.'

It was indeed like old times when, at that hour, I found myself seated beside him in a hansom,* my revolver in my pocket and the thrill of adventure in my heart. Holmes was cold and stern and silent. As the gleam of the street-lamps flashed upon his austere features, I saw that his brows were drawn down in thought and his thin lips compressed. I knew not what wild beast we were about to hunt down in the dark jungle of criminal London, but I was well assured from the bearing of this master huntsman that the adventure was a most grave one, while the sardonic smile which occasionally broke through his ascetic gloom boded little good for the object of our quest.

I had imagined that we were bound for Baker Street, but Holmes stopped the cab at the corner of Cavendish Square.* I observed that as he stepped out he gave a most searching glance to right and left, and at every subsequent street corner he took the utmost pains to assure that he was not followed. Our route was certainly a singular one. Holmes's knowledge of the byways of London was extraordinary, and on this occasion he passed rapidly, and with an assured step, through a network of mews and stables the very existence of which I had never known. We emerged at last into a small road, lined with old, gloomy houses, which led us into Manchester Street, and so to Blandford Street. Here he turned swiftly down a narrow passage, passed

through a wooden gate into a deserted yard, and then
opened with a key the back door of a house. We entered
together, and he closed it behind us.

The place was pitch dark, but it was evident to me that
it was an empty house. Our feet creaked and crackled over
the bare planking, and my outstretched hand touched a
wall from which the paper was hanging in ribbons.* Holmes's cold, thin fingers closed round my wrist and led me
forward down a long hall, until I dimly saw the murky
fanlight over the door. Here Holmes turned suddenly to the
right, and we found ourselves in a large, square, empty
room, heavily shadowed in the corners, but faintly lit in the
centre from the lights of the street beyond. There was no
lamp near, and the window was thick with dust, so that we
could only just discern each other's figures within. My
companion put his hand upon my shoulder, and his lips
close to my ear.

'Do you know where we are?' he whispered.

'Surely that is Baker Street,' I answered, staring through
the dim window.

'Exactly. We are in Camden House, which stands opposite
to our own old quarters.'*

'But why are we here?'

'Because it commands so excellent a view of that picturesque pile. Might I trouble you, my dear Watson, to draw
a little nearer to the window, taking every precaution not to
show yourself, and then to look up at our old rooms—the
starting-point of so many of our little adventures.* We will
see if my three years of absence have entirely taken away
my power to surprise you.'

I crept forward and looked across at the familiar window.
As my eyes fell upon it I gave a gasp and a cry of
amazement. The blind was down, and a strong light was
burning in the room. The shadow of a man who was seated
in a chair within was thrown in hard, black outline upon the
luminous screen of the window. There was no mistaking the
poise of the head, the squareness of the shoulders, the
sharpness of the features. The face was turned half-round,

and the effect was that of one of those silhouettes which our grandparents loved to frame. It was a perfect reproduction of Holmes. So amazed was I that I threw out my hand to make sure that the man himself was standing beside me. He was quivering with silent laughter.

'Well?' said he.

'Good heavens!' I cried. 'It's marvellous.'

'I trust that age doth not wither nor custom stale my infinite variety,'* said he, and I recognized in his voice the joy and pride which the artist takes in his own creation. 'It really is rather like me, is it not?'

'I should be prepared to swear that it was you.'

'The credit of the execution is due to Monsieur Oscar Meunier, of Grenoble,* who spent some days in doing the moulding. It is a bust in wax. The rest I arranged myself during my visit to Baker Street this afternoon.'

'But why?'

'Because, my dear Watson, I had the strongest possible reason for wishing certain people to think that I was there when I was really elsewhere.'

'And you thought the rooms were watched?'

'I *knew* that they were watched.'

'By whom?'

'By my old enemies, Watson. By the charming society whose leader lies in the Reichenbach Fall. You must remember that they knew, and only they knew, that I was still alive. Sooner or later they believed that I should come back to my rooms. They watched them continuously, and this morning they saw me arrive.'

'How do you know?'

'Because I recognized their sentinel when I glanced out of my window. He is a harmless enough fellow, Parker by name, a garrotter by trade,* and a remarkable performer upon the jew's harp.* I cared nothing for him. But I cared a great deal for the much more formidable person who was behind him, the bosom friend of Moriarty, the man who dropped the rocks over the cliff, the most cunning and dangerous criminal in London. That is the man who is after me tonight, Watson, and that is the man who is quite unaware that we are after *him.*'

My friend's plans were gradually revealing themselves. From this convenient retreat the watchers were being watched and the trackers tracked. That angular shadow up yonder was the bait, and we were the hunters. In silence we stood together in the darkness and watched the hurrying figures who passed and repassed in front of us. Holmes was silent and motionless; but I could tell that he was keenly alert, and that his eyes were fixed intently upon the stream of passers-by. It was a bleak and boisterous night, and the wind whistled shrilly down the long street. Many people were moving to and fro, most of them muffled in their coats and cravats. Once or twice it seemed to me that I had seen the same figure before, and I especially noticed two men who appeared to be sheltering themselves from the wind in the doorway of a house some distance up the street. I tried to draw my companion's attention to them, but he gave a little ejaculation of impatience, and continued to stare into the street. More than once he fidgeted with his feet and tapped rapidly with his fingers upon the wall. It was evident to me that he was becoming uneasy, and that his plans were not working out altogether as he had hoped. At last, as midnight approached and the street gradually cleared, he paced up and down the room in uncontrollable agitation. I was about to make some remark to him, when I raised my eyes to the lighted window, and again experienced almost as great a surprise as before. I clutched Holmes's arm and pointed upwards.

'The shadow has moved!' I cried.

It was, indeed, no longer the profile, but the back, which was turned towards us.

Three years had certainly not smoothed the asperities of his temper, or his impatience with a less active intelligence than his own.

'Of course it has moved,' said he. 'Am I such a farcical bungler, Watson, that I should erect an obvious dummy and expect that some of the sharpest men in Europe would be

16

deceived by it? We have been in this room two hours, and
Mrs Hudson has made some change in that figure eight
times, or once every quarter of an hour. She works it from
the front so that her shadow may never be seen. Ah!' He
drew in his breath with a shrill, excited intake. In the dim
light I saw his head thrown forward, his whole attitude rigid
with attention. Those two men might still be crouching in
the doorway, but I could no longer see them. All was still
and dark, save only that brilliant yellow screen in front of
us with the black figure outlined upon its centre. Again in
the utter silence I heard that thin, sibilant note which spoke
of intense suppressed excitement. An instant later he pulled
me back into the blackest corner of the room, and I felt his
warning hand upon my lips. The fingers which clutched me
were quivering. Never had I known my friend more moved,
and yet the dark street still stretched lonely and motionless
before us.

But suddenly I was aware of that which his keener senses
had already distinguished. A low, stealthy sound came to my
ears, not from the direction of Baker Street, but from the
back of the very house in which we lay concealed. A door
opened and shut. An instant later steps crept down the
passage—steps which were meant to be silent, but which
reverberated harshly through the empty house. Holmes
crouched back against the wall, and I did the same, my
hand closing upon the handle of my revolver. Peering
through the gloom, I saw the vague outline of a man a shade
blacker than the blackness of the open door. He stood for
an instant, and then he crept forward, crouching, menacing,
into the room. He was within three yards of us, this sinister
figure, and I had braced myself to meet his spring, before I
realized that he had no idea of our presence. He passed
close beside us, stole over to the window, and very softly and
noiselessly raised it for half a foot. As he sank to the level of
this opening the light of the street, no longer dimmed by the
dusty glass, fell full upon his face. The man seemed to be
beside himself with excitement. His two eyes shone like
stars, and his features were working convulsively. He was an

elderly man, with a thin projecting nose, a high, bald forehead, and a huge grizzled moustache. An opera-hat was pushed to the back of his head, and an evening dress shirt-front gleamed out through his open overcoat. His face was gaunt and swarthy, scored with deep, savage lines. In his hand he carried what appeared to be a stick, but as he laid it down upon the floor it gave a metallic clang. Then from the pocket of his overcoat he drew a bulky object, and he busied himself in some task which ended with a loud, sharp click, as if a spring or bolt had fallen into its place. Still kneeling upon the floor, he bent forward and threw all his weight and strength upon some lever, with the result that there came a long, whirling, grinding noise, ending once more in a powerful click. He straightened himself then, and I saw that what he held in his hand was a sort of gun, with a curiously misshapen butt. He opened it at the breech, put something in, and snapped the breech-block. Then, crouching down, he rested the end of the barrel upon the ledge of the open window, and I saw his long moustache droop over the stock and his eye gleam as it peered along the sights. I heard a little sigh of satisfaction as he cuddled the butt into his shoulder, and saw that amazing target, the black man on the yellow ground, standing clear at the end of his foresight. For an instant he was rigid and motionless. Then his finger tightened on the trigger. There was a strange, loud whiz and a long, silvery tinkle of broken glass. At that instant Holmes sprang like a tiger on to the marksman's back and hurled him flat upon his face. He was up again in a moment, and with convulsive strength he seized Holmes by the throat; but I struck him on the head with the butt of my revolver, and he dropped again upon the floor. I fell upon him, and as I held him my comrade blew a shrill call upon a whistle. There was the clatter of running feet upon the pavement, and two policemen in uniform, with one plain-clothes detective, rushed through the front entrance and into the room.

'That you, Lestrade?' said Holmes.

'Yes, Mr Holmes. I took the job myself. It's good to see you back in London, sir.'

'I think you want a little unofficial help. Three undetected murders in one year won't do, Lestrade. But you handled the Molesey Mystery* with less than your usual—that's to say, you handled it fairly well.'

We had all risen to our feet, our prisoner breathing hard, with a stalwart constable on each side of him. Already a few loiterers had begun to collect in the street. Holmes stepped up to the window, closed it, and dropped the blinds. Lestrade had produced two candles, and the policemen had uncovered their lanterns. I was able at last to have a good look at our prisoner.

It was a tremendously virile and yet sinister face which was turned towards us. With the brow of a philosopher above and the jaw of a sensualist below, the man must have started with great capacities for good or for evil. But one could not look upon his cruel blue eyes, with their drooping, cynical lids, or upon the fierce, aggressive nose and the threatening, deep-lined brow, without reading Nature's plainest danger-signals. He took no heed of any of us, but his eyes were fixed upon Holmes's face with an expression in which hatred and amazement were equally blended. 'You devil!' he kept on muttering—'you clever, clever devil!'*

'Ah, Colonel,' said Holmes, arranging his crumpled collar, ' "journeys end in lovers' meetings," as the old play says.* I don't think I have had the pleasure of seeing you since you favoured me with those attentions as I lay on the ledge above the Reichenbach Fall.'

The colonel still stared at my friend like a man in a trance. 'You cunning, cunning devil!'* was all that he could say.

'I have not introduced you yet,' said Holmes. 'This, gentlemen, is Colonel Sebastian Moran,* once of Her Majesty's Indian Army, and the best heavy game shot that our Eastern Empire has ever produced. I believe I am correct, Colonel, in saying that your bag of tigers still remains unrivalled?'

The fierce old man said nothing, but still glared at my companion; with his savage eyes and bristling moustache, he was wonderfully like a tiger himself.*

'I wonder that my very simple stratagem could deceive so old a shikari,'* said Holmes. 'It must be very familiar to you. Have you not tethered a young kid under a tree, lain above it with your rifle, and waited for the bait to bring up your tiger? This empty house is my tree, and you are my tiger. You have possibly had other guns in reserve in case there should be several tigers, or in the unlikely supposition of your own aim failing you. These', he pointed around, 'are my other guns. The parallel is exact.'

Colonel Moran sprang forward with a snarl of rage, but the constables dragged him back. The fury upon his face was terrible to look at.

'I confess that you had one small surprise for me,' said Holmes. 'I did not anticipate that you would yourself make use of this empty house and this convenient front window. I had imagined you as operating from the street, where my friend Lestrade and his merry men* were awaiting you. With that exception, all has gone as I expected.'

Colonel Moran turned to the official detective.

'You may or may not have just cause for arresting me,' said he, 'but at least there can be no reason why I should submit to the gibes of this person. If I am in the hands of the law, let things be done in a legal way.'

'Well, that's reasonable enough,' said Lestrade. 'Nothing further you have to say, Mr Holmes, before we go?'

Holmes had picked up the powerful air-gun* from the floor and was examining its mechanism.

'An admirable and unique weapon,' said he, 'noiseless and of tremendous power. I knew Von Herder, the blind German mechanic,* who constructed it to the order of the late Professor Moriarty. For years I have been aware of its existence, though I have never before had an opportunity of handling it. I commend it very specially to your attention, Lestrade, and also the bullets which fit it.'

'You can trust us to look after that, Mr Holmes,' said Lestrade, as the whole party moved towards the door. 'Anything further to say?'

'Only to ask what charge you intend to prefer?'

'What charge, sir? Why, of course, the attempted murder of Mr Sherlock Holmes.'

'Not so, Lestrade. I do not propose to appear in the matter at all. To you, and to you only, belongs the credit of the remarkable arrest which you have effected. Yes, Lestrade, I congratulate you! With your usual happy mixture of cunning and audacity you have got him.'

'Got him! Got whom, Mr Holmes?'

'The man whom the whole Force has been seeking in vain—Colonel Sebastian Moran, who shot the Honourable Ronald Adair with an expanding bullet from an air-gun through the open window of the second-floor front of No. 427 Park Lane, upon the 30th of last month. That's the charge, Lestrade. And now, Watson, if you can endure the draught from a broken window, I think that half an hour in my study over a cigar may afford you some profitable amusement.'

Our old chambers had been left unchanged, through the supervision of Mycroft Holmes and the immediate care of Mrs Hudson.* As I entered I saw, it is true, an unwonted tidiness, but the old landmarks were all in their places. There were the chemical corner and the acid-stained deal-topped table. There upon a shelf was the row of formidable scrap-books and books of reference which many of our fellow citizens would have been so glad to burn. The diagrams, the violin-case, and the pipe-rack—even the Persian slipper which contained the tobacco—all met my eye as I glanced round me. There were two occupants of the room—one Mrs Hudson, who beamed upon us both as we entered; the other, the strange dummy which had played so important a part in the evening's adventures. It was a wax-coloured model of my friend, so admirably done that it was a perfect facsimile. It stood on a small pedestal table with an old dressing-gown of Holmes's so draped round it that the illusion from the street was absolutely perfect.

'I hope you preserved all precautions, Mrs Hudson?' said Holmes.

'I went to it on my knees, sir, just as you told me.'

'Excellent. You carried the thing out very well. Did you observe where the bullet went?'

'Yes, sir. I'm afraid it has spoilt your beautiful bust, for it passed right through the head and flattened itself on the wall. I picked it up from the carpet. Here it is!'

Holmes held it out to me. 'A soft revolver bullet, as you perceive, Watson. There's genius in that—for who would expect to find such a thing fired from an air-gun? All right, Mrs Hudson, I am much obliged for your assistance. And now, Watson, let me see you in your old seat once more, for there are several points which I should like to discuss with you.'

He had thrown off the seedy frock-coat, and now he was the Holmes of old, in the mouse-coloured dressing-gown* which he took from his effigy.

'The old shikari's nerves have not lost their steadiness nor his eyes their keenness,' said he, with a laugh, as he inspected the shattered forehead of his bust.

'Plumb in the middle of the back of the head and smack through the brain.* He was the best shot in India, and I expect that there are few better in London. Have you heard the name?'

'No, I have not.'

'Well, well, such is fame! But then, if I remember aright, you had not heard the name of Professor James Moriarty,* who had one of the great brains of the century. Just give me down my index of biographies* from the shelf.'

He turned over the pages lazily, leaning back in his chair, and blowing great clouds of smoke from his cigar.

'My collection of M's is a fine one,' said he. 'Moriarty himself is enough to make any letter illustrious, and here is Morgan the poisoner,* and Merridew of abominable memory,* and Mathews, who knocked out my left canine* in the waiting-room at Charing Cross, and, finally, here is our friend of to-night.'

He handed over the book, and I read: '*Moran, Sebastian, Colonel*. Unemployed. Formerly 1st Bengalore Pioneers. Born London, 1840. Son of Sir Augustus Moran, CB, once British Minister to Persia. Educated Eton and Oxford. Served in

22

Jowaki Campaign, Afghan Campaign, Charasiab (dispat-
ches), Sherpur, and Cabul. Author of *Heavy Game of the
Western Himalayas*, 1881; *Three Months in the Jungle*, 1884.
Address: Conduit Street. Clubs: The Anglo-Indian, the
Tankerville, the Bagatelle Card Club.'*

On the margin was written in Holmes's precise hand:
'The second most dangerous man in London.'

'This is astonishing,' said I, as I handed back the volume.
'The man's career is that of a honourable soldier.'

'It is true,' Holmes answered. 'Up to a certain point he
did well. He was always a man of iron nerve, and the story
is still told in India how he crawled down a drain after a
wounded man-eating tiger.* There are some trees, Watson,
which grow to a certain height and then suddenly develop
some unsightly eccentricity. You will see it often in humans.
I have a theory that the individual represents in his development the whole procession of his ancestors, and that such
a sudden turn to good or evil stands for some strong
influence which came into the line of his pedigree. The
person becomes, as it were, the epitome of the history of his
own family.'

'It is surely rather fanciful.'

'Well, I don't insist upon it. Whatever the cause, Colonel
Moran began to go wrong. Without any open scandal, he
still made India too hot to hold him. He retired, came to
London, and again acquired an evil name. It was at this
time that he was sought out by Professor Moriarty, to whom
for a time he was chief of the staff.* Moriarty supplied him
liberally with money, and used him only in one or two very
high-class jobs which no ordinary criminal could have
undertaken. You may have some recollection of the death of
Mrs Stewart, of Lauder,* in 1887. Not? Well, I am sure
Moran was at the bottom of it; but nothing could be proved.
So cleverly was the colonel concealed that even when the
Moriarty gang was broken up we could not incriminate him.
You remember at that date, when I called upon you in your
rooms, how I put up the shutters for fear of air-guns?* No
doubt you thought me fanciful. I knew exactly what I was

doing, for I knew of the existence of this remarkable gun, and I knew also that one of the best shots in the world would be behind it. When we were in Switzerland he followed us with Moriarty, and it was undoubtedly he who gave me that evil five minutes on the Reichenbach ledge.

'You may think that I read the papers with some attention during my sojourn in France, on the look-out for any chance of laying him by the heels. So long as he was free in London my life would really not have been worth living. Night and day the shadow would have been over me, and sooner or later his chance must have come. What could I do? I could not shoot him at sight, or I should myself be in the dock. There was no use appealing to a magistrate. They cannot interfere on the strength of what would appear to them to be a wild suspicion. So I could do nothing. But I watched the criminal news, knowing that sooner or later I should get him. Then came the death of this Ronald Adair. My chance had come at last! Knowing what I did, was it not certain that Colonel Moran had done it? He had played cards with the lad; he had followed him home from the club; he had shot him through the open window. There was not a doubt of it. The bullets alone are enough to put his head in a noose. I came over at once. I was seen by the sentinel, who would, I knew, direct the colonel's attention to my presence. He could not fail to connect my sudden return with his crime, and to be terribly alarmed. I was sure that he would make an attempt to get me out of the way *at once*, and would bring round his murderous weapon for that purpose. I left him an excellent mark in the window, and, having warned the police that they might be needed—by the way, Watson, you spotted their presence in that doorway with unerring accuracy—I took up what seemed to me to be a judicious post for observation, never dreaming that he would choose the same spot for his attack. Now, my dear Watson, does anything remain for me to explain?'

'Yes,' said I. 'You have not made it clear what was Colonel Moran's motive in murdering the Honourable Ronald Adair.'

'Ah! my dear Watson, there we come into those realms of conjecture where the most logical mind may be at fault. Each may form his own hypothesis upon the present evidence, and yours is as likely to be correct as mine.'

'You have formed one, then?'

'I think that it is not difficult to explain the facts. It came out in evidence that Colonel Moran and young Adair had between them won a considerable amount of money. Now, Moran undoubtedly played foul—of that I have long been aware. I believe that on the day of the murder, Adair had discovered that Moran was cheating. Very likely he had spoken to him privately, and had threatened to expose him unless he voluntarily resigned his membership of the club and promised not to play cards again. It is unlikely that a youngster like Adair would at once make a hideous scandal by exposing a well-known man so much older than himself. Probably he acted as I suggest. The exclusion from his clubs would mean ruin to Moran, who lived by his ill-gotten card gains. He therefore murdered Adair, who at the time was endeavouring to work out how much money he should himself return, since he could not profit by his partner's foul play. He locked the door, lest the ladies should surprise him and insist upon knowing what he was doing with these names and coins. Will it pass?'

'I have no doubt that you have hit upon the truth.'

'It will be verified or disproved at the trial. Meanwhile, come what may, Colonel Moran will trouble us no more, the famous air-gun of Von Herder will embellish the Scotland Yard Museum,* and once again Mr Sherlock Holmes is free to devote his life to examining those interesting little problems which the complex life of London so plentifully presents.'

The Norwood Builder

'FROM the point of view of the criminal expert,' said Mr Sherlock Holmes, 'London has become a singularly uninteresting city since the death of the late lamented Professor Moriarty.'*

'I can hardly think that you would find many decent citizens to agree with you,' I answered.

'Well, well, I must not be selfish,' said he, with a smile, as he pushed back his chair from the breakfast-table. 'The community is certainly the gainer, and no one the loser, save the poor out-of-work specialist, whose occupation has gone. With that man in the field one's morning paper presented infinite possibilities. Often it was only the smallest trace, Watson, the faintest indication, and yet it was enough to tell me that the great malignant brain was there, as the gentlest tremors of the edges of the web remind one of the foul spider which lurks in the centre. Petty thefts, wanton assaults, purposeless outrage—to the man who held the clue all could be worked into one connected whole. To the scientific student of the higher criminal world no capital in Europe offered the advantages which London then possessed. But now—' He shrugged his shoulders in humorous deprecation of the state of things which he had himself done so much to produce.

At the time of which I speak, Holmes had been back for some months, and I, at his request, had sold my practice and returned to share the old quarters in Baker Street.* A young doctor, named Verner,* had purchased my small Kensington practice, and given with astonishingly little demur the highest price that I ventured to ask—an incident which only explained itself some years later, when I found that Verner was a distant relation of Holmes's, and that it was my friend who had really found the money.

26

Our months of partnership had not been so uneventful as he had stated, for I find, on looking over my notes, that this period includes the case of the papers of ex-President Murillo,* and also the shocking affair of the Dutch steamship *Friesland*,* which so nearly cost us both our lives. His cold and proud nature was always averse, however, to anything in the shape of public applause, and he bound me in the most stringent terms to say no further word of himself, his methods, or his successes—a prohibition which, as I have explained, has only now been removed.

Mr Sherlock Holmes was leaning back in his chair after his whimsical protest, and was unfolding his morning paper in a leisurely fashion, when our attention was arrested by a tremendous ring at the bell, followed immediately by a hollow drumming sound, as if someone were beating on the outer door with his fist. As it opened there came a tumultuous rush into the hall, rapid feet clattered up the stair, and an instant later a wild-eyed and frantic young man, pale, dishevelled, and palpitating, burst into the room. He looked from one to the other of us, and under our gaze of inquiry he became conscious that some apology was needed for this unceremonious entry.

'I'm sorry, Mr Holmes,' he cried. 'You mustn't blame me. I am nearly mad. Mr Holmes, I am the unhappy John Hector McFarlane.'*

He made the announcement as if the name alone would explain both his visit and its manner, but I could see by my companion's unresponsive face that it meant no more to him than to me.

'Have a cigarette, Mr McFarlane,' said he, pushing his case across. 'I am sure that with your symptoms my friend Dr Watson here would prescribe a sedative. The weather has been so very warm these last few days. Now, if you feel a little more composed, I should be glad if you would sit down in that chair and tell us very slowly and quietly who you are and what it is that you want. You mentioned your name as if I should recognize it, but I assure you that, beyond obvious facts that you are a bachelor, a solicitor, a

27

Freemason, and an asthmatic, I know nothing whatever about you.'

Familiar as I was with my friend's methods, it was not difficult for me to follow his deductions, and to observe the untidiness of attire, the sheaf of legal papers, the watch-charm, and the breathing which had prompted them. Our client, however, stared in amazement.

'Yes, I am all that, Mr Holmes, and in addition I am the most unfortunate man at this moment in London. For God's sake* don't abandon me, Mr Holmes! If they come to arrest me before I have finished my story, make them give me time, so that I may tell you the whole truth. I could go to gaol happy if I knew that you were working for me outside.'

'Arrest you!' said Holmes. 'This is really most grati—most interesting. On what charge do you expect to be arrested?'

'Upon the charge of murdering Mr Jonas Oldacre,* of Lower Norwood.'*

My companion's expressive face showed a sympathy which was not, I am afraid, entirely* unmixed with satisfaction.

'Dear me!' said he; 'it was only this moment at breakfast that I was saying to my friend, Dr Watson, that sensational cases had disappeared out of our papers.'

Our visitor stretched forward a quivering hand and picked up the *Daily Telegraph*, which still lay upon Holmes's knee.

'If you had looked at it, sir, you would have seen at a glance what the errand is on which I have come to you this morning. I feel as if my name and my misfortune must be in every man's mouth.' He turned it over to expose the central page. 'Here it is, and with your permission I will read it to you. Listen to this, Mr Holmes. The headlines are: MYSTERIOUS AFFAIR AT LOWER NORWOOD.* DISAPPEARANCE OF A WELL-KNOWN BUILDER. SUSPICION OF MURDER AND ARSON. A CLUE TO THE CRIMINAL. That is the clue which they are already following, Mr Holmes, and I know that it leads infallibly to me. I have been followed from London Bridge Station,* and I am sure that they are only waiting for the warrant to arrest me. It will break my mother's heart—it will break her heart!' He wrung his hands in an agony of apprehension, and swayed backwards and forwards in his chair.

I looked with interest upon this man, who was accused of being the perpetrator of a crime of violence. He was flaxen-haired and handsome in a washed-out, negative fashion, with frightened blue eyes and a clean-shaven face, with a weak, sensitive mouth. His age may have been about twenty-seven; his dress and bearing, that of a gentleman. From the pocket of his light summer overcoat protruded the bundle of endorsed papers which proclaimed his profession.

'We must use what time we have,' said Holmes. 'Watson, would you have the kindness to take the paper and to read me the paragraph in question?'

Underneath the vigorous headlines which our client had quoted I read the following suggestive narrative:

'Late last night, or early this morning, an incident oc- curred at Lower Norwood which points, it is feared, to a serious crime. Mr Jonas Oldacre is a well-known resident of that suburb, where he has carried on his business as a builder for many years. Mr Oldacre is a bachelor, fifty-two years of age, and lives in Deep Dene House, at the Syden- ham end of the road of that name.* He has had the reputation of being a man of eccentric habits, secretive and retiring. For some years he has practically withdrawn from the business, in which he is said to have amassed consider- able wealth. A small timber-yard still exists, however, at the back of the house, and last night, about twelve o'clock, an alarm was given that one of the stacks was on fire. The engines were soon upon the spot, but the dry wood burned with great fury, and it was impossible to arrest the confla- gration until the stack had been entirely consumed. Up to this point the incident bore the appearance of an ordinary accident, but fresh indications seem to point to serious crime. Surprise was expressed at the absence of the master of the establishment from the scene of the fire, and an inquiry followed, which showed that he had disappeared from the house. An examination of his room revealed that the bed had not been slept in, that a safe which stood in it was open, that a number of important papers were scattered about the room, and, finally, that there were signs of a murderous struggle, slight traces of blood being found within the room, and an oaken walking-stick which also showed stains of blood upon the handle. It is known that Mr Jonas Oldacre had received a late visitor in his bedroom upon that night, and the stick found has been identified as the property of this person, who is a young London solicitor named John Hector McFarlane, junior partner of Graham & McFarlane, of 426 Gresham Buildings, EC.* The police believe that they have evidence in their possession which supplies a very convincing motive for the crime, and altogether it cannot be doubted that sensational developments will follow.

'LATER—It is rumoured as we go to press that Mr John Hector McFarlane has actually been arrested on the charge of the murder of Mr Jonas Oldacre. It is at least certain that a warrant has been issued. There have been further and sinister developments in the investigation at Norwood. Besides the signs of a struggle in the room of the unfortunate builder, it is now known that the French windows of his bedroom (which is on the ground floor) were found to be open, that there were marks as if some bulky object had been dragged across to the wood-pile, and, finally, it is asserted that charred remains* have been found among the charcoal ashes of the fire. The police theory is that a most sensational crime has been committed, that the victim was clubbed to death in his own bedroom, his papers rifled, and his dead body dragged across to the wood-stack, which was then ignited so as to hide all traces of the crime. The conduct of the criminal investigation has been left in the experienced hands of Inspector Lestrade, of Scotland Yard, who is following up the clues with his accustomed energy and sagacity.'

Sherlock Holmes listened with closed eyes and finger-tips together to this remarkable account.

'The case has certainly some points of interest,' said he, in his languid fashion. 'May I ask, in the first place, Mr McFarlane, how it is that you are still at liberty, since there appears to be enough evidence to justify your arrest?'

'I live at Torrington Lodge, Blackheath,* with my parents, Mr Holmes; but last night, having to do business very late with Mr Jonas Oldacre, I stayed at an hotel in Norwood, and came to my business from there. I knew nothing of this affair until I was in the train, when I read what you have just heard. I at once saw the horrible danger of my position, and I hurried to put the case into your hands. I have no doubt that I should have been arrested either at my City office or at my home. A man followed me from London Bridge Station, and I have no doubt—Great heaven, what is that?'

It was a clang of the bell, followed instantly by heavy steps upon the stair. A moment later our old friend Lestrade appeared in the doorway. Over his shoulder I caught a glimpse of one or two uniformed policemen outside.

'Mr John Hector McFarlane,' said Lestrade.

Our unfortunate client rose with a ghastly face.

'I arrest you for the wilful murder of Mr Jonas Oldacre of Lower Norwood.'

McFarlane turned to us with a gesture of despair, and sank into his chair once more like one who is crushed.

'One moment, Lestrade,' said Holmes. 'Half an hour more or less can make no difference to you, and the gentleman was about to give us an account of this very interesting affair, which might aid us in clearing it up.'

'I think there will be no difficulty in clearing it up,' said Lestrade grimly.

'None the less, with your permission, I should be much interested to hear his account.'

'Well, Mr Holmes, it is difficult for me to refuse you anything, for you have been of use to the Force once or twice in the past, and we owe you a good turn at Scotland Yard,' said Lestrade. 'At the same time, I must remain with my prisoner, and I am bound to warn him that anything he may say will appear in evidence against him.'

'I wish nothing better,' said our client. 'All I ask is that you should hear and recognize the absolute truth.'

Lestrade looked at his watch. 'I'll give you half an hour,' said he.

'I must explain first,' said McFarlane, 'that I knew nothing of Mr Jonas Oldacre. His name was familiar to me; for many years ago my parents were acquainted with him, but they drifted apart. I was very much surprised, therefore, when yesterday, about three o'clock in the afternoon, he walked into my office in the City. But I was still more astonished when he told me the object of his visit. He had in his hand several sheets of a note-book, covered with scribbled writing—here they are—and he laid them on my table.

' "Here is my will," said he. "I want you, Mr McFarlane, to cast it into proper legal shape. I will sit here while you do so."

'I set myself to copy it, and you can imagine my astonishment when I found that, with some reservations, he had left all his property to me. He was a strange, little, ferret-like man, with white eyelashes, and when I looked up at him I found his keen grey eyes fixed upon me with an amused expression.* I could hardly believe my own senses as I read the terms of the will; but he explained that he was a bachelor with hardly any living relation, that he had known my parents in his youth, and that he had always heard of me as a very deserving young man, and was assured that his money would be in worthy hands. Of course, I could only stammer out my thanks. The will was duly finished, signed, and witnessed by my clerk.* This is it on the blue paper, and these slips, as I have explained, are the rough draft. Mr Jonas Oldacre then informed me that there were a number of documents—building leases, title-deeds, mortgages, scrip, and so forth—which it was neces-sary that I should see and understand. He said that his mind would not be easy until the whole thing was settled, and he begged me to come out to his house at Norwood that night, bringing the will with me, and to arrange matters. "Remem-

32

ber, my boy, not one word to your parents about the affair until everything is settled. We will keep it as a little surprise for them." He was very insistent upon this point, and made me promise it faithfully.

'You can imagine, Mr Holmes, that I was not in a humour to refuse him anything that he might ask. He was my benefactor, and all my desire was to carry out his wishes in every particular. I sent a telegram home, therefore, to say that I had important business on hand, and that it was impossible for me to say how late I might be. Mr Oldacre had told me that he would like me to have supper with him at nine, as he might not be home before that hour. I had some difficulty in finding his house, however, and it was nearly half-past before I reached it. I found him—'

'One moment!' said Holmes. 'Who opened the door?'

'A middle-aged woman, who was, I suppose, his housekeeper.'*

'And it was she, I presume, who mentioned your name?'

'Exactly,' said McFarlane.

'Pray proceed.'

Mr* McFarlane wiped his damp brow, and then continued his narrative:

'I was shown by this woman into a sitting-room, where a frugal supper was laid out. Afterwards Mr Jonas Oldacre led me into his bedroom, in which there stood a heavy safe. This he opened and took out a mass of documents, which we went over together. It was between eleven and twelve when we finished. He remarked that we must not disturb the housekeeper. He showed me out through his own French window, which had been open all this time.'

'Was the blind down?' asked Holmes.

'I will not be sure, but I believe that it was only half down. Yes, I remember how he pulled it up in order to swing open the window. I could not find my stick, and he said, "Never mind, my boy; I shall see a good deal of you now, I hope, and I will keep your stick until you come back to claim it." I left him there, the safe open, and the papers made up in packets upon the table. It was so late that I could not get back to Blackheath, so I spent the night at the Anerley Arms,* and I knew nothing more until I read of this horrible affair in the morning.'

'Anything more that you would like to ask, Mr Holmes?' said Lestrade, whose eyebrows had gone up once or twice during this remarkable explanation.

'Not until I have been to Blackheath.'

'You mean to Norwood,' said Lestrade.

'Oh, yes; no doubt that is what I must have meant,' said Holmes, with his enigmatical smile. Lestrade had learned by more experiences than he would care to acknowledge that that razor-like brain could cut through that which was impenetrable to him. I saw him look curiously at my companion.

'I think I should like to have a word with you presently, Mr Sherlock Holmes,' said he. 'Now, Mr McFarlane, two of my constables are at the door, and there is a four-wheeler* waiting.' The wretched young man arose, and with a last beseeching glance at us he walked from the room. The officers conducted him to the cab, but Lestrade remained.

Holmes had picked up the pages which formed the rough draft of the will, and was looking at them with the keenest interest upon his face.

'There are some points about that document, Lestrade, are there not?' said he, pushing them over.

The official looked at them with a puzzled expression.

'I can read the first few lines, and these in the middle of the second page, and one or two at the end. Those are as clear as print,' said he; 'but the writing in between is very bad, and there are three places where I cannot read it at all.'

'What do you make of that?' said Holmes.

'Well, what do *you* make of it?'

'That it was written in a train; the good writing represents stations, the bad writing, movement, and the very bad writing, passing over points. A scientific expert would pronounce at once that this was drawn up on a suburban line, since nowhere save in the immediate vicinity of a great city could there be so quick a succession of points. Granting that his whole journey was occupied in drawing up the will, then the train was an express, only stopping once between Norwood and London Bridge.'

Lestrade began to laugh.

'You are too many for me when you begin to get on your theories, Mr Holmes,' said he. 'How does this bear on the case?'

'Well, it corroborates the young man's story to the extent that the will was drawn up by Jonas Oldacre in his journey yesterday. It is curious—is it not?—that a man should draw up so important a document in so haphazard a fashion. It suggests that he did not think it was going to be of much practical importance. If a man drew up a will which he did not intend ever to be effective he might do it so.'

'Well, he drew up his own death-warrant at the same time,' said Lestrade.

'Oh, you think so?'

'Don't you?'

'Well, it is quite possible; but the case is not clear to me yet.'

'Not clear? Well, if that isn't clear, what *could* be clearer?* Here is a young man who learns suddenly that if a certain older man dies he will succeed to a fortune. What does he do? He says nothing to anyone, but he arranges that he shall go out on some pretext to see his client that night; he waits until the only other person in the house is in bed, and then in the solitude of the man's room he murders him, burns his body in the wood-pile, and departs to a neighbouring hotel. The blood-stains in the room and also on the stick are very slight. It is probable that he imagined his crime to be a bloodless one, and hoped that if the body were consumed it would hide all traces of the method of his death—traces which for some reason must have pointed to him. Is all this not obvious?'

'It strikes me, my good Lestrade, as being just a trifle too obvious,' said Holmes. 'You do not add imagination to your other great qualities; but if you could for one moment put yourself in the place of this young man, would you choose the very night after the will had been made to commit your crime? Would it not seem dangerous to you to make so very close a relation between the two incidents? Again, would you choose an occasion when you are known to be in the house, when a servant has let you in? And, finally, would you take the great pains to conceal the body and yet leave your own stick as a sign that you were the criminal? Confess, Lestrade, that all this is very unlikely.'

'As to the stick, Mr Holmes, you know as well as I do that a criminal is often flurried and does things which a cool man would avoid. He was very likely afraid to go back to the room. Give me another theory that would fit the facts.'

'I could very easily give you half a dozen,' said Holmes. 'Here, for example, is a very possible and even probable one. I make you a free present of it. The older man is showing documents which are of evident value. A passing tramp sees them through the window, the blind of which is only half down. Exit the solicitor. Enter the tramp! He seizes a stick, which he observes there, kills Oldacre, and departs after burning the body.'

'Why should the tramp burn the body?'

'For the matter of that, why should McFarlane?'

'To hide some evidence.'

'Possibly the tramp wanted to hide that any murder at all had been committed.'

'And why did the tramp take nothing?'

'Because they were papers that he could not negotiate.'

Lestrade shook his head, though it seemed to me that his manner was less absolutely assured than before.

'Well, Mr Sherlock Holmes, you may look for your tramp, and while you are finding him we will hold on to our man. The future will show which is right. Just notice this point, Mr Holmes—that so far as we know none of the papers were removed, and that the prisoner is the one man in the world who had no reason for removing them since he was heir-at-law and would come into them in any case.'

My friend seemed struck by this remark.

'I don't mean to deny that the evidence is in some ways very strongly in favour of your theory,' said he. 'I only wish to point out that there are other theories possible. As you say, the future will decide. Good morning! I dare say that in the course of the day I shall drop in at Norwood and see how you are getting on.'

When the detective departed my friend rose and made his preparations for the day's work with the alert air of a man who has a congenial task before him.

'My first movement, Watson,' said he, as he bustled into his frock-coat, 'must, as I said, be in the direction of Blackheath.'*

'And why not Norwood?'

'Because we have in this case one singular incident coming close to the heels of another singular incident. The police are making the mistake of concentrating their attention upon the second because it happens to be the one which is actually criminal. But it is evident to me that the logical way to approach the case is to begin by trying to throw some light upon the first incident—the curious will, so suddenly made, and to so unexpected an heir. It may do something to simplify what followed. No, my dear fellow, I don't think you can help me. There is no prospect of danger, or I should not dream of stirring out without you. I trust that when I see you in the evening I will be able to report that I have been able to do something for this unfortunate youngster who has thrown himself upon my protection.'

It was late when my friend returned, and I could see by a glance at his haggard and anxious face that the high hopes with which he had started had not been fulfilled. For an hour he droned away upon his violin, endeavouring to soothe his own ruffled spirits. At last he flung down the instrument and plunged into a detailed account of his misadventures.

'It's all going wrong, Watson—all as wrong as it can go. I kept a bold face before Lestrade, but, upon my soul, I believe that for once the fellow is on the right track and we are on the wrong. All my instincts are one way, and all the facts are the other, and I much fear that British juries have not yet attained that pitch of intelligence when they will give the preference to my theories over Lestrade's facts.'

'Did you go to Blackheath?'

'Yes, Watson, I went there, and I found very quickly that the late lamented Oldacre was a pretty considerable black-guard. The father was away in search of his son. The mother was at home—a little, fluffy, blue-eyed person, in a tremor of fear and indignation. Of course, she would not admit even the possibility of his guilt. But she would not express either surprise or regret over the fate of Oldacre. On the contrary, she spoke of him with such bitterness that she was unconsciously considerably strengthening the case of the police; for, of course, if the son had heard her speak of the man in that fashion it would predispose him towards hatred and violence. "He was more like a malignant and cunning ape than a human being," said she, "and he always was, ever since he was a young man."

' "You knew him at the* time?" said I.

' "Yes, I knew him well; in fact, he was an old suitor of mine. Thank God* that I had the sense to turn away from him and to marry a better, if a poorer, man. I was engaged to him, Mr Holmes, when I heard a shocking story of how he had turned a cat loose in an aviary, and I was so horrified at his brutal cruelty that I would have nothing more to do with him." She rummaged in a bureau, and presently she produced a photograph of a woman, shame-fully defaced and mutilated with a knife. "That is my own photograph," said she. "He sent it to me in that state, with his curse, upon my wedding morning."

' "Well," said I, "at least he has forgiven you now, since he has left all his property to your son."

' "Neither my son nor I want anything from Jonas Old-acre, dead or alive," she cried, with a proper spirit. "There is a God in heaven, Mr Holmes, and that same God who has punished that wicked man will show in His own good time that my son's hands are guiltless of his blood."

'Well, I tried one or two leads, but could get at nothing which would help our hypothesis, and several points which would make against it. I gave it up at last, and off I went to Norwood.

'This place, Deep Dene House, is a big modern villa of staring brick, standing back in its own grounds, with a laurel-clumped lawn in front of it. To the right and some distance back from the road was the timber-yard which had been the scene of the fire. Here's a rough plan on a leaf of my note-book. This window on the left is the one which opens into Oldacre's room. You can look into it from the road, you see. That is about the only bit of consolation I have had to-day. Lestrade was not there, but his head constable did the honours. They had just made a great treasure-trove. They had spent the morning raking among the ashes of the burned wood-pile and besides the charred organic remains they had secured several discoloured metal discs. I examined them with care, and there was no doubt that they were trouser buttons. I even distinguished that one of them was marked with the name of "Hyams",* who was Oldacre's tailor. I then worked the lawn very carefully for signs and traces, but this drought has made everything as hard as iron. Nothing was to be seen save that somebody or a bundle* had been dragged through a low privet hedge which is in a line with the wood-pile. All that, of course, fits in with the official theory. I crawled about the lawn with an August sun on my back. But I got up at the end of an hour no wiser than before.

'Well, after this fiasco I went into the bedroom and examined that also. The blood-stains were very slight, mere smears and discolorations, but undoubtedly fresh. The stick had been removed, but there also the marks were slight. There is no doubt about the stick belonging to our client. He admits it. Footmarks of both men could be made out on the carpet, but none of any third person, which again is a trick for the other side. They were piling up their score all the time, and we were at a standstill.

'Only one little gleam of hope did I get—and yet it amounted to nothing. I examined the contents of the safe, most of which had been taken out and left on the table. The papers had been made up into sealed envelopes, one or two of which had been opened by the police. They were not, so far as I could judge, of any great value, nor did the bankbook show that Mr Oldacre was in such very affluent circumstances. But it seemed to me that all the papers were not there. There were allusions to some deeds—possibly the more valuable—which I could not find. This, of course, if we could definitely prove it, would turn Lestrade's argument against himself, for who would steal a thing if he knew that he would shortly inherit it?

'Finally, having drawn every other cover and picked up no scent, I tried my luck with the housekeeper. Mrs Lexington is her name, a little, dark, silent person, with suspicious and sidelong eyes. She could tell us something if she would—I am convinced of it. But she was as close as wax. Yes, she had let Mr McFarlane in at half-past nine. She wished her hand had withered before she had done so. She had gone to bed at half-past ten. Her room was at the other end of the house, and she could hear nothing of what passed. Mr McFarlane had left his hat, and to the best of her belief his stick, in the hall. She had been awakened by the alarm of fire. Her poor, dear master had certainly been murdered. Had he any enemies? Well, every man had enemies, but Mr Oldacre kept himself very much to himself, and only met people in the way of business. She had seen the buttons, and was sure that they belonged to the clothes which he had worn last night. The wood-pile was very dry, for it had not rained for a month. It burned like a tinder, and by the time she reached the spot nothing could be seen but flames. She and all the firemen smelled the burned flesh from inside it. She knew nothing of the papers, nor of Mr Oldacre's private affairs.

'So, my dear Watson, there's my report of a failure. And yet—and yet'—he clenched his thin hands in a paroxysm of conviction—'I *know* it's all wrong. I feel it in my bones. There is something that has not come out, and that housekeeper knows it. There was a sort of sulky defiance in her eyes which only goes with guilty knowledge. However, there's no good talking any more about it, Watson; but unless some lucky chance comes our way I fear that the Norwood Disappearance Case will not figure in that chronicle of our successes which I foresee that a patient public will sooner or later have to endure.'

'Surely,' said I, 'the man's appearance would go far with any jury?'

'That is a dangerous argument, my dear Watson. You remember that terrible murderer, Bert Stevens, who wanted us to get him off in '87? Was there ever a more mild-mannered, Sunday-school young man?'*

'It is true.'

'Unless we succeed in establishing an alternative theory, this man is lost. You can hardly find a flaw in the case which can now be presented against him, and all further investigation has served to strengthen it. By the way, there is one curious little point about those papers which may serve us as the starting-point for an inquiry. On looking over the bank book I found that the low state of the balance was principally due to large cheques which have been made out during the last year to Mr Cornelius.* I confess that I should be interested to know who this Mr Cornelius may be with whom a retired builder has such very large transactions. Is it possible that he has had a hand in the affair? Cornelius might be a broker, but we have found no scrip to correspond with these large payments. Failing any other indication, my researches must now take the direction of an inquiry at the bank for the gentleman who has cashed these cheques. But I fear, my dear fellow, that our case will end ingloriously by Lestrade hanging our client, which will certainly be a triumph for Scotland Yard.'

I do not know how far Sherlock Holmes took any sleep that night, but when I came down to breakfast I found him pale and harassed, his bright eyes the brighter for the dark shadows round them. The carpet round his chair was littered with cigarette ends and with the early editions of the morning papers. An open telegram lay upon the table.

'What do you think of this, Watson?' he asked, tossing it across.

It was from Norwood, and ran as follows:

IMPORTANT FRESH EVIDENCE TO HAND. MCFARLANE'S GUILT DEFINITELY ESTABLISHED. ADVISE YOU TO ABANDON CASE. LESTRADE

'This sounds serious,' said I.

'It is Lestrade's little cock-a-doodle of victory,' Holmes answered, with a bitter smile. 'And yet it may be premature to abandon the case. After all, important fresh evidence is a two-edged thing, and may possibly cut in a very different direction to that which Lestrade imagines. Take your breakfast, Watson, and we will go out together and see what we can do. I feel as if I shall need your company and your moral support to-day.'

My friend had no breakfast himself, for it was one of his peculiarities that in his more intense moments he would permit himself no food, and I have known him presume upon his iron strength until he has fainted from pure inanition.* 'At present I cannot spare energy and nerve force for digestion,' he would say, in answer to my medical remonstrances. I was not surprised, therefore, when this morning he left his untouched meal behind him and started with me for Norwood. A crowd of morbid sightseers were still gathered round Deep Dene House, which was just such a suburban villa as I had pictured. Within the gates Lestrade met us, his face flushed with victory, his manner grossly triumphant.

'Well, Mr Holmes, have you proved us to be wrong yet? Have you found your tramp?' he cried.

'I have formed no conclusion whatever,' my companion answered.

'But we formed ours yesterday, and now it proves to be correct; so you must acknowledge that we have been a little in front of you this time, Mr Holmes.'

'You certainly have the air of something unusual having occurred,' said Holmes.

Lestrade laughed loudly.

'You don't like being beaten any more than the rest of us do,' said he. 'A man can't expect always to have it his own way—can he, Dr Watson? Step this way, if you please, gentlemen, and I think I can convince you once for all that it was John McFarlane who did this crime.'

He led us through the passage and out into a dark hall beyond.

'This is where young McFarlane must have come out to get his hat after the crime was done,' said he. 'Now look at this.' With dramatic suddenness he struck a match, and by its light exposed a stain of blood* upon the whitewashed* wall. As he held the match nearer I saw that it was more than a stain. It was the well-marked print of a thumb.

'Look at that with your magnifying glass, Mr Holmes.'

'Yes, I am doing so.'

'You are aware that no two thumb-marks are alike?'

'I have heard something of the kind.'

'Well, then, will you please compare that print with this wax impression of young McFarlane's right thumb, taken by my orders this morning?'

As he held the waxen print close to the blood-stain it did not take a magnifying glass to see that the two were undoubtedly from the same thumb. It was evident to me that our unfortunate client was lost.

'That is final,' said Lestrade.

'Yes, that is final,' I involuntarily echoed.

'It is final,' said Holmes.

Something in his tone caught my ear, and I turned to look at him. An extraordinary change had come over his face. It was writhing with inward merriment.

His two eyes were shining like stars. It seemed to me that he was making desperate efforts to restrain a convulsive attack of laughter.

'Dear me! Dear me!' he said at last. 'Well, now, who would have thought it? And how deceptive appearances may be, to be sure! Such a nice young man to look at! It is a lesson to us not to trust our own judgement—is it not, Lestrade?'

'Yes, some of us are a little too much inclined to be cock-sure, Mr Holmes,' said Lestrade. The man's insolence was maddening, but we could not resent it.

'What a providential thing that this young man should press his right thumb against the wall in taking his hat from the peg! Such a very natural action, too, if you come to think of it.' Holmes was outwardly calm, but his whole body gave a wriggle of suppressed excitement as he spoke. 'By the way, Lestrade, who made this remarkable discovery?'

'It was the housekeeper, Mrs Lexington,* who drew the night constable's attention to it.'

'Where was the night constable?'

'He remained on guard in the bedroom where the crime was committed, so as to see that nothing was touched.'

'But why didn't the police see this mark yesterday?'

'Well, we had no particular reason to make a careful examination of the hall. Besides, it's not in a very prominent place, as you see.'

'No, no, of course not. I suppose there is no doubt that the mark was there yesterday?'

Lestrade looked at Holmes as if he thought he was going out of his mind. I confess that I was myself surprised both at his hilarious manner and at his rather wild observation.

'I don't know whether you think that McFarlane came out of gaol in the dead of the night in order to strengthen the evidence against himself,' said Lestrade. 'I leave it to any expert in the world whether that is not the mark of his thumb.'

'It is unquestionably the mark of his thumb.'

'There, that's enough,' said Lestrade. 'I am a practical man, Mr Holmes, and when I have got my evidence I come to my conclusions. If you have anything to say you will find me writing my report in the sitting-room.'

Holmes had recovered his equanimity, though I still seemed to detect gleams of amusement in his expression.

'Dear me, this is a very sad development, Watson, is it not?' said he. 'And yet there are singular points about it which hold out some hopes for our client.'

44

'I am delighted to hear it,' said I heartily. 'I was afraid it was all up with him.'

'I would hardly go so far as to say that, my dear Watson. The fact is that there is one really serious flaw in this evidence to which our friend attaches so much importance.'

'Indeed, Holmes! What is it?'

'Only this—that I *know* that that mark was not there when I examined the hall yesterday. And now, Watson, let us have a little stroll round in the sunshine.'

With a confused brain, but with a heart into which some warmth of hope was returning, I accompanied my friend in a walk round the garden. Holmes took each face of the house in turn and examined it with great interest. He then led the way inside, and went over the whole building from basement to attics. Most of the rooms were unfurnished, but none the less Holmes inspected them all minutely. Finally, on the top corridor, which ran outside three untenanted bedrooms, he again was seized with a spasm of merriment.

'There are really some very unique features about this case, Watson,' said he. 'I think it is time now that we took our friend Lestrade into our confidence. He has had his little smile at our expense, and perhaps we may do as much by him if my reading of this problem proves to be correct. Yes, yes; I think I see how we should approach it.'

The Scotland Yard inspector was still writing in the parlour when Holmes interrupted him.

'I understood that you were writing a report of this case,' said he.

'So I am.'

'Don't you think it may be a little premature? I can't help thinking that your evidence is not complete.'

Lestrade knew my friend too well to disregard his words. He laid down his pen and looked curiously at him.

'What do you mean, Mr Holmes?'

'Only that there is an important witness whom you have not seen.'

'Can you produce him?'

45

'I think I can.'

'Then do so.'

'I will do my best. How many constables have you?'

'There are three within call.'

'Excellent!' said Holmes. 'May I ask if they are all large, able-bodied men with powerful voices?'

'I have no doubt they are, though I fail to see what their voices have to do with it.'

'Perhaps I can help you to see that, and one or two other things as well,' said Holmes. 'Kindly summon your men, and I will try.'

Five minutes later three policemen had assembled in the hall.

'In the outhouse you will find a considerable quantity of straw,' said Holmes. 'I will ask you to carry in two bundles of it. I think it will be of the greatest assistance in producing the witness whom I require. Thank you very much. I believe you have some matches in your pocket, Watson. Now, Mr Lestrade, I will ask you all to accompany me to the top landing.'

As I have said, there was a broad corridor there, which ran outside three empty bedrooms. At one end of the corridor we were all marshalled by Sherlock Holmes, the constables grinning, and Lestrade staring at my friend with amazement, expectation, and derision chasing each other across his features. Holmes stood before us with an air of a conjurer who is performing a trick.

'Would you kindly send one of your constables for two buckets of water? Put the straw on the floor here, free from the wall on either side. Now I think that we are all ready.'

Lestrade's face had begun to grow red and angry.

'I don't know whether you are playing a game with us, Mr Sherlock Holmes,' said he. 'If you know anything, you can surely say it without all this tomfoolery.'

'I assure you, my good Lestrade, that I have an excellent reason for everything that I do. You may possibly remember that you chaffed me a little some hours ago, when the sun

46

seemed on your side of the hedge, so you must not grudge me a little pomp and ceremony now. Might I ask you, Watson, to open that window, and then to put a match to the edge of the straw?'

I did so, and, driven by the draught, a coil of grey smoke swirled down the corridor, while the dry straw crackled and flamed.

'Now we must see if we can find this witness for you, Lestrade. Might I ask you all to join in the cry of "Fire"? Now, then: one, two, three—'

'Fire!' we all yelled.

'Thank you. I will trouble you once again.'

'Fire!'

'Just once more, gentlemen, and all together.'

'Fire!' The shout must have rung over Norwood.

It had hardly died away when an amazing thing happened. A door suddenly flew open out of what appeared to be solid wall at the end of the corridor, and a little wizened man darted out of it, like a rabbit out of its burrow.

'Capital!' said Holmes calmly. 'Watson, a bucket of water over the straw. That will do! Lestrade, allow me to present you with your principal missing witness, Mr Jonas Oldacre.'

The detective stared at the newcomer with blank amazement. The latter was blinking in the bright light of the corridor, and peering at us and at the smouldering fire. It was an odious face—crafty, vicious, malignant, with shifty, light-grey eyes and white eyelashes.

'What's this, then?' said Lestrade at last. 'What have you been doing all this time, eh?'

Oldacre gave an uneasy laugh, shrinking back from the furious red face of the angry detective.

'I have done no harm.'

'No harm? You have done your best to get an innocent man hanged. If it wasn't for this gentleman here, I am not sure that you would not have succeeded.'

The wretched creature began to whimper.

'I am sure, sir, it was only my practical joke.'

'Oh! a joke, was it? You won't find the laugh on your side, I promise you. Take him down and keep him in the sitting-room until I come. Mr Holmes,' he continued, when they had gone, 'I could not speak before the constables, but I don't mind saying, in the presence of Dr Watson, that this is the brightest thing that you have done yet, though it is a mystery to me how you did it. You have saved an innocent man's life, and you have prevented a very grave scandal, which would have ruined my reputation in the Force.'

Holmes smiled and clapped Lestrade upon the shoulder.

'Instead of being ruined, my good sir, you will find that your reputation has been enormously enhanced. Just make a few alterations in that report which you were writing, and they will understand how hard it is to throw dust in the eyes of Inspector Lestrade.'

'And you don't want your name to appear?'

'Not at all. The work is its own reward. Perhaps I shall get the credit also at some distant day when I permit my zealous historian to lay out his foolscap once more—eh, Watson? Well, now, let us see where this rat has been lurking.'

A lath-and-plaster partition had been run across the passage six feet from the end, with a door cunningly concealed in it. It was lit within by slits under the eaves. A few articles of furniture and a supply of food and water were within, together with a number of books and papers.

'There's the advantage of being a builder,' said Holmes as we came out. 'He was able to fix up his own little hiding-place without any confederate—save, of course, that precious housekeeper of his, whom I should lose no time in adding to your bag, Lestrade.'

'I will take your advice. But how did you know of this place, Mr Holmes?'

'I made up my mind that the fellow was in hiding in the house. When I paced one corridor and found it six feet shorter than the corresponding one below, it was pretty clear where he was. I thought he had not the nerve to lie

48

quiet before an alarm of fire. We could, of course, have gone
in and taken him, but it amused me to make him reveal
himself; besides, I owed you a little mystification, Lestrade,
for your chaff in the morning.'

'Well, sir, you certainly got equal with me on that. But
how in the world did you know that he was in the house at
all?'

'The thumb-mark, Lestrade. You said it was final; and so
it was, in a very different sense. I knew it had not been there
the day before. I pay a good deal of attention to matters of
detail, as you may have observed, and I had examined the
hall, and was sure that the wall was clear. Therefore, it had
been put on during the night.'

'But how?'

'Very simply. When those packets were sealed up, Jonas
Oldacre got McFarlane to secure one of the seals by putting
his thumb upon the soft wax. It would be done so quickly
and so naturally that I dare say the young man himself has
no recollection of it. Very likely it just so happened, and
Oldacre had himself no notion of the use he would put it to.
Brooding over the case in that den of his, it suddenly struck
him what absolutely damning evidence he could make
against McFarlane by using that thumb-mark. It was the
simplest thing in the world for him to take a wax impression
from the seal, to moisten it in as much blood as he could get
from a pin-prick, and to put the mark upon the wall during
the night, either with his own hand or with that of his
housekeeper. If you examine among these documents which
he took with him into his retreat, I will lay you a wager that
you find the seal with the thumb-mark upon it.'

'Wonderful!' said Lestrade. 'Wonderful! It's all as clear as
crystal, as you put it. But what is the object of this deep
deception, Mr Holmes?'

It was amusing to me to see how the detective's overbear-
ing manner had changed suddenly to that of a child asking
questions of its teacher.

'Well, I don't think that is very hard to explain. A very
deep, malicious, vindictive person is the gentleman who is

now awaiting us downstairs. You know that he was once refused by McFarlane's mother? You don't! I told you that you should go to Blackheath first and Norwood afterwards. Well, this injury, as he would consider it, has rankled in his wicked, scheming brain, and all his life he has longed for vengeance, but never seen his chance. During the last year or two things have gone against him—secret speculation, I think—and he finds himself in a bad way. He determines to swindle his creditors, and for this purpose he pays large cheques to a certain Mr Cornelius, who is, I imagine, himself under another name. I have not traced these cheques yet, but I have no doubt that they were banked under that name at some provincial town where Oldacre from time to time led a double existence. He intended to change his name altogether, draw this money, and vanish, starting life again elsewhere.'

'Well, that's likely enough.'

'It would strike him that in disappearing he might throw all pursuit off his track, and at the same time have an ample and crushing revenge upon his old sweetheart, if he could give the impression that he had been murdered by her only child. It was a masterpiece of villainy, and he carried it out like a master. The idea of the will, which would give an obvious motive for the crime, the secret visit unknown to his own parents, the retention of the stick, the blood, and the animal remains and buttons in the wood-pile, all were admirable. It was a net from which it seemed to me a few hours ago that there was no possible escape. But he had not that supreme gift of the artist, the knowledge of when to stop. He wished to improve that which was already perfect—to draw the rope tighter yet round the neck of his unfortunate victim—and so he ruined all. Let us descend, Lestrade. There are just one or two questions that I would ask him.'

The malignant creature was seated in his own parlour with a policeman upon each side of him.

'It was a joke, my good sir; a practical joke, nothing more,' he whined incessantly. 'I assure you, sir, that I simply concealed myself in order to see the effect of my disappearance, and I am sure that you would not be so unjust as to imagine that I would have allowed any harm to befall poor young Mr McFarlane.'

'That's for the jury to decide,' said Lestrade. 'Anyhow, we shall have you on a charge of conspiracy, if not for attempted murder.'

'And you'll probably find that your creditors will impound the banking account of Mr Cornelius,' said Holmes.

The little man started and turned his malignant eyes upon my friend.

'I have to thank you for a good deal,' said he. 'Perhaps I'll pay my debt some day.'

Holmes smiled indulgently.

'I fancy that for some few years you will find your time very fully occupied,' said he. 'By the way, what was it you put into the wood-pile besides your old trousers? A dead dog, or rabbits, or what? You won't tell? Dear me, how very unkind of you! Well, well, I dare say that a couple of rabbits would account both for the blood and for the charred ashes. If ever you write an account, Watson, you can make rabbits serve your turn.'

The Solitary Cyclist

FROM the years 1894 to 1901 inclusive, Mr Sherlock Holmes was a very busy man. It is safe to say that there was no public case of any difficulty in which he was not consulted during those eight* years, and there were hundreds of private cases, some of them of the most intricate and extraordinary character, in which he played a prominent part. Many startling successes and a few unavoidable failures were the outcome of this long period of continuous work. As I have preserved very full notes of all these cases, and was myself personally engaged in many of them, it may be imagined that it is no easy task to know which I should select to lay before the public. I shall, however, preserve my former rule, and give the preference to those cases which derive their interest not so much from the brutality of the crime as from the ingenuity and dramatic quality of the solution.* For this reason I will now lay before the reader the facts connected with Miss Violet Smith, the solitary cyclist of Charlington,* and the curious sequel of our investigation, which culminated in unexpected tragedy.* It is true that the circumstances did not permit of any striking illustration of those powers for which my friend was famous, but there were some points about the case which made it stand out in those long records of crime from which I gather the material for these little narratives.

On referring to my note-book for the year 1895, I find that it was upon Saturday, April 23rd,* that we first heard of Miss Violet Smith. Her visit was, I remember, extremely unwelcome to Holmes, for he was immersed at the moment in a very abstruse and complicated problem concerning the peculiar persecution to which John Vincent Harden* the well-known tobacco millionaire, had been subjected. My friend, who loved above all things precision and concentration of thought, resented anything which distracted his attention from the matter in hand. And yet without a harshness which was foreign to his nature it was impossible to refuse to listen to the story of the young and beautiful woman, tall, graceful and queenly, who presented herself at Baker Street late in the evening and implored his assistance and advice. It was vain to urge that his time was already fully occupied, for the young lady had come with the determination to tell her story, and it was evident that nothing short of force could get her out of the room until she had done so. With a resigned air and a somewhat weary smile, Holmes begged the beautiful intruder to take a seat and to inform us what it was that was troubling her.

'At least it cannot be your health,' said he, as his keen eyes darted over her; 'so ardent a bicyclist must be full of energy.'

She glanced down in surprise at her own feet, and I observed the slight roughening of the side of the sole caused by the friction of the edge of the pedal.

'Yes, I bicycle a good deal, Mr Holmes, and that has something to do with my visit to you to-day.'

My friend took the lady's ungloved hand and examined it with as close an attention and as little sentiment as a scientist would show to a specimen.

'You will excuse me, I am sure. It is my business,' said he, as he dropped it. 'I nearly fell into the error of supposing that you were typewriting. Of course, it is obvious that it is music. You observe the spatulate finger end,* Watson, which is common to both professions? There is a spirituality about the face, however'—he gently turned it towards the light*—'which the typewriter does not generate. This lady is a musician.'

'Yes, Mr Holmes, I teach music.'

'In the country, I presume, from your complexion.'

'Yes, sir; near Farnham, on the borders of Surrey.'*

'A beautiful neighbourhood, and full of the most interesting associations. You remember, Watson, that it was near there that we took Archie Stamford, the forger.* Now, Miss Violet, what has happened to you near Farnham, on the borders of Surrey?'

53

The young lady, with great clearness and composure, made the following curious statement:

'My father is dead, Mr Holmes. He was James Smith, who conducted the orchestra at the old Imperial Theatre.* My mother and I were left without a relation in the world except one uncle, Ralph Smith, who went to Africa twenty-five years ago, and we have never had a word from him since. When Father died we were left very poor, but one day we were told that there was an advertisement in *The Times* inquiring for our whereabouts. You can imagine how excited we were, for we thought that someone had left us a fortune. We went at once to the lawyer whose name was given in the paper. There we met two gentlemen, Mr Carruthers and Mr Woodley,* who were home on a visit from South Africa. They said that my uncle was a friend of theirs, that he died some months before in great poverty in Johannesburg, and that he had asked them with his last breath to hunt up his relations and see that they were in no want. It seemed strange to us that Uncle Ralph, who took no notice of us when he was alive, should be so careful to look after us when he was dead; but Mr Carruthers explained that the reason was that my uncle had just heard of the death of his brother, and so felt responsible for our fate.'

'Excuse me,' said Holmes; 'when was this interview?'

'Last December—four months ago.'

'Pray proceed.'

'Mr Woodley seemed to me to be a most odious person. He was for ever making eyes at me—a coarse, puffy-faced, red-moustached young man, with his hair plastered down on each side of his forehead. I thought that he was perfectly hateful—and I was sure that Cyril would not wish me to know such a person.'

'Oh, Cyril is his name!' said Holmes, smiling.

The young lady blushed and laughed.

'Yes, Mr Holmes; Cyril Morton,* an electrical engineer, and we hope to be married at the end of the summer. Dear me, how *did* I get talking about him? What I wished to say was that Mr Woodley was perfectly odious, but that Mr

Carruthers, who was a much older man, was more agree-able. He was a dark, sallow, clean-shaven, silent person; but he had polite manners and a pleasant smile. He inquired how we were left, and on finding that we were very poor he suggested that I should come and teach music to his only daughter, aged ten. I said that I did not like to leave my mother, on which he suggested that I should go home to her every week-end, and he offered me a hundred a year, which was certainly splendid pay. So it ended by my accepting, and I went down to Chiltern Grange, about six miles from Farnham.* Mr Carruthers was a widower, but he had en-gaged a lady-housekeeper, a very respectable, elderly per-son, called Mrs Dixon, to look after his establishment. The child was a dear, and everything promised well. Mr Car-ruthers was very kind and very musical, and we had most pleasant evenings together. Every week-end I went home to my mother in town.

'The first flaw in my happiness was the arrival of the red-moustached Mr Woodley. He came for a visit of a week, and oh, it seemed three months to me! He was a dreadful person, a bully to everyone else, but to me something infinitely worse. He made odious love to me,* boasted of his wealth, said that if I married him I would have the finest diamonds in London, and finally, when I would have nothing to do with him, he seized me in my arms one day after dinner—he was hideously strong—and he swore that he would not let me go until I had kissed me. Mr Carru-thers came in, and tore him off from me, on which he turned upon his own host, knocking him down and cutting his face open. That was the end of his visit, as you can imagine. Mr Carruthers apologized to me next day, and assured me that I should never be exposed to such an insult again. I have not seen Mr Woodley since.

'And now, Mr Holmes, I come at last to the special thing which has caused me to ask your advice to-day. You must know that every Saturday forenoon I ride on my bicycle to Farnham Station in order to get the 12.22 to town. The road from Chiltern Grange is a lonely one, and at one spot it is

particularly so, for it lies for over a mile between Charlington Heath upon one side and the woods which lie round
Charlington Hall upon the other.* You could not find a
more lonely tract of road anywhere, and it is quite rare to
meet so much as a cart, or a peasant, until you reach the
high-road near Crooksbury Hill.* Two weeks ago I was
passing this place when I chanced to look back over my
shoulder, and about two hundred yards behind me I saw a
man, also on a bicycle. He seemed to be a middle-aged
man, with a short, dark beard. I looked back before I
reached Farnham, but the man was gone, so I thought no
more about it. But you can imagine how surprised I was, Mr
Holmes, when on my return on the Monday I saw the same
man on the same stretch of road. My astonishment was
increased when the incident occurred again, exactly as
before, on the following Saturday and Monday. He always
kept his distance, and did not molest me in any way, but still
it certainly was very odd. I mentioned it to Mr Carruthers,
who seemed interested in what I said,* and told me that he
had ordered a horse and trap, so that in future I should not
pass over these lonely roads without some companion.

'The horse and trap were to have come this week, but for
some reason they were not delivered, and again I had to
cycle to the station. That was this morning. You can think
that I looked out when I came to Charlington Heath, and
there, sure enough, was the man, exactly as he had been the
two weeks before. He always kept so far from me that I
could not clearly see his face, but it was certainly someone
whom I did not know. He was dressed in a dark suit with a
cloth cap. The only thing about his face that I could clearly
see was his dark beard. To-day I was not alarmed, but I was
filled with curiosity, and I determined to find out who he
was and what he wanted. I slowed down my machine, but
he slowed down his. Then I stopped altogether, but he
stopped also. Then I laid a trap for him. There is a sharp
turning of the road, and I pedalled very quickly round this,
and then I stopped and waited. I expected him to shoot
round and pass me before he could stop. But he never

appeared. Then I went back and looked round the corner. I could see a mile of road, but he was not on it. To make it the more extraordinary there was no side-road at this point down which he could have gone.'

Holmes chuckled and rubbed his hands.

'This case certainly presents some features of its own,' said he. 'How much time elapsed between your turning the corner and your discovery that the road was clear?'

'Two or three minutes.'

'Then he could not have retreated down the road, and you say that there are no side-roads?'

'None.'

'Then he certainly took a footpath on one side or the other.'

'It could not have been on the side of the heath or I should have seen him.'

'So by the process of exclusion we arrive at the fact that he made his way towards Charlington Hall, which, as I understand, is situated in its own grounds on one side of the road. Anything else?'

'Nothing, Mr Holmes, save that I was so perplexed that I felt I should not be happy until I had seen you and had your advice.'

Holmes sat in silence for some little time.

'Where is the gentleman to whom you are engaged?' he asked at last.

'He is in the Midland Electric Company, at Coventry.'*

'He would not pay you a surprise visit?'

'Oh, Mr Holmes! As if I should not know him!'

'Have you had any other admirers?'

'Several before I knew Cyril.'

'And since?'

'There was this dreadful man, Woodley, if you can call him an admirer.'

'No one else?'

Our fair client seemed a little confused.

'Who was he?' asked Holmes.

'Oh, it may be a mere fancy of mine; but it has seemed to me sometimes that my employer, Mr Carruthers, takes a great deal of interest in me. We are thrown rather together. I play his accompaniments in the evening. He has never said anything. He is a perfect gentleman. But a girl always knows.'

'Ha!' Holmes looked grave. 'What does he do for a living?'

'He is a rich man.'

'No carriages or horses?'

'Well, at least he is fairly well-to-do. But he goes into the City two or three times a week. He is deeply interested in South African gold shares.'

'You will let me know any fresh development, Miss Smith. I am very busy just now, but I will find time to make some inquiries into your case. In the meantime, take no step without letting me know. Good-bye, and I trust that we shall have nothing but good news from you.'

'It is part of the settled order of Nature that such a girl should have followers,' said Holmes, as he pulled at his meditative pipe, 'but for choice not on bicycles in lonely country roads. Some secretive lover, beyond all doubt. But there are curious and suggestive details about the case, Watson.'

'That he should appear only at that point?'

'Exactly. Our first effort must be to find who are the tenants of Charlington Hall. Then, again, how about the connection between Carruthers and Woodley, since they appear to be men of such different types? How came they *both* to be so keen upon looking up Ralph Smith's relations? One more point. What sort of a *ménage** is it which pays double the market price for a governess, but does not keep a horse although six miles from the station? Odd, Watson—very odd.'

'You will go down?'

'No, my dear fellow, *you* will go down. This may be some trifling intrigue, and I cannot break my other important research for the sake of it. On Monday you will arrive early at Farnham; you will conceal yourself near Charlington Heath; you will observe these facts for yourself, and act as your own judgement advises. Then, having inquired as to the occupants of the Hall, you will come back to me and report. And now, Watson, not another word of the matter until we have a few solid stepping-stones on which we may hope to get across to our solution.'

We had ascertained from the lady that she went down upon the Monday by the train which leaves Waterloo at 9.50, so I started early and caught the 9.13. At Farnham Station I had no difficulty in being directed to Charlington Heath. It was impossible to mistake the scene of the young lady's adventure, for the road runs between the open heath on one side, and an old yew hedge upon the other, surrounding a park which is studded with magnificent trees. There was a main gateway of lichen-studded stone, each side-pillar surmounted by mouldering heraldic emblems; but besides this central carriage-drive I observed several points where there were gaps in the hedge and paths leading through them. The house was invisible from the road, but the surroundings all spoke of gloom and decay.

The heath was covered with golden patches of flowering gorse, gleaming magnificently in the light of the bright spring sunshine. Behind one of these clumps I took up my position, so as to command both the gateway of the Hall and a long stretch of the road upon either side. It had been deserted when I left it, but now I saw a cyclist riding down it from the opposite direction to that in which I had come. He was clad in a dark suit, and I saw that he had a black beard. On reaching the end of the Charlington grounds he sprang from his machine and led it through a gap in the hedge, disappearing from my view.

A quarter of an hour passed and then a second cyclist appeared. This time it was the young lady coming from the station. I saw her look about her as she came to the Charlington hedge. An instant later the man emerged from his hiding place, sprang upon his bicycle, and followed her. In all the broad landscape those were the only moving figures, the graceful girl sitting very straight upon her machine and the man behind her bending low over his handle-bar, with a curiously furtive suggestion in every movement. She looked back at him and slowed her pace. He slowed also. She stopped. He at once stopped, too, keeping two hundred yards behind her. Her next movement was as unexpected as it was spirited. She suddenly whisked her wheels round and dashed straight at him! He was as quick as she, however, and darted off in desperate flight. Presently she came back up the road again, her head haughtily in the air, not deigning to take further notice of her silent attendant. He had turned also, and still kept his distance until the curve of the road hid them from my sight.

I remained in my hiding-place, and it was well that I did so, for presently the man reappeared, cycling slowly back. He turned in at the Hall gates and dismounted from his machine. For some few minutes I could see him standing among the trees. His hands were raised, and he seemed to be settling his necktie. Then he mounted his bicycle and rode away from me down the drive towards the Hall. I ran across the heath and peered through the trees. Far away I could catch glimpses of the old grey building with its bristling Tudor chimneys, but the drive ran through a dense shrubbery, and I saw no more of my man.

However, it seemed to me that I had done a fairly good morning's work, and I walked back in high spirits to Farnham. The local house agent could tell me nothing about Charlington Hall, and referred me to a well-known firm in Pall Mall.* There I halted on my way home, and met with courtesy from the representative. No, I could not have Charlington Hall for the summer. I was just too late. It had been let about a month ago. Mr Williamson* was the name of the tenant. He was a respectable elderly gentleman. The polite agent was afraid he could say no more, as the affairs of his clients were not matters which he could discuss.

Mr Sherlock Holmes listened with attention to the long report which I was able to present to him that evening, but it did not elicit that word of curt praise which I had hoped for and should have valued. On the contrary, his austere face was even more severe than usual as he commented upon the things that I had done and the things that I had not.

'Your hiding-place, my dear Watson, was very faulty. You should have been behind the hedge; then you would have had a close view of this interesting person. As it is you were some hundreds of yards away, and can tell me even less than Miss Smith. She thinks she does not know the man; I am convinced she does. Why, otherwise, should he be so desperately anxious that she should not get so near him as to see his features? You describe him as bending over the handle-bar. Concealment again, you see. You really have done remarkably badly. He returns to the house, and you want to find out who he is. You come to a London house-agent!'

'What should I have done?' I cried, with some heat.

'Gone to the nearest public house. That is the centre of country gossip. They would have told you every name, from the master to the scullery-maid. Williamson! It conveys nothing to my mind. If he is an elderly man he is not this active cyclist who springs away from that athletic young lady's pursuit. What have we gained by your expedition? The knowledge that the girl's story is true. I never doubted it. That there is a connection between the cyclist and the Hall. I never doubted that either. That the Hall is tenanted by Williamson. Who's the better for that? Well, well, my dear sir, don't look so depressed. We can do little more until next Saturday, and in the meantime I may make one or two inquiries myself.'

Next morning we had a note from Miss Smith, recounting shortly and accurately the very incidents which I had seen, but the pith of the letter lay in the postscript:

I am sure that you will respect my confidence, Mr Holmes, when I tell you that my place here has become difficult owing to the fact that my employer has proposed marriage to me. I am convinced that his feelings are most deep and most honourable. At the same time my promise is, of course, given. He took my refusal very seriously, but also very gently. You can understand, however, that the situation is a little strained.

'Our young friend seems to be getting into deep waters,' said Holmes thoughtfully, as he finished the letter. 'The case certainly presents more features of interest and more possibility of development than I had originally thought. I should be none the worse for a quiet, peaceful day in the country, and I am inclined to run down this afternoon and test one or two theories which I have formed.'

Holmes's quiet day in the country had a singular termination, for he arrived at Baker Street late in the evening with a cut lip and a discoloured lump upon his forehead, besides a general air of dissipation which would have made his own person the fitting object of a Scotland Yard investigation. He was immensely tickled by his own adventures, and laughed heartily as he recounted them.

'I get so little active exercise that it is always a treat,' said he. 'You are aware that I have some proficiency in the good old British sport of boxing.* Occasionally it is of service. Today, for example, I should have come to very ignominious grief without it.'

I begged him to tell me what had occurred.

'I found that country pub which I had already recommended to your notice, and there I made my discreet inquiries. I was in the bar, and a garrulous landlord was giving me all that I wanted. Williamson is a white-bearded man, and he lives alone with a small staff of servants at the Hall. There is some rumour that he is or has been a clergyman; but one or two incidents of his short residence at the Hall struck me as peculiarly unecclesiastical. I have already made some inquiries at a clerical agency,* and they tell me that there *was* a man of that name in orders whose career has been a singularly dark one. The landlord further informed me that there are usually week-end visitors—"a warm lot, sir"—at the Hall, and especially one gentleman with a red moustache, Mr Woodley by name, who was always there. We had got as far as this when who should walk in but the gentleman himself, who had been drinking his beer in the tap-room, and had heard the whole conversation. Who was I? What did I want? What did I mean by asking questions? He had a fine flow of language, and his adjectives were very vigorous. He ended a string of abuse by a vicious back-hander, which I failed to entirely avoid. The next few minutes were delicious. It was a straight left against a slogging ruffian. I emerged as you see me. Mr Woodley went home in a cart. So ended my country trip, and it must be confessed that, however enjoyable, my day on the Surrey border has not been much more profitable than your own.'

The Thursday brought us another letter from our client:

You will not be surprised, Mr Holmes [said she], to hear that I am leaving Mr Carruthers's employment. Even the high pay cannot reconcile me to the discomforts of my situation. On Saturday I come up to town, and I do not intend to return. Mr Carruthers has got a trap, and so the dangers of the lonely road, if there ever were any dangers, are now over.

As to the special cause of my leaving, it is not merely the strained situation with Mr Carruthers, but it is the reappearance of that odious man, Mr Woodley. He was always hideous, but he looks more awful than ever now, for he appears to have had an accident and he is much disfigured. I saw him out of the window, but I am glad to say I did not meet him. He had a long talk with Mr Carruthers, who seemed much excited afterwards. Woodley must be staying in the neighbourhood, for he did not sleep here, and yet I caught a glimpse of him again this morning slinking about in the shrubbery. I would sooner have a savage wild animal loose about the place. I loathe and fear him more than I can say. How *can* Mr Carruthers endure such a creature for a moment? However, all my troubles will be over on Saturday.

'So I trust, Watson, so I trust,' said Holmes gravely. 'There is some deep intrigue going on round that little woman, and it is our duty to see that no one molests her upon that last journey. I think, Watson, that we must spare time to run down together on Saturday morning, and make sure that this curious and inconclusive investigation has no untoward ending.'

I confess that I had not up to now taken a very serious view of the case, which had seemed to me rather grotesque and bizarre than dangerous. That a man should lie in wait for and follow a very handsome woman is no unheard-of thing, and if he had so little audacity that he not only dared not address her, but even fled from her approach, he was not a very formidable assailant. The ruffian Woodley was a very different person, but, except on the one occasion, he had not molested our client, and now he visited the house of Carruthers without intruding upon her presence. The man on the bicycle was doubtless a member of those week-end parties at the Hall of which the publican had spoken; but who he was or what he wanted was as obscure as ever. It was the severity of Holmes's manner and the fact that he slipped a revolver into his pocket before leaving our rooms which impressed me with the feeling that tragedy might prove to lurk behind this curious train of events.

A rainy night had been followed by a glorious morning, and the heath-covered countryside, with the glowing clumps of flowering gorse, seemed all the more beautiful to eyes which were weary of the duns and drabs and slate-greys of London.* Holmes and I walked along the broad, sandy road inhaling the fresh morning air, and rejoicing in the music of the birds and the fresh breath of the spring. From a rise of the road on the shoulder of Crooksbury Hill we could see the grim Hall bristling out from amidst the ancient oaks, which, old as they were, were still younger than the building which they surrounded. Holmes pointed down the long tract of road which wound, a reddish-yellow band, between the brown of the heath and the budding green of the woods. Far away, a black dot, we could see a vehicle moving in our direction. Holmes gave an exclamation of impatience.

'I had given a margin of half an hour,' said he. 'If that is her trap she must be making for the earlier train. I fear, Watson, that she will be past Charlington before we can possibly meet her.'

From the instant that we passed the rise we could no longer see the vehicle, but we hastened onwards at such a pace that my sedentary life began to tell upon me, and I was compelled to fall behind. Holmes, however, was always in training, for he had inexhaustible stores of nervous energy upon which to draw. His springy step never slowed, until suddenly, when he was a hundred yards in front of me, he halted, and I saw him throw up his hand with a gesture of grief and despair. At the same instant an empty dog-cart, the horse cantering, the reins trailing, appeared round the curve of the road and rattled swiftly towards us.

'Too late, Watson; too late!' cried Holmes, as I ran panting to his side. 'Fool that I was not to allow for the earlier train! It's abduction, Watson—abduction! Murder! God* knows what! Block the road! Stop the horse! That's right. Now jump in, and let us see if I can repair the consequences of my own blunder.'

We had sprung into the dog-cart, and Holmes, after turning the horse, gave it a sharp cut with a whip, and we flew back along the road. As we turned the curve the whole stretch of road between the Hall and the heath was opened up. I grasped Holmes's arm.

'That's the man!' I gasped.

A solitary cyclist was coming towards us. His head was down and his shoulders rounded as he put every ounce of energy that he possessed on to the pedals. He was flying like a racer. Suddenly he raised his bearded face, saw us close to him, and pulled up, springing from his machine. That coal-black beard was in singular contrast to the pallor of his face, and his eyes were as bright as if he had a fever. He stared at us and at the dog-cart. Then a look of amazement came over his face.

'Hullo! Stop there!' he shouted, holding his bicycle to block our road. 'Where did you get that dog-cart? Pull up, man!' he yelled, drawing a pistol from his side-pocket. 'Pull up, I say, or, by George, I'll put a bullet into your horse!'

Holmes threw the reins into my lap and sprang down from the cart.

'You're the man we want to see. Where is Miss Violet Smith?' he said in his quick, clear way.

'That's what I am asking you. You're in her dog-cart. You ought to know where she is.'

'We met the dog-cart on the road. There was no one in it. We drove back to help the young lady.'

'Good Lord! Good Lord! What shall I do?' cried the stranger, in an ecstasy of despair. 'They've got her, that hell-hound Woodley and the blackguard parson. Come, man, come, if you really are her friend. Stand by me and we'll save her, if I have to leave my carcass in Charlington Wood.'

He ran distractedly, his pistol in his hand, towards a gap in the hedge. Holmes followed him, and I, leaving the horse grazing beside the road, followed Holmes.

'This is where they came through,' said he, pointing to the marks of several feet upon the muddy path. 'Hullo! Stop a minute! Who's this in the bush?'

It was a young fellow about seventeen, dressed like an ostler, with leather cords and gaiters. He lay upon his back, his knees drawn up, a terrible cut upon his head. He was insensible, but alive. A glance at his wound told me that it had not penetrated the bone.

'That's Peter, the groom,' cried the stranger. 'He drove her. The beasts have pulled him off and clubbed him. Let him lie; we can't do him any good, but we may save her from the worst fate that can befall a woman.'

We ran frantically down the path, which wound among the trees. We had reached the shrubbery which surrounded the house when Holmes pulled up.

'They didn't go to the house. Here are their marks on the left—here, beside the laurel bushes! Ah, I said so!'

As he spoke a woman's shrill scream*—a scream which vibrated with a frenzy of horror—burst from the thick green clump of bushes in front of us. It ended suddenly on its highest note with a choke and gurgle.

'This way! This way! They are in the bowling alley,' cried the stranger, darting through the bushes. 'Ah, the cowardly dogs! Follow me, gentlemen! Too late! too late! by the living Jingo!'*

We had broken suddenly into a lovely glade of green-sward* surrounded by ancient trees. On the farther side of it, under the shadow of a mighty oak, there stood a singular group of three people. One was a woman, our client, drooping and faint, a handkerchief round her mouth. Opposite her stood a brutal, heavy-faced, red-moustached young man, his gaitered legs parted wide, one arm akimbo,* the other waving a riding-crop, his whole attitude suggestive of a triumphant bravado. Between them an elderly, grey-bearded man, wearing a short surplice* over a light tweed suit, had evidently just completed the wedding service, for he pocketed his Prayer-Book as we appeared, and slapped the sinister bridegroom upon the back in jovial congratulation.

'They're married!' I gasped.

'Come, on!' cried our guide; 'come on!' He rushed across the glade, Holmes and I at his heels. As we approached, the lady staggered against the trunk of the tree for support. Williamson, the ex-clergyman, bowed to us with mock politeness, and the bully Woodley advanced with a shout of brutal and exultant laughter.

'You can take your beard off, Bob,' said he. 'I know you right enough. Well, you and your pals have just come in time for me to be able to introduce you to Mrs Woodley.'

Our guide's answer was a singular one. He snatched off the dark beard which had disguised him and threw it on the ground, disclosing a long, sallow, clean-shaven face below it. Then he raised his revolver and covered the young ruffian, who was advancing upon him with his dangerous riding-crop swinging in his hand.

'Yes,' said our ally, 'I *am* Bob Carruthers, and I'll see this woman righted if I have to swing for it. I told you what I'd do if you molested her, and, by the Lord, I'll be as good as my word!'

'You're too late. She's my wife!'

'No, she's your widow.'

His revolver cracked, and I saw the blood spurt from the front of Woodley's waistcoat. He spun round with a scream and fell upon his back, his hideous red face turning suddenly to a dreadful mottled pallor. The old man, still clad in his surplice, burst into such a string of foul oaths as I have never heard, and pulled out a revolver of his own, but before he could raise it he was looking down the barrel of Holmes's weapon.

'Enough of this,' said my friend coldly. 'Drop that pistol! Watson, pick it up! Hold it to his head! Thank you. You, Carruthers, give me that revolver. We'll have no more violence. Come, hand it over!'

'Who are you, then?'

'My name is Sherlock Holmes.'

'Good Lord!'

'You have heard of me, I see. I will represent the official police until their arrival. Here, you!' he shouted to the frightened groom, who had appeared at the edge of the glade. 'Come here. Take this note as hard as you can ride to Farnham.' He scribbled a few words upon a leaf from his notebook. 'Give it to the superintendent at the police-station. Until he comes, I must detain you all under my personal custody.'

The strong, masterful personality of Holmes dominated the tragic scene, and all were equally puppets in his hands. Williamson and Carruthers found themselves carrying the wounded Woodley into the house, and I gave my arm to the frightened girl. The injured man was laid on his bed, and at Holmes's request I examined him. I carried my report to where he sat in the old tapestry-hung dining-room with his two prisoners before him.

'He will live,' said I.

'What!' cried Carruthers, springing out of his chair. 'I'll go upstairs and finish him first. Do you tell me that that girl, that angel, is to be tied to Roaring Jack Woodley* for life?'

'You need not concern yourself about that,' said Holmes. 'There are two very good reasons why she should under no circumstances be his wife. In the first place, we are very safe in questioning Mr Williamson's right to solemnize a marriage.'

'I have been ordained,' cried the old rascal.

'And also unfrocked.'*

'Once a clergyman, always a clergyman.'

'I think not. How about the licence?'

'We had a licence for the marriage. I have it here in my pocket.'

'Then you got it by a trick. But in any case a forced marriage is no marriage, but it is a very serious felony, as you will discover before you have finished. You'll have time to think the point out during the next ten years or so, unless I am mistaken. As to you, Carruthers, you would have done better to keep your pistol in your pocket.'

'I begin to think so, Mr Holmes; but when I thought of all the precaution I had taken to shield this girl—for I loved her, Mr Holmes, and it is the only time that ever I knew what love was—it fairly drove me mad to think that she was in the power of the greatest brute and bully in South Africa, a man whose name is a holy terror from Kimberley to Johannesburg.* Why, Mr Holmes, you'll hardly believe it, but ever since that girl has been in my employment I never once let her go past this house, where I knew these rascals were lurking, without following her on my bicycle just to see that she came to no harm. I kept my distance from her, and I wore a beard so that she should not recognize me, for she is a good and high-spirited girl, and she wouldn't have stayed in my employment long if she had thought that I was following her about the country roads.'

'Why didn't you tell her of her danger?'

'Because then, again, she would have left me, and I couldn't bear to face that. Even if she couldn't love me it was a great deal to me just to see her dainty form about the house, and to hear the sound of her voice.'

'Well,' said I, 'you call that love, Mr Carruthers, but I should call it selfishness.'*

'Maybe the two things go together. Anyhow, I couldn't let her go. Besides, with this crowd about, it was well that she should have someone near to look after her. Then when the cable* came I knew they were bound to make a move.'

'What cable?'

Carruthers took a telegram from his pocket.

'That's it!' said he. It was short and concise:

THE OLD MAN IS DEAD.

'Hum!' said Holmes. 'I think I see how things worked, and I can understand how this message would, as you say, bring them to a head. But while we wait, you might tell me what you can.'

The old reprobate with the surplice burst into a volley of bad language.

'By God,'* said he, 'if you squeal on us, Bob Carruthers, I'll serve you as you served Jack Woodley! You can bleat about the girl to your heart's content, for that's your own affair, but if you round on your pals to this plain-clothes copper it will be the worst day's work that ever you did.'

'Your reverence need not be excited,' said Holmes, lighting a cigarette. 'The case is clear enough against you, and all I ask is a few details for my private curiosity. However, if there's any difficulty in your telling me I'll do the talking, and then you will see how far you have a chance of holding back your secrets. In the first place, three of you came from South Africa on this game—you, Williamson, you, Carruthers, and Woodley.'

'Lie number one,' said the old man; 'I never saw either of them until two months ago, and I have never been in Africa in my life, so you can put that in your pipe and smoke it, Mr Busybody Holmes!'

'What he says is true,' said Carruthers.

'Well, well, two of you came over. His reverence is our own home-made article. You had known Ralph Smith in South Africa. You had reason to believe he would not live long. You found out that his niece would inherit his fortune. How's that—eh?'

Carruthers nodded, and Williamson swore.

'She was next-of-kin, no doubt, and you were aware that the old fellow would make no will.'

'Couldn't read or write,' said Carruthers.

'So you came over, the two of you, and hunted up the girl. The idea was that one of you was to marry her, and the other have a share of the plunder. For some reason Woodley was chosen as the husband. Why was that?'

'We played cards for her on the voyage. He won.'

'I see. You got the young lady into your service, and there Woodley was to do the courting. She recognized the drunken brute that he was, and would have nothing to do with him. Meanwhile, your arrangement was rather upset by the fact that you had yourself fallen in love with the lady. You could no longer bear the idea of this ruffian owning her.'

'No, by George, I couldn't!'

'There was a quarrel between you. He left you in a rage, and began to make his own plans independently of you.'

'It strikes me, Williamson, there isn't very much that we can tell this gentleman,' cried Carruthers, with a bitter laugh. 'Yes, we quarrelled, and he knocked me down. I am level with him on that, anyhow. Then I lost sight of him. That was when he picked up with this cast padre* here. I found that they had set up housekeeping together at this place on the line that she had to pass for the station. I kept my eye on her after that, for I knew there was some devilry in the wind. I saw them from time to time, for I was anxious to know what they were after. Two days ago Woodley came up to my house with this cable, which showed that Ralph Smith was dead. He asked me if I would stand by the bargain. I said I would not. He asked me if I would marry the girl myself and give him a share. I said I would willingly do so, but that she would not have me. He said, "Let us get her married first, and after a week or two she may see things a bit different." I said I would have nothing to do with violence. So he went off cursing, like the foul-mouthed blackguard that he was, and swearing that he would have her yet. She was leaving me this week-end, and I had got a trap to take her to the station, but I was so uneasy in my mind that I followed her on my bicycle. She had got a start, however, and before I could catch her the mischief was done. The first thing I knew about it was when I saw you two gentlemen driving back in her dog-cart.'

Holmes rose and tossed the end of his cigarette into the grate. 'I have been very obtuse, Watson,' said he. 'When in your report you said that you had seen the cyclist as you thought arrange his necktie in the shrubbery, that alone should have told me all. However, we may congratulate ourselves upon a curious and in some respects a unique case. I perceive three of the county constabulary in the drive, and I am glad to see that the little ostler is able to keep pace with them; so it is likely that neither he nor the interesting bridegroom will be permanently damaged by their morning's adventures. I think, Watson, that in your medical capacity you might wait upon Miss Smith and tell her that if she is sufficiently recovered we shall be happy to escort her to her mother's home. If she is not quite convalescent you will find that a hint that we were about to telegraph to a young electrician in the Midlands would probably complete the cure. As to you, Mr Carruthers, I think that you have done what you could to make amends for your share in an evil plot. There is my card, sir, and if my evidence can be of help to you in your trial it shall be at your disposal.'

In the whirl of our incessant activity it has often been difficult for me, as the reader has probably observed, to round off my narratives, and to give those final details which the curious might expect. Each case has been the prelude to another, and the crisis once over, the actors have passed for ever out of our busy lives. I find, however, a short note at the end of my manuscripts dealing with this case, in which I have put it upon record that Miss Violet Smith did indeed inherit a large fortune, and that she is now the wife of Cyril Morton, the senior partner of Morton and Kennedy, the famous Westminster electricians. Williamson and Woodley were both tried for abduction and assault, the former getting seven years and the latter ten. Of the fate of Carruthers I have no record, but I am sure that his assault was not viewed very gravely by the Court, since Woodley had the reputation of being a most dangerous ruffian, and I think that a few months were sufficient to satisfy the demands of justice.

The Dancing Men

HOLMES had been seated for some hours in silence, with his long, thin back curved over a chemical vessel in which he was brewing a particularly malodorous product. His head was sunk upon his breast, and he looked from my point of view like a strange, lank bird, with dull grey plumage and a black top-knot.

'So, Watson,' said he suddenly, 'you do not propose to invest in South African securities?'*

I gave a start of astonishment. Accustomed as I was to Holmes's curious faculties, this sudden intrusion into my most intimate thoughts was utterly inexplicable.

'How on earth do you know that?' I asked.

He wheeled round upon his stool, with a steaming test-tube in his hand and a gleam of amusement in his deep-set eyes.

'Now, Watson, confess yourself utterly taken aback,' said he.

'I am.'

'I ought to make you sign a paper to that effect.'

'Why?'

'Because in five minutes you will say that it is all so absurdly simple.'

'I am sure that I shall say nothing of the kind.'

'You see, my dear Watson'—he propped his test-tube in the rack and began to lecture with the air of a professor addressing his class*—'it is not really difficult to construct a series of inferences, each dependent upon its predecessor and each simple in itself. If, after doing so, one simply knocks out all the central inferences and presents one's audience with the starting-point and the conclusion, one may produce a startling, though possibly a meretricious, effect. Now, it was not really difficult, by an inspection of the groove between your left forefinger and thumb, to feel

73

sure that you did *not* propose to invest your small capital in the goldfields.'

'I see no connection.'

'Very likely not; but I can quickly show you a close connection. Here are the missing links of the very simple chain: 1. You had chalk between your left finger and thumb when you returned from the club last night. 2. You put chalk there when you play billiards to steady the cue. 3. You never play billiards except with Thurston.* 4. You told me four weeks ago that Thurston had an option on some South African property which would expire in a month, and which he desired you to share with him. 5. Your cheque-book is locked in my drawer, and you have not asked for the key. 6. You do not propose to invest your money in this manner.'

'How absurdly simple!' I cried.

'Quite so!' said he, a little nettled. 'Every problem becomes very childish when once it is explained to you. Here is an unexplained one. See what you can make of that, friend Watson.' He tossed a sheet of paper upon the table, and turned once more to his chemical analysis.

I looked with amazement at the absurd hieroglyphics upon the paper.

'Why, Holmes, it is a child's drawing!' I cried.

'Oh, that's your idea!'

'What else should it be?'

'That is what Mr Hilton Cubitt,* of Ridling Thorpe Manor, Norfolk,* is very anxious to know. This little conundrum came by the first post, and he was to follow by the next train. There's a ring at the bell, Watson. I should not be very much surprised if this were he.'

A heavy step was heard upon the stairs, and an instant later there entered a tall, ruddy, clean-shaven gentleman, whose clear eyes and florid cheeks told of a life led far from the fogs of Baker Street. He seemed to bring a whiff of his strong, fresh, bracing, east-coast air with him as he entered. Having shaken hands with each of us, he was about to sit down, when his eye rested upon the paper with the curious markings, which I had just examined and left upon the table.

'Well, Mr Holmes, what do you make of these?' he cried. 'They told me that you were fond of queer mysteries, and I don't think you can find a queerer one than that. I sent the paper on ahead so that you might have time to study it before I came.'

'It is certainly rather a curious production,' said Holmes. 'At first sight it would appear to be some childish prank. It consists of a number of absurd little figures dancing across the paper upon which they are drawn. Why should you attribute any importance to so grotesque an object?'

'I never should, Mr Holmes. But my wife does. It is frightening her to death. She says nothing, but I can see terror in her eyes. That's why I want to sift the matter to the bottom.'

Holmes held up the paper so that the sunlight shone full upon it. It was a page torn from a note-book. The markings were done in pencil, and ran in this way:

Holmes examined it for some time, and then, folding it carefully up, he placed it in his pocket-book.

'This promises to be a most interesting and unusual case,' said he. 'You gave me a few particulars in your letter, Mr Hilton Cubitt, but I should be very much obliged if you would kindly go over it all again for the benefit of my friend, Dr Watson.'

'I'm not much of a story-teller,' said our visitor, nervously clasping and unclasping his great, strong hands. 'You'll just ask me anything that I don't make clear. I'll begin at the time of my marriage last year; but I want to say first of all that, though I'm not a rich man, my people have been at Ridling Thorpe for a matter of five centuries, and there is no better-known family in the county of Norfolk. Last year I came up to London for the Jubilee,* and I stopped at a boarding-house in Russell Square, because Parker, the vicar of our parish,* was staying in it. There was an American

young lady there—Patrick was the name—Elsie Patrick.*
In some way we became friends, until before my month was
up I was as much in love as a man could be. We were
quietly married at a registry office, and we returned to
Norfolk a wedded couple. You'll think it very mad, Mr
Holmes, that a man of a good old family should marry a
wife in this fashion, knowing nothing of her past or of her
people; but if you saw her and knew her it would help you
to understand.

'She was very straight about it, was Elsie. I can't say that
she did not give me every chance of getting out of it if I
wished to do so. "I have had some very disagreeable
associations in my life," said she; "I wish to forget all about
them. I would rather never allude to the past, for it is very
painful to me. If you take me, Hilton,* you will take a
woman who has nothing that she need be personally
ashamed of; but you will have to be content with my word
for it, and to allow me to be silent as to all that passed up
to the time when I became yours. If these conditions are too
hard, then go back to Norfolk and leave me to the lonely
life in which you found me." It was only the day before our
wedding that she said those very words to me. I told her that
I was content to take her on her own terms, and I have been
as good as my word.

'Well, we have been married now for a year, and very
happy we have been. But about a month ago, at the end of
June, I saw for the first time signs of trouble. One day my
wife received a letter from America. I saw the American
stamp. She turned deadly white, read the letter, and threw
it into the fire. She made no allusion to it afterwards and I
made none, for a promise is a promise; but she has never
known an easy hour from that moment. There is always a
look of fear upon her face—a look as if she were waiting and
expecting. She would do better to trust me. She would find
that I was her best friend. But until she speaks I can say
nothing. Mind you, she is a truthful woman, Mr Holmes,
and whatever trouble there may have been in her past life,
it has been no fault of hers. I am only a simple Norfolk

squire, but there is not a man in England who ranks his family honour more highly than I do. She knows it well, and she knew it well before she married me. She would never bring any stain upon it—of that I am sure.*

'Well, now I come to the queer part of my story. About a week ago—it was the Tuesday of last week—I found on one of the window-sills a number of absurd little dancing figures, like these upon the paper. They were scrawled with chalk. I thought that it was the stable-boy who had drawn them, but the lad swore he knew nothing about it. Anyhow, they had come there during the night. I had them washed out, and I only mentioned the matter to my wife afterwards. To my surprise she took it very seriously, and begged me if any more came to let her see them. None did come for a week, and then yesterday morning I found this paper lying on the sun-dial in the garden. I showed it to Elsie, and down she dropped in a dead faint. Since then she has looked like a woman in a dream, half dazed, and with terror always lurking in her eyes. It was then that I wrote and sent the paper to you, Mr Holmes. It was not a thing that I could take to the police, for they would have laughed at me, but you will tell me what to do. I am not a rich man; but if there is any danger threatening my little woman, I would spend my last copper to shield her.'

He was a fine creature, this man of the old English soil, simple, straight and gentle, with his great, earnest, blue eyes and broad, comely face. His love for his wife and his trust in her shone in his features. Holmes had listened to his story with the utmost attention, and now he sat for some time in silent thought.

'Don't you think, Mr Cubitt,' said he at last, 'that your best plan would be to make a direct appeal to your wife, and to ask her to share her secret with you?'

Hilton Cubitt shook his massive head.

'A promise is a promise, Mr Holmes. If Elsie wished to tell me, she would. If not, it is not for me to force her confidence. But I am justified in taking my own line—and I will.'

'Then I will help you with all my heart. In the first place, have you heard of any strangers being seen in your neighbourhood?'

'No.'

'I presume that it is a very quiet place. Any fresh face would cause comment?'

'In the immediate neighbourhood, yes. But we have several small watering-places not very far away. And the farmers take in lodgers.'

'These hieroglyphics have evidently a meaning. If it is a purely arbitrary one, it may be impossible for us to solve it. If, on the other hand, it is systematic, I have no doubt that we shall get to the bottom of it. But this particular sample is so short that I can do nothing, and the facts which you have brought me are so indefinite that we have no basis for an investigation. I would suggest that you return to Norfolk, that you keep a keen look-out, and that you take an exact copy of any fresh dancing men which may appear. It is a thousand pities that we have not a reproduction of those which were done in chalk upon the window-sill. Make a discreet inquiry, also, as to any strangers in the neighbourhood. When you have collected some fresh evidence, come to me again. That is the best advice which I can give you, Mr Hilton Cubitt. If there are any pressing fresh developments, I shall be always ready to run down and see you in your Norfolk home.'

The interview left Sherlock Holmes very thoughtful, and several times in the next few days I saw him take his slip of paper from his note-book and look long and earnestly at the curious figures inscribed upon it. He made no allusion to the affair, however, until one afternoon a fortnight or so later. I was going out, when he called me back.

'You had better stay here, Watson.'

'Why?'

'Because I had a wire from Hilton Cubitt this morning—you remember Hilton Cubitt, of the dancing men? He was to reach Liverpool Street at one-twenty.* He may be here at any moment. I gather from his wire that there have been some new incidents of importance.'

We had not long to wait, for our Norfolk squire came straight from the station as fast as a hansom could bring him. He was looking worried and depressed, with tired eyes and a lined forehead.

'It's getting on my nerves, this business, Mr Holmes,' said he, as he sank, like a wearied man, into an arm-chair. 'It's bad enough to feel that you are surrounded by unseen, unknown folk who have some kind of design upon you; but when, in addition to that, you know that it is just killing your wife by inches, then it becomes as much as flesh and blood can endure. She's wearing away under it—just wearing away before my eyes.'

'Has she said anything yet?'

'No, Mr Holmes, she has not. And yet there have been times when the poor girl has wanted to speak, and yet could not quite bring herself to take the plunge. I have tried to help her; but I dare say I did it clumsily, and scared her off from it. She has spoken about my old family, and our reputation in the county, and our pride in our unsullied honour, and I always felt it was leading to the point; but somehow it turned off before we got there.'

'But you have found out something for yourself?'

'A good deal, Mr Holmes. I have several fresh dancing men pictures for you to examine, and, what is more important, I have seen the fellow.'

'What—the man who draws them?'

'Yes, I saw him at his work. But I will tell you everything in order. When I got back after my visit to you, the very first thing I saw next morning was a fresh crop of dancing men. They had been drawn in chalk upon the black wooden door of the tool-house, which stands beside the lawn in full view of the front windows. I took an exact copy, and here it is.' He unfolded a paper and laid it upon the table. Here is a copy of the hieroglyphics:

79

'Excellent!' said Holmes. 'Excellent! Pray continue.'

'When I had taken the copy I rubbed out the marks; but two mornings later a fresh inscription had appeared. I have a copy of it here':

Holmes rubbed his hands and chuckled with delight.

'Our material is rapidly accumulating,' said he.

'Three days later a message was left scrawled upon paper, and placed under a pebble upon the sun-dial. Here it is. The characters are, as you see, exactly the same as the last one. After that I determined to lie in wait; so I got out my revolver and I sat up in my study, which overlooks the lawn and garden. About two in the morning I was seated by the window, all being dark save for the moonlight outside, when I heard steps behind me, and there was my wife in her dressing-gown. She implored me to come to bed. I told her frankly that I wished to see who it was who played such absurd tricks upon us. She answered that it was some senseless practical joke, and that I should not take any notice of it.

' "If it really annoys you, Hilton, we might go and travel, you and I, and so avoid this nuisance."

' "What, be driven out of our own house by a practical joker?" said I. "Why, we should have the whole county laughing at us!"

' "Well, come to bed," said she, "and we can discuss it in the morning."

'Suddenly, as she spoke, I saw her white face grow whiter yet in the moonlight, and her hand tightened upon my shoulder. Something was moving in the shadow of the tool-house. I saw a dark, creeping figure which crawled round the corner and squatted in front of the door. Seizing my pistol I was rushing out, when my wife threw her arms round me and held me with convulsive strength. I tried to throw her off, but she clung to me most desperately. At last

I got clear, but by the time I had opened the door and reached the house the creature was gone. He had left a trace of his presence, however, for there on the door was the very same arrangement of dancing men which had already twice appeared, and which I have copied on that paper. There was no other sign of the fellow anywhere, though I ran all over the grounds. And yet the amazing thing is that he must have been there all the time, for when I examined the door again in the morning he had scrawled some more of his pictures under the line which I had already seen.'

'Have you that fresh drawing?'

'Yes; it is very short, but I made a copy of it, and here it is.'

Again he produced a paper. The new dance was in this form:

'Tell me,' said Holmes—and I could see by his eyes that he was much excited—'was this a mere addition to the first, or did it appear to be entirely separate?'

'It was on a different panel of the door.'

'Excellent! This is far the most important of all for our purpose. It fills me with hopes. Now, Mr Hilton Cubitt, please continue your most interesting statement.'

'I have nothing more to say, Mr Holmes, except that I was angry with my wife that night for having held me back when I might have caught the skulking rascal. She said that she feared that I might come to harm. For an instant it had crossed my mind that perhaps what she really feared was that *he* might come to harm, for I could not doubt that she knew who this man was and what he meant by these strange signals. But there is a tone in my wife's voice, Mr Holmes, and a look in her eyes which forbid doubt, and I am sure that it was indeed my own safety that was in her mind. There's the whole case, and now I want your advice as to what I ought to do. My own inclination is to put half a dozen of my farm lads in the shrubbery, and when this fellow comes again to give him such a hiding that he will leave us in peace for the future.'

'I fear it is too deep a case for such simple remedies,' said Holmes. 'How long can you stop in London?'

'I must go back to-day. I would not leave my wife alone at night for anything. She is very nervous and begged me to come back.'

'I dare say you are right. But if you could have stopped I might possibly have been able to return with you in a day or two. Meanwhile, you will leave me these papers, and I think that it is very likely that I shall be able to pay you a visit shortly and to throw some light upon your case.'

Sherlock Holmes preserved his calm professional manner until our visitor had left us, although it was easy for me, who knew him so well, to see that he was profoundly excited. The moment that Hilton Cubitt's broad back had disappeared through the door my comrade rushed to the table, laid out all the slips of paper containing dancing men in front of him, and threw himself into an intricate and elaborate calculation.

For two hours I watched him as he covered sheet after sheet of paper with figures and letters, so completely absorbed in his task that he had evidently forgotten my presence. Sometimes he was making progress, and whistled and sang at his work; sometimes he was puzzled and would sit for a long spell with a furrowed brow and a vacant eye. Finally he sprang from his chair with a cry of satisfaction, and walked up and down the room rubbing his hands together. Then he wrote a long telegram upon a cable form. 'If my answer to this is as I hope, you will have a very pretty case to add to your collection, Watson,' said he. 'I expect that we shall be able to go down to Norfolk to-morrow, and to take our friend some very definite news as to the secret of his annoyance.'

I confess that I was filled with curiosity, but I was aware that Holmes liked to make his disclosures at his own time and in his own way; so I waited until it should suit him to take me into his confidence.

But there was a delay in that answering telegram, and two days of impatience followed, during which Holmes pricked up his ears at every ring of the bell. On the evening of the second there came a letter from Hilton Cubitt. All was quiet with him, save that a long inscription had appeared that morning upon the pedestal of the sun-dial. He enclosed a copy of it, which is here reproduced:

Holmes bent over this grotesque frieze for some minutes and then suddenly sprang to his feet with an exclamation of surprise and dismay. His face was haggard with anxiety.

'We have let this affair go far enough,' said he. 'Is there a train to North Walsham* to-night?'

I turned up the time-table. The last had just gone.

'Then we shall breakfast early and take the very first in the morning,' said Holmes. 'Our presence is most urgently needed. Ah, here is our expected cablegram. One moment, Mrs Hudson—there may be an answer. No, that is quite as I expected. This message makes it even more essential that we should not lose an hour in letting Hilton Cubitt know how matters stand, for it is a singular and dangerous web in which our simple Norfolk squire is entangled.'

So, indeed, it proved, and as I come to the dark conclusion of a story which had seemed to me to be only childish and bizarre, I experience once again the dismay and horror with which I was filled. Would that I had some brighter ending to communicate to my readers; but these are the chronicles of facts, and I must follow to their dark crisis the strange chain of events which for some days made Ridling Thorpe Manor a household word through the length and breadth of England.

We had hardly alighted at North Walsham, and mentioned the name of our destination, when the station-master hurried towards us. 'I suppose that you are the detectives from London?' said he.

A look of annoyance passed over Holmes's face.

'What makes you think such a thing?'

'Because Inspector Martin from Norwich has just passed through. But maybe you are the surgeons. She's not dead—or wasn't by last accounts. You may be in time to save her yet—though it be for the gallows.'

Holmes's brow was dark with anxiety.

'We are going to Ridling Thorpe Manor,' said he, 'but we have heard nothing of what has passed there.'

'It's a terrible business,' said the station-master. 'They are shot, both Mr Hilton Cubitt and his wife. She shot him and then herself—so the servants say. He's dead, and her life is despaired of. Dear, dear! one of the oldest families in the county of Norfolk, and one of the most honoured.'

Without a word Holmes hurried to a carriage, and during the long, seven-miles drive he never opened his mouth. Seldom have I seen him so utterly despondent. He had been uneasy during all our journey from town, and I had observed that he had turned over the morning papers with anxious attention; but now this sudden realization of his worst fears left him in a blank melancholy. He leaned back in his seat, lost in gloomy speculation. Yet there was much around us to interest us, for we were passing through as singular a country-side as any in England, where a few scattered cottages represented the population of today, while on every hand enormous square-towered churches bristled up from the flat, green landscape and told of the glory and prosperity of old East Anglia. At last the violet rim of the German Ocean* appeared over the green edge of the Norfolk coast, and the driver pointed with his whip to two old brick and timber gables which projected from a grove of trees. 'That's Ridling Thorpe Manor,' said he.

As we drove up to the porticoed front door I observed in front of it, beside the tennis lawn, the black tool-house and the pedestalled sun-dial with which we had such strange associations. A dapper little man, with a quick, alert manner and a waxed moustache, had just descended from a high dog-cart. He introduced himself as Inspector Martin, of the Norfolk Constabulary, and he was considerably astonished when he heard the name of my companion.

'Why, Mr Holmes, the crime was only committed at three this morning! How could you hear of it in London and get to the spot as soon as I?'

'I anticipated it. I came in the hope of preventing it.'

'Then you must have important evidence of which we are ignorant, for they were said to be a most united couple.'

'I have only the evidence of the dancing men,' said Holmes. 'I will explain the matter to you later. Meanwhile, since it is too late to prevent this tragedy, I am very anxious that I should use the knowledge which I possess in order to ensure that justice be done. Will you associate me in your investigation, or will you prefer that I should act independently?'

'I should be proud to feel that we were acting together, Mr Holmes,' said the inspector earnestly.

'In that case I should be glad to hear the evidence and to examine the premises without an instant of unnecessary delay.'

Inspector Martin had the good sense to allow my friend to do things in his own fashion, and contented himself with carefully noting the results. The local surgeon, an old, white-haired man, had just come down from Mrs Hilton Cubitt's room, and he reported that her injuries were serious, but not necessarily fatal. The bullet had passed through the front of her brain, and it would probably be some time before she could regain consciousness. On the question of whether she had been shot or had shot herself he would not venture to express any decided opinion. Certainly the bullet had been discharged at very close quarters. There was only the one pistol found in the room, two barrels of which had been emptied. Mr Hilton Cubitt had been shot through the heart. It was equally conceivable that he had shot her and then himself, or that she had been the criminal, for the revolver lay upon the floor midway between them.

'Has he been moved?' asked Holmes.

'We have moved nothing except the lady. We could not leave her lying wounded upon the floor.'

'How long have you been here, doctor?'

'Since four o'clock.'

'Anyone else?'

'Yes, the constable here.'

'And you have touched nothing?'

'Nothing.'

'You have acted with great discretion. Who sent for you?'

'The housemaid, Saunders.'

'Was it she who gave the alarm?'

'She and Mrs King, the cook.'

'Where are they now?'

'In the kitchen, I believe.'

'Then I think we had better hear their story at once.'

The old hall, oak-panelled and high-windowed, had been turned into a court of investigation. Holmes sat in a great, old-fashioned chair, his inexorable eyes gleaming out of his haggard face. I could read in them a set purpose to devote his life to this quest until the client whom he had failed to save should at last* be avenged. The trim Inspector Martin, the old grey-headed* country doctor, myself and a stolid village policeman made up the rest of that strange company.

The two women told their story clearly enough. They had been aroused from their sleep by the sound of an explosion, which had been followed a minute later by a second one. They slept in adjoining rooms, and Mrs King had rushed in to Saunders. Together they had descended the stairs. The door of the study was open and a candle was burning upon the table. Their master lay upon his face in the centre of the room. He was quite dead. Near the window his wife was crouching, her head leaning against the wall. She was horribly wounded, and the side of her face was red with blood. She breathed heavily, but was incapable of saying anything. The passage, as well as the room, was full of smoke and the smell of powder. The window was certainly shut and fastened upon the inside. Both women were positive upon the point. They had at once sent for the doctor and for the constable. Then, with the aid of the groom and the stable-boy, they had conveyed their injured mistress to her room. Both she and her husband had occupied the bed. She was clad in her dress—he in his dressing-gown, over his night-clothes. Nothing had been moved in the study. So far as they knew, there had never been any quarrel between husband and wife. They had always looked upon them as a very united couple.

These were the main points of the servants' evidence. In answer to Inspector Martin they were clear that every door was fastened upon the inside and that no one could have escaped from the house. In answer to Holmes, they both remembered that they were conscious of the smell of powder from the moment that they ran out of their rooms upon the top floor. 'I commend that fact very carefully to your attention,' said Holmes to his professional colleague. 'And now I think that we are in a position to undertake a thorough examination of the room.'

The study proved to be a small chamber, lined on three sides with books, and with a writing-table facing an ordinary window, which looked out upon the garden. Our first attention was given to the body of the unfortunate squire, whose huge frame lay stretched across the room. His disordered dress showed that he had been hastily aroused from sleep. The bullet had been fired at him from the front, and had remained in his body after penetrating the heart. His death had certainly been instantaneous and painless. There was no powder-marking either upon his dressing-gown or on his hands. According to the country surgeon, the lady had stains upon her face, but none upon her hand.

'The absence of the latter means nothing, though its presence may mean everything,' said Holmes. 'Unless the powder from a badly fitting cartridge happens to spurt backwards, one may fire many shots without leaving a sign. I would suggest that Mr Cubitt's body may now be removed. I suppose, doctor, you have not recovered the bullet which wounded the lady?'

'A serious operation will be necessary before that can be done. But there are still four cartridges in the revolver. Two have been fired and two wounds inflicted, so that each bullet can be accounted for.'

'So it would seem,' said Holmes. 'Perhaps you can account also for the bullet which has so obviously struck the edge of the window?'

He had turned suddenly, and his long, thin finger was pointing to a hole which had been drilled right through the lower window-sash about an inch above the bottom.

'By George!' cried the inspector. 'How ever did you see that?'

'Because I looked for it.'

'Wonderful!' said the country doctor. 'You are certainly right, sir. Then a third shot has been fired, and therefore a third person must have been present. But who could that have been, and how could he have got away?'

'That is the problem which we are now about to solve,' said Sherlock Holmes. 'You remember, Inspector Martin, when the servants said that on leaving their room they were at once conscious of a smell of powder, I remarked that the point was an extremely important one?'

'Yes, sir; but I confess I did not quite follow you.'

'It suggested that at the time of the firing the window as well as the door of the room had been open. Otherwise the fumes of powder could not have been blown so rapidly through the house. A draught in the room was necessary for that. Both door and window were only open for a* short time, however.'

'How do you prove that?'

'Because the candle has not guttered.'

'Capital!' cried the inspector. 'Capital!'

'Feeling sure that the window had been open at the time of the tragedy, I conceived that there might have been a third person in the affair, who stood outside this opening and fired through it. Any shot directed at this person might hit the sash. I looked, and there, sure enough, was the bullet mark!'

'But how came the window to be shut and fastened?'

'The woman's first instinct would be to shut and fasten the window. But, hullo! what is this?'

It was a lady's hand-bag which stood upon the study table—a trim little hand-bag of crocodile-skin and silver. Holmes opened it and turned the contents out. There were twenty fifty-pound notes of the Bank of England, held together by an India-rubber band—nothing else.

'This must be preserved, for it will figure in the trial,' said Holmes, as he handed the bag with its contents to the inspector. 'It is now necessary that we should try to throw some light upon this third bullet, which has clearly, from the splintering of the wood, been fired from inside the room. I should like to see Mrs King, the cook, again . . . You said, Mrs King, that you were awakened by a *loud* explosion. When you said that, did you mean that it seemed to you to be louder than the second one?'

'Well, sir, it wakened me from my sleep, and so it is hard to judge. But it did seem very loud.'

'You don't think that it might have been two shots fired almost at the same instant?'

'I am sure I couldn't say, sir.'

'I believe that it was undoubtedly so. I rather think, Inspector Martin, that we have now exhausted all that this room can teach us. If you will kindly step round with me we shall see what fresh evidence the garden has to offer.'

A flower-bed extended up to the study window, and we all broke into an exclamation as we approached it. The flowers were trampled down, and the soft soil was imprinted all over with footmarks. Large, masculine feet they were, with peculiarly long, sharp toes. Holmes hunted about among the grass and leaves like a retriever after a wounded bird. Then, with a cry of satisfaction, he bent forward and picked up a little brazen cylinder.

'I thought so,' said he; 'the revolver had an ejector, and here is the third cartridge. I really think, Inspector Martin, that our case is almost complete.'

The country inspector's face had shown his intense amazement at the rapid and masterful progress of Holmes's investigations. At first he had shown some disposition to assert his own position; but now he was overcome with admiration, and ready to follow without question wherever Holmes led.

'Whom do you suspect?' he asked.

'I'll go into that later. There are several points in this problem which I have not been able to explain to you yet. Now that I have got so far I had best proceed on my own lines, and then clear the whole matter up once and for all.'

'Just as you wish, Mr Holmes, so long as we get our man.'

'I have no desire to make mysteries, but it is impossible at the moment of action to enter into long and complex explanations. I have the threads of this affair all in my hand. Even if this lady should never recover consciousness we can still reconstruct the events of last night and ensure that justice be done. First of all I wish to know whether there is any inn in this neighbourhood known as "Elrige's?"'*

The servants were cross-questioned, but none of them had heard of such a place. The stable-boy threw a light upon the matter by remembering that a farmer of that name lived some miles off in the direction of East Ruston.*

'Is it a lonely farm?'

'Very lonely, sir.'

'Perhaps they have not heard yet of all that happened here during the night?'

'Maybe not, sir.'

Holmes thought for a little, and then a curious smile played over his face.

'Saddle a horse, my lad,' said he. 'I shall wish you to take a note to Elrige's Farm.'

He took from his pocket the various slips of the dancing men. With these in front of him he worked for some time at the study-table. Finally he handed a note to the boy, with directions to put it into the hands of the person to whom it was addressed, and especially to answer no questions of any sort which might be put to him. I saw the outside of the note, addressed in straggling, irregular characters, very unlike Holmes's usual precise hand. It was consigned to Mr Abe Slaney,* Elrige's Farm, East Ruston, Norfolk.

'I think, Inspector,' Holmes remarked, 'that you would do well to telegraph for an escort, as, if my calculations prove to be correct, you may have a particularly dangerous prisoner to convey to the county gaol. The boy who takes this note could no doubt forward your telegram. If there is an afternoon train to town, Watson, I think we should do well to take it, as I have a chemical analysis of some interest to finish, and this investigation draws rapidly to a close.'

When the youth had been dispatched with the note, Sherlock Holmes gave his instructions to the servants. If any visitor were to call asking for Mrs Hilton Cubitt no information should be given as to her condition, but he was to be shown at once into the drawing-room. He impressed these points upon them with the utmost earnestness. Finally he led the way into the drawing-room, with the remark that the business was now out of our hands, and that we must while away the time as best we might until we could see what was in store for us. The doctor had departed to his patients, and only the inspector and myself remained.

'I think I can help you to pass an hour in an interesting and profitable manner,' said Holmes, drawing his chair up to the table and spreading out in front of him the various papers upon which were recorded the antics of the dancing men. 'As to you, friend Watson, I owe you every atonement for having allowed your natural curiosity to remain so long unsatisfied. To you, inspector, the whole incident may appeal as a remarkable professional study. I must tell you first of all the interesting circumstances connected with the previous consultations which Mr Hilton Cubitt has had with me in Baker Street.' He then shortly recapitulated the facts which have already been recorded.

'I have here in front of me these singular productions, at which one might smile had they not proved themselves to be the forerunners of so terrible a tragedy. I am fairly familiar with all forms of secret writings, and am myself the author of a trifling monograph upon the subject, in which I analyse one hundred and sixty separate ciphers; but I confess that this is entirely new to me. The object of those who invented the system has apparently been to conceal that these characters convey a message, and to give the idea that they are the mere random sketches of children.

'Having once recognized, however, that the symbols stood for letters, and having applied the rules which guide us in all forms of secret writings, the solution was easy enough. The first message submitted to me was so short that it was impossible for me to do more than say with some confidence that the symbol 𐊠 stood for E.* As you are aware, E is the most common letter in the English alphabet and it predominates to so marked an extent that even in a short sentence one would expect to find it most often. Out of fifteen symbols in the first message four were the same, so it was reasonable to set this down as E. It is true that in some cases the figure was bearing a flag, and in some cases not, but it was probable from the way in which the flags were distributed that they were used to break the sentence up into words. I accepted this as an hypothesis, and noted that E was represented by

'But now came the real difficulty of the inquiry. The order of the English letters after E is by no means well marked, and any preponderance which may be shown in an average of a printed sheet may be reversed in a single short sentence. Speaking roughly, T, A, O, I, N, S, H, R, D, and L are the numerical order in which letters occur;* but T, A, O, and I are very nearly abreast of each other, and it would be an endless task to try each combination until a meaning was arrived at. I, therefore, waited for fresh material. In my second interview with Mr Hilton Cubitt he was able to give me two other short sentences and one message, which appeared—since there was no flag—to be a single word. Here are the symbols:

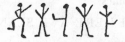

Now, in the single word I have already got the two E's coming second and fourth in a word of five letters. It might be "sever", or "lever", or "never". There can be no question that the latter as a reply to an appeal is far the most probable, and the circumstances pointed to its being a reply written by the lady. Accepting it as correct we are now able to say that the symbols

stand respectively for N, V, and R.

'Even now I was in considerable difficulty, but a happy thought put me in possession of several other letters. It occurred to me that if these appeals came, as I expected, from someone who had been intimate with the lady in her early life, a combination which contained two E's with three letters between might very well stand for the name "ELSIE". On examination I found that such a combination formed the termination of the message which was three times repeated. It was certainly some appeal to "Elsie". In this way I had got my L, S, and I. But what appeal could it be? There were only four letters in the word which preceded "Elsie", and it ended in E. Surely the word must be "COME". I tried all other four letters ending in E, but could find none to fit the case. So now I was in possession of C, O, and M, and I was in a position to attack the first message once more, dividing it into words and putting dots for each symbol which was still unknown. So treated it worked out in this fashion:

.M.ERE..E SL.NE.

'Now, the first letter can only be A, which is a most useful discovery, since it occurs no fewer than three times in this short sentence, and the H is also apparent in the second word. Now it becomes:

AM HERE A . E SLANE.

Or, filling in the obvious vacancies in the name:

AM HERE ABE SLANEY

I had so many letters now that I could proceed with considerable confidence to the second message, which worked out in this fashion:

A . ELRI . ES

Here I could only make sense by putting T and G for the missing letters, and supposing that the name was that of some house or inn at which the writer was staying.'

Inspector Martin and I had listened with the utmost interest to the full and clear account of how my friend had produced results which had led to so complete a command over our difficulties.

'What did you do then, sir?' asked the inspector.

'I had every reason to suppose that this Abe Slaney was an American, since Abe is an American contraction, and since a letter from America had been the starting-point of all the trouble. I had also every cause to think that there was some criminal secret in the matter. The lady's allusions to her past and her refusal to take her husband into her confidence both pointed in that direction. I therefore cabled to my friend, Wilson Hargreave, of the New York Police Bureau, who has more than once made use of my knowledge of London crime. I asked him whether the name of Abe Slaney was known to him. Here is his reply: "The most dangerous crook in Chicago." On the very evening upon which I had his answer Hilton Cubitt sent me the last message from Slaney. Working with known letters it took this form:

ELSIE . RE . ARE TO MEET THY GO .

The addition of a P and a D completed a message which showed me that the rascal was proceeding from persuasion to threats, and my knowledge of the crooks of Chicago prepared me to find that he might very rapidly put his words into action. I at once came to Norfolk with my friend and colleague, Dr Watson, but, unhappily, only in time to find that the worst had already occurred.'

'It is a privilege to be associated with you in the handling of a case,' said the inspector warmly. 'You will excuse me, however, if I speak frankly to you. You are only answerable to yourself, but I have to answer to my superiors. If this Abe Slaney, living at Elrige's, is indeed the murderer, and if he has made his escape while I am seated here, I should certainly get into serious trouble.'

'You need not be uneasy. He will not try to escape.'

'How do you know?'

'To fly would be a confession of guilt.'

'Then let us go to arrest him.'

'I expect him here every instant.'

'But why should he come?'

'Because I have written and asked him.'

'But this is incredible, Mr Holmes! Why should he come because you have asked him? Would not such a request rather rouse his suspicions and cause him to fly?'

'I think I have known how to frame the letter,' said Sherlock Holmes. 'In fact, if I am not very much mistaken, here is the gentleman himself coming up the drive.'

A man was striding up the path which led to the door. He was a tall, handsome, swarthy fellow, clad in a suit of grey flannel, with a Panama hat, a bristling black beard and a great, aggressive, hooked nose, and flourishing a cane as he walked. He swaggered up the path as if the place belonged to him, and we heard his loud, confident peal at the bell.

'I think, gentlemen,' said Holmes quietly, 'that we had best take up our position behind the door. Every precaution is necessary when dealing with such a fellow. You will need your handcuffs, Inspector. You can leave the talking to me.'

We waited in silence for a minute—one of those minutes

95

which one can never forget. Then the door opened, and the man stepped in. In an instant Holmes clapped a pistol to his head, and Martin slipped the handcuffs over his wrists. It was all done so swiftly and deftly that the fellow was helpless before he knew that he was attacked. He glared from one to the other of us with a pair of blazing black eyes. Then he burst into a bitter laugh.

'Well, gentlemen, you have the drop on me this time. I seem to have knocked up against something hard. But I came here in answer to a letter from Mrs Hilton Cubitt. Don't tell me that she is in this? Don't tell me that she helped to set a trap for me?'

'Mrs Hilton Cubitt was seriously injured, and is at death's door.'

The man gave a hoarse cry of grief which rang through the house.

'You're crazy!' he cried fiercely. 'It was he that was hurt, not she. Who would have hurt little Elsie? I may have threatened her, God forgive me, but I would not have touched a hair of her pretty head. Take it back—you! Say that she is not hurt!'

'She was found badly wounded by the side of her dead husband.'

He sank with a deep groan on to the settee, and buried his face in his manacled hands. For five minutes he was silent. Then he raised his face once more, and spoke with the cold composure of despair.

'I have nothing to hide from you, gentlemen,' said he. 'If I shot the man he had his shot at me, and there's no murder in that. But if you think I could have hurt that woman, then you don't know either me or her. I tell you there was never a man in this world loved a woman more than I loved her. I had a right to her. She was pledged to me years ago. Who was this Englishman that he should come between us? I tell you that I had the first right to her, and that I was only claiming my own.'

'She broke away from your influence when she found the man that you are,' said Holmes sternly. 'She fled from

America to avoid you, and she married an honourable
gentleman in England. You dogged her and followed her,
and made her life a misery to her in order to induce her to
abandon the husband whom she loved and respected in
order to fly with you, whom she feared and hated. You have
ended by bringing about the death of a noble man and driving
his wife to suicide. That is your record in this business, Mr Abe
Slaney, and you will answer for it to the law.'

'If Elsie dies I care nothing what becomes of me,' said the
American. He opened one of his hands and looked at a note
crumpled up in his palm. 'See here, mister,' he cried, with
a gleam of suspicion in his eyes, 'you're not trying to scare
me over this, are you? If the lady is hurt as bad as you say,
who was it that wrote this note?' He tossed it forward on to
the table.

'I wrote it to bring you here.'

'You wrote it? There was no one on earth outside the
Joint who knew the secret of the dancing men.* How came
you to write it?'

'What one man can invent another can discover,' said
Holmes. 'There is a cab coming to convey you to Norwich,
Mr Slaney. But, meanwhile, you have time to make some
small reparation for the injury you have wrought. Are you
aware that Mrs Hilton Cubitt has herself lain under grave
suspicion of the murder of her husband, and that it was only
my presence here and the knowledge which I happened to
possess which has saved her from the accusation? The least
that you owe her is to make it clear to the whole world that
she was in no way, directly or indirectly, responsible for his
tragic end.'

'I ask nothing better,' said the American. 'I guess the very
best case I can make for myself is the absolute naked truth.'

'It is my duty to warn you that it will be used against you,'
cried the inspector, with the magnificent fair-play of the
British criminal law.

Slaney shrugged his shoulders.

'I'll chance that,' said he. 'First of all, I want you
gentlemen to understand that I have known this lady since

she was a child. There were seven of us in a gang in Chicago, and Elsie's father was the boss of the Joint. He was a clever man, was old Patrick. It was he who invented that writing, which would pass as a child's scrawl unless you just happened to have the key to it. Well, Elsie learned some of our ways; but she couldn't stand the business, and she had a bit of honest money of her own, so she gave us all the slip and got away to London. She had been engaged to me, and she would have married me, I believe, if I had taken over another profession; but she would have nothing to do with anything on the cross. It was only after her marriage to this Englishman that I was able to find out where she was. I wrote to her, but got no answer. After that I came over, and, as letters were of no use, I put my messages where she could read them.

'Well, I have been here a month now. I lived in that farm, where I had a room down below, and could get in and out every night, and no one the wiser. I tried all I could to coax Elsie away. I knew that she read the messages, for once she wrote an answer under one of them. Then my temper got the better of me, and I began to threaten her. She sent me a letter then, imploring me to go away, and saying that it would break her heart if any scandal should come upon her husband. She said that she would come down when her husband was asleep at three in the morning, and speak with me through the end window, if I would go away afterwards and leave her in peace. She came down and brought money with her, trying to bribe me to go. This made me mad, and I caught her arm and tried to pull her through the window. At that moment in rushed the husband with his revolver in his hand. Elsie had sunk down upon the floor, and we were face to face. I was heeled also, and I held up my gun to scare him off and let me get away. He fired and missed me. I pulled off almost at the same instant, and down he dropped. I made away across the garden, and as I went I heard the window shut behind me. That's God truth, gentlemen, every word of it, and I heard no more about it until that lad came riding up with a note which made me walk in here, like a jay, and give myself into your hands.'

A cab had driven up whilst the American had been talking. Two uniformed policemen sat inside. Inspector Martin rose and touched his prisoner on the shoulder.

'It is time for us to go.'

'Can I see her first?'

'No, she is not conscious. Mr Sherlock Holmes, I only hope that if ever again I have an important case I shall have the good fortune to have you by my side.'

We stood at the window and watched the cab drive away. As I turned back my eye caught the pellet of paper which the prisoner had tossed upon the table. It was the note with which Holmes had decoyed him.

'See if you can read it, Watson,' said he, with a smile.

It contained no word, but this little line of dancing men:

'If you use the code which I have explained,' said Holmes, 'you will find that it simply means "Come here at once." I was convinced that it was an invitation which he would not refuse, since he could never imagine that it could come from anyone but the lady. And so, my dear Watson, we have ended by turning the dancing men to good when they have so often been the agents of evil, and I think that I have fulfilled my promise of giving you something unusual for your notebook. Three-forty is our train, and I fancy we should be back in Baker Street for dinner.'*

Only one word of epilogue. The American, Abe Slaney, was condemned to death at the winter assizes at Norwich; but his penalty was changed to penal servitude in consideration of mitigating circumstances, and the certainty that Hilton Cubitt had fired the first shot. Of Mrs Hilton Cubitt I only know that I have heard she recovered entirely, and that she still remains a widow, devoting her whole life to the care of the poor and to the administration of her husband's estate.

The Priory School

WE have had some dramatic entrances and exits upon our small stage at Baker Street, but I cannot recollect anything more sudden and startling than the first appearance of Dr Thorneycroft Huxtable,* M.A., Ph.D., etc. His card, which seemed too small to carry the weight of his academic distinctions, preceded him by a few seconds, and then he entered himself—so large, so pompous, and so dignified that he was the very embodiment of self-possession and solidity. And yet his first action when the door had closed behind him was to stagger against the table, whence he slipped down upon the floor, and there was that majestic figure prostrate and insensible upon our bearskin hearthrug.

We had sprung to our feet, and for a few moments we stared in silent amazement at this ponderous piece of wreckage, which told of some sudden and fatal storm far out on the ocean of life. Then Holmes hurried with a cushion for his head, and I with brandy for his lips. The heavy white face was seamed with lines of trouble, the hanging pouches under the closed eyes were leaden in colour, the loose mouth drooped dolorously at the corners, the rolling chins were unshaven. Collar and shirt bore the grime of a long journey, and the hair bristled unkempt from the well-shaped head. It was a sorely stricken man who lay before us.

'What is it, Watson?' asked Holmes.

'Absolute exhaustion—possibly mere hunger and fatigue,' said I, with my finger on the thready pulse, where the stream of life trickled thin and small.

'Return ticket from Mackleton, in the North of England,'* said Holmes, drawing it from the watch-pocket. 'It is not twelve o'clock* yet. He has certainly been an early starter.'

The puckered eyelids had begun to quiver, and now a pair of vacant, grey eyes looked up at us. An instant later the man had scrambled on to his feet, his face crimson with shame.

'Forgive this weakness, Mr Holmes; I have been a little overwrought. Thank you, if I might have a glass of milk and a biscuit I have no doubt that I should be better. I came personally, Mr Holmes, in order to ensure that you would return with me. I feared that no telegram would convince you of the absolute urgency of the case.'

'When you are quite restored—'

'I am quite well again. I cannot imagine how I came to be so weak. I wish you, Mr Holmes, to come to Mackleton with me by the next train.'

My friend shook his head.

'My colleague, Dr Watson, could tell you that we are very busy at present. I am retained in this case of the Ferrers Documents,* and the Abergavenny murder* is coming up for trial. Only a very important issue could call me from London at present.'

'Important!' Our visitor threw up his hands. 'Have you heard nothing of the abduction of the only son of the Duke of Holdernesse?'*

'What! the late Cabinet Minister?'*

'Exactly. We had tried to keep it out of the papers, but there was some rumour in the *Globe** last night. I thought it might have reached your ears.'

Holmes shot out his long, thin arm and picked out Volume 'H' in his encyclopaedia of reference.*

' "Holdernesse, sixth Duke, K.G., P.C."—half the alphabet! "Baron Beverley, Earl of Carston"—dear me, what a list! "Lord-Lieutenant of Hallamshire since 1900. Married Edith, daughter of Sir Charles Appledore, 1888. Heir and only child, Lord Saltire. Owns about two hundred and fifty thousand acres. Minerals in Lancashire and Wales. Address: Carlton House Terrace; Holdernesse Hall, Hallamshire; Carston Castle, Bangor, Wales. Lord of the Admiralty, 1872; Chief Secretary of State for—"* Well, well, this man is certainly one of the greatest subjects of the Crown!'

'The greatest and perhaps the wealthiest. I am aware, Mr Holmes, that you take a very high line in professional matters, and that you are prepared to work for the work's sake. I may tell you, however, that his Grace has already intimated that a cheque for five thousand pounds* will be handed over to the person who can tell him where his son is, and another thousand to him who can name the man, or men, who have taken him.'

'It is a princely offer,' said Holmes. 'Watson, I think that we shall accompany Dr Huxtable back to the North of England. And now, Dr Huxtable, when you have consumed that milk you will kindly tell me what has happened, when it happened, how it happened, and, finally, what Dr Thorneycroft Huxtable, of the Priory School, near Mackleton, has to do with the matter, and why he comes three days after an event—the state of your chin gives the date—to ask for my humble services.'

Our visitor had consumed his milk and biscuits. The light had come back to his eyes and the colour to his cheeks as he set himself with great vigour and lucidity to explain the situation.

'I must inform you, gentlemen, that the Priory is a preparatory school, of which I am the founder and principal. *Huxtable's Sidelights on Horace* * may possibly recall my name to your memories. The Priory is, without exception, the best and most select preparatory school in England. Lord Leverstoke, the Earl of Blackwater, Sir Cathcart Soames*—they all have entrusted their sons to me. But I felt that my school had reached its zenith when, three weeks ago, the Duke of Holdernesse sent Mr James Wilder, his secretary, with the intimation that young Lord Saltire, ten years old, his only son and heir, was about to be committed to my charge. Little did I think that this would be the prelude to the most crushing misfortune of my life.

'On May 1st the boy arrived, that being the beginning of the summer term. He was a charming youth, and he soon fell into our ways. I may tell you—I trust that I am not indiscreet, but half-confidences are absurd in such a case— that he was not entirely happy at home. It is an open secret that the Duke's married life had not been a peaceful one, and the matter had ended in a separation by mutual consent, the

Duchess taking up her residence in the South of France.*
This had occurred very shortly before, and the boy's sympathies are known to have been strongly with his mother.
He moped after her departure from Holdernesse Hall, and
it was for this reason that the Duke desired to send him to
my establishment. In a fortnight the boy was quite at home
with us, and was apparently absolutely happy.

'He was last seen on the night of May 13th—that is, the
night of last Monday. His room was on the second floor, and
was approached through another larger room in which two
boys were sleeping. These boys saw and heard nothing, so
that it is certain that young Saltire did not pass out that way.
His window was open, and there is a stout ivy plant leading
to the ground. We could trace no footmarks below, but it is
sure that this is the only possible exit.

'His absence was discovered at seven o'clock on Tuesday
morning. His bed had been slept in. He had dressed himself
fully before going off in his usual school suit of black Eton
jacket* and dark grey trousers. There were no signs that
anyone had entered the room, and it is quite certain that
anything in the nature of cries or a struggle would have been
heard, since Caunter,* the elder boy in the inner room, is a
very light sleeper.

'When Lord Saltire's disappearance was discovered I
at once called a roll of the whole establishment—boys,
masters, and servants. It was then that we ascertained that
Lord Saltire had not been alone in his flight. Heidegger,*
the German master, was missing. His room was on the
second floor, at the farther end of the building, facing the
same way as Lord Saltire's. His bed had also been slept
in; but he had apparently gone away partly dressed, since
his shirt and socks were lying on the floor. He had undoubtedly let himself down by the ivy, for we could see the
marks of his feet where he had landed on the lawn. His
bicycle was kept in a small shed beside this lawn, and it also
was gone.

'He had been with me for two years, and came with the
best references; but he was a silent, morose man, not very

popular with either masters or boys. No trace could be found of the fugitives, and now on Thursday morning we are as ignorant as we were on Tuesday. Inquiry was, of course, made at once at Holdernesse Hall. It is only a few miles away, and we imagined that in some sudden attack of homesickness he had gone back to his father; but nothing had been heard of him. The Duke is greatly agitated— and as to me, you have seen yourselves the state of nervous prostration to which the suspense and the responsibility have reduced me. Mr Holmes, if ever you put forward your full powers, I implore you to do so now, for never in your life could you have a case which is more worthy of them.'

Sherlock Holmes had listened with the utmost intentness to the statement of the unhappy schoolmaster. His drawn brows and the deep furrow between them showed that he needed no exhortation to concentrate all his attention upon a problem which, apart from the tremendous interests involved, must appeal so directly to his love of the complex and the unusual. He now drew out his note-book and jotted down one or two memoranda.

'You have been very remiss in not coming to me sooner,' said he severely. 'You start me on my investigation with a very serious handicap. It is inconceivable, for example, that this ivy and this lawn would have yielded nothing to an expert observer.'

'I am not to blame, Mr Holmes. His Grace was extremely desirous to avoid all public scandal. He was afraid of his family unhappiness being dragged before the world. He has a deep horror of anything of the kind.'

'But there has been some official investigation?'

'Yes, sir, and it has proved most disappointing. An apparent clue was at once obtained, since a boy and a young man were reported to have been seen leaving a neighbouring station by an early train. Only last night we had news that the couple had been hunted down in Liverpool, and they prove to have no connection whatever with the matter in hand. Then it was that in my despair and disappointment, after a sleepless night, I came straight to you by the early train.'

'I suppose the local investigation was relaxed while this false clue was being followed up?'

'It was entirely dropped.'

'So that three days have been wasted. The affair has been most deplorably handled.'

'I feel it, and admit it.'

'And yet the problem should be capable of ultimate solution. I shall be very happy to look into it. Have you been able to trace any connection between the missing boy and this German master?'

'None at all.'

'Was he in the master's class?'

'No; he never exchanged a word with him, so far as I know.'

'That is certainly very singular. Had the boy a bicycle?'

'No.'

'Was any other bicycle missing?'

'No.'

'Is that certain?'

'Quite.'

'Well, now, you do not mean to seriously suggest that this German rode off upon a bicycle in the dead of the night bearing the boy in his arms?'

'Certainly not.'

'Then what is the theory in your mind?'

'The bicycle may have been a blind. It may have been hidden somewhere, and the pair gone off on foot.'

'Quite so; but it seems rather an absurd blind, does it not? Were there other bicycles in this shed?'

'Several.'

'Would he not have hidden *a couple* had he desired to give the idea that they had gone off upon them?'

'I suppose he would.'

'Of course he would. The blind theory won't do. But the incident is an admirable starting-point for an investigation. After all, a bicycle is not an easy thing to conceal or to destroy. One other question. Did anyone call to see the boy on the day before he disappeared?'

'No.'

'Did he get any letters?'

'Yes; one letter.'

'From whom?'

'From his father.'

'Do you open the boys' letters?'

'No.'

'How do you know it was from the father?'

'The coat-of-arms was on the envelope, and it was addressed in the Duke's peculiar stiff hand. Besides, the duke remembers having written.'

'When had he a letter before that?'

'Not for several days.'

'Had he ever had one from France?'

'No; never.'

'You see the point of my questions, of course. Either the boy was carried off by force or he went of his own free will. In the latter case you would expect that some prompting from outside would be needed to make so young a lad do such a thing. If he has had no visitors, that prompting must have come in letters. Hence I try to find out who were his correspondents.'

'I fear I cannot help you much. His only correspondent, so far as I know, was his own father.'

'Who wrote to him on the very day of his disappearance. Were the relations between father and son very friendly?'

'His Grace is never very friendly with anyone. He is completely immersed in large public questions, and is rather inaccessible to all ordinary emotions. But he was always kind to the boy in his own way.'

'But the sympathies of the latter were with the mother?'

'Yes.'

'Did he say so?'

'No.'

'The Duke, then?'

'Good heavens, no!'

'Then how could you know?'

'I have had some confidential talk with Mr James Wilder, his Grace's secretary. It was he who gave me the information about Lord Saltire's feelings.'

'I see. By the way, that last letter of the Duke's—was it found in the boy's room after he was gone?'

'No; he had taken it with him. I think, Mr Holmes, it is time that we were leaving for Euston.'

'I will order a four-wheeler. In a quarter of an hour we shall be at your service. If you are telegraphing home, Mr Huxtable, it would be well to allow the people in your neighbourhood to imagine that the inquiry is still going on in Liverpool, or wherever else that red herring led your pack. In the meantime, I will do a little quiet work at your own doors, and perhaps the scent is not so cold but that two old hounds like Watson and myself* may get a sniff of it.'

That evening found us in the cold, bracing atmosphere of the Peak country, in which Dr Huxtable's famous school is situated. It was already dark when we reached it. A card was lying on the hall table, and the butler whispered something to his master, who turned to us with agitation in every heavy feature.

'The Duke is here,' said he. 'The Duke and Mr Wilder are in the study. Come, gentlemen, and I will introduce you.'

I was, of course, familiar with the pictures of the famous statesman, but the man himself was very different from his representation. He was a tall and stately person, scrupulously dressed, with a drawn, thin face, and a nose which was grotesquely curved and long. His complexion was of a dead pallor, which was more startling by contrast with a long, dwindling beard of vivid red, which flowed down over his white waistcoat, with his watch-chain gleaming through its fringe. Such was the stately presence who looked stonily at us from the centre of Dr Huxtable's hearthrug. Beside him stood a very young man, whom I understood to be Wilder, the private secretary. He was small, nervous, alert, with intelligent, light blue eyes and mobile features. It was he who at once, in an incisive and positive tone, opened the conversation.

'I called this morning, Dr Huxtable, too late to prevent you from starting for London. I learned that your object was to invite Mr Sherlock Holmes to undertake the conduct of this case. His Grace is surprised, Dr Huxtable, that you should have taken such a step without consulting him.'

'When I learned the police had failed—'

'His Grace is by no means convinced that the police have failed.'

'But surely, Mr Wilder—'

'You are well aware, Dr Huxtable, that his Grace is particularly anxious to avoid all public scandal. He prefers to take as few people as possible into his confidence.'

'The matter can be easily remedied,' said the brow-beaten doctor. 'Mr Sherlock Holmes can return to London by the morning train.'

'Hardly that, Doctor, hardly that,' said Holmes, in his blandest voice. 'This northern air is invigorating and pleasant, so I propose to spend a few days upon your moors, and to occupy my mind as best I may. Whether I have the shelter of your roof or of the village inn is, of course, for you to decide.'

I could see that the unfortunate doctor was in the last stage of indecision, from which he was rescued by the deep, sonorous voice of the red-bearded Duke, which boomed out like a dinner-gong.

'I agree with Mr Wilder, Dr Huxtable, that you would have done wisely to consult me. But since Mr Holmes has already been taken into your confidence, it would indeed be absurd that we should not avail ourselves of his services. Far from going to the inn, Mr Holmes, I should be pleased if you would come and stay with me at Holdernesse Hall?'

'I thank your Grace. For the purposes of my investigation I think that it would be wiser for me to remain at the scene of the mystery.'

'Just as you like, Mr Holmes. Any information which Mr Wilder or I can give you is, of course, at your disposal.'

'It will probably be necessary for me to see you at the Hall,' said Holmes. 'I would only ask you now, sir, whether you have formed any explanation in your own mind as to the mysterious disappearance of your son?'

'No, sir, I have not.'

'Excuse me if I allude to that which is painful to you, but I have no alternative. Do you think that the Duchess had anything to do with the matter.'

The great Minister showed perceptible hesitation.

'I do not think so,' he said, at last.

'The other most obvious explanation is that the child has been kidnapped for the purpose of levying ransom. You have not had any demand of the sort?'

'No, sir.'

'One more question, your Grace. I understand that you wrote to your son upon the day when this incident occurred.'

'No; I wrote upon the day before.'

'Exactly. But he received it on that day?'

'Yes.'

'Was there anything in your letter which might have unbalanced him or induced him to take such a step?'

'No, sir, certainly not.'

'Did you post that letter yourself?'

The nobleman's reply was interrupted by his secretary, who broke in with some heat.

'His Grace is not in the habit of posting letters himself,' said he. 'This letter was laid with others upon the study table, and I myself put them in the post-bag.'

'You are sure this one was among them?'

'Yes; I observed it.'

'How many letters did your Grace write that day?'

'Twenty or thirty. I have a large correspondence. But surely this is somewhat irrelevant?'

'Not entirely,' said Holmes.

'For my own part,' the Duke continued, 'I have advised the police to turn their attention to the South of France. I have already said that I do not believe that the Duchess would encourage so monstrous an action, but the lad had the most wrong-headed opinions, and it is possible that he may have fled to her, aided and abetted by this German. I think, Dr Huxtable, that we will now return to the Hall.'

I could see that there were other questions which Holmes would have wished to put; but the nobleman's abrupt manner showed that the interview was at end. It was evident that to his intensely aristocratic nature this discussion of his intimate family affairs with a stranger was most abhorrent, and that he feared lest every fresh question would throw a fiercer light into the discreetly shadowed corners of his ducal history.

When the nobleman and his secretary had left, my friend flung himself at once with characteristic eagerness into the investigation.

The boy's chamber was carefully examined, and yielded nothing save the absolute conviction that it was only through the window that he could have escaped. The German master's room and effects gave no further clue. In his case a trailer of ivy had given way under his weight, and we saw by the light of a lantern the mark on the lawn where his heels had come down. That one dent in the short green grass was the only material witness left of this inexplicable nocturnal flight.

Sherlock Holmes left the house alone, and only returned after eleven. He had obtained a large ordnance map of the neighbourhood, and this he brought into my room, where he laid it out on the bed, and, having balanced the lamp in the middle of it, he began to smoke over it, and occasionally to point out objects of interest with the reeking amber of his pipe.

'This case grows upon me, Watson,' said he. 'There are decidedly some points of interest in connection with it. In this early stage I want you to realize these geographical features, which may have a good deal to do with our investigation.

'Look at this map.* This dark square is the Priory School. I'll put a pin in it. Now, this line is the main road.* You see

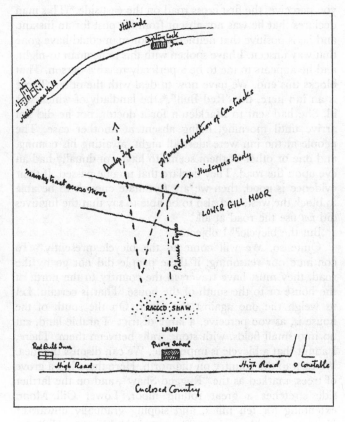

SKETCH MAP SHOWING THE LOCALITY

that it runs east and west past the school, and you see also there is no side road for a mile either way. If these two folk passed away by road it was *this* road.'

'Exactly.'

'By a singular and happy chance we are able to some extent to check what passed along this road during the night in question. At this point, where my pipe is now resting, a country constable was on duty from twelve to six. It is, as

III

you perceive, the first cross road on the east side.* This man declares that he was not absent from his post for an instant, and he is positive that neither boy nor man could have gone that way unseen. I have spoken with this policeman to-night, and he appears to me to be a perfectly reliable person. That blocks this end. We have now to deal with the other. There is an inn here, the "Red Bull",* the landlady of which was ill. She had sent to Mackleton for a doctor, but he did not arrive until morning, being absent at another case. The people at the inn were alert all night, awaiting his coming, and one or other of them seems to have continually had an eye upon the road. They declare that no one passed. If their evidence is good, then we are fortunate enough to be able to block the west, and also to be able to say that the fugitives did *not* use the road at all.'

'But the bicycle?' I objected.

'Quite so. We will come to the bicycle presently.* To continue our reasoning: if these people did not go by the road, they must have traversed the country to the north of the house or to the south of the house. That is certain. Let us weigh the one against the other. On the south of the house is, as you perceive, a large district of arable land, cut up into small fields, with stone walls between them. There, I admit that a bicycle is impossible. We can dismiss the idea. We turn to the country on the north. Here there lies a grove of trees, marked as the "Ragged Shaw", and on the farther side stretches a great rolling moor, Lower Gill Moor, extending for ten miles, and sloping gradually upwards.* Here, at one side of this wilderness, is Holdernesse Hall, ten miles by road, but only six across the moor. It is a peculiarly desolate plain. A few moor farmers have small holdings, where they rear sheep and cattle.* Except these, the plover and the curlew are the only inhabitants until you come to the Chesterfield high road.* There is a church there, you see, a few cottages, and an inn. Beyond that the hills become precipitous. Surely it is here to the north that our quest must lie.'

'But the bicycle?' I persisted.

'Well, well!' said Holmes impatiently. 'A good cyclist does not need a high road. The moor is intersected with paths, and the moon was at the full. Hullo! What is this?'

There was an agitated knock at the door, and an instant afterwards Dr Huxtable was in the room. In his hand he held a blue cricket-cap, with a white chevron on the peak.*

'At last we have a clue,' he cried. 'Thank Heaven at last we are on the dear boy's track! It is his cap.'

'Where was it found?'

'In the van of the gipsies who camped on the moor. They left on Tuesday. To-day the police traced them down and examined their caravan. This was found.'

'How do they account for it?'

'They shuffled and lied—said that they found it on the moor on Tuesday morning. They know where he is, the rascals! Thank goodness, they are all safe under lock and key. Either the fear of the law or the Duke's purse will certainly get out of them all that they know.'

'So far, so good,' said Holmes, when the doctor had at last left the room. 'It at least bears out the theory that it is on the side of the Lower Gill Moor that we must hope for results. The police have really done nothing locally, save the arrest of these gipsies. Look here, Watson! There is a watercourse across the moor. You see it marked here in the map. In some parts it widens into a morass. This is particularly so in the region between Holdernesse Hall and the school. It is vain to look elsewhere for tracks in this dry weather; but at *that* point there is certainly a chance of some record being left. I will call you early to-morrow morning, and you and I will try if we can to throw some light upon the mystery.'

The day was just breaking when I woke to find the long, thin form of Holmes by my bedside. He was fully dressed, and had apparently already been out.

'I have done the lawn and the bicycle shed,' said he. 'I have also had a ramble through the Ragged Shaw. Now, Watson, there is cocoa ready in the next room. I must beg you to hurry, for we have a great day before us.'

His eyes shone, and his cheek was flushed with the exhilaration of the master workman who sees his work lies ready before him.* A very different Holmes, this active, alert man, from the introspective and pallid dreamer of Baker Street. I felt, as I looked upon that supple figure, alive with nervous energy, that it was indeed a strenuous day that awaited us.

And yet it opened in the blackest disappointment. With high hopes we struck across the peaty, russet moor, intersected with a thousand sheep paths, until we came to the broad, light-green belt which marked the morass between us and Holdernesse. Certainly, if the lad had gone homewards, he must have passed this, and he could not pass it without leaving his trace. But no sign of him or the German could be seen. With a darkening face my friend strode along the margin, eagerly observant of every muddy stain upon the mossy surface. Sheep-marks there were in profusion, and at one place, some miles down, cows had left their tracks.* Nothing more.

'Check number one,' said Holmes, looking gloomily over the rolling expanse of the moor. 'There is another morass down yonder, and a narrow neck between. Hullo! hullo! hullo! What have we here?'

We had come on a small black ribbon of pathway. In the middle of it, clearly marked on the sodden soil, was the track of a bicycle.

'Hurrah!' I cried. 'We have it.'

But Holmes was shaking his head, and his face was puzzled and expectant rather than joyous.

'A bicycle certainly, but not *the* bicycle,' said he. 'I am familiar with forty-two different impressions left by tyres.* This, as you perceive, is a Dunlop, with a patch upon the outer cover.* Heidegger's tyres were Palmers, leaving longitudinal stripes. Aveling,* the mathematical master, was sure upon the point. Therefore it is not Heidegger's track.'

'The boy's, then?'

'Possibly, if we could prove a bicycle to have been in his possession. But this we have utterly failed to do. This track, as you perceive, was made by a rider who was going from the direction of the school.'

'Or towards it?'

'No, no, my dear Watson. The more deeply sunk impression is, of course, the hind wheel, upon which the weight rests. You perceive several places where it has passed across and obliterated the more shallow mark of the front one. It was undoubtedly heading away from the school. It may or may not be connected with our inquiry, but we will follow it backwards before we go any farther.'

We did so, and at the end of a few hundred yards lost the tracks as we emerged from the boggy portion of the moor. Following the path backwards, we picked out another spot, where a spring trickled across it. Here, once again, was the mark of the bicycle, though nearly obliterated by the hoofs of cows. After that there was no sign, but the path ran right on into Ragged Shaw, the wood which backed on to the school. From this wood the cycle must have emerged. Holmes sat down on a boulder and rested his chin in his hands. I had smoked two cigarettes before he moved.

'Well, well,' said he at last. 'It is, of course, possible that a cunning man might change the tyre of his bicycle in order to leave unfamiliar tracks. A criminal who was capable of such a thought is a man whom I should be proud to do business with. We will leave this question undecided and hark back to our morass again, for we have left a good deal unexplored.'

We continued our systematic survey of the edge of the sodden portion of the moor, and soon our perseverance was gloriously rewarded. Right across the lower part of the bog lay a miry path. Holmes gave a cry of delight as he approached it. An impression like a fine bundle of telegraph wires ran down the centre of it. It was the Palmer tyre.

'Here is Herr Heidegger, sure enough!' cried Holmes exultantly. 'My reasoning* seems to have been pretty sound, Watson.'

'I congratulate you.'

'But we have a long way still to go. Kindly walk clear of the path. Now let us follow the trail. I fear that it will not lead very far.'

We found, however, as we advanced, that this portion of the moor was intersected with soft patches, and, though we frequently lost sight of the track, we always succeeded in picking it up once more.

'Do you observe,' said Holmes, 'that the rider is now undoubtedly forcing the pace? There can be no doubt of it. Look at this impression, where you get both tyres clear. The one is as deep as the other. That can only mean that the rider is throwing his weight on to the handle-bar as a man does when he is sprinting. By Jove! he has had a fall.'

There was a broad irregular smudge covering some yards of the track. Then there were a few footmarks, and the tyre reappeared once more.

'A side-slip,' I suggested.

Holmes held up a crumpled branch of flowering gorse. To my horror I perceived that the yellow blossoms were all dabbled with crimson. On the path, too, and among the heather were dark stains of clotted blood.

'Bad!' said Holmes. 'Bad! Stand clear, Watson! Not an unnecessary footstep! What do I read here? He fell wounded, he stood up, he remounted, he proceeded. But there is no other track. Cattle on this side path. He was surely not gored by a bull? Impossible! But I see no traces of anyone else. We must push on, Watson. Surely, with stains as well as the track to guide us, he cannot escape us now.'

Our search was not a very long one. The tracks of the tyre began to curve fantastically upon the wet and shining path. Suddenly, as I looked ahead, the gleam of metal caught my eye from amid the thick gorse bushes. Out of them we dragged a bicycle, Palmer-tyred, one pedal bent, and the whole front of it horribly smeared and slobbered with blood. On the other side of the bushes a shoe was projecting. We ran round, and there lay the unfortunate rider. He was a tall man, full bearded, with spectacles, one glass of which had been knocked out. The cause of his death was a frightful blow upon the head, which had crushed in part of his skull. That he could have gone on after receiving such an injury said much for the vitality and courage of the man. He wore shoes, but no socks, and his open coat disclosed a night-shirt beneath it. It was undoubtedly the German master.

Holmes turned the body over reverently, and examined it with great attention. He then sat in deep thought for a time, and I could see by his ruffled brow that this grim discovery had not, in his opinion, advanced us much in our inquiry.

'It is a little difficult to know what to do, Watson,' said he, at last. 'My own inclinations are to push this inquiry on, for we have already lost so much time that we cannot afford to waste another hour. On the other hand, we are bound to inform the police of this discovery, and to see that this poor fellow's body is looked after.'

'I could take a note back.'

'But I need your company and assistance. Wait a bit! There is a fellow cutting peat up yonder. Bring him over here, and he will guide the police.'

I brought the peasant across, and Holmes dispatched the frightened man with a note to Dr Huxtable.

'Now, Watson,' said he, 'we have picked up two clues this morning. One is the bicycle with the Palmer tyre, and we see what that has led to. The other is the bicycle with the patched Dunlop. Before we start to investigate that, let us try to realize what we *do* know, so as to make the most of it, and to separate the essential from the accidental.

'First of all, I wish to impress upon you that the boy certainly left of his own free will. He got down from his window and he went off, either alone or with someone. That is sure.'

I assented.

'Well, now, let us turn to this unfortunate German master. The boy was fully dressed when he fled. Therefore he foresaw what he would do. But the German went without his socks. He certainly acted on very short notice.'

'Undoubtedly.'

'Why did he go? Because, from his bedroom window, he saw the flight of the boy. Because he wished to overtake him and bring him back. He seized his bicycle, pursued the lad, and in pursuing him met his death.'

'So it would seem.'

'Now I come to the critical part of my argument. The natural action of a man in pursuing a little boy would be to run after him. He would know that he could overtake him. But the German does not do so. He turns to his bicycle. I am told that he was an excellent cyclist. He would not do this if he did not see that the boy had some swift means of escape.'

'The other bicycle.'

'Let us continue our reconstruction. He meets his death five miles* from the school—not by a bullet, mark you, which even a lad might conceivably discharge, but by a savage blow dealt by a vigorous arm. The lad, then, *had* a companion in his flight. And the flight was a swift one, since it took five miles before an expert cyclist could overtake them. Yet we survey the ground round the scene of the tragedy. What do we find? A few cattle tracks, nothing more. I took a wide sweep round, and there is no path within fifty yards. Another cyclist could have had nothing to do with the actual murder. Nor were there any human footmarks.'

'Holmes,' I cried, 'this is impossible.'

'Admirable!' he said. 'A most illuminating remark. It *is* impossible as I state it, and therefore I must in some respect have stated it wrong. Yet you saw for yourself. Can you suggest any fallacy?'

'He could not have fractured his skull in a fall?'

'In a morass, Watson?'

'I am at my wits' end.'

'Tut, tut; we have solved some worse problems. At least we have plenty of material, if we can only use it. Come, then, and, having exhausted the Palmer, let us see what the Dunlop with the patched cover has to offer us.'

We picked up the track and followed it onwards for some distance; but soon the moor rose into a long, heather-tufted curve, and we left the watercourse behind us. No further help from tracks could be hoped for. At the spot where we saw the last of the Dunlop tyre it might equally have led to Holdernesse Hall, the stately towers of which rose some miles to our left, or to a low, grey village which lay in front of us, and marked the position of the Chesterfield high road.

As we approached the forbidding and squalid inn, with the sign of a game-cock* above the door, Holmes gave a sudden groan and clutched me by the shoulder to save himself from falling. He had had one of those violent strains of the ankle which leave a man helpless. With difficulty he limped up to the door, where a squat, dark, elderly man was smoking a black clay pipe.

'How are you, Mr Reuben Hayes?'* said Holmes.

'Who are you, and how do you get my name so pat?' the countryman answered, with a suspicious flash of a pair of cunning eyes.

'Well, it's printed on the board above your head. It's easy to see a man who is master of his own house. I suppose you haven't such a thing as a carriage in your stables?'

'No; I have not.'

'I can hardly put my foot to the ground.'

'Don't put it to the ground.'

'But I can't walk.'

'Well, then, hop.'

Mr Reuben Hayes's manner was far from gracious, but Holmes took it with admirable good humour.

'Look here, my man,' said he. 'This is really rather an awkward fix for me. I don't mind how I get on.'

'Neither do I,' said the morose landlord.

'The matter is very important. I would offer you a sovereign for the use of a bicycle.'

The landlord pricked up his ears.

'Where do you want to go?'

'To Holdernesse Hall.'

'Pals of the Dook, I suppose?' said the landlord, surveying our mud-stained garments with ironical eyes.

Holmes laughed good-naturedly.

'He'll be glad to see us, anyhow.'

'Why?'

'Because we bring him news of his lost son.'

The landlord gave a very visible start.

'What, you're on his track?'

'He has been heard of in Liverpool.* They expect to get him every hour.'

Again a swift change passed over the heavy, unshaven face. His manner was suddenly genial.

'I've less reason to wish the Dook well than most men,' said he, 'for I was his head coachman once, and cruel bad he treated me. It was him that sacked me without a character on the word of a lying corn-chandler.* But I'm glad to hear that the young lord was heard of in Liverpool, and I'll help you to take the news to the Hall.'

'Thank you,' said Holmes. 'We'll have some food first. Then you can bring round the bicycle.'

'I haven't got a bicycle.'

Holmes held up a sovereign.

'I tell you, man, that I haven't got one. I'll let you have two horses as far as the Hall.'

'Well, well,' said Holmes, 'we'll talk about it when we've had something to eat.'

When we were left alone in the stone-flagged kitchen it was astonishing how rapidly that sprained ankle recovered. It was nearly nightfall, and we had eaten nothing since early morning, so that we spent some time over our meal. Holmes was lost in thought, and once or twice he walked over to the window and stared earnestly out. It opened on to a squalid courtyard. In the far corner was a smithy, where a grimy lad was at work. On the side were the stables. Holmes had sat down again after one of these excursions, when he suddenly sprang out of his chair with a loud exclamation.

'By Heaven, Watson, I believe that I've got it!' he cried. 'Yes, yes, it must be so. Watson, do you remember seeing any cow-tracks to-day?'

'Yes, several.'

'Where?'

'Well, everywhere. They were at the morass, and again on the path, and again near where poor Heidegger met his death.'

'Exactly. Well, now, Watson, how many cows did you see on the moor?'

'I don't remember seeing any.'

'Strange, Watson, that we should see tracks all along our line, but never a cow on the whole moor; very strange, Watson, eh?'

'Yes, it is strange.'

'Now, Watson, make an effort; throw your mind back! Can you see those tracks upon the path?'

'Yes, I can.'

'Can you recall that the tracks were sometimes like that, Watson'—he arranged a number of breadcrumbs in this fashion*— : : : : : —'and sometimes like this'—:· :· :· :· —'and occasionally like this'—. · . · . ·

'Can you remember that?'

'No, I cannot.'

'But I can. I could swear to it. However, we will go back at our leisure and verify it. What a blind beetle I have been not to draw my conclusion!'

'And what is your conclusion?'

'Only that it is a remarkable cow which walks, canters, and gallops. By George, Watson, it was no brain of a country publican that thought out such a blind as that! The coast seems to be clear, save for that lad in the smithy. Let us slip out and see what we can see.'

There were two rough-haired, unkempt horses in the tumble-down stable. Holmes raised the hind leg of one of them and laughed loud.

'Old shoes, but newly shod—old shoes, but new nails. This case deserves to be a classic. Let us go across to the smithy.'

The lad continued his work without regarding us. I saw Holmes's eye darting to right and left among the litter of iron and wood, which was scattered about the floor. Suddenly, however, we heard a step behind us, and there was the landlord, his heavy eyebrows drawn down over his savage eyes, his swarthy features convulsed with passion.

He held a short metal-headed stick in his hand, and he advanced in so menacing a fashion that I was right glad to feel the revolver in my pocket.

'You infernal spies!' the man cried. 'What are you doing there?'

'Why, Mr Reuben Hayes,' said Holmes coolly, 'one might think that you were afraid of our finding something out.'

The man mastered himself with a violent effort, and his grim mouth loosened into a false laugh, which was more menacing than his frown.

'You're welcome to all you can find out in my smithy,' said he. 'But look here, mister, I don't care for folk poking about my place without my leave, so the sooner you pay your score and get out of this the better I shall be pleased.'

'All right, Mr Hayes—no harm meant,' said Holmes. 'We have been having a look at your horses; but I think I'll walk after all. It's not far, I believe.'

'Not more than two miles to the Hall gates. That's the road to the left.' He watched us with sullen eyes until we had left his premises.

We did not go very far along the road, for Holmes stopped the instant that the curve hid us from the landlord's view.

'We were warm, as the children say, at that inn,' said he. 'I seem to grow colder every step that I take away from it. No, no; I can't possibly leave it.'

'I am convinced,' said I, 'that this Reuben Hayes knows all about it. A more self-evident villain I never saw.'

'Oh! he impressed you in that way, did he? There are the horses, there is the smithy. Yes, it is an interesting place, this "Fighting Cock". I think we shall have another look at it in an unobtrusive way.'

A long, sloping hill-side, dotted with grey limestone boulders, stretched behind us. We had turned off the road, and were making our way up the hill, when, looking in the direction of Holdernesse Hall, I saw a cyclist coming swiftly along.

'Get down, Watson!' cried Holmes, with a heavy hand upon my shoulder. We had hardly sunk from view when the man flew past us on the road. Amid a rolling could of dust I caught a glimpse of a pale, agitated face—a face with horror in every lineament, the mouth open, the eyes staring wildly in front. It was like some strange caricature of the dapper James Wilder whom we had seen the night before.

'The Duke's secretary!' cried Holmes. 'Come, Watson, let us see what he does.'

We scrambled from rock to rock until in a few moments we had made our way to a point from which we could see the front door of the inn. Wilder's bicycle was leaning against the wall beside it. No one was moving about the house, nor could we catch a glimpse of any faces at the windows. Slowly the twilight crept down as the sun sank behind the high towers of Holdernesse Hall. Then in the gloom we saw the two side-lamps of a trap light up in the stable-yard of the inn, and shortly afterwards heard the rattle of hoofs, as it wheeled out into the road and tore off at a furious pace in the direction of Chesterfield.

'What do you make of that, Watson?' Holmes whispered. 'It looks like a flight.'*

'A single man in a dog-cart, so far as I could see. Well, it certainly was not Mr James Wilder, for there he is at the door.'

A red square of light had sprung out of the darkness. In the middle of it was the black figure of the secretary, his head advanced, peering out into the night. It was evident that he was expecting someone. Then at last there were steps in the road, a second figure was visible for an instant against the light, the door shut, and all was black once more. Five minutes later a lamp was lit in a room upon the first floor.

'It seems to be a curious class of custom that is done by the "Fighting Cock",' said Holmes.

'The bar is on the other side.'

'Quite so. These are what one may call the private guests. Now, what in the world is Mr James Wilder doing in that den at this hour of night, and who is the companion who comes to meet him there? Come, Watson, we must really take a risk and try to investigate this a little more closely.'

Together we stole down to the road and crept across to the door of the inn. The bicycle still leaned against the wall. Holmes struck a match and held it to the back wheel, and I heard him chuckle as the light fell upon a patched Dunlop tyre.* Up above us was the lighted window.

'I must have a peep throught that, Watson. If you bend your back and support yourself upon the wall, I think that I can manage.'

An instant later his feet were on my shoulders. But he was hardly up before he was down again.

'Come, my friend,' said he, 'our day's work has been quite long enough. I think that we have gathered all that we can. It's a long walk to the school, and the sooner we get started the better.'

He hardly opened his lips during that weary trudge across the moor, nor would he enter the school when he reached it, but went on to Mackleton Station, whence he could send some telegrams. Late at night I heard him consoling Dr Huxtable, prostrated by the tragedy of his master's death, and later still he entered my room as alert and vigorous as he had been when he started in the morning. 'All goes well, my friend,' said he. 'I promise that before to-morrow evening we shall have reached the solution of the mystery.'

At eleven o'clock next morning my friend and I were walking up the famous yew avenue of Holdernesse Hall. We were ushered through the magnificent Elizabethan doorway and into his Grace's study. There we found Mr James Wilder, demure and courtly, but with some trace of that wild terror of the night before still lurking in his furtive eyes and in his twitching features.

'You have come to see his Grace? I am sorry; but the fact

is that the Duke is far from well. He has been very much upset by the tragic news. We received a telegram from Dr Huxtable yesterday afternoon, which told us of your discovery.'

'I must see the Duke, Mr Wilder.'

'But he is in his room.'

'Then I must go to his room.'

'I believe he is in his bed.'

'I will see him there.'

Holmes's cold and inexorable manner showed the secretary that it was useless to argue with him.

'Very good, Mr Holmes; I will tell him that you are here.'

After half an hour's delay* the great nobleman appeared. His face was more cadaverous than ever, his shoulders had rounded, and he seemed to me to be an altogether older man than he had been the morning before. He greeted us with a stately courtesy, and seated himself at his desk, his red beard streaming down on to the table.

'Well, Mr Holmes?' said he.

But my friend's eyes were fixed upon the secretary, who stood by his master's chair.

'I think, your Grace, that I could speak more freely in Mr Wilder's absence.'

The man turned a shade paler and cast a malignant glance at Holmes.

'If your Grace wishes—'

'Yes, yes; you had better go. Now, Mr Holmes, what have you to say?'

My friend waited until the door had closed behind the retreating secretary.

'The fact is, your Grace,' said he, 'that my colleague, Dr Watson, and myself had an assurance from Dr Huxtable that a reward had been offered in this case. I should like to have this confirmed from your own lips.'

'Certainly, Mr Holmes.'

'It amounted, if I am correctly informed, to five thousand pounds to anyone who will tell you where your son is?'

'Exactly.'

'And another thousand to the man who will name the person or persons who keep him in custody?'

'Exactly.'

'Under the latter heading is included, no doubt, not only those who may have taken him away, but also those who conspire to keep him in his present position?'

'Yes, yes,' cried the Duke impatiently. 'If you do your work well, Mr Sherlock Holmes, you will have no reason to complain of niggardly treatment.'

My friend rubbed his thin hands together with an appearance of avidity which was a surprise to me, who knew his frugal tastes.

'I fancy that I see your Grace's cheque-book upon the table,' said he. 'I should be glad if you would make me out a cheque for six thousand pounds. It would be as well, perhaps, for you to cross it. The Capital and Counties Bank, Oxford Street branch, are my agents.'*

His Grace sat very stern and upright in his chair, and looked stonily at my friend.

'Is this a joke, Mr Holmes? It is hardly a subject for pleasantry.'

'Not at all, your Grace. I was never more earnest in my life.'

'What do you mean, then?'

'I mean that I have earned the reward, I know where your son is, and I know some, at least, of those who are holding him.'

The Duke's beard had turned more aggressively red than ever against his ghastly white face.

'Where is he?' he gasped.

'He is, or was last night, at the "Fighting Cock Inn", about two miles from your park gate.'

The Duke fell back in his chair.

'And whom do you accuse?'

Sherlock Holmes's answer was an astounding one. He stepped swiftly forward and touched the Duke upon the shoulder.

'I accuse *you*,' said he. 'And now, your Grace, I'll trouble you for that cheque.'

Never shall I forget the Duke's appearance as he sprang up and clawed with his hands like one who is sinking into an abyss. Then, with an extraordinary effort of aristocratic self-command, he sat down and sank his face in his hands. It was some minutes before he spoke.

'How much do you know?' he asked at last, without raising his head.

'I saw you together last night.'

'Does anyone else besides your friend know?'

'I have spoken to no one.'

The Duke took a pen in his quivering fingers and opened his cheque-book.

'I shall be as good as my word, Mr Holmes. I am about to write your cheque, however unwelcome the information which you have gained may be to me. When the offer was first made I little thought the turn which events would take. But you and your friend are men of discretion, Mr Holmes?'

'I hardly understand your Grace.'

'I must put it plainly, Mr Holmes. If only you two know of the incident, there is no reason why it should go any farther. I think twelve thousand pounds is the sum that I owe you, is it not?'

But Holmes smiled, and shook his head.

'I fear, your Grace, that matters can hardly be arranged so easily. There is the death of this schoolmaster to be accounted for.'

'But James knew nothing of that. You cannot hold him responsible for that. It was the work of this brutal ruffian whom he had the misfortune to employ.'

'I must take the view, your Grace, that when a man embarks upon a crime he is morally guilty of any other crime which may spring from it.'

'Morally, Mr Holmes. No doubt you are right. But surely not in the eyes of the law. A man cannot be condemned for a murder at which he was not present, and which he loathes and abhors as much as you do. The instant that he heard of it he made a complete confession to me, so filled was he with horror and remorse. He lost not an hour in breaking entirely

THE RETURN OF SHERLOCK HOLMES

with the murderer. Oh, Mr Holmes, you must save him—
you must save him! I tell you that you must save him!' The
Duke had dropped the last attempt at self-command, and
was pacing the room with a convulsed face and with his
clenched hands raving in the air. At last he mastered himself
and sat down once more at his desk. 'I appreciate your
conduct in coming here before you spoke to anyone else,'
said he. 'At least we may take counsel how far we can
minimize this hideous scandal.'

'Exactly,' said Holmes. 'I think, your Grace, that this can
only be done by absolute and complete frankness between
us. I am disposed to help your Grace to the best of my
ability; but in order to do so I must understand to the last
detail how the matter stands. I realize that your words
applied to Mr James Wilder, and that he is not the murderer.'

'No; the murderer has escaped.'

Sherlock Holmes smiled demurely.

'Your Grace can hardly have heard of any small reputation which I possess, or you would not imagine that it is so
easy to escape me. Mr Reuben Hayes was arrested at
Chesterfield on my information at eleven o'clock last night.
I had a telegram from the head of the local police before I
left the school this morning.'

The Duke leaned back in his chair and stared with
amazement at my friend.

'You seem to have powers that are hardly human,' said
he. 'So Reuben Hayes is taken? I am right glad to hear it,
if it will not react upon the fate of James.'

'Your secretary?'

'No, sir; my son.'

It was Holmes's turn to look astonished.

'I confess that this is entirely new to me, your Grace, I
must beg of you to be more explicit.'

'I will conceal nothing from you. I agree with you that
complete frankness, however painful it may be to me, is the
best policy in this desperate situation to which James's folly
and jealousy have reduced us. When I was a young man,

Mr Holmes, I loved with such a love as comes only once in a lifetime. I offered the lady marriage, but she refused it on the grounds that such a match might mar my career. Had she lived, I would certainly have never married anyone else. She died, and left this one child, whom for her sake I have cherished and cared for. I could not acknowledge the paternity to the world; but I gave him the best of educations, and since he came to manhood I have kept him near my person. He surprised my secret, and has presumed ever since upon the claim which he has upon me and upon his power of provoking a scandal, which would be abhorrent to me. His presence had something to do with the unhappy issue of my marriage. Above all, he hated my young legitimate heir from the first with a persistent hatred.* You may well ask me why, under these circumstances, I still kept James under my roof. I answer that it was because I could see his mother's face in his, and that for her dear sake there was no end to my long-suffering. All her pretty ways, too—there was not one of them which he could not suggest and bring back to my memory. I *could* not send him away. But I feared so lest he should do Arthur—that is, Lord Saltire—a mischief that I dispatched him for safety to Dr Huxtable's school.

'James came into contact with this fellow Hayes because the man was a tenant of mine, and James acted as agent. The fellow was a rascal from the beginning; but in some extraordinary way James became intimate with him. He had always a taste for low company. When James determined to kidnap Lord Saltire it was of this man's service that he availed himself. You remember that I wrote to Arthur upon that last day. Well, James opened the letter and inserted a note asking Arthur to meet him in a little wood called the Ragged Shaw which is near to the school. He used the Duchess's name, and in that way got the boy to come. That evening James cycled over—I am telling you what he has himself confessed to me—and he told Arthur, whom he met in the wood, that his mother longed to see him, that she was awaiting him on the moor, and that if he would come back into the wood at midnight he would find a man with a horse, who would take him to her. Poor Arthur fell into the trap. He came to the appointment and found this fellow Hayes with a led pony.* Arthur mounted, and they set off together. It appears—though this James only heard yesterday—that they were pursued, that Hayes struck the pursuer with his stick, and that the man died of his injuries. Hayes brought Arthur to his public-house, the "Fighting Cock", where he was confined in an upper room, under the care of Mrs Hayes, who is a kindly woman, but entirely under the control of her brutal husband.

'Well, Mr Holmes, that was the state of affairs when I first saw you two days ago. I had no more idea of the truth than you. You will ask me what was James's motive in doing such a deed. I answer that there was a great deal which was unreasoning and fanatical in the hatred which he bore my heir. In his view he himself should have been heir of all my estates, and he deeply resented those social laws which made it impossible. At the same time, he had a definite motive also. He was eager that I should break the entail, and he was of opinion that it lay in my power to do so. He intended to make a bargain with me—to restore Arthur if I would break the entail, and so make it possible for the estate to be left to him by will. He knew well that I should never willingly invoke the aid of the police against him. I say that he would have proposed such a bargain to me, but he did not actually do so, for events moved too quickly for him, and he had not time to put his plans into practice.

'What brought all his wicked scheme to wreck was your discovery of this man Heidegger's dead body. James was seized with horror at the news. It came to us yesterday as we sat together in this study. Dr Huxtable had sent a telegram. James was so overwhelmed with grief and agitation that my suspicions, which had never been entirely absent, rose instantly to a certainty, and I taxed him with the deed. He made a complete voluntary confession. Then he implored me to keep his secret for three days longer, so as to give his wretched accomplice a chance of saving his guilty life. I yielded—as I have always yielded—to his prayers, and instantly James hurried off to the "Fighting Cock" to warn Hayes and give him the means of flight. I could not go there by daylight without provoking comment, but as soon as night fell I hurried off to see my dear Arthur. I found him safe and well, but horrified beyond expression by the dreadful deed he had witnessed. In deference to my promise, and much against my will, I consented to leave him there for three days under the charge of Mrs Hayes, since it was evident that it was impossible to inform the police where he was without telling them also who was the murderer, and I could not see how that murderer could be punished without ruin to my unfortunate James. You asked for frankness, Mr Holmes, and I have taken you at your word, for I have now told you everything without an attempt at circumlocution or concealment. Do you in your turn be as frank with me.'

'I will,' said Holmes. 'In the first place, your Grace, I am bound to tell you that you have placed yourself in a most serious position in the eyes of the law. You have condoned a felony, and you have aided the escape of a murderer; for I cannot doubt that any money which was taken by James Wilder to aid his accomplice in his flight came from your Grace's purse.'

The Duke bowed his assent.

'This is indeed a most serious matter. Even more culpable, in my opinion, your Grace, is your attitude towards your younger son. You leave him in this den for three days.'

'Under solemn promises—'

'What are promises to such people as these? You have no guarantee that he will not be spirited away again. To humour your guilty elder son you have exposed your innocent younger son to imminent and unnecessary danger. It was a most unjustifiable action.'

The proud lord of Holdernesse was not accustomed to be so rated in his own ducal hall. The blood flushed into his high forehead, but his conscience held him dumb.

'I will help you, but on one condition only. It is that you ring for the footman and let me give such orders as I like.'

Without a word the Duke pressed the electric button. A servant entered.

'You will be glad to hear', said Holmes, 'that your young master is found. It is the Duke's desire that the carriage shall go at once to the "Fighting Cock Inn" to bring Lord Saltire home.'

'Now,' said Holmes, when the rejoicing lackey had disappeared, 'having secured the future we can afford to be more lenient with the past. I am not in an official position, and there is no reason, so long as the ends of justice are served, why I should disclose all that I know. As to Hayes I say nothing. The gallows awaits him, and I would do nothing to save him from it. What he will divulge I cannot tell, but I have no doubt that your Grace could make him understand that it is to his interest to be silent. From the police point of view he will have kidnapped the boy for the purpose of ransom. If they do not themselves find it out I see no reason why I should prompt them to take a broader view. I would warn your Grace, however, that the continued presence of Mr James Wilder in your household can only lead to misfortune.'

'I understand that, Mr Holmes, and it is already settled that he shall leave me for ever and go to seek his fortune in Australia.'

'In that case, your Grace, since you have yourself stated that any unhappiness in your married life was caused by his presence, I would suggest that you make such amends as you can to the Duchess, and that you try to resume those relations which have been so unhappily interrupted.'

'That also I have arranged, Mr Holmes. I wrote to the Duchess this morning.'

'In that case,' said Holmes, rising, 'I think that my friend and I can congratulate ourselves upon several most happy results from our little visit to the North. There is one other small point upon which I desire some light. This fellow

Hayes had shod his horses with shoes which counterfeited the tracks of cows. Was it from Mr Wilder that he learned so extraordinary a device?'

The Duke stood in thought for a moment, with a look of intense surprise on his face. Then he opened a door and showed us into a large room furnished as a museum. He led the way to a glass case in a corner, and pointed to the inscription.

'These shoes', it ran, 'were dug up in the moat of Holdernesse Hall. They are for the use of horses; but they are shaped below with a cloven foot of iron, so as to throw pursuers off the track. They are supposed to have belonged to some of the marauding Barons of Holdernesse in the Middle Ages.'

Holmes opened the case, and, moistening his finger, he passed it along the shoe. A thin film of recent mud was left upon his skin.

'Thank you,' said he, as he replaced the glass. 'It is the second most interesting object that I have seen in the North.'

'And the first?'

Holmes folded up his cheque, and placed it carefully in his note-book. 'I am a poor man,' said he, as he patted it affectionately, and thrust it into the depths of his inner pocket.

Black Peter

I HAVE never known my friend to be in better form, both mental and physical, than in the year '95. His increasing fame had brought with it an immense practice, and I should be guilty of an indiscretion if I were even to hint at the identity of some of the illustrious clients who crossed our humble threshold in Baker Street. Holmes, however, like all great artists, lived for his art's sake, and, save in the case of the Duke of Holdernesse, I have seldom known him claim any large reward for his inestimable services. So unworldly was he—or so capricious—that he frequently refused his help to the powerful and wealthy where the problem made no appeal to his sympathies, while he would devote weeks of most intense application to the affairs of some humble client whose case presented those strange and dramatic qualities which appealed to his imagination and challenged his ingenuity.

In this memorable year '95 a curious and incongruous succession of cases had engaged his attention, ranging from his famous investigation of the sudden death of Cardinal Tosca*—an inquiry which was carried out by him at the express desire of his Holiness the Pope—down to his arrest of Wilson, the notorious canary-trainer,* which removed a plague-spot from the East End of London. Close on the heels of these two famous cases came the tragedy of Woodman's Lee,* and the very obscure circumstances which surrounded the death of Captain Peter Carey.* No record of the doings of Mr Sherlock Holmes would be complete which did not include some account of this very unusual affair.

During the first week of July my friend had been absent so often and so long from our lodgings that I knew he had something on hand. The fact that several rough-looking men called during that time and inquired for Captain Basil* made me understand that Holmes was working somewhere under one of the numerous disguises and names with which he concealed his own formidable identity. He had at least five small refuges in different parts of London in which he was able to change his personality.* He said nothing of his business to me, and it was not my habit to force a confidence. The first positive sign which he gave me of the direction which his investigation was taking was an extraordinary one. He had gone out before breakfast, and I had sat down to mine, when he strode into the room, his hat upon his head, and a huge barb-headed spear* tucked like an umbrella under his arm.

'Good gracious, Holmes!' I cried. 'You don't mean to say that you have been walking about London with that thing?'

'I drove to the butcher's and back.'

'The butcher's?'

'And I return with an excellent appetite. There can be no question, my dear Watson, of the value of exercise before breakfast. But I am prepared to bet that you will not guess the form that my exercise has taken.'

'I will not attempt it.'

He chuckled as he poured out the coffee.

'If you could have looked into Allardyce's back shop* you would have seen a dead pig swung from a hook in the ceiling, and a gentleman in his shirt-sleeves furiously stabbing at it with this weapon. I was that energetic person, and I have satisfied myself that by no exertion of my strength can I transfix the pig with a single blow. Perhaps you would care to try?'

'Not for worlds. But why were you doing this?'

'Because it seemed to me to have an indirect bearing upon the mystery of Woodman's Lee. Ah, Hopkins, I got your wire last night, and I have been expecting you. Come and join us.'

Our visitor was an exceedingly alert man, thirty years of age, dressed in a quiet tweed suit, but retaining the erect bearing of one who was accustomed to official uniform. I recognized him at once as Stanley Hopkins,* a young police inspector for whose future Holmes had high hopes, while he in turn professed the admiration and respect of a pupil for the scientific methods of the famous amateur. Hopkins's brow was clouded and he sat down with an air of deep dejection.

'No, thank you, sir. I breakfasted before I came round. I spend the night in town, for I came up yesterday to report.'

'And what had you to report?'

'Failure, sir—absolute failure.'

'You have made no progress?'

'None.'

'Dear me! I must have a look at the matter.'

'I wish to heavens that you would, Mr Holmes. It's my first big chance, and I am at my wits' end. For goodness' sake come down and lend me a hand.'

'Well, well, it happens that I have already read all the available evidence, including the report of the inquest, with some care. By the way, what do you make of that tobacco-pouch found on the scene of the crime? Is there no clue there?'

Hopkins looked surprised.

'It was the man's own pouch, sir. His initials were inside it. And it was of sealskin—and he was an old sealer.'*

'But he had no pipe.'

'No, sir, we could find no pipe; indeed, he smoked very little. And yet he might have kept some tobacco for his friends.'

'No doubt. I only mention it because if I had been handling the case I should have been inclined to make that the starting-point of my investigation. However, my friend Dr Watson knows nothing of this matter, and I should be none the worse for hearing the sequence of events once more. Just give us some short sketch of the essentials.'

Stanley Hopkins drew a slip of paper from his pocket.

'I have a few dates here which will give you the career of the dead man, Captain Peter Carey. He was born in '45—fifty years of age. He was a most daring and successful seal and whale fisher. In 1883 he commanded the steam sealer *Sea Unicorn*, of Dundee.* He had then had several successful voyages in succession, and in the following year, 1884, he retired. After that he travelled for some years, and finally he bought a small place called Woodman's Lee, near Forest Row, in Sussex.* There he has lived for six years, and there he died just a week ago to-day.

'There were some most singular points about the man. In ordinary life he was a strict Puritan*—a silent, gloomy fellow. His household consisted of his wife, his daughter, aged twenty, and two female servants. These last were continually changing, for it was never a very cheery situation, and sometimes it became past all bearing. The man was an intermittent drunkard, and when he had the fit on him he was a perfect fiend. He has been known to drive his wife and his daughter out of doors in the middle of the night, and flog them through the park until the whole village outside the gates was aroused by their screams.

'He was summoned once for a savage assault upon the old vicar, who had called upon him to remonstrate with him upon his conduct. In short, Mr Holmes, you would go far before you found a more dangerous man than Peter Carey, and I have heard that he bore the same character when he commanded his ship. He was known in the trade as Black Peter, and the name was given him, not only on account of his swarthy features and the colour of his huge beard, but for the humours which were the terror of all around him. I need not say that he was loathed and avoided by every one of his neighbours, and that I have not heard one single word of sorrow about his terrible end.

'You must have read in the account of the inquest about the man's cabin, Mr Holmes; but perhaps your friend here has not heard of it. He had built himself a wooden out-house—he always called it "the cabin"*—a few hundred yards from his house, and it was here that he slept every night. It was a little, single-roomed hut, sixteen feet by ten. He kept the key in his pocket, made his own bed, cleaned it himself, and allowed no other foot to cross the threshold. There are small windows on each side, which were covered by curtains, and never opened. One of these windows was turned towards the high road, and when the light burned in it at night the folk used to point it out to each other, and wonder what Black Peter was doing in there. That's the window, Mr Holmes, which gave us one of the few bits of positive evidence that came out at the inquest.

'You remember that a stonemason, named Slater,* walking from Forest Row about one o'clock in the morning—two days before the murder—stopped as he passed the grounds and looked at the square of light still shining among the trees. He swears that the shadow of a man's head turned sideways was clearly visible on the blind, and that this shadow was certainly not that of Peter Carey, whom he knew well. It was that of a bearded man, but the beard was short, and bristled forwards in a way very different from that of the captain. So he says, but he had been two hours in the public-house, and it is some distance from the road to the window. Besides, this refers to the Monday, and the crime was done upon the Wednesday.

'On the Tuesday Peter Carey was in one of his blackest moods, flushed with drink and as savage as a dangerous wild beast. He roamed about the house, and the women ran for it when they heard him coming. Late in the evening he went down to his own hut. About two o'clock the following morning his daughter, who slept with her window open, heard a most fearful yell from that direction, but it was no unusual thing for him to bawl and shout when he was in drink, so no notice was taken. On rising at seven one of the maids noticed that the door of the hut was open, but so great was the terror which the man caused that it was midday before anyone would venture down to see what had become of him. Peeping into the open door, they saw a sight which sent them flying with white faces into the village. Within an hour I was on the spot, and had taken over the case.

'Well, I have fairly steady nerves, as you know, Mr Holmes, but I give you my word that I got a shake when I put my head into that little house. It was droning like a harmonium with the flies and bluebottles, and the floor and walls were like a slaughter-house. He had called it a cabin, and a cabin it was, sure enough, for you would have thought that you were in a ship. There was a bunk at one end, a sea-chest, maps and charts, a picture of the *Sea Unicorn*, a line of log-books on a shelf, all exactly as one would expect to find it in a captain's room. And there in the middle of it was the man himself, his face twisted like a lost soul in hell,* and his great brindled* beard stuck upwards in his agony. Right through his broad breast a steel harpoon had been driven, and it had sunk deep into the wood of the wall behind him. He was pinned like a beetle on a card. Of course, he was quite dead, and had been so from the instant that he uttered that last yell of agony.

'I know your methods, sir, and I applied them. Before I permitted anything to be moved I examined most carefully the ground outside, and also the floor of the room. There were no footmarks.'

'Meaning that you saw none?'

'I assure you, sir, that there were none.'

'My good Hopkins, I have investigated many crimes, but I have never yet seen one which was committed by a flying creature. As long as the criminal remains upon two legs so long must there be some indentation, some abrasion, some trifling displacement which can be detected by the scientific searcher. It is incredible that this blood-bespattered room contained no trace which could have aided us. I understand, however, from the inquest that there were some objects which you failed to overlook?'

The young inspector winced at my companion's ironical comments.

'I was a fool not to call you in at the time, Mr Holmes. However, that's past praying for now. Yes, there were several objects in the room which called for special attention. One was the harpoon with which the deed was committed. It had been snatched down from a rack on the wall. Two others remained there, and there was a vacant place for the third. On the stock* was engraved "S.S. *Sea*

Unicorn, Dundee". This seemed to establish that the crime had been done in a moment of fury, and that the murderer had seized the first weapon which came in his way. The fact that the crime was committed at two in the morning, and yet Peter Carey was fully dressed, suggested that he had an appointment with the murderer, which is borne out by the fact that a bottle of rum and two dirty glasses stood upon the table.'

'Yes,' said Holmes; 'I think that both inferences are permissible. Was there any other spirit but rum in the room?'

'Yes; there was a tantalus* containing brandy and whisky on the sea-chest. It is of no importance to us, however, since the decanters were full and it had therefore not been used.'

'For all that its presence has some significance,' said Holmes. 'However, let us hear some more about the objects which do seem to you to bear upon the case.'

'There was this tobacco-pouch upon the table.'

'What part of the table?'

'It lay in the middle. It was of coarse sealskin—the straight-haired skin, with a leather thong to bind it. Inside was "PC" on the flap. There was half an ounce of strong ship's tobacco* in it.'

'Excellent! What more?'

Stanley Hopkins drew from his pocket a drab-covered note-book. The outside was rough and worn, the leaves were discoloured. On the first page were written the initials 'JHN', and the date '1883'. Holmes laid it on the table and examined it in his minute way, while Hopkins and I gazed over each shoulder. On the second page were printed the letters 'CPR', and then came several sheets of numbers. Another heading was Argentine, another Costa Rica, and another San Paulo,* each with pages of signs and figures after it.

'What do you make of these?' asked Holmes.

'They appear to be lists of Stock Exchange securities. I thought that "JHN" were the initials of a broker, and that "CPR" may have been his client.'

'Try Canadian Pacific Railway,'* said Holmes.

Stanley Hopkins swore between his teeth, and struck his thigh with his clenched hand.

'What a fool I have been!' he cried. 'Of course it is as you say. Then "JHN" are the only initials we have to solve. I have already examined the old Stock Exchange lists, and I can find no one in 1883 either in the House or among the outside brokers* whose initials correspond with these. Yet I feel that the clue is the most important one that I hold. You will admit, Mr Holmes, that there is a possibility that these initials are those of the second person who was present—in other words, of the murderer. I would also urge that the introduction into the case of a document relating to large masses of valuable securities gives us for the first time some indication of a motive for the crime.'

Sherlock Holmes's face showed that he was thoroughly taken aback by this new development.

'I must admit both your points,' said he. 'I confess that this note-book, which did not appear at the inquest, modifies any views which I may have formed. I had come to a theory of the crime in which I can find no place for this. Have you endeavoured to trace any of the securities here mentioned?'

'Inquiries are now being made at the offices, but I fear that the complete register of the stock-holders of these South American concerns is in South America, and that some weeks must elapse before we can trace the shares.'

Holmes had been examining the cover of the note-book with his magnifying lens.

'Surely there is some discoloration here,' said he.

'Yes, sir, it is a blood-stain. I told you that I picked the book off the floor.'

'Was the blood-stain above or below?'

'On the side next to the boards.'

'Which proves, of course, that the book was dropped after the crime was committed.'

'Exactly, Mr Holmes. I appreciated that point, and I conjectured that it was dropped by the murderer on his hurried flight. It lay near the door.'

'I suppose that none of these securities have been found among the property of the dead man?'

'No, sir.'

'Have you any reason to suspect robbery?'

'No, sir. Nothing seemed to have been touched.'

'Dear me, it is certainly a very interesting case. Then there was a knife, was there not?'

'A sheath-knife,* still in its sheath. It lay at the feet of the dead man. Mrs Carey has identified it as being her husband's property.'

Holmes was lost in thought for some time.

'Well,' said he, at last, 'I suppose I shall have to come out and have a look at it.'

Stanley Hopkins gave a cry of joy.

'Thank you, sir. That will indeed be a weight off my mind.'

Holmes shook his finger at the inspector.

'It would have been an easier task a week ago,' said he. 'But even now my visit may not be entirely fruitless. Watson, if you can spare the time, I should be very glad of your company. If you will call a four-wheeler, Hopkins, we shall be ready to start for Forest Row in a quarter of an hour.'

Alighting at the small wayside station, we drove for some miles through the remains of widespread woods, which were once part of that great forest which for so long held the Saxon invaders at bay—the impenetrable 'weald', for sixty years the bulwark of Britain.* Vast sections of it have been cleared, for this is the seat of the first ironworks of the country, and the trees have been felled to smelt the ore. Now the richer fields of the North have absorbed the trade, and nothing save these ravaged groves and great scars in the earth show the work of the past. Here in a clearing upon the green slope of a hill stood a long, low stone house, approached by a curving drive running through the fields. Nearer the road, and surrounded on three sides by bushes, was a small outhouse, one window and the door facing in our direction. It was the scene of the murder.

Stanley Hopkins led us first to the house, where he introduced us to a haggard, grey-haired woman, the widow of the murdered man, whose gaunt and deep-lined face, with the furtive look of terror in the depths of her red-rimmed eyes, told of the years of hardship and ill-usage which she had endured. With her was her daughter, a pale, fair-haired girl, whose eyes blazed defiantly at us as she told us that she was glad that her father was dead, and that she blessed the hand which had struck him down. It was a terrible household that Black Peter Carey had made for himself, and it was with a sense of relief that we found ourselves in the sunlight again and making our way along the path which had been worn across the fields by the feet of the dead man.

The outhouse was the simplest of dwellings, wooden-walled, single-roofed,* one window beside the door, and one on the farther side. Stanley Hopkins drew the key from his pocket, and had stooped to the lock, when he paused with a look of attention and surprise upon his face.

'Someone has been tampering with it,' he said.

There could be no doubt of the fact. The woodwork was cut, and the scratches showed white through the paint, as if they had been that instant done. Holmes had been examining the window.

'Someone has tried to force this also. Whoever it was has failed to make his way in. He must have been a very poor burglar.'

'This is a most extraordinary thing,' said the inspector; 'I could swear that these marks were not here yesterday evening.'

'Some curious person from the village, perhaps,' I suggested.

'Very unlikely. Few of them would dare to set foot in the grounds, far less try to force their way into the cabin. What do you think of it, Mr Holmes?'

'I think that fortune is very kind to us.'

'You mean that the person will come again?'

'It is very probable. He came expecting to find the door open. He tried to get in with the blade of a very small penknife.* He could not manage it. What would he do?'

'Come again next night with a more useful tool.'

'So I should say. It will be our fault if we are not there to receive him. Meanwhile, let me see the inside of the cabin.'

The traces of the tragedy had been removed, but the furniture of the little room still stood as it had been on the night of the crime. For two hours, with the most intense concentration, Holmes examined every object in turn, but his face showed that his quest was not a successful one. Once only he paused in his patient investigation.

'Have you taken anything off this shelf, Hopkins?'

'No; I have moved nothing.'

'Something has been taken. There is less dust in this corner of the shelf than elsewhere. It may have been a book lying on its side. It may have been a box. Well, well, I can do nothing more. Let us walk in these beautiful woods, Watson, and give a few hours to the birds and the flowers. We shall meet you here later, Hopkins, and see if we can come to closer quarters with the gentleman who has paid this visit in the night.'

It was past eleven o'clock when we formed our little ambuscade.* Hopkins was for leaving the door of the hut open, but Holmes was of the opinion that this would rouse the suspicions of the stranger. The lock was a perfectly simple one, and only a strong blade was needed to push it back. Holmes also suggested that we should wait, not inside the hut, but outside it among the bushes which grew round the farther window. In this way we should be able to watch our man if he struck a light, and see what his object was in this stealthy nocturnal visit.

It was a long and melancholy vigil, and yet it brought with it something of the thrill which the hunter feels when he lies beside the water-pool and waits for the coming of the thirsty beast of prey. What savage creature was it which might steal upon us out of the darkness? Was it a fierce tiger of crime, which could only be taken fighting hard with flashing fang and claw, or would it prove to be some skulking jackal, dangerous only to the weak and unguarded? In absolute silence we crouched amongst the bushes, waiting for whatever might come. At first the steps of a few belated villagers, or the sound of voices from the village, lightened our vigil; but one by one these interruptions died away, and an absolute stillness fell upon us; save for the chimes of the distant church, which told us of the progress of the night, and for the rustle and whisper of a fine rain falling amid the foliage which roofed us in.*

Half-past two had chimed,* and it was the darkest hour which precedes the dawn, when we all started as a low but sharp click came from the direction of the gate. Someone had entered the drive. Again there was a long silence, and I had begun to fear that it was a false alarm, when a stealthy step was heard upon the other side of the hut, and a moment later a metallic scraping and clicking. The man was trying to force the lock! This time his skill was greater or his tool was better, for there was a sudden snap and the creak of the hinges. Then a match was struck, and next instant the steady light from a candle filled the interior of the hut. Through the gauze curtain our eyes were all riveted upon the scene within.

The nocturnal visitor was a young man, frail and thin, with a black moustache which intensified the deadly pallor of his face. He could not have been much above twenty years of age. I have never seen any human being who appeared to be in such a pitiable fright, for his teeth were visibly chattering, and he was shaking in every limb. He was dressed like a gentleman, in Norfolk jacket* and knickerbockers, with a cloth cap upon his head. We watched him staring round with frightened eyes. Then he laid the candle-end upon the table and disappeared from our view into one of the corners. He returned with a large book, one of the log-books which formed a line upon the shelves. Leaning on the table, he rapidly turned over the leaves of this volume until he came to the entry which he sought. Then, with an angry gesture of his clenched hand, he closed the book, replaced it in the corner, and put out the light. He had hardly turned to leave the hut when Hopkins's hand was on the fellow's collar, and I heard his loud gasp of terror as he understood that he was taken. The candle was re-lit, and there was our wretched captive shivering and cowering in the grasp of the detective. He sank down upon the sea-chest, and looked helplessly from one of us to the other.

'Now, my fine fellow,' said Stanley Hopkins, 'who are you, and what do you want here?'

The man pulled himself together and faced us with an effort at self-composure.

'You are detectives, I suppose?' said he. 'You imagine I am connected with the death of Captain Peter Carey. I assure you that I am innocent.'

'We'll see about that,' said Hopkins. 'First of all, what is your name?'

'It is John Hopley Neligan.'*

I saw Holmes and Hopkins exchange a quick glance.

'What are you doing here?'

'Can I speak confidentially?'

'No, certainly not.'

'Why should I tell you?'

'If you have no answer it may go badly with you at the trial.'

The young man winced.

'Well, I will tell you,' he said. 'Why should I not? And yet I hate to think of this old scandal gaining a new lease of life. Did you ever hear of Dawson & Neligan?'*

I could see from Hopkins's face that he never had; but Holmes was keenly interested.

'You mean the West Country bankers,' said he. 'They failed for a million, ruined half the county families of Cornwall, and Neligan disappeared.'

'Exactly. Neligan was my father.'

At last we were getting something positive, and yet it seemed a long gap between an absconding banker and Captain Peter Carey pinned against the wall with one of his own harpoons. We all listened intently to the young man's words.

'It was my father who was really concerned. Dawson had retired. I was only ten years of age at the time, but I was old enough to feel the shame and horror of it all. It has always been said that my father stole all the securities and fled. It is not true. It was his belief that if he were given time in which to realize them all would be well, and every creditor paid in full. He started in his little yacht for Norway just before the warrant was issued for his arrest. I can remember that last night when he bade farewell to my mother. He left us a list of the securities he was taking,* and he swore that he would come back with his honour cleared, and that none who had trusted him would suffer. Well, no word was ever heard from him again. Both the yacht and he vanished utterly. We believed, my mother and I, that he and it, with the securities that he had taken with him, were at the bottom of the sea. We had a faithful friend, however, who is a business man, and it was he who discovered some time ago that some of the securities which my father had with him have reappeared on the London market. You can imagine our amazement. I spent months in trying to trace them, and at last, after many doublings and difficulties, I discovered that the original seller had been Captain Peter Carey, the owner of this hut.

'Naturally I made some inquiries about the man. I found that he had been in command of a whaler which was due to return from the Arctic seas at the very time when my father was crossing to Norway. The autumn of that year was a stormy one and there was a long succession of southerly gales. My father's yacht may well have been blown to the north, and there met by Captain Peter Carey's ship. If that were so, what had become of my father? In any case, if I could prove from Peter Carey's evidence how these securities came in the market, it would be a proof that my father had not sold them, and that he had no view to personal profit when he took them.

'I came down to Sussex with the intention of seeing the captain, but it was at this moment that his terrible death occurred. I read at the inquest a description of his cabin, in which it stated that the old log-books of his vessel were preserved in it. It struck me that if I could see what occurred in the month of August, 1883, on board the *Sea Unicorn*, I might settle the mystery of my father's fate. I tried last night to get at these log-books, but was unable to open the door. To-night I tried again, and succeeded; but I find that the pages which deal with that month have been torn from the book. It was at that moment I found myself a prisoner in your hands.'*

'Is that all?' asked Hopkins.

'Yes, that is all.' His eyes shifted as he said it.

'You have nothing else to tell us?'

He hesitated.

'No; there is nothing.'

'You have not been here before last night?'

'No.'

'Then how do you account for *that*?' cried Hopkins, as he held up the damning notebook, with the initials of our prisoner on the first leaf, and the blood-stain on the cover.

The wretched man collapsed. He sank his face in his hands and trembled all over.

'Where did you get it?' he groaned. 'I did not know. I thought I had lost it at the hotel.'

'That is enough,' said Hopkins sternly. 'Whatever else you have to say you must say in court. You will walk down with me now to the police-station. Well, Mr Holmes, I am very much obliged to you and to your friend for coming down to help me. As it turns out your presence was unnecessary, and I would have brought the case to this successful issue without you; but none the less I am very grateful. Rooms have been reserved for you at the Brambletye* Hotel, so we can all walk down to the village together.'

'Well, Watson, what do you think of it?' asked Holmes as we travelled back next morning.

'I can see that you are not satisfied.'

'Oh, yes, my dear Watson, I am perfectly satisfied. At the same time Stanley Hopkins's methods do not commend themselves to me. I am disappointed in Stanley Hopkins. I had hoped for better things from him. One should always look for a possible alternative and provide against it. It is the first rule of criminal investigation.'

'What, then, is the alternative?'

'The line of investigation which I have myself been pursuing. It may give nothing. I cannot tell. But at least I shall follow it to the end.'

Several letters were waiting for Holmes at Baker Street. He snatched one of them up, opened it, and burst out into a triumphant chuckle of laughter.

'Excellent, Watson. The alternative develops. Have you telegraph forms? Just write a couple of messages for me: "Sumner, Shipping Agent, Ratcliff Highway.* Send three men on, to arrive ten to-morrow morning.—Basil." That's my name in those parts. The other is "Inspector Stanley Hopkins, 46, Lord Street, Brixton.* Come breakfast to-morrow at nine-thirty. Important. Wire if unable to come.—Sherlock Holmes." There, Watson, this infernal case has haunted me for ten days. I hereby banish it completely from my presence. To-morrow I trust that we shall hear the last of it for ever.'

Sharp at the hour named Inspector Stanley Hopkins appeared, and we sat down together to the excellent breakfast which Mrs Hudson had prepared. The young detective was in high spirits at his success.

'You really think that your solution must be correct?' asked Holmes.

'I could not imagine a more complete case.'

'It did not seem to me conclusive.'

'You astonish me, Mr Holmes. What more could one ask for?'

'Does your explanation cover every point?'

'Undoubtedly. I find that young Neligan arrived at the Brambletye Hotel on the very day of the crime. He came on the pretence of playing golf. His room was on the ground-floor, and he could get out when he liked. That very night he went down to Woodman's Lee, saw Peter Carey at the hut, quarrelled with him, and killed him with the harpoon.

149

Then, horrified by what he had done, he fled out of the hut, dropping the note-book which he had brought with him in order to question Peter Carey about these different securities. You may have observed that some of them were marked with ticks, and the others—the great majority—were not. Those which are ticked have been traced on the London market; but the others presumably were still in the possession of Carey, and young Neligan, according to his own account, was anxious to recover them in order to do the right thing by his father's creditors. After his flight he did not dare to approach the hut again for some time; but at last he forced himself to do so in order to obtain the information which he needed. Surely that is all simple and obvious?'

Holmes smiled and shook his head.

'It seems to me to have only one drawback, Hopkins, and that is that it is intrinsically impossible. Have you tried to drive a harpoon through a body? No? Tut, tut, my dear sir, you must really pay attention to these details. My friend Watson could tell you that I spent a whole morning in that exercise. It is no easy matter, and requires a strong and practised arm. But this blow was delivered with such violence that the head of the weapon sank deep into the wall. Do you imagine that this anaemic youth was capable of so frightful an assault? Is he the man who hob-nobbed* in rum and water with Black Peter in the dead of the night? Was it his profile that was seen on the blind two nights before? No, no, Hopkins; it is another and a more formidable person for whom we must seek.'

The detective's face had grown longer and longer during Holmes's speech. His hopes and his ambitions were all crumbling about him. But he would not abandon his position without a struggle.

'You can't deny that Neligan was present that night, Mr Holmes. The book will prove that. I fancy that I have evidence enough to satisfy a jury, even if you are able to pick a hole in it. Besides, Mr Holmes, I have laid my hand upon *my* man. As to this terrible person of yours, where is he?'

'I rather fancy that he is on the stair,' said Holmes, serenely. 'I think, Watson, that you would do well to put that revolver where you can reach it.' He rose, and laid a written paper upon a side-table. 'Now we are ready,' said he.

There had been some talking in gruff voices outside, and now Mrs Hudson opened the door to say that there were three men inquiring for Captain Basil.

'Show them in one by one,' said Holmes.

The first who entered was a little ribston-pippin of a man, with ruddy cheeks and fluffy white side-whiskers.* Holmes had drawn a letter from his pocket.

'What name?' he asked.

'James Lancaster.'*

'I am sorry, Lancaster, but the berth is full. Here is half a sovereign for your trouble. Just step into this room and wait there for a few minutes.'

The second man was a long, dried-up creature, with lank hair and sallow cheeks. His name was Hugh Pattins.* He also received his dismissal, his half-sovereign, and the order to wait.

The third applicant was a man of remarkable appearance. A fierce, bull-dog face was framed in a tangle of hair and beard, and two bold dark eyes gleamed behind the cover of thick, tufted, overhung eyebrows. He saluted and stood sailor-fashion, turning his cap round in his hands.

'Your name?' asked Holmes.

'Patrick Cairns.'

'Harpooner?'

'Yes, sir. Twenty-six voyages.'

'Dundee, I suppose?'

'Yes, sir.'

'And ready to start with an exploring ship?'

'Yes, sir.'

'What wages?'

'Eight pounds a month.'*

'Could you start at once?'

'As soon as I get my kit.'

'Have you your papers?'

'Yes, sir.' He took a sheaf of worn and greasy forms from his pocket. Holmes glanced over them and returned them.

'You are just the man I want,' said he. 'Here's the agreement on the side-table. If you sign it the whole matter will be settled.'

The seaman lurched across the room and took up the pen.

'Shall I sign here?' he asked, stooping over the table.

Holmes leaned over his shoulder and passed both hands over his neck.

'This will do,' said he.

I heard a click of steel and a bellow like an enraged bull. The next instant Holmes and the seaman were rolling on the ground together. He was a man of such gigantic strength that, even with the handcuffs which Holmes had so deftly fastened upon his wrist, he would have quickly overpowered my friend had Hopkins and I not rushed to his rescue. Only when I pressed the cold muzzle of the revolver to his temple did he at last understand that resistance was vain. We lashed his ankles with cord and rose breathless from the struggle.

'I must really apologize, Hopkins,' said Sherlock Holmes; 'I fear that the scrambled eggs are cold. However, you will enjoy the rest of your breakfast all the better, will you not, for the thought that you have brought your case to a triumphant conclusion?'

Stanley Hopkins was speechless with amazement.

'I don't know what to say, Mr Holmes,' he blurted out at last, with a very red face. 'It seems to me that I have been making a fool of myself from the beginning. I understand now, what I should never have forgotten, that I am the pupil and you are the master. Even now I see what you have done, but I don't know how you did it, or what it signifies.'

'Well, well,' said Holmes good-humouredly. 'We all learn by experience, and your lesson this time is that you should never lose sight of the alternative. You were so absorbed in young Neligan that you could not spare a thought to Patrick Cairns, the true murderer of Peter Carey.'

The hoarse voice of the seaman broke in on our conversation.

'See here, mister,' said he, 'I make no complaint of being man-handled in this fashion, but I would have you call things by their right names. You say I murdered Peter Carey; I say I *killed* Peter Carey, and there's all the difference. Maybe you don't believe what I say. Maybe you think I am just slinging you a yarn.'

'Not at all,' said Holmes. 'Let us hear what you have to say.'

'It's soon told, and, by the Lord, every word of it is truth. I knew Black Peter, and when he pulled out his knife I whipped a harpoon through him sharp, for I knew that it was him or me. That's how he died. You can call it murder. Anyhow, I'd as soon die with a rope round my neck as with Black Peter's knife in my heart.'

'How came you there?' asked Holmes.

'I'll tell it you from the beginning. Just sit me up a little so I can speak easy. It was in '83 that it happened—August of that year. Peter Carey was master of the *Sea Unicorn*, and I was spare harpooner.* We were coming out of the ice-pack on our way home, with head winds and a week's southerly gale, when we picked up a little craft that had been blown north. There was one man on her—a landsman. The crew had thought she would founder, and had made for the Norwegian coast in the dinghy. I guess they were all drowned. Well, we took him on board, this man, and he and the skipper had some long talks in the cabin. All the baggage we took off with him was one tin box. So far as I know the man's name was never mentioned, and on the second night he disappeared as if he had never been. It was given out that he had either thrown himself overboard or fallen overboard in the heavy weather that we were having. Only one man knew what had happened to him, and that was me, for with my own eyes I saw the skipper tip up his heels and put him over the rail in the middle watch of a dark night, two days before we sighted the Shetland lights.*

'Well, I kept my knowledge to myself and waited to see what would come of it. When we got back to Scotland it was easily hushed up, and nobody asked any questions. A stranger died by an accident, and it was nobody's business to inquire. Shortly after Peter Carey gave up the sea, and it was long years before I could find where he was. I guessed that he had done the deed for the sake of what was in that tin box, and that he could afford now to pay me well for keeping my mouth shut.

'I found out where he was through a sailor man that had met him in London, and down I went to squeeze him. The first night he was reasonable enough, and was ready to give me what would make me free of the sea for life. We were to fix it all two nights later. When I came I found him three-parts drunk and full of the devil.* We sat down and we drank and we yarned about old times, but the more he drank the less I liked the look on his face. I spotted that harpoon upon the wall, and I thought I might need it before I was through. Then at last he broke out at me spitting and cursing, with murder in his eyes and a great clasp-knife in his hand. He had not time to get it from the sheath before I had the harpoon through him. My God!* what a yell he gave; and his face gets between me and my sleep! I stood there, with his blood splashing round me, and I waited for a bit; but all was quiet, so I took heart once more. I looked round, and there was the tin box on a shelf. I had as much right to it as Peter Carey, anyhow, so I took it with me and left the hut. Like a fool I left my baccy-pouch upon the table.

'Now I'll tell you the queerest part of the whole story. I had hardly got outside the hut when I heard someone coming, and I hid among the bushes. A man came slinking along, went into the hut, gave a cry as if he had seen a ghost, and legged it as hard as he could run until he was out of sight. Who he was or what he wanted is more than I can tell. For my part, I walked ten miles, got a train at Tunbridge Wells, and so reached London, and no one the wiser.

'Well, when I came to examine the box I found there was no money in it, and nothing but papers that I would not dare to sell. I had lost my hold on Black Peter, and was stranded in London without a shilling. There was only my trade left. I saw these advertisements about harpooners and high wages, so I went to the shipping agents, and they sent me here. That's all I know, and I say again that if I killed Black Peter, the law should give me thanks, for I saved them the price of a hempen rope.'*

'A very clear statement,' said Holmes, rising and lighting his pipe. 'I think, Hopkins, that you should lose no time in conveying your prisoner to a place of safety. This room is not well adapted for a cell, and Mr Patrick Cairns occupies too large a portion of our carpet.'*

'Mr Holmes,' said Hopkins, 'I do not know how to express my gratitude. Even now I do not understand how you attained this result.'

'Simply by having the good fortune to get the right clue from the beginning. It is very possible that if I had known about this note-book it might have led away my thoughts, as it did yours. But all I heard pointed in the one direction. The amazing strength, the skill in the use of the harpoon, the rum and water, the seal-skin tobacco-pouch, with the coarse tobacco—all these pointed to a seaman, and one who had been a whaler. I was convinced that the initals "PC" upon the pouch were a coincidence, and not those of Peter Carey,* since he seldom smoked, and no pipe was found in his cabin. You remember that I asked whether whisky and brandy were in the cabin. You said they were. How many landsmen are there who would drink rum when they could get these other spirits? Yes, I was certain it was a seaman.'

'And how did you find him?'

'My dear sir, the problem had become a very simple one. If it were a seaman, it could only be a seaman who had been with him on the *Sea Unicorn*. So far as I could learn, he had sailed in no other ship. I spent three days in wiring to Dundee, and at the end of that time I had ascertained the names of the crew of the *Sea Unicorn* in 1883. When I found Patrick Cairns among the harpooners my research was nearing its end. I argued that the man was probably in London, and that he would desire to leave the country for a time. I therefore spent some days in the East End, devised an Arctic expedition, put forward tempting terms for harpooners who would serve under Captain Basil—and behold the result!'

'Wonderful!' cried Hopkins. 'Wonderful!'

'You must obtain the release of young Neligan as soon as possible.' said Holmes. 'I confess that I think you owe him some apology. The tin box must be returned to him, but of course, the securities which Peter Carey has sold are lost for ever. There's the cab, Hopkins, and you can remove your man. If you want me for the trial, my address and that of Watson will be somewhere in Norway*—I'll send particulars later.'

Charles Augustus Milverton

I T is years since the incidents of which I speak took place, and yet it is with diffidence that I allude to them. For a long time, even with the utmost discretion and reticence, it would have been impossible to make the facts public; but now the principal person concerned is beyond the reach of human law, and with due suppression the story may be told in such fashion as to injure no one. It records an absolutely unique experience in the career both of Mr Sherlock Holmes and of myself. The reader will excuse me if I conceal the date or any other fact by which he might trace the actual occurrence.

We had been out for one of our evening rambles, Holmes and I, and had returned about six o'clock on a cold, frosty winter's evening. As Holmes turned up the lamp the light fell upon a card on the table. He glanced at it, and then, with an ejaculation of disgust, threw it on the floor. I picked it up and read:

CHARLES AUGUSTUS MILVERTON,
APPLEDORE TOWERS,*
HAMPSTEAD.

Agent

'Who is he?' I asked.

'The worst man in London,' Holmes answered, as he sat down and stretched his legs before the fire. 'Is anything on the back of the card?'

I turned it over.

'Will call at 6.30.—CAM,' I read.

'Hum! He's about due. Do you feel a creeping, shrinking sensation, Watson, when you stand before the serpents in the Zoo* and see the slithery, gliding, venomous creatures, with their deadly eyes and wicked, flattened faces? Well, that's how Milverton impresses me. I've had to do with fifty murderers in my career, but the worst of them never gave me the repulsion which I have for this fellow. And yet I can't get out of doing business with him—indeed, he is here at my invitation.'

'But who is he?'

'I'll tell you, Watson. He is the king of all the black-mailers. God* help the man, and still more the woman, whose secret and reputation come into the power of Milverton. With a smiling face and a heart of marble he will squeeze and squeeze until he has drained them dry. The fellow is a genius in his way, and would have made his mark in some more savoury trade. His method is as follows: he allows it to be known that he is prepared to pay very high sums for letters which compromise people of wealth or position. He receives these wares not only from treacherous valets or maids, but frequently from genteel ruffians who have gained the confidence and affection of trusting women. He deals with no niggard hand.* I happen to know that he paid seven hundred pounds to a footman for a note two lines in length, and that the ruin of a noble family was the result. Everything which is in the market goes to Milverton, and there are hundreds in this great city who turn white at his name. No one knows where his grip may fall, for he is far too rich and far too cunning to work from hand to mouth. He will hold a card back for years in order to play it at the moment when the stake is best worth winning. I have said that he is the worst man in London, and I would ask you how could one compare the ruffian who in hot blood bludgeons his mate with this man, who methodically and at his leisure tortures the soul and wrings the nerves in order to add to his already swollen money-bags?'

I had seldom heard my friend speak with such intensity of feeling.

'But surely,' said I, 'the fellow must be within the grasp of the law?'

'Technically, no doubt, but practically not. What would it profit a woman, for example, to get him a few months' imprisonment if her own ruin must immediately follow? His victims dare not hit back. If ever he blackmailed an innocent person, then, indeed, we should have him; but he is as cunning as the Devil.* No, no; we must find other ways to fight him.'

'And why is he here?'

'Because an illustrious client has placed her piteous case in my hands. It is the Lady Eva Brackwell,* the most beautiful *débutante* of last season.* She is to be married in a fortnight to the Earl of Dovercourt.* This fiend has several imprudent letters—imprudent, Watson, nothing worse—which were written to an impecunious young squire in the country. They would suffice to break off the match. Milverton will send the letters to the Earl unless a large sum of money is paid him. I have been commissioned to meet him, and—to make the best terms I can.'

At that instant there was a clatter and a rattle in the street below. Looking down I saw a stately carriage and pair,* the brilliant lamps gleaming on the glossy haunches of the noble chestnuts. A footman opened the door, and a small, stout man in a shaggy astrakhan* overcoat descended. A minute later he was in the room.

Charles Augustus Milverton was a man of fifty, with a large, intellectual head, a round, plump, hairless face, a perpetual frozen smile, and two keen grey eyes, which gleamed brightly from behind broad, golden-rimmed glasses. There was something of Mr Pickwick's benevolence* in his appearance, marred only by the insincerity of the fixed smile and by the hard glitter of those restless and penetrating eyes. His voice was as smooth and suave as his countenance, as he advanced with a plump little hand extended, murmuring his regret for having missed us at his first visit.

Holmes disregarded the outstretched hand and looked at him with a face of granite. Milverton's smile broadened; he shrugged his shoulders, removed his overcoat, folded it with great deliberation over the back of a chair, and then took a seat.

'This gentleman,' said he, with a wave in my direction. 'Is it discreet? Is it right?'

'Dr Watson is my friend and partner.'

'Very good, Mr Holmes. It is only in your client's interests that I protested. The matter is so very delicate—'

'Dr Watson has already heard of it.'

'Then we can proceed to business. You say that you are acting for Lady Eva. Has she empowered you to accept my terms?'

'What are your terms?'

'Seven thousand pounds.'

'And the alternative?'

'My dear sir, it is painful to me to discuss it; but if the money is not paid on the 14th there certainly will be no marriage on the 18th.' His insufferable smile was more complacent than ever. Holmes thought for a little.

'You appear to me', he said at last, 'to be taking matters too much for granted. I am, of course, familiar with the contents of these letters. My client will certainly do what I may advise. I shall counsel her to tell her future husband the whole story and to trust to his generosity.'

Milverton chuckled.

'You evidently do not know the Earl,' said he.

From the baffled look upon Holmes's face I could clearly see that he did.

'What harm is there in the letters?' he asked.

'They are sprightly—very sprightly,' Milverton answered. 'The lady was a charming correspondent. But I can assure you that the Earl of Dovercourt would fail to appreciate them. However, since you think otherwise, we will let it rest at that. It is purely a matter of business. If you think that it is in the best interests of your client that these letters should be placed in the hands of the Earl, then you would indeed be foolish to pay so large a sum of money to regain them.' He rose and seized his astrakhan coat.

Holmes was grey with anger and mortification.

'Wait a little,' he said. 'You go too fast. We would certainly make every effort to avoid scandal in so delicate a matter.'

Milverton relapsed into his chair.

'I was sure that you would see it in that light,' he purred.

'At the same time,' Holmes continued, 'Lady Eva is not a wealthy woman. I assure you that two thousand pounds would be a drain upon her resources, and that the sum you name is utterly beyond her power. I beg, therefore, that you will moderate your demands, and that you will return the letters at the price I indicate, which is, I assure you, the highest that you can get.'

Milverton's smile broadened and his eyes twinkled humorously.

'I am aware that what you say is true about the lady's resources,' said he. 'At the same time, you must admit that the occasion of a lady's marriage is a very suitable time for her friends and relatives to make some little effort upon her behalf. They may hesitate as to an acceptable wedding present. Let me assure them that this little bundle of letters would give more joy than all the candelabra and butter-dishes in London.'

'It is impossible,' said Holmes.

'Dear me, dear me, how unfortunate!' cried Milverton, taking out a bulky pocket-book. 'I cannot help thinking that ladies are ill-advised in not making an effort. Look at this!' He held up a little note with a coat-of-arms upon the envelope.* 'That belongs to—well, perhaps it is hardly fair to tell the name until to-morrow morning. But at that time it will be in the hands of the lady's husband. And all because she will not find a beggarly sum which she could get in an hour by turning her diamonds into paste. It *is* such a pity. Now, you remember the sudden end of the engagement between the Honourable Miss Miles and Colonel Dorking?* Only two days before the wedding there was a paragraph in the *Morning Post** to say that it was all off. And why? It is almost incredible, but the absurd sum of twelve hundred pounds would have settled the whole question. Is it not pitiful? And there I find you, a man of sense, boggling* about terms when your client's future and honour are at stake. You surprise me, Mr Holmes.'

'What I say is true,' Holmes answered. 'The money cannot be found. Surely it is better for you to take the substantial sum which I offer than to ruin this woman's career, which can profit you in no way?'

'There you make a mistake, Mr Holmes. An exposure would profit me indirectly to a considerable extent. I have eight or ten similar cases maturing. If it was circulated among them that I had made a severe example of the Lady Eva I should find all of them much more open to reason. You see my point?'

Holmes sprang from his chair.

'Get behind him, Watson. Don't let him out! Now, sir, let us see the contents of that note-book.'

Milverton had glided as quick as a rat* to the side of the room, and stood with his back against the wall.

'Mr Holmes, Mr Holmes!' he said, turning the front of his coat and exhibiting the butt of a large revolver, which projected from the inside pocket. 'I have been expecting you to do something original. This has been done so often, and what good has ever come from it? I assure you that I am armed to the teeth, and I am perfectly prepared to use my weapon, knowing that the law will support me. Besides, your supposition that I would bring the letters here in a note-book is entirely mistaken. I would do nothing so foolish. And now, gentlemen, I have one or two little interviews this evening, and it is a long drive to Hampstead.' He stepped forward, took up his coat, laid his hand on his revolver, and turned to the door. I picked up a chair, but Holmes shook his head, and I laid it down again. With a bow, a smile, and a twinkle Milverton was out of the room, and a few moments after we heard the slam of the carriage door and the rattle of the wheels as he drove away.

Holmes sat motionless by the fire, his hands buried deep in his trouser pockets, his chin sunk upon his breast, his eyes fixed upon the glowing embers. For half an hour he was silent and still. Then, with the gesture of a man who has taken his decision, he sprang to his feet and passed into his bedroom. A little later a rakish young workman with a goatee beard* and a swagger lit his clay pipe at the lamp before descending into the street. 'I'll be back some time,

Watson,' said he, and vanished into the night. I understood that he had opened his campaign against Charles Augustus Milverton; but I little dreamed the strange shape which that campaign was destined to take.

For some days Holmes came and went at all hours in this attire, but beyond a remark that his time was spent at Hampstead, and that it was not wasted, I knew nothing of what he was doing. At last, however, on a wild, tempestuous evening, when the wind screamed and rattled against the windows, he returned from his last expedition, and, having removed his disguise, he sat before the fire and laughed heartily in his silent, inward fashion.

'You would not call me a marrying man, Watson?'

'No, indeed!'

'You will be interested to hear that I am engaged.'

'My dear fellow! I congrat—'

'To Milverton's housemaid.'

'Good heavens, Holmes!'

'I wanted information, Watson.'

'Surely you have gone too far?'

'It was a most necessary step. I am a plumber with a rising business, Escott by name.* I have walked out with her each evening, and I have talked with her. Good heavens, those talks! However, I have got all I wanted. I know Milverton's house as I know the palm of my hand.'

'But the girl, Holmes?'

He shrugged his shoulders.

'You can't help it, my dear Watson. You must play your cards as best you can when such a stake is on the table. However, I rejoice to say that I have a hated rival who will certainly cut me out the instant that my back is turned. What a splendid night it is!'

'You like this weather?'

'It suits my purpose. Watson, I mean to burgle Milverton's house to-night.'

I had a catching of the breath, and my skin went cold at the words, which were slowly uttered in a tone of concentrated resolution. As a flash of lightning in the night shows up in an instant every detail of a wide landscape, so at one glance I seemed to see every possible result of such an action—the detection, the capture, the honoured career ending in irreparable failure and disgrace, my friend himself lying at the mercy of the odious Milverton.

'For God's sake,* Holmes, think what you are doing!' I cried.

'My dear fellow, I have given it every consideration. I am never precipitate in my actions, nor would I adopt so energetic and indeed so dangerous a course if any other were possible. Let us look at the matter clearly and fairly. I suppose that you will admit that the action is morally justifiable, though technically criminal. To burgle his house is no more than to forcibly take his pocket-book—an action in which you were prepared to aid me.'

I turned it over in my mind.

'Yes,' I said; 'it is morally justifiable so long as our object is to take no articles save those which are used for an illegal purpose.'

'Exactly. Since it is morally justifiable, I have only to consider the question of personal risk. Surely a gentleman should not lay much stress upon this when a lady is in most desperate need of his help?'

'You will be in such a false position.'

'Well, that is part of the risk. There is no other possible way of regaining these letters. The unfortunate lady has not the money, and there are none of her people in whom she could confide. To-morrow is the last day of grace, and unless we can get the letters to-night this villain will be as good as his word, and will bring about her ruin. I must, therefore, abandon my client to her fate, or I must play this last card. Between ourselves, Watson, it's a sporting duel between this fellow Milverton and me. He had, as you saw, the best of the first exchanges; but my self-respect and my reputation are concerned to fight it to a finish.'

'Well, I don't like it; but I suppose it must be,' said I. 'When do we start?'

'You are not coming.'*

'Then you are not going,' said I. 'I give you my word of honour—and I never broke it in my life—that I will take a cab straight to the police-station and give you away unless you let me share this adventure with you.'

'You can't help me.'

'How do you know that? You can't tell what may happen. Anyway, my resolution is taken. Other people besides you have self-respect and even reputations.'

Holmes had looked annoyed, but his brow cleared, and he clapped me on the shoulder.

'Well, well, my dear fellow, be it so. We have shared the same room for some years, and it would be amusing if we ended by sharing the same cell. You know, Watson, I don't mind confessing to you that I have always had an idea that I would have made a highly efficient criminal. This is the chance of my lifetime in that direction. See here!' He took a neat little leather case out of a drawer, and opening it he exhibited a number of shining instruments. 'This is a first-class, up-to-date burgling kit, with nickel-plated jemmy, diamond-tipped glass-cutter, adaptable keys,* and every modern improvement which the march of civilization demands. Here, too, is my dark lantern. Everything is in order. Have you a pair of silent shoes?'

'I have rubber-soled tennis shoes.'

'Excellent. And a mask?'

'I can make a couple out of black silk.'

'I can see that you have a strong natural turn for this sort of thing. Very good; do you make the masks. We shall have some cold supper before we start. It is now nine-thirty. At eleven we shall drive as far as Church Row.* It is a quarter of an hour's walk from there to Appledore Towers. We shall be at work before midnight. Milverton is a heavy sleeper, and retires punctually at ten-thirty. With any luck we should be back here by two, with the Lady Eva's letters in my pocket.'

Holmes and I put on our dress-clothes, so that we might appear to be two theatre-goers homeward bound. In Oxford Street we picked up a hansom* and drove to an address in

Hampstead. Here we paid off our cab, and with our great-coats buttoned up—for it was bitterly cold, and the wind seemed to blow through us—we walked along the edge of the Heath.

'It's a business that needs delicate treatment,' said Holmes. 'These documents are contained in a safe* in the fellow's study, and the study is the ante-room of his bed-chamber. On the other hand, like all these stout, little men who do themselves well, he is a plethoric sleeper.* Agatha—that's my *fiancée*—says it is a joke in the servants' hall that it's impossible to wake the master. He has a secretary who is devoted to his interests and never budges from the study all day. That's why we are going at night. Then he has a beast of a dog which roams the garden. I met Agatha late the last two evenings, and she locks the brute up so as to give me a clear run. This is the house, this big one in its own grounds. Through the gate—now to the right among the laurels. We might put on our masks here, I think. You see, there is not a glimmer of light in any of the windows, and everything is working splendidly.'

With our black silk face-coverings, which turned us into two of the most truculent figures in London,* we stole up to the silent, gloomy house. A sort of tiled veranda* extended along one side of it, lined by several windows and two doors.

'That's his bedroom,' Holmes whispered. 'This door opens straight into the study. It would suit us best, but it is bolted as well as locked, and we should make too much noise getting in. Come round here. There's a greenhouse which opens into the drawing-room.'

The place was locked, but Holmes removed a circle of glass and turned the key from the inside.* An instant afterwards he had closed the door behind us, and we had become felons in the eyes of the law. The thick, warm air of the conservatory and the rich, choking fragrance of exotic plants took us by the throat. He seized my hand in the darkness and led me swiftly past banks of shrubs which brushed against our faces. Holmes had remarkable powers, carefully cultivated, of seeing in the dark.* Still holding my hand in one of his, he opened a door, and I was vaguely conscious that we had entered a large room in which a cigar had been smoked not long before. He felt his way among the furniture, opened another door, and closed it behind us. Putting out my hand I felt several coats hanging from the wall, and I understood that I was in a passage. We passed along it, and Holmes very gently opened a door upon the right-hand side. Something rushed out at us, and my heart sprang into my mouth, but I could have laughed when I realized that it was the cat. A fire was burning in this new room, and again the air was heavy with tobacco smoke. Holmes entered on tiptoe, waited for me to follow, and then very gently closed the door. We were in Milverton's study, and a *portière* * at the farther side showed the entrance to his bedroom.

It was a good fire, and the room was illuminated by it. Near the door I saw the gleam of an electric switch, but it was unnecessary, even if it had been safe, to turn it on. At one side of the fireplace was a heavy curtain, which covered the bay window we had seen from outside. On the other side was the door which communicated with the veranda. A desk stood in the centre, with a turning chair of shining red leather. Opposite was a large bookcase, with a marble burst of Athene* on the top. In the corner between the bookcase and the wall there stood a tall green safe, the firelight flashing back from the polished brass knobs upon its face. Holmes stole across and looked at it. Then he crept to the door of the bedroom, and stood with slanting head listening intently. No sound came from within. Meanwhile it had struck me that it would be wise to secure our retreat through the outer door, so I examined it. To my amazement it was neither locked nor bolted! I touched Holmes on the arm, and he turned his masked face in that direction. I saw him start, and he was evidently as surprised as I.

'I don't like it,' he whispered, putting his lips to my very ear. 'I can't quite make it out. Anyhow, we have no time to lose.'

'Can I do anything?'

'Yes; stand by the door. If you hear anyone come, bolt it on the inside, and we can get away as we came. If they come the other way, we can get through the door if our job is done, or hide behind these window curtains if it is not. Do you understand?'

I nodded and stood by the door. My first feeling of fear had passed away, and I thrilled now with a keener zest than I had ever enjoyed when we were the defenders of the law instead of its defiers. The high object of our mission, the consciousness that it was unselfish and chivalrous, the villainous character of our opponent, all added to the sporting interest of the adventure. Far from feeling guilty, I rejoiced and exulted in our dangers. With a glow of admiration I watched Holmes unrolling his case of instruments and choosing his tool with the calm, scientific accuracy of a surgeon who performs a delicate operation. I knew that the opening of safes was a particular hobby with him, and I understood the joy which it gave him to be confronted with this green and gold monster, the dragon which held in its maw* the reputations of many fair ladies. Turning up the cuffs of his dress-coat—he had placed his overcoat on a chair—Holmes laid out two drills, a jemmy, and several skeleton keys. I stood at the centre door with my eyes glancing at each of the others, ready for any emergency; though, indeed, my plans were somewhat vague as to what I should do if we were interrupted. For half an hour Holmes worked with concentrated energy, laying down one tool, picking up another, handling each with the strength and delicacy of the trained mechanic. Finally I heard a click, the broad green door swung open, and inside I had a glimpse of a number of paper packets, each tied, sealed, and inscribed. Holmes picked one out, but it was hard to read by the flickering fire, and he drew out his little dark lantern, for it was too dangerous, with Milverton in the next room, to switch on the electric light. Suddenly I saw him halt, listen intently, and then in an instant he had swung the door of the safe to, picked up his coat, stuffed his tools into the pockets, and darted behind the window curtain, motioning me to do the same.

It was only when I had joined him there that I heard what had alarmed his quicker senses. There was a noise somewhere within the house. A door slammed in the distance. Then a confused, dull murmur broke itself into the measured thud of heavy footsteps rapidly approaching. They were in the passage outside the room. They paused at the door. The door opened. There was a sharp snick as the electric light was turned on.* The door closed once more, and the pungent reek of a strong cigar was borne to our nostrils. Then the footsteps continued backwards and forwards, backwards and forwards, within a few yards of us. Finally, there was a creak from a chair, and the footsteps ceased. Then a key clicked in a lock, and I heard the rustle of papers.

So far I had not dared to look out, but now I gently parted the division of the curtains in front of me and peeped through. From the pressure of Holmes's shoulder against mine I knew that he was sharing my observations. Right in front of us, and almost within our reach, was the broad, rounded back of Milverton. It was evident that we had entirely miscalculated his movements, that he had never been to his bedroom, but that he had been sitting up in some smoking- or billiard room in the farther wing of the house, the windows of which we had not seen. His broad, grizzled head, with its shining patch of baldness, was in the immediate foreground of our vision. He was leaning far back in the red leather chair, his legs outstretched, a long black cigar projecting at an angle from his mouth. He wore a semi-military smoking-jacket, claret-coloured, with a black velvet collar. In his hand he held a long legal document, which he was reading in an indolent fashion, blowing rings of tobacco smoke from his lips as he did so. There was no promise of a speedy departure in his composed bearing and his comfortable attitude.

I felt Holmes's hand steal into mine and give me a reassuring shake, as if to say that the situation was within his powers, and that he was easy in his mind. I was not sure whether he had seen what was only too obvious from my position—that the door of the safe was imperfectly closed, and that Milverton might at any moment observe it. In my own mind I had determined that if I were sure, from the rigidity of his gaze, that it had caught his eye, I would at once spring out, throw my great-coat over his head, pinion him, and leave the rest to Holmes. But Milverton never looked up. He was languidly interested by the papers in his hand, and page after page was turned as he followed the argument of the lawyer. At least, I thought, when he has finished the document and the cigar he will go to his room; but before he had reached the end of either there came a remarkable development which turned our thoughts into quite another channel.

Several times I had observed that Milverton looked at his watch, and once he had risen and sat down again, with a gesture of impatience. The idea, however, that he might have an appointment at so strange an hour never occurred to me until a faint sound reached my ears from the veranda outside. Milverton dropped his papers and sat rigid in his chair. The sound was repeated, and then there came a gentle tap at the door. Milverton rose and opened it.

'Well,' said he curtly, 'you are nearly half an hour late.'

So this was the explanation of the unlocked door and of the nocturnal vigil of Milverton. There was the gentle rustle of a woman's dress. I had closed the slit between the curtains as Milverton's face turned in our direction, but now I ventured very carefully to open it once more. He had resumed his seat, the cigar still projecting at an insolent angle from the corner of his mouth. In front of him, in the full glare of the electric light, there stood a tall, slim, dark woman, a veil over her face, a mantle drawn round her chin. Her breath came quick and fast and every inch of the lithe figure was quivering with strong emotion.

'Well,' said Milverton, 'you've made me lose a good night's rest, my dear. I hope you'll prove worth it. You couldn't come any other time—eh?'

The woman shook her head.

'Well, if you couldn't you couldn't. If the Countess is a hard mistress you have your chance to get level with her now. Bless the girl, what are you shivering about? That's right! Pull yourself together! Now, let us get down to business.' He took a note from the drawer of his desk. 'You say that you have five letters which compromise the Countess d'Albert.* You want to sell them. I want to buy them. So far so good. It only remains to fix a price. I should want to inspect the letters, of course. If they are really good specimens—Good God,* is it you?'

The woman without a word had raised her veil and dropped the mantle from her chin. It was a dark, handsome, clear-cut face which confronted Milverton, a face with a curved nose, strong, dark eyebrows, shading hard, glittering eyes, and a straight, thin-lipped mouth set in a dangerous smile.

'It is I,' she said—'the woman whose life you have ruined.'

Milverton laughed, but fear vibrated in his voice. 'You were so very obstinate,' said he. 'Why did you drive me to such extremities? I assure you I wouldn't hurt a fly of my own accord, but every man has his business, and what was I to do? I put the price well within your means. You would not pay.'

'So you sent the letters to my husband, and he—the noblest gentleman that ever lived, a man whose boots I was never worthy to lace—he broke his gallant heart and died. You remember that last night when I came through that door I begged and prayed you for mercy, and you laughed in my face as you are trying to laugh now, only your coward heart cannot keep your lips from twitching? Yes; you never thought to see me here again, but it was that night which taught me how I could meet you face to face, and alone. Well, Charles Milverton, what have you to say?'

'Don't imagine that you can bully me,' said he, rising to his feet. 'I have only to raise my voice, and I could call my servants and have you arrested. But I will make allowance for your natural anger. Leave the room at once as you came, and I will say no more.'

The woman stood with her hand buried in her bosom, and the same deadly smile on her thin lips.

'You will ruin no more lives as you ruined mine. You will wring no more hearts as you wrung mine. I will free the world of a poisonous thing. Take that, you hound, and that!—and that!—and that!—and that!'

She had drawn a little gleaming revolver, and emptied barrel after barrel into Milverton's body, the muzzle within two feet of his shirt front. He shrank away, and then fell forward upon the table, coughing furiously and clawing among the papers. Then he staggered to his feet, received another shot, and rolled upon the floor. 'You've done me,' he cried, and lay still. The woman looked at him intently and ground her heel into his upturned face. She looked again, but there was no sound or movement. I heard a sharp rustle, the night air blew into the heated room, and the avenger was gone.

No interference upon our part could have saved the man from his fate; but as the woman poured bullet after bullet into Milverton's shrinking body, I was about to spring out, when I felt Holmes's cold, strong grasp upon my wrist. I understood the whole argument of that firm, restraining grip—that it was no affair of ours; that justice had overtaken a villain; that we had our own duties and our own objects which were not to be lost sight of. But hardly had the woman rushed from the room when Holmes, with swift, silent steps, was over at the other door. He turned the key in the lock. At the same instant we heard voices in the house and the sound of hurrying feet. The revolver shots had roused the household. With perfect coolness Holmes slipped across to the safe, filled his two arms with bundles of letters, and poured them all into the fire. Again and again he did it, until the safe was empty. Someone turned the handle and beat upon the outside of the door. Holmes looked swiftly round. The letter which had been the messenger of death for Milverton lay, all mottled with his blood, upon the table. Holmes tossed it in among the blazing papers. Then he drew the key from the outer door, passed through after me, and locked it on the outside. 'This way, Watson,' said he; 'we can scale the garden wall in this direction.'

I could not have believed that an alarm could have spread so swiftly. Looking back, the huge house was one blaze of light. The front door was open, and figures were rushing down the drive. The whole garden was alive with people, and one fellow raised a view-halloo as we emerged from the veranda and followed hard at our heels. Holmes seemed to know the ground perfectly, and he threaded his way swiftly among a plantation of small trees, I close at his heels, and our foremost pursuer panting behind us. It was a six-foot wall which barred our path, but he sprang to the top and over. As I did the same I felt the hand of the man behind me grab my ankle; but I kicked myself free, and scrambled over a glass-strewn coping. I fell upon my face among some bushes; but Holmes had me on my feet in an instant, and together we dashed away across the huge expanse of Hampstead Heath. We had run two miles, I suppose, before Holmes at last halted and listened intently. All was absolutely silence behind us. We had shaken off our pursuers, and were safe.

We had breakfasted and were smoking our morning pipe, on the day after the remarkable experience which I have recorded, when Mr Lestrade, of Scotland Yard, very solemn and impressive, was ushered into our modest sitting-room.

'Good morning, Mr Holmes,' said he—'good morning. May I ask if you are very busy just now?'

'Not too busy to listen to you.'

'I thought that, perhaps, if you had nothing particular on hand, you might care to assist us in a most remarkable case which occurred only last night at Hampstead.'

'Dear me!' said Holmes. 'What was that?'

'A murder—a most dramatic and remarkable murder. I know how keen you are upon these things, and I would take it as a great favour if you would step down to Appledore Towers and give us the benefit of your advice. It is no ordinary crime. We have had our eyes upon this Mr

Milverton for some time, and, between ourselves, he was a bit of a villain. He is known to have held papers which he used for blackmailing purposes. These papers have all been burned by the murderers. No article of value was taken, as it is probable that the criminals were men of good position, whose sole object was to prevent social exposure.'

'Criminals!' exclaimed Holmes. 'Plural!'

'Yes, there were two of them. They were, as nearly as possible, captured red-handed. We have their footmarks, we have their description; it's ten to one that we trace them. The first fellow was a bit too active, but the second was caught by the under-gardener, and only got away after a struggle. He was a middle-sized, strongly built man—square jaw, thick neck, moustache, a mask over his eyes.'*

'That's rather vague,' said Sherlock Holmes. 'Why, it might be a description of Watson!'

'It's true,' said the inspector, with much amusement. 'It might be a description of Watson.'

'Well, I am afraid I can't help you, Lestrade,' said Holmes. 'The fact is that I knew this fellow Milverton, that I considered him one of the most dangerous men in London, and that I think there are certain crimes which the law cannot touch, and which therefore, to some extent, justify private revenge. No, it's no use arguing. I have made up my mind. My sympathies are with the criminals rather than with the victim, and I will not handle this case.'

Holmes had not said one word to me about the tragedy which we had witnessed, but I observed all the morning that he was in the most thoughtful mood, and he gave me the impression, from his vacant eyes and his abstracted manner, of a man who is striving to recall something to his memory. We were in the middle of our lunch, when he suddenly sprang to his feet. 'By Jove, Watson! I've got it!' he cried.* 'Take your hat! Come with me!' He hurried at his top speed down Baker Street and along Oxford Street, until we had almost reached Regent Circus. Here on the left hand there stands a shop window filled with photographs of the celebrities and beauties of the day.* Holmes's eyes fixed themselves upon one of them, and following his gaze I saw the picture of a regal and stately lady in Court dress,* with a high diamond tiara upon her noble head. I looked at that delicately curved nose, at the marked eyebrows, at the straight mouth, and the strong little chin beneath it. Then I caught my breath as I read the time-honoured title of the great nobleman and statesman whose wife she had been. My eyes met those of Holmes, and he put his finger to his lips as we turned away from the window.

The Six Napoleons

CHAPTER ... THE SIX NAPOLEONS

I T was no very unusual thing for Mr Lestrade, of Scotland Yard, to look in upon us of an evening, and his visits were welcome to Sherlock Holmes, for they enabled him to keep in touch with all that was going on at the police headquarters.* In return for the news which Lestrade would bring, Holmes was always ready to listen with attention to the details of any case upon which the detective was engaged, and was able occasionally, without any active interference, to give some hint or suggestion drawn from his own vast knowledge and experience.

On this particular evening Lestrade had spoken of the weather and the newspapers. Then he had fallen silent, puffing thoughtfully at his cigar. Holmes looked keenly at him.

'Anything remarkable on hand?' he asked.

'Oh, no, Mr Holmes, nothing very particular.'

'Then tell me all about it.'*

Lestrade laughed.

'Well, Mr Holmes, there is no use denying that there *is* something on my mind. And yet it is such an absurd business that I hesitated to bother you about it. On the other hand, although it is trivial, it is undoubtedly queer, and I know that you have a taste for all that is out of the common. But in my opinion it comes more in Dr Watson's line that ours.'

'Disease?' said I.

'Madness, anyhow. And a queer madness too! You wouldn't think there was anyone living at this time of day who had such a hatred of Napoleon the First* that he would break any image of him that he could see.'

Holmes sank back in his chair.

'That's no business of mine,' said he.

'Exactly. That's what I said. But then, when the man commits burglary in order to break images which are not his own, that brings it away from the doctor and on to the policeman.'

Holmes sat up again.

'Burglary! This is more interesting. Let me hear the details.'

Lestrade took out his official note-book and refreshed his memory from its pages.

'The first case reported was four days ago,' said he. 'It was at the shop of Morse Hudson,* who has a place for the sale of pictures and statues in the Kennington Road. The assistant had left the front shop for an instant, when he heard a crash, and, hurrying in found a plaster bust of Napoleon, which stood with several other works of art upon the counter, lying shivered into fragments. He rushed out into the road, but, although several passers-by declared that they had noticed a man run out of the shop, he could neither see anyone nor could he find any means of identifying the rascal. It seemed to be one of those senseless acts of hooliganism* which occur from time to time, and it was reported to the constable on the beat as such. The plaster cast was not worth more than a few shillings, and the whole affair appeared to be too childish for any particular investigation.

'The second case, however, was more serious and also more singular. It occurred only last night.

'In Kennington Road, and within a few hundred yards of Morse Hudson's shop, there lives a well-known medical practitioner, named Dr Barnicot,* who has one of the largest practices upon the south side of the Thames. His residence and principal consulting-room is at Kennington Road, but he has a branch surgery and dispensary at Lower Brixton Road,* two miles away. This Dr Barnicot is an enthusiastic admirer of Napoleon, and his house is full of books, pictures, and relics of the French Emperor. Some little time ago he purchased from Morse Hudson two duplicate plaster casts of the famous head of Napoleon by the French sculptor Devine.* One of these he placed in his hall in the house at Kennington Road, and the other on the mantelpiece of the surgery at Lower Brixton. Well, when Dr Barnicot came down this morning he was astonished to find that his house had been burgled during the night, but that nothing had been taken save the plaster head from the hall. It had been carried out, and had been dashed savagely against the garden wall, under which its splintered fragments were discovered.'

Holmes rubbed his hands.

'This is certainly very novel,' said he.

'I thought it would please you. But I have not got to the end yet. Dr Barnicot was due at his surgery at twelve o'clock, and you can imagine his amazement when, on arriving there, he found that the window had been opened in the night, and that the broken pieces of his second bust were strewn all over the room. It had been smashed to atoms where it stood. In neither case were there any signs which could give us a clue as to the criminal or lunatic who had done the mischief. Now, Mr Holmes, you have got the facts.'

'They are singular, not to say grotesque,' said Holmes. 'May I ask whether the two busts smashed in Dr Barnicot's rooms were the exact duplicates of the one which was destroyed in Morse Hudson's shop?'

'They were taken from the same mould.'

'Such a fact must tell against the theory that the man who breaks them is influenced by any general hatred of Napoleon. Considering how many hundreds of statues of the great Emperor must exist in London, it is too much to suppose such a coincidence as that a promiscuous iconoclast* should chance to begin upon three specimens of the same bust.'

'Well, I thought as you do,' said Lestrade. 'On the other hand, this Morse Hudson is the purveyor of busts in that part of London, and these three were the only ones which had been in his shop for years. So although, as you say, there are many hundreds of statues in London, it is very probable that these three were the only ones in that district. Therefore a local fanatic would begin with them. What do you think, Dr Watson?'

'There are no limits to the possibilities of monomania,' I answered. 'There is the condition which the modern French psychologists have called the "*idée fixe*",* which may be trifling in character, and accompanied by complete sanity in every other way. A man who had read deeply about Napoleon, or who had possibly received some hereditary family injury through the great war, might conceivably form such an "*idée fixe*", and under its influence be capable of any fantastic outrage.'

'That won't do, my dear Watson,' said Holmes, shaking his head; 'for no amount of "*idée fixe*" would enable your interesting monomaniac to find out where these busts were situated.'

'Well, how you do *you* explain it?'

'I don't attempt to do so. I would only observe that there is a certain method in the gentleman's eccentric proceedings. For example, in Dr Barnicot's hall, where a sound might arouse the family, the bust was taken outside before being broken, whereas in the surgery, where there was less danger of an alarm, it was smashed where it stood. The affair seems absurdly trifling, and yet I dare call nothing trivial when I reflect that some of my most classic cases have had the least promising commencement. You will remember, Watson, how the dreadful business of the Abernetty family* was first brought to my notice by the depth which the parsley had sunk into the butter upon a hot day. I can't afford, therefore, to smile at your three broken busts, Lestrade, and I shall be very much obliged to you if you will let me hear of any fresh developments of so singular a chain of events.'

The development for which my friend had asked came in a quicker and an infinitely more tragic form than he could have imagined. I was still dressing in my bedroom next morning, when there was a tap at the door, and Holmes entered, a telegram in his hand. He read it aloud:

Come instantly, 131, Pitt Street, Kensington.* LESTRADE.

'What is it, then?' I asked.

'Don't know—may be anything. But I suspect it is the sequel of the story of the statues. In that case our friend the image-breaker has begun operations in another quarter of London. There's coffee on the table, Watson, and I have a cab at the door.'

In half an hour we had reached Pitt Street, a quiet little backwater just beside one of the briskest currents of London life. No. 131 was one of a row, all flat-chested, respectable, and most unromantic dwellings. As we drove up we found the railings in front of the house lined by a curious crowd. Holmes whistled.

'By George! it's attempted murder at the least. Nothing less will hold the London message boy. There's a deed of violence indicated in that fellow's round shoulders and outstretched neck. What's this, Watson? The top step swilled down and the other ones dry. Footsteps enough, anyhow! Well, well, there's Lestrade at the front window, and we shall soon know all about it.'

The official received us with a very grave face and showed us into a sitting-room, where an exceedingly unkempt and agitated elderly man, clad in a flannel dressing-gown, was pacing up and down. He was introduced to us as the owner of the house—Mr Horace Harker,* of the Central Press Syndicate.*

'It's the Napoleon bust business again,' said Lestrade. 'You seemed interested last night, Mr Holmes, so I thought perhaps you would be glad to be present now that the affair has taken a very much graver turn.'

'What has it turned to, then?'

'To murder. Mr Harker, will you tell these gentlemen exactly what has occurred?'

The man in the dressing-gown turned upon us with a most melancholy face.

'It's an extraordinary thing,' said he, 'that all my life I have been collecting other people's news, and now that a real piece of news has come my own way I am so confused and bothered that I can't put two words together. If I had come in here as a journalist I should have interviewed myself and had two columns in every evening paper. As it is, I am giving away valuable copy by telling my story over and over to a string of different people, and I can make no use of it myself. However, I've heard your name, Mr Sherlock Holmes, and if you'll only explain this queer business I shall be paid for my trouble in telling you the story.'

Holmes sat down and listened.

'It all seems to centre round that bust of Napoleon which I bought for this very room about four months ago. I picked it up cheap from Harding Brothers,* two doors from the High Street Station. A great deal of my journalistic work is done at night, and I often write until the early morning. So it was to-day. I was sitting in my den, which is at the back of the top of the house, about three o'clock, when I was convinced that I heard some sounds downstairs. I listened, but they were not repeated, and I concluded that they came from outside. Then suddenly, about five minutes later, there came a most horrible yell—the most dreadful sound, Mr Holmes, that ever I heard. It will ring in my ears as long as I live. I sat frozen with horror for a minute or two. Then I seized the poker and went downstairs. When I entered this room I found the window wide open, and I at once observed that the bust was gone from the mantelpiece. Why any burglar should take such a thing passes my understanding, for it was only a plaster cast, and of no real value whatever.

'You can see for yourself that anyone going out through that open window could reach the front doorstep by taking a long stride. This was clearly what the burglar had done, so I went round and opened the door. Stepping out into the dark I nearly fell over a dead man who was lying there. I ran back for a light, and there was the poor devil,* a great gash in his throat and the whole place swimming in blood. He lay on his back, his knees drawn up, and his mouth horribly open. I shall see him in my dreams. I had just time to blow on my police-whistle, and then I must have fainted, for I knew nothing more until I found the policeman standing over me in the hall.'

'Well, who was the murdered man?' asked Holmes.

'There's nothing to show who he was,' said Lestrade. 'You shall see the body at the mortuary, but we have made nothing of it up to now. He is a tall man, sunburnt, very powerful, not more than thirty. He is poorly dressed, and yet does not appear to be a labourer. A horn-handled clasp-knife was lying in a pool of blood beside him. Whether it was the weapon which did the deed, or whether it belonged to the dead man, I do not know. There was no name on his clothing, and nothing in his pockets save an apple, some string, a shilling map of London, and a photograph. Here it is.'

It was evidently taken by a snap-shot from a small camera. It represented an alert, sharp-featured simian man with thick eyebrows, and a very peculiar projection of the lower part of the face like the muzzle of a baboon.

'And what became of the bust?' asked Holmes, after a careful study of this picture.

'We had news of it just before you came. It has been found in the front garden of an empty house in Campden House Road. It was broken into fragments. I am going round now to see it. Will you come?'

'Certainly. I must just take one look round.' He examined the carpet and the window. 'The fellow had either very long legs or was a most active man,' said he. 'With an area beneath, it was no mean feat to reach that window-ledge and open that window. Getting back was comparatively simple. Are you coming with us to see the remains of your bust, Mr Harker?'

The disconsolate journalist had seated himself at a writing-table.

'I must try and make something of it,' said he, 'though I have no doubt that the first editions of the evening papers are out already with full details. It's like my luck! You remember when the stand fell at Doncaster?* Well, I was the only journalist in the stand, and my journal the only one that had no account of it, for I was too shaken to write it. And now I'll be too late with a murder done on my own doorstep.'

As we left the room we heard his pen travelling shrilly over the foolscap.

The spot where the fragments of the bust had been found was only a few hundred yards away. For the first time our eyes rested upon this presentment of the great Emperor, which seemed to raise such frantic and destructive hatred in the mind of the unknown. It lay scattered in splintered shards upon the grass. Holmes picked up several of them and examined them carefully. I was convinced from his intent face and purposeful manner that at last he was upon a clue.

'Well?' asked Lestrade.

Holmes shrugged his shoulders.

'We have a long way to go yet,' said he. 'And yet—and yet—well, we have some suggestive facts to act upon. The possession of this trifling bust was worth more in the eyes of this strange criminal than a human life. That is one point. Then there is the singular fact that he did not break it in the house, or immediately outside the house, if to break it was his sole object.'

'He was rattled and hustled* by meeting this other fellow. He hardly knew what he was doing.'

'Well, that's likely enough. But I wish to call your attention very particularly to the position of this house in the garden of which the bust was destroyed.'

Lestrade looked about him.

'It was an empty house, and so he knew that he would not be disturbed in the garden.'

'Yes, but there is another empty house farther up the street which he must have passed before he came to this one. Why did he not break it there, since it is evident that every yard that he carried it increased the risk of someone meeting him?'

'I give it up,' said Lestrade.

Holmes pointed to the street-lamp above our heads.

183

'He could see what he was doing here, and he could not there. That was the reason.'

'By Jove! that's true,' said the detective. 'Now that I come to think of it, Dr Barnicot's bust was broken not far from his red lamp.* Well, Mr Holmes, what are we to do with that fact?'

'To remember it—to docket it.* We may come on something later which will bear upon it. What steps do you propose to take now, Lestrade?'

'The most practical way of getting at it, in my opinion, is to identify the dead man. There should be no difficulty about that. When we have found who he is and who his associates are, we should have a good start in learning what he was doing in Pitt Street last night, and who it was who met him and killed him on the doorstep of Mr Horace Harker. Don't you think so?'

'No doubt; and yet it is not quite the way in which I should approach the case.'

'What would you do then?'

'Oh, you must not let me influence you in any way. I suggest that you go on your line and I on mine. We can compare notes afterwards, and each will supplement the other.'

'Very good,' said Lestrade.

'If you are going back to Pitt Street you might see Mr Horace Harker. Tell him from me that I have quite made up my mind, and that it is certain that a dangerous homicidal lunatic with Napoleonic delusions was in his house last night. It will be useful for his article.'

Lestrade stared.

'You don't seriously believe that?'

Holmes smiled.

'Don't I? Well, perhaps I don't. But I am sure that it will interest Mr Horace Harker and the subscribers of the Central Press Syndicate. Now, Watson, I think that we shall find that we have a long and rather complex day's work before us. I should be glad, Lestrade, if you could make it convenient to meet us at Baker Street at six o'clock this evening. Until then I should like to keep this photograph found in the dead man's pocket. It is possible that I may have to ask your company and assistance upon a small expedition which will have to be undertaken to-night, if my chain of reasoning should prove to be correct. Until then, good-bye, and good luck!'

Sherlock Holmes and I walked together to the High Street, where he stopped at the shop of Harding Brothers, whence the bust had been purchased. A young assistant informed us that Mr Harding would be absent until after noon, and that he was himself a newcomer, who could give us no information. Holmes's face showed his disappointment and annoyance.

'Well, well, we can't expect to have it all our own way, Watson,' he said at last. 'We must come back in the afternoon, if Mr Harding will not be here until then. I am, as you have no doubt surmised, endeavouring to trace these busts to their source, in order to find if there is not something peculiar which may account for their remarkable fate. Let us make for Mr Morse Hudson, of the Kennington Road, and see if he can throw any light upon the problem.'

A drive of an hour brought us to the picture-dealer's establishment. He was a small, stout man with a red face and a peppery manner.

'Yes, sir. On my very counter, sir,' said he. 'What we pay rates and taxes for I don't know, when any ruffian can come in and break one's goods. Yes, sir, it was I who sold Dr Barnicot his two statues. Disgraceful, sir! A Nihilist plot, that's what I make it. No one but an Anarchist would go about breaking statues. Red republicans, that's what I call 'em. Who did I get the statues from? I don't see what that has to do with it. Well, if you really want to know, I got them from Gelder & Co.,* in Church Street, Stepney.* They are a well-known house in the trade, and have been this twenty years. How many had I? Three—two and one are three—two of Dr Barnicot's and one smashed in broad daylight on my own counter. Do I know that photograph? No, I don't. Yes, I do though. Why, it's Beppo!* He was a kind of Italian piece-work man, who made himself useful in the shop. He could carve a bit, and gild a frame, and do odd jobs. The fellow left me last week, and I've heard nothing of him since. No, I don't know where he came from nor where he went to. I had nothing against him while he was here. He was gone two days before the bust was smashed.'

'Well, that's all we could reasonably expect to get from Morse Hudson,' said Holmes, as we emerged from the shop. 'We have this Beppo as a common factor, both in Kennington and in Kensington, so that is worth a ten-mile drive. Now, Watson, let us make for Gelder & Co., of Stepney, the source and origin of busts. I shall be surprised if we don't get some help down there.'

In rapid succession we passed through the fringe of fashionable London, hotel London, theatrical London, literary London, commercial London, and, finally, maritime London,* till we came to a riverside city of a hundred thousand souls, where the tenement houses swelter and reek with the outcasts of Europe. Here, in a broad thoroughfare, once the abode of wealthy city merchants we found the sculpture works for which we searched. Outside was a considerable yard full of monumental masonry. Inside was a large room in which fifty workers were carving or moulding. The manager, a big blond German, received us civilly, and gave a clear answer to all Holmes's questions. A reference to his books showed that hundreds of casts had been taken from a marble copy of Devine's head of Napoleon, but that the three which had been sent to Morse Hudson a year or so before had been half of a batch of six, the other three being sent to Harding Brothers, of Kensington. There was no reason why those six should be different to any of the other casts. He could suggest no possible cause why anyone should wish to destroy them—in fact, he laughed at the idea. Their wholesale price was six shillings, but the retailer would get twelve or more. The cast was taken in two moulds from each side of the face, and then these two profiles of plaster of Paris were joined together to make the complete bust. The work was usually done by Italians in the room we were in. When finished the busts were put on a table in the passage to dry, and afterwards stored. That was all he could tell us.

But the production of the photograph had a remarkable effect upon the manager. His face flushed with anger, and his brows knotted over his blue Teutonic eyes.

'Ah, the rascal!' he cried. 'Yes, indeed, I know him very well. This has always been a respectable establishment, and the only time that we have ever had the police in it was over this very fellow. It was more than a year ago now. He knifed another Italian in the street, and then he came to the works with the police on his heels, and he was taken here. Beppo was his name—his second name I never knew. Serve me right for engaging a man with such a face. But he was a good workman—one of the best.'

'What did he get?'

'The man lived, and he got off with a year. I have no doubt he is out now; but he has not dared to show his nose here. We have a cousin of his here, and I dare say he could tell you where he is.'

'No, no,' cried Holmes, 'not a word to the cousin—not a word, I beg you. The matter is very important, and the farther I go with it the more important it seems to grow. When you referred in your ledger to the sale of those casts I observed that the date was 3rd June of last year. Could you give me the date when Beppo was arrested?'

'I could tell you roughly by the pay-list,' the manager answered. 'Yes,' he continued, after some turning over of pages, 'he was paid last on May 20th.'

'Thank you,' said Holmes. 'I don't think that I need intrude upon your time and patience any more.' With a last word of caution that he should say nothing as to our researches we turned our faces westward once more.

The afternoon was far advanced before we were able to snatch a hasty luncheon at a restaurant. A news-bill at the entrance announced 'Kensington Outrage. Murder by a Madman', and the contents of the paper showed that Mr Horace Harker had got his account into print after all. Two columns were occupied with a highly sensational and flowery rendering of the whole incident. Holmes propped it against the cruet stand and read it while he ate. Once or twice he chuckled.

'This is all right, Watson,' said he. 'Listen to this: "It is satisfactory to know that there can be no difference of opinion upon this case, since Mr Lestrade, one of the most experienced members of the official force, and Mr Sherlock Holmes, the well-known consulting expert, have each come to the conclusion that the grotesque series of incidents, which have ended in so tragic a fashion, arise from lunacy rather than from deliberate crime. No explanation save mental aberration can cover the facts." The Press, Watson, is a most valuable institution, if you only know how to use it. And now, if you have quite finished, we will hark back to Kensington, and see what the manager of Harding Brothers has to say to the matter.'*

The founder of that great emporium proved to be a brisk, crisp little person, very dapper and quick, with a clear head and a ready tongue.

'Yes, sir, I have already read the account in the evening papers. Mr Horace Harker is a customer of ours. We supplied him with the bust some months ago. We ordered three busts of that sort from Gelder & Co., of Stepney. They are all sold now. To whom? Oh, I dare say by consulting our sales book we could very easily tell you. Yes, we have the entries here. One to Mr Harker, you see, and one to Mr Josiah Brown, of Laburnum Lodge, Laburnum Vale, Chiswick,* and one to Mr Sandeford, of Lower Grove Road, Reading.* No, I have never seen this face which you show me in the photograph. You would hardly forget it—would you, sir?—for I've seldom seen an uglier.* Have we any Italians on the staff? Yes, sir, we have several among our workpeople and cleaners. I dare say they might get a peep at that sales book if they wanted to. There is no particular reason for keeping a watch upon that book. Well, well, it's a very strange business, and I hope that you'll let me know if anything comes of your inquiries.'

Holmes had taken several notes during Mr Harding's evidence, and I could see that he was thoroughly satisfied by the turn which affairs were taking. He made no remark, however, save that, unless we hurried, we should be late for our appointment with Lestrade. Sure enough, when we reached Baker Street the detective was already there, and we found him pacing up and down in a fever of impatience. His look of importance showed that his day's work had not been in vain.

'Well?' he asked. 'What luck, Mr Holmes?'

'We have had a very busy day, and not entirely a wasted one,' my friend explained. 'We have seen both the retailers and also the wholesale manufacturers. I can trace each of the busts now from the beginning.'

'The busts!' cried Lestrade. 'Well, well, you have your own methods, Mr Sherlock Holmes, and it is not for me to say a word against them, but I think I have done a better day's work than you. I have identified the dead man.'

'You don't say so?'

'And found a cause for the crime.'

'Splendid!'

'We have an inspector who makes a speciality of Saffron Hill and the Italian quarter.* Well, this dead man had some Catholic emblem round his neck,* and that, along with his colour, made me think he was from the South. Inspector Hill knew him the moment he caught sight of him. His name is Pietro Venucci, from Naples,* and he is one of the greatest cut-throats in London. He is connected with the Mafia,* which, as you know, is a secret political society, enforcing its decrees by murder. Now you see how the affair begins to clear up. The other fellow is probably an Italian also, and a member of the Mafia. He has broken the rules in some fashion. Pietro is set upon his track. Probably the photograph we found in his pocket is the man himself, so that he may not knife the wrong person. He dogs the fellow, he sees him enter a house, he waits outside for him, and in the scuffle receives his own death-wound. How is that, Mr Sherlock Holmes?'

Holmes clapped his hands approvingly.

'Excellent, Lestrade, excellent!' he cried. 'But I didn't quite follow your explanation of the destruction of the busts.'

'The busts! You never can get those busts out of your head. After all, that is nothing; petty larceny, six months at the most. It is the murder that we are really investigating, and I tell you that I am gathering all the threads into my hands.'

'And the next stage?'

'Is a very simple one. I shall go down with Hill to the Italian quarter, find the man whose photograph we have got, and arrest him on the charge of murder. Will you come with us?'

'I think not. I fancy we can attain our end in a simpler way. I can't say for certain, because it all depends—well, it all depends upon a factor which is completely outside our control. But I have great hopes—in fact, the betting is exactly two to one*—that if you will come with us tonight I shall be able to help you to lay him by the heels.'

'In the Italian quarter?'

'No; I fancy Chiswick is an address which is more likely to find him. If you will come with me to Chiswick tonight, Lestrade, I'll promise to go to the Italian quarter with you to-morrow, and no harm will be done by the delay. And now I think that a few hours' sleep would do us all good, for I do not propose to leave before eleven o'clock, and it is unlikely that we shall be back before morning. You'll dine with us, Lestrade, and then you are welcome to the sofa until it is time for us to start. In the meantime, Watson, I should be glad if you would ring for an express messenger,* for I have a letter to send, and it is important that it should go at once.'

Holmes spent the evening in rummaging among the files of the old daily papers with which one of our lumber-rooms was packed. When at last he descended it was with triumph in his eyes, but he said nothing to either of us as to the result of his researches. For my own part, I had followed step by step the methods by which he had traced the various windings of this complex case, and, though I could not yet perceive the goal which we would reach, I understood clearly that Holmes expected this grotesque criminal to make an attempt upon the two remaining busts, one of which, I remembered, was at Chiswick. No doubt the object of our journey was to catch him in the very act, and I could not but admire the cunning with which my friend had inserted the wrong clue in the evening paper so as to give the fellow the idea that he could continue his scheme with impunity. I was not surprised when Holmes suggested that I should take my revolver with me. He had himself picked up the loaded hunting-crop* which was his favourite weapon.

A four-wheeler was at the door at eleven, and in it we drove to a spot at the other side of Hammersmith Bridge.* Here the cabman was directed to wait. A short walk brought us to a secluded road fringed with pleasant houses, each standing in its own grounds. In the light of a street lamp we read 'Laburnum Villa' upon the gate-post of one of them. The occupants had evidently retired to rest, for all was dark save for a fanlight over the hall door, which shed a single blurred circle on to the garden path. The wooden fence which separated the grounds from the road threw a dense black shadow upon the inner side, and here it was that we crouched.

'I fear that you'll have a long time to wait,' Holmes whispered. 'We may thank our stars that it is not raining. I don't think we can even venture to smoke to pass the time. However, it's a two to one chance that we get something to pay us for our trouble.'

It proved, however, that our vigil was not to be so long as Holmes had led us to fear, and it ended in a very sudden and singular fashion. In an instant, without the least sound to warn us of his coming, the garden gate swung open, and a lithe, dark figure, as swift and active as an ape, rushed up the garden path. We saw it whisk past the light thrown from over the door and disappear against the black shadow of the house. There was a long pause, during which we held our breath, and then a very gentle creaking sound came to our ears. The window was being opened. The noise ceased, and again there was a long silence. The fellow was making his way into the house. We saw the sudden flash of a dark lantern inside the room. What he sought was evidently not there, for again we saw the flash through another blind, and then through another.

'Let us get to the open window. We will nab him as he climbs out,' Lestrade whispered.

But before we could move the man had emerged again. As he came out into the glimmering patch of light we saw that he carried something white under his arm. He looked stealthily all round him. The silence of the deserted street reassured him. Turning his back upon us, he laid down his burden, and the next instant there was the sound of a sharp tap, followed by a clatter and rattle. The man was so intent upon what he was doing that he never heard our steps as we stole across the grass plot. With the bound of a tiger Holmes was on his back, and an instant later Lestrade and I had him by either wrist, and the handcuffs had been fastened. As we turned him over I saw his hideous, sallow face, with writhing, furious features glaring up at us, and I knew that it was indeed the man of the photograph whom we had secured.

But it was not our prisoner to whom Holmes was giving his attention. Squatted on the doorstep, he was engaged in most carefully examining that which the man had brought from the house. It was a bust of Napoleon like the one which we had seen that morning, and it had been broken into similar fragments. Carefully Holmes held each separate shard to the light, but in no way did it differ from any other shattered piece of plaster. He had just completed his examination, when the hall lights flew up, the door opened* and the owner of the house, a jovial, rotund figure in shirt and trousers,* presented himself.

'Mr Josiah Brown, I suppose?' said Holmes.

'Yes, sir; and you no doubt are Mr Sherlock Holmes? I had the note which you sent by the express messenger, and

I did exactly what you told me. We locked every door in the inside and awaited developments. Well, I'm very glad to see that you have got the rascal. I hope, gentlemen, that you will come in and have some refreshment.'

However, Lestrade was anxious to get his man into safe quarters, so within a few minutes our cab had been summoned and we were all four upon our way to London. Not a word would our captive say; but he glared at us from the shadow of his matted hair,* and once, when my hand seemed within his reach, he snapped at it like a hungry wolf. We stayed long enough at the police-station to learn that a search of his clothing revealed nothing save shillings and a long sheath knife, the handle of which bore copious traces of recent blood.

'That's all right,' said Lestrade, as we parted. 'Hill knows all these gentry, and he will give a name to him. You'll find that my theory of the Mafia will work out all right. But I'm sure I am exceedingly obliged to you, Mr Holmes, for the workmanlike way in which you laid hands upon him. I don't quite understand it all yet.'

'I fear it is rather too late an hour for explanations,' said Holmes. 'Besides, there are one or two details which are not finished off, and it is one of those cases which are worth working out to the very end. If you will come round once more to my rooms at six o'clock to-morrow I think I shall be able to show you that even now you have not grasped the entire meaning of this business, which presents some features which make it absolutely original in the history of crime. If ever I permit you to chronicle any more of my little problems, Watson, I foresee that you will enliven your pages by an account of the singular adventure of the Napoleonic busts.'

When we met again next evening, Lestrade was furnished with much information concerning our prisoner. His name, it appeared, was Beppo, second name unknown. He was a well-known ne'er-do-well among the Italian colony. He had once been a skilful sculptor and had earned an honest living, but he had taken to evil courses, and had twice already been in gaol—once for a petty theft and once, as we had already heard, for stabbing a fellow-countryman. He could talk English perfectly well. His reasons for destroying the busts were still unknown, and he refused to answer any questions upon the subject; but the police had discovered that these same busts might very well have been made by his own hands, since he was engaged in this class of work at the establishment of Gelder & Co. To all this information, much of which we already knew, Holmes listened with polite attention; but I, who knew him so well, could clearly see that his thoughts were elsewhere, and I detected a mixture of mingled uneasiness and expectation beneath that mask which he was wont to assume. At last he started in his chair and his eyes brightened. There had been a ring at the bell. A minute later we heard steps upon he stairs, and an elderly, red-faced man with grizzled side-whiskers was ushered in. In his right hand he carried an old-fashioned carpet-bag, which he placed upon the table.

'Is Mr Sherlock Holmes here?'

My friend bowed and smiled 'Mr Sandeford, of Reading, I suppose?' said he.

'Yes, sir. I fear that I am a little late; but the trains were awkward. You wrote to me about a bust that is in my possession.'

'Exactly.'

'I have your letter here. You said, "I desire to possess a copy of Devine's Napoleon and am prepared to pay you ten pounds for the one which is in your possession." Is that right?'

'Certainly.'

'I was very much surprised at your letter, for I could not imagine how you knew that I owned such a thing.'

'Of course you must have been surprised, but the explanation is very simple. Mr Harding, of Harding Brothers, said that they had sold you their last copy, and he gave me your address.'

'Oh, that was it, was it? Did he tell you what I paid for it?'

'No, he did not.'

'Well, I am an honest man, though not a very rich one. I only gave fifteen shillings for the bust, and I think you ought to know that before I take ten pounds from you.'

'I am sure the scruple does you honour, Mr Sandeford. But I have named that price, so I intend to stick to it.'

'Well, it is very handsome of you, Mr Holmes. I brought the bust up with me, as you asked me to do. Here it is!' He opened his bag, and at last we saw placed upon our table a complete specimen of that bust which we had already seen more than once in fragments.

Holmes took a paper from his pocket and laid a ten-pound note upon the table.

'You will kindly sign that paper, Mr Sandeford, in the presence of these witnesses. It is simply to say that you transfer every possible right that you ever had in the bust to me. I am a methodical man, you see, and you never know what turn events might take afterwards. Thank you, Mr Sandeford; here is your money, and I wish you a very good evening.'

When our visitor had disappeared Sherlock Holmes's movements were such as to rivet our attention. He began by taking a clean white cloth from a drawer and laying it over the table. Then he placed his newly acquired bust in the centre of the cloth. Finally he picked up his hunting-crop and struck Napoleon a sharp blow on the top of the head. The figure broke into fragments, and Holmes bent eagerly over the shattered remains. Next instant, with a loud shout of triumph, he held up one splinter, in which a round, dark object was fixed like a plum in a pudding.

'Gentlemen,' he cried, 'let me introduce you to the famous black pearl of the Borgias.'*

Lestrade and I sat silent for a moment, and then, with a spontaneous impulse, we both broke out clapping as at the well-wrought crisis of a play. A flush of colour sprang to Holmes's pale cheeks, and he bowed to us like the master dramatist who receives the homage of his audience. It was at such moments that for an instant he ceased to be a

195

reasoning machine and betrayed his human love for admiration and applause. The same singularly proud and reserved nature which turned away with disdain from popular notoriety was capable of being moved to its depth by spontaneous wonder and praise from a friend.

'Yes, gentlemen,' said he, 'it is the most famous pearl now existing in the world, and it has been my good fortune, by a connected chain of inductive reasoning, to trace it from the Prince of Colonna's* bedroom at the Dacre Hotel,* where it was lost, to the interior of this, the last of the six busts of Napoleon which were manufactured by Gelder & Co., of Stepney. You will remember, Lestrade, the sensation caused by the disappearance of this valuable jewel, and the vain efforts of the London police to recover it. I was myself consulted upon the case; but I was unable to throw any light upon it. Suspicion fell upon the maid of the Princess, who was an Italian, and it was proved that she had a brother in London, but we failed to trace any connection between them. The maid's name was Lucretia Venucci, and there is no doubt in my mind that this Pietro who was murdered two nights ago was the brother. I have been looking up the dates in the old files of the paper, and I find that the disappearance of the pearl was exactly two days before the arrest of Beppo for some crime of violence—an event which took place in the factory of Gelder & Co., at the very moment when these busts were being made. Now you clearly see the sequence of events, though you see them, of course, in the inverse order to the way in which they presented themselves to me. Beppo had the pearl in his possession. He may have stolen it from Pietro, he may have been Pietro's confederate, he may have been the go-between of Pietro and his sister. It is of no consequence to us which is the correct solution.

'The main fact is that he *had* the pearl, and at that moment, when it was on his person, he was pursued by the police. He made for the factory in which he worked, and he knew that he had only a few minutes in which to conceal this enormously valuable prize, which would otherwise be found on him when he was searched. Six plaster casts of

Napoleon were drying in the passage. One of them was still soft. In an instant Beppo, a skilful workman, made a small hole in the wet plaster, dropped in the pearl, and with a few touches covered over the aperture once more. It was an admirable hiding-place. No one could possibly find it. But Beppo was condemned to a year's imprisonment, and in the meanwhile his six busts were scattered over London. He could not tell which contained his treasure. Only by breaking them could he see. Even shaking would tell him nothing for as the plaster was wet it was probable that the pearl would adhere to it—as, in fact, it has done. Beppo did not despair, and he conducted his search with considerable ingenuity and perseverance. Through a cousin who works with Gelder he found out the retail firms who had bought the busts. He managed to find employment with Morse Hudson, and in that way tracked down three of them. The pearl was not there. Then with the help of some Italian employee, he succeeded in finding out where the other three busts had gone. The first was at Harker's. There he was dogged by his confederate, who held Beppo responsible for the loss of the pearl, and he stabbed him in the scuffle which followed.'

'If he was his confederate, why should he carry his photograph?' I asked.

'As a means of tracing him if he wished to inquire about him from any third person. That was the obvious reason. Well, after the murder I calculated that Beppo would probably hurry rather than delay his movements. He would fear that the police would read his secret, and so hastened on before they should get ahead of him. Of course, I could not say that he had not found the pearl in Harker's bust. I had not even concluded for certain that it was the pearl; but it was evident to me that he was looking for something, since he carried the bust past the other houses in order to break it in the garden which had a lamp overlooking it. Since Harker's bust was one in three, the chances were exactly as I told you—two to one against the pearl being inside it. There remained two busts, and it was obvious that he would go for the London one first. I warned the inmates of the house, so as to avoid a second tragedy, and we went down, with the happiest results. By that time, of course, I knew for certain that it was the Borgia pearl that we were after. The name of the murdered man linked the one event with the other. There only remained a single bust—the Reading one—and the pearl must be there. I bought it in your presence from the owner—and there it lies.'

We sat in silence for a moment.

'Well,' said Lestrade, 'I've seen you handle a good many cases, Mr Holmes, but I don't know that I ever knew a more workmanlike one than that. We're not jealous of you at Scotland Yard. No, sir, we are damned proud of you,* and if you come down tomorrow there's not a man, from the oldest inspector to the youngest constable, who wouldn't be glad to shake you by the hand.'

'Thank you!' said Holmes. 'Thank you!' and as he turned away it seemed to me that he was more nearly moved by the softer human emotions than I had ever seen him. A moment later he was the cold and practical thinker once more. 'Put the pearl in the safe, Watson,' said he, 'and get out the papers of the Conk-Singleton forgery case.* Good-bye, Lestrade. If any little problem comes your way I shall be happy, if I can, to give you a hint or two as to its solution.'

The Three Students

IT was in the year '95 that a combination of events, into which I need not enter, caused Mr Sherlock Holmes and myself to spend some weeks in one of our great University towns,* and it was during this time that the small but instructive adventure which I am about to relate befell us. It will be obvious that any details which would help the reader to exactly identify the college or the criminal would be injudicious and offensive. So painful a scandal may well be allowed to die out. With due discretion the incident itself may, however, be described, since it serves to illustrate some of those qualities for which my friend was remarkable. I will endeavour in my statement to avoid such terms as would serve to limit the events to any particular place, or give a clue as to the people concerned.

We were residing at the time in furnished lodgings close to a library where Sherlock Holmes was pursuing some laborious researches* in early English charters*—researches which led to results so striking that they may be the subject of one of my future narratives. Here it was that one evening we received a visit from an acquaintance, Mr Hilton Soames,* tutor and lecturer at the College of St Luke's.* Mr Soames was a tall, spare man, of a nervous and excitable temperament. I had always known him to be restless in his manner, but on this particular occasion he was in such a state of uncontrollable agitation that it was clear something very unusual had occurred.

'I trust, Mr Holmes, that you can spare me a few hours of your valuable time. We have had a very painful incident at St Luke's, and really, but for the happy chance of your being in the town, I should have been at a loss what to do.'

'I am very busy just now, and I desire no distractions,' my friend answered. 'I should much prefer that you called in the aid of the police.'

'No, no, my dear sir; such a course is utterly impossible. When once the law is evoked it cannot be stayed again, and this is just one of those cases where, for the credit of the college, it is most essential to avoid scandal. Your discretion is as well known as your powers, and you are the one man in the world who can help me. I beg you, Mr Holmes, to do what you can.'

My friend's temper had not improved since he had been deprived of the congenial surroundings of Baker Street. Without his scrap-books, his chemicals, and his homely untidiness, he was an uncomfortable man. He shrugged his shoulders in ungracious acquiescence, while our visitor in hurried words and with much excitable gesticulation poured forth his story.

'I must explain to you, Mr Holmes, that to-morrow is the first day of the examination for the Fortescue Scholarship.* I am one of the examiners. My subject is Greek, and the first of the papers consists of a large passage of Greek translation which the candidate has not seen.* This passage is printed on the examination paper, and it would naturally be an immense advantage if the candidate could prepare it in advance. For this reason great care is taken to keep the paper secret.

'To-day about three o'clock the proofs of this paper arrived from the printers. The exercise consists of half a chapter of Thucydides.* I had to read it over carefully, as the text must be absolutely correct.* At four-thirty my task was not yet completed. I had, however, promised to take tea in a friend's rooms, so I left the proof upon my desk. I was absent rather more than an hour. You are aware, Mr Holmes, that our college doors are double—a green baize one within and a heavy oak one without. As I approached my outer door I was amazed to see a key in it. For an instant I imagined that I had left my own there, but on feeling in my pocket I found that it was all right. The only duplicate which existed, so far as I knew, was that which belonged to my servant, Bannister,* a man who has looked after my room for ten years, and whose honesty is absolutely above suspicion. I found that the key was indeed his, that he had entered my room to know if I wanted tea, and that he had very carelessly left the key in the door when he came out. His visit to my room must have been within a very few minutes of my leaving it. His forgetfulness about the key would have mattered little upon any other occasion, but on this one day it has produced the most deplorable consequences.

'The moment I looked at my table I was aware that someone had rummaged among my papers. The proof was in three long slips.* I had left them all together. Now I found that one of them was lying on the floor, one was on the side-table near the window, and the third was where I had left it.'

Holmes stirred for the first time.

'The first page on the floor, the second in the window, and the third where you left it,' said he.

'Exactly, Mr Holmes. You amaze me. How could you possibly know that?'

'Pray continue your very interesting statement.'

'For an instant I imagined that Bannister had taken the unpardonable liberty of examining my papers. He denied it, however, with the utmost earnestness, and I am convinced that he was speaking the truth. The alternative was that someone passing had observed the key in the door, had known that I was out, and had entered to look at the papers. A large sum of money is at stake, for the scholarship is a very valuable one, and an unscrupulous man might very well run a risk in order to gain advantage over his fellows.

'Bannister was very much upset by the incident. He had nearly fainted when we found that the papers had undoubtedly been tampered with. I gave him a little brandy and left him collapsed in a chair while I made a most careful examination of the room. I soon saw that the intruder had left other traces of his presence besides the rumpled papers. On the table in the window were several shreds from a pencil which had been sharpened. A broken tip of lead was lying there also. Evidently the rascal had copied the paper in a great hurry, had broken his pencil, and had been compelled to put a fresh point to it.'

'Excellent!' said Holmes, who was recovering his good humour as his attention became more engrossed by the case. 'Fortune has been your friend.'

'This was not all. I have a new writing-table with a fine surface of red leather. I am prepared to swear, and so is Bannister, that it was smooth and unstained. Now I found a clean cut in it about three inches long—not a mere scratch, but a positive cut. Not only this, but on the table I found a small ball of black dough, or clay, with specks of something which looks like sawdust in it. I am convinced that these marks were left by the man who rifled the papers. There were no footmarks and no other evidence as to his identity. I was at my wits' end, when suddenly the happy thought occurred to me that you were in the town, and I came straight round to put the matter into your hands. Do help me, Mr Holmes! You see my dilemma. Either I must find the man, or else the examination must be postponed until fresh papers are prepared, and since this cannot be done without explanation, there will ensue a hideous scandal, which will throw a cloud not only on the college but on the University. Above all things, I desire to settle the matter quietly and discreetly.'

'I shall be happy to look into it and to give you such advice as I can,' said Holmes, rising and putting on his overcoat. 'This case is not entirely devoid of interest. Has anyone visited you in your room after the papers came to you?'

'Yes, young Daulat Ras, an Indian student* who lives on the same stair, came in to ask me some particulars about the examination.'

'For which he was entered?'

'Yes.'

'And the papers were on your table?'

'To the best of my belief they were rolled up.'

'But might be recognized as proofs?'

'Possibly.'

'No one else in your room?'

'No.'

'Did anyone know that these proofs would be there?'

'No one save the printer.'

'Did this man Bannister know?'

'No, certainly not. No one knew.'

'Where is Bannister now?'

'He was very ill, poor fellow! I left him collapsed in the chair. I was in such a hurry to come to you.'

'You left your door open?'

'I locked the papers up first.'

'Then it amounts to this, Mr Soames, that unless the Indian student recognized the roll as being proofs, the man who tampered with them came upon them accidentally without knowing that they were there.'

'So it seems to me.'

Holmes gave an enigmatic smile.

'Well,' said he, 'let us go round. Not one of your cases, Watson—mental, not physical. All right; come if you want to. Now, Mr Soames—at your disposal!'

The sitting-room of our client opened by a long, low, latticed window on to the ancient lichen-tinted court of the old college. A Gothic arched door led to a worn stone staircase. On the ground floor was the tutor's room. Above were three students, one on each storey. It was already twilight when we reached the scene of our problem. Holmes halted and looked earnestly at the window. Then he approached it, and, standing on tiptoe, with his neck craned, he looked into the room.

'He must have entered through the door. There is no opening except the one pane,' said our learned guide.

'Dear me!' said Holmes, and he smiled in a singular way as he glanced at our companion. 'Well, if there is nothing to be learned here we had best go inside.'

The lecturer unlocked the outer door and ushered us into his room. We stood at the entrance while Holmes made an examination of the carpet.

'I am afraid there are no signs here,' said he. 'One could hardly hope for any upon so dry a day. Your servant seems to have quite recovered. You left him in a chair, you say; which chair?'

'By the window there.'

'I see. Near this little table. You can come in now. I have finished with the carpet. Let us take the little table first. Of course, what has happened is very clear. The man entered and took the papers, sheet by sheet, from the central table. He carried them over to the window table, because from there he could see if you came across the courtyard, and so could effect an escape.'

'As a matter of fact, he could not,' said Soames, 'for I entered by the side-door.'

'Ah, that's good! Well, anyhow, that was in his mind. Let me see the three strips. No finger impressions—no! Well, he carried over this one first and he copied it. How long would it take him to do that, using every possible contraction? A quarter of an hour, not less. Then he tossed it down and seized the next. He was in the midst of that when your return caused him to make a very hurried retreat—*very* hurried, since he had not time to replace the papers which would tell you that he had been there. You were not aware of any hurrying feet on the stair as you entered the outer door?'

'No, I can't say I was.'

'Well, he wrote so furiously that he broke his pencil, and had, as you observe, to sharpen it again. This is of interest, Watson. The pencil was not an ordinary one. It was above the usual size with a soft lead; the outer colour was dark blue, the maker's name was printed in silver lettering, and the piece remaining is only about an inch and a half long. Look for such a pencil, Mr Soames, and you have got your man. When I add that he possesses a large and very blunt knife, you have an additional aid.'

Mr Soames was somewhat overwhelmed by this flood of information. 'I can follow the other points,' said he, 'but really in this matter of the length—'

Holmes held out a small chip with the letters NN and a space of clear wood after them.

'You see?'

'No, I fear that even now——'

'Watson, I have always done you an injustice. There are others. What could this NN be? It is at the end of a word. You are aware that Johann Faber* is the most common maker's name. Is it not clear that there is just as much of the pencil left as usually follows the Johann?' He held the small table sideways to the electric light. 'I was hoping that if the paper on which he wrote was thin some trace of it might come through upon this polished surface. No, I see nothing. I don't think there is anything more to be learned here. Now for the central table. This small pellet is, I presume, the black doughy mass you spoke of. Roughly pyramidal in shape and hollowed out, I perceive. As you say, there appear to be grains of sawdust in it. Dear me, this is very interesting. And the cut—a positive tear, I see. It began with a thin scratch and ended in a jagged hole. I am much indebted to you for directing my attention to this case, Mr Soames. Where does that door lead to?'

'To my bedroom.'

'Have you been in it since your adventure?'

'No; I came straight away for you.'

'I should like to have a glance round. What a charming, old-fashioned room! Perhaps you will kindly wait a minute until I have examined the floor. No, I see nothing. What about this curtain? You hang your clothes behind it. If anyone were forced to conceal himself in this room he must do it there, since the bed is too low and the wardrobe too shallow. No one there, I suppose?'

As Holmes drew the curtain I was aware, from some little rigidity and alertness of his attitude, that he was prepared for an emergency. As a matter of fact the drawn curtain disclosed nothing but three or four suits of clothes hanging from a line of pegs. Holmes turned away, and stooped suddenly to the floor.

'Hullo! What's this?' said he.

It was a small pyramid of black, putty-like stuff, exactly like the one upon the table of the study. Holmes held it out on his open palm in the glare of the electric light.

'Your visitor seems to have left traces in your bedroom as well as in your sitting-room, Mr Soames.'

'What could he have wanted there?'

'I think it is clear enough. You came back by an unexpected way, and so he had no warning until you were at the very door. What could he do? He caught up everything which would betray him, and he rushed into your bedroom to conceal himself.'

'Good gracious, Mr Holmes, do you mean to tell me that all the time I was talking to Bannister in this room we had the man prisoner if we had only known it?'

'So I read it.'

'Surely there is another alternative, Mr Holmes? I don't know whether you observed my bedroom window.'

'Lattice-paned, lead framework, three separate windows, one swinging on a hinge and large enough to admit a man.'

'Exactly. And it looks out on an angle of the courtyard so as to be partly invisible. The man might have effected his entrance there, left traces as he passed through the bedroom, and, finally, finding the door open, have escaped that way.'

Holmes shook his head impatiently.

'Let us be practical,' said he. 'I understand you to say that there are three students who use this stair and are in the habit of passing your door?'

'Yes, there are.'

'And they are all in this examination?'

'Yes.'

'Have you any reason to suspect any one of them more than the others?'

Soames hesitated.

'It is a very delicate question,' said he. 'One hardly likes to throw suspicion where there are no proofs.'

'Let us hear the suspicions. I will look after the proofs.'

'I will tell you, then, in a few words, the character of the three men who inhabit these rooms. The lower of the three is Gilchrist,* a fine scholar and athlete; plays in the Rugby team and the cricket team for the college, and got his Blue for the hurdles and the long jump.* He is a fine, manly fellow. His father was the notorious Sir Jabez Gilchrist, who ruined himself on the Turf. My scholar has been left very poor, but he is hard-working and industrious. He will do well.

'The second floor is inhabited by Daulat Ras, the Indian. He is a quiet, inscrutable fellow, as most of those Indians are. He is well up in his work, though his Greek is his weak subject. He is steady and methodical.

'The top floor belongs to Miles McLaren.* He is a brilliant fellow when he chooses to work—one of the brightest intellects of the University, but he is wayward, dissipated, and unprincipled. He was nearly expelled over a card scandal in his first year. He has been idling all this term, and he must look forward with dread to the examination.'

'Then it is he whom you suspect?'

'I dare not go so far as that. But of the three he is perhaps the least unlikely.'

'Exactly. Now, Mr Soames, let us have a look at your servant, Bannister.'

He was a little, white-faced, clean-shaven, grizzly-haired fellow of fifty. He was still suffering from this sudden disturbance of the quiet routine of his life. His plump face was twitching with his nervousness, and his fingers could not keep still.

'We are investigating this unhappy business, Bannister,' said his master.

'Yes, sir.'

'I understand,' said Holmes, 'that you left your key in the door?'

'Yes, sir.'

'Was it not very extraordinary that you should do this on the very day when there were these papers inside?'

'It was most unfortunate, sir. But I have occasionally done the same thing at other times.'

'When did you enter the room?'

'It was about half-past four. That is Mr Soames's tea-time.'

'How long did you stay?'

'When I saw that he was absent I withdrew at once.'

'Did you look at these papers on the table?'

'No, sir; certainly not.'

'How came you to leave the key in the door?'

'I had the tea-tray in my hand. I thought I would come back for the key. Then I forgot.'

'Has the outer door a spring lock?'

'No, sir.'

'Then it was open all the time?'

'Yes, sir.'

'Anyone in the room could get out?'

'Yes, sir.'

'When Mr Soames returned and called for you, you were very much disturbed?'

'Yes, sir. Such a thing has never happened during the many years that I have been here. I nearly fainted, sir.'

'So I understand. Where were you when you began to feel bad?'

'Where was I, sir? Why, here, near the door.'

'That is singular, because you sat down in that chair over yonder near the corner. Why did you pass these other chairs?'

'I don't know, sir. It didn't matter to me where I sat.'

'I really don't think he knew much about it, Mr Holmes. He was looking very bad—quite ghastly.'

'You stayed here when your master left?'

'Only for a minute or so. Then I locked the door and went to my room.'

'Whom do you suspect?'

'Oh, I would not venture to say, sir. I don't believe there is any gentleman in this University who is capable of profiting by such an action. No, sir, I'll not believe it.'

'Thank you; that will do,' said Holmes. 'Oh, one more word. You have not mentioned to any of the three gentlemen whom you attend that anything is amiss?'

'No, sir; not a word.'

'You haven't seen any of them?'

'No, sir.'

'Very good. Now, Mr Soames, we will take a walk in the quadrangle, if you please.'

Three yellow squares of light shone above us in the gathering gloom.

'Your three birds are all in their nests,' said Holmes, looking up. 'Hullo! What's that? One of them seems restless enough.'

It was the Indian, whose dark silhouette appeared suddenly upon the blind. He was pacing swiftly up and down his room.

'I should like to have a peep at each of them,' said Holmes. 'Is it possible?'

'No difficulty in the world,' Soames answered. 'This set of rooms is quite the oldest in the college, and it is not unusual for visitors to go over them. Come along, and I will personally conduct you.'

'No names, please!' said Holmes, as we knocked at Gilchrist's door. A tall, flaxen-haired, slim young fellow opened it, and made us welcome when he understood our errand. There were some really curious pieces of medieval domestic architecture within. Holmes was so charmed with one of them that he insisted on drawing it on his notebook, broke his pencil, had to borrow one from our host, and finally borrowed a knife to sharpen his own. The same curious accident happened to him in the rooms of the Indian—a silent, little, hook-nosed fellow, who eyed us askance and was obviously glad when Holmes's architectural studies had come to an end. I could not see that in either case Holmes had come upon the clue for which he was searching. Only at the third did our visit prove abortive. The outer door would not open to our knock, and nothing more substantial than a torrent of bad language came from behind it. 'I don't care who you are. You can go to blazes!' roared the angry voice. 'To-morrow's the exam, and I won't be drawn by anyone.'

'A rude fellow,' said our guide, flushing with anger as we withdrew down the stair. 'Of course, he did not realize that it was I who was knocking, but none the less his conduct was very uncourteous, and, indeed, under the circumstances, rather suspicious.'

Holmes's response was a curious one.

'Can you tell me his exact height?' he asked.

'Really, Mr Holmes, I cannot undertake to say. He is taller than the Indian, not so tall as Gilchrist. I suppose five foot six would be about it.'

'That is very important,' said Holmes. 'And now, Mr Soames, I wish you good-night.'

Our guide cried aloud in his astonishment and dismay. 'Good gracious, Mr Holmes, you are surely not going to leave me in this abrupt fashion! You don't seem to realize the position. To-morrow is the examination. I must take some definite action tonight. I cannot allow the examination to be held if one of the papers has been tampered with. The situation must be faced.'

'You must leave it as it is. I shall drop round early to-morrow morning and chat the matter over. It is possible that I may be in a position then to indicate some course of action. Meanwhile you change nothing—nothing at all.'

'Very good, Mr Holmes.'

'You can be perfectly easy in your mind. We shall certainly find some way out of your difficulties. I will take the black clay with me, also the pencil cuttings. Good-bye.'

When we were out in the darkness of the quadrangle we again looked up at the windows. The Indian still paced his room. The others were invisible.

'Well, Watson, what do you think of it?' Holmes asked as we came out into the main street. 'Quite a little parlour game—sort of three-card trick,* is it not? There are your three men. It must be one of them. You take your choice. Which is yours?'

'The foul-mouthed fellow at the top. He is the one with the worst record. And yet that Indian was a sly fellow also. Why should he be pacing his room all the time?'

'There is nothing in that. Many men do it when they are trying to learn anything by heart.'

'He looked at us in a queer way.'

'So would you if a flock of strangers came in on you when you were preparing for an examination next day, and every moment was of value. No, I see nothing in that. Pencils, too, and knives—all was satisfactory. But that fellow *does* puzzle me.'

'Who?'

'Why, Bannister, the servant. What's his game in the matter?'

'He impressed me as being a perfectly honest man.'

'So he did me. That's the puzzling part. Why should a perfectly honest man—well, well, here's a large stationer's. We shall begin our researches here.'

There were only four stationers of any consequence in the town, and at each Holmes produced his pencil chips and bid high for a duplicate. All were agreed that one could be ordered, but that it was not a usual size of pencil, and that it was seldom kept in stock. My friend did not appear to be depressed by his failure, but shrugged his shoulders in half-humorous resignation.

'No good, my dear Watson. This, the best and only final clue, has run to nothing. But, indeed, I have little doubt that we can build up a sufficient case without it. By Jove! my dear fellow, it is nearly nine, and the landlady babbled of green peas at seven-thirty.* What with your eternal tobacco, Watson, and your irregularity at meals, I expect that you will get notice to quit, and that I shall share your downfall— not, however, before we have solved the problem of the nervous tutor, the careless servant, and the three enterprising students.'

Holmes made no further allusion to the matter that day, though he sat lost in thought for a long time after our belated dinner. At eight in the morning he came into my room just as I finished my toilet.

'Well, Watson,' said he, 'it is time we went down to St Luke's. Can you do without breakfast?'

'Certainly.'

'Soames will be in a dreadful fidget until we are able to tell him something positive.'

'Have you anything positive to tell him?'

'I think so.'

'You have formed a conclusion?'

'Yes, my dear Watson; I have solved the mystery.'

'But what fresh evidence could you have got?'

'Aha! It is not for nothing that I have turned myself out of bed at the untimely hour of six. I have put in two hours' hard work and covered at least five miles,* with something to show for it. Look at that!'

He held out his hand. On the palm were three little pyramids of black, doughy clay.*

'Why, Holmes, you had only two yesterday!'

'And one more this morning. It is a fair argument, that wherever No. 3 came from is also the source of Nos. 1 and 2. Eh, Watson? Well, come along and put friend Soames out of his pain.'

The unfortunate tutor was certainly in a state of pitiable agitation when we found him in his chambers. In a few hours the examinations would commence and he was still in the dilemma between making the facts public and allowing the culprit to compete for the valuable scholarship. He could hardly stand still, so great was his mental agitation, and he ran towards Holmes with two eager hands outstretched.

'Thank God* that you have come! I feared that you had given it up in despair. What am I to do? Shall the examination proceed?'

'Yes; let it proceed by all means.'

'But this rascal—?'

'He shall not compete.'

'You know him?'

'I think so. If this matter is not to become public we must give ourselves certain powers, and resolve ourselves into a small private court-martial. You there, if you please,

Soames! Watson, you here! I'll take the arm-chair in the middle. I think that we are now sufficiently imposing to strike terror into a guilty breast. Kindly ring the bell!'

Bannister entered, and shrank back in evident surprise and fear at our judicial appearance.

'You will kindly close the door,' said Holmes. 'Now, Bannister, will you please tell us the truth about yesterday's incident?'

The man turned white to the roots of his hair.

'I have told you everything, sir.'

'Nothing to add?'

'Nothing at all, sir.'

'Well, then, I must make some suggestions to you. When you sat down on that chair yesterday, did you do so in order to conceal some object which would have shown who had been in the room?'

Bannister's face was ghastly.

'No, sir; certainly not.'

'It is only a suggestion,' said Holmes, suavely. 'I frankly admit that I am unable to prove it. But it seems probable enough, since the moment that Mr Soames's back was turned you released the man who was hiding in that bedroom.'

Bannister licked his dry lips.

'There was no man, sir.'

'Ah, that's a pity, Bannister. Up to now you may have spoken the truth, but now I know that you have lied.'

The man's face set in sullen defiance.

'There was no man, sir.'

'Come, come, Bannister.'

'No, sir; there was no one.'

'In that case you can give us no further information. Would you please remain in the room? Stand over there near the bedroom door. Now, Soames, I am going to ask you to have the great kindness to go up to the room of young Gilchrist, and to ask him to step down into yours.'

An instant later the tutor returned, bringing with him the student. He was a fine figure of a man, tall, lithe, and agile, with a springy step and a pleasant, open face. His troubled blue eyes glanced at each of us, and finally rested with an expression of blank dismay upon Bannister in the farther corner.

'Just close the door,' said Holmes. 'Now, Mr Gilchrist, we are all quite alone here, and no one need ever know one word of what passes between us. We can be perfectly frank with each other. We want to know, Mr Gilchrist, how you, an honourable man, ever came to commit such an action as that of yesterday?'

The unfortunate young man staggered back, and cast a look full of horror and reproach at Bannister.

'No, no, Mr Gilchrist, sir; I never said a word—never one word!' cried the servant.

'No, but you have now,' said Holmes. 'Now, sir, you must see that after Bannister's words your position is hopeless, and that your only chance lies in a frank confession.'

For a moment Gilchrist, with upraised hand, tried to control his writhing features. The next he had thrown himself on his knees beside the table, and, burying his face in his hands, he burst into a storm of passionate sobbing.

'Come, come,' said Holmes kindly; 'it is human to err,* and at least no one can accuse you of being a callous criminal. Perhaps it would be easier for you if I were to tell Mr Soames what occurred, and you can check me where I am wrong. Shall I do so? Well, well, don't trouble to answer. Listen, and see that I do you no injustice.

'From the moment, Mr Soames, that you said to me that no one, not even Bannister, could have told that the papers were in your room, the case began to take a definite shape in my mind. The printer one could, of course, dismiss. He could examine the papers in his own office. The Indian I also thought nothing of. If the proofs were in the roll he could not possibly know what they were. On the other hand, it seemed an unthinkable coincidence that a man should dare to enter the room, and that by chance on that very day the papers were on the table. I dismissed that. The man who entered knew that the papers were there. How did he know?

'When I approached your room I examined the window. You amused me by supposing that I was contemplating the possibility of someone having in broad daylight, under the eyes of all these opposite rooms, forced himself through it. Such an idea was absurd. I was measuring how tall a man would need to be in order to see as he passed what papers were on the central table. I am six feet high, and I could do it with an effort. No one less than that would have a chance. Already, you see, I had reason to think that if one of your three students was a man of unusual height he was the most worth watching of the three.

'I entered, and I took you into my confidence as to the suggestions of the side-table. Of the centre table I could make nothing, until in your description of Gilchrist you mentioned that he was a long-distance jumper. Then the whole thing came to me in an instant, and I only needed certain corroborative proofs, which I speedily obtained.

'What happened was this. This young fellow had employed his afternoon at the athletic grounds, where he had been practising the jump. He returned carrying his jumping-shoes, which are provided, as you are aware, with several* spikes. As he passed your window he saw, by means of his great height, these proofs upon your table, and conjectured what they were. No harm would have been done had it not been that as he passed your door he perceived the key which had been left by the carelessness of your servant. A sudden impulse came over him to enter and see if they were indeed the proofs. It was not a dangerous exploit, for he could always pretend that he had simply looked in to ask a question.

'Well, when he saw that they were indeed the proofs, it was then that he yielded to temptation. He put his shoes on the table. What was it you put on that chair near the window?'

'Gloves,' said the young man.

Holmes looked triumphantly at Bannister.

'He put his gloves on the chair, and he took the proofs, sheet by sheet, to copy them. He thought the tutor must return by the main gate, and that he would see him. As we know, he came back by the side gate. Suddenly he heard him at the very door. There was no possible escape. He forgot his gloves, but he caught up his shoes and darted into the bedroom. You observe that the scratch on that table is slight at one side, but deepens in the direction of the bedroom door. That in itself is enough to show us that the shoes had been drawn in that direction, and that the culprit had taken refuge there. The earth round the spike had been left on the table, and a second sample was loosened and fell in the bedroom. I may add that I walked out to the athletic grounds this morning, saw that tenacious black clay is used in the jumping-pit, and carried away a specimen of it, together with some of the fine tan* or sawdust which is strewn over it to prevent the athlete from slipping. Have I told the truth, Mr Gilchrist?'

The student had drawn himself erect.

'Yes, sir, it is true,' said he.

'Good God,* have you nothing to add?' cried Soames.

'Yes, sir, I have, but the shock of this disgraceful exposure has bewildered me. I have a letter here, Mr Soames, which I wrote to you early this morning in the middle of a restless night. It was before I knew that my sin had found me out.* Here it is, sir. You will see that I have said, "I have determined not to go in for the examination. I have been offered a commission in the Rhodesian Police,* and I am going out to South Africa at once." '

'I am indeed pleased to hear that you did not intend to profit by your unfair advantage,' said Soames. 'But why did you change your purpose?'

Gilchrist pointed to Bannister.

'There is the man who sent me in the right path,' said he.

'Come now, Bannister,' said Holmes. 'It will be clear to you from what I have said that only you could have let this young man out, since you were left in the room and must have locked the door when you went out. As to his escaping by that window, it was incredible. Can you not clear up the last point in this mystery, and tell us the reason for your action?'

'It was simple enough, sir, if you had only known; but with all your cleverness it was impossible that you could know. Time was, sir, when I was butler to old Sir Jabez Gilchrist, this young gentleman's father. When he was ruined I came to the college as servant, but I never forgot my old employer because he was down in the world. I watched his son all I could for the sake of the old days. Well, sir, when I came into this room yesterday when the alarm was given, the first thing I saw was Mr Gilchrist's tan gloves* a-lying in that chair. I knew those gloves well, and I understood their message. If Mr Soames saw them the game was up. I flopped down into that chair, and nothing would budge me until Mr Soames he went for you.* Then out came my poor young master, whom I had dandled on my knee, and confessed it all to me. Wasn't it natural, sir, that I should save him, and wasn't it natural also that I should try to speak to him as his dead father would have done, and make him understand that he could not profit by such a deed? Could you blame me, sir?'

'No, indeed!' said Holmes heartily, springing to his feet. 'Well, Soames, I think we have cleared your little problem up, and our breakfast awaits us at home. Come, Watson! As to you, sir, I trust that a bright future awaits you in Rhodesia. For once you have fallen low. Let us see in the future how high you can rise.'

The Golden Pince-Nez

WHEN I look at the three massive manuscript volumes which contain our work for the year 1894 I confess that it is very difficult for me, out of such a wealth of material, to select the cases which are most interesting in themselves and at the same time most conducive to a display of those peculiar powers for which my friend was famous. As I turn over the pages I see my notes upon the repulsive story of the red leech and the terrible death of Crosby the banker.* Here also I find an account of the Addleton tragedy and the singular contents of the ancient British barrow.* The famous Smith-Mortimer succession case* comes also within this period, and so does the tracking and arrest of Huret, the Boulevard assassin*—an exploit which won for Holmes an autograph letter of thanks from the French President* and the Order of the Legion of Honour.* Each of these would furnish a narrative, but on the whole I am of opinion that none of them unite so many singular points of interest as the episode of Yoxley Old Place,* which includes, not only the lamentable death of young Willoughby Smith, but also those subsequent developments which threw so curious a light upon the causes of the crime.

It was a wild, tempestuous night towards the close of November. Holmes and I sat together in silence all the evening, he engaged with a powerful lens deciphering the remains of the original inscription upon a palimpsest,* I deep in a recent treatise upon surgery. Outside the wind howled down Baker Street, while the rain beat fiercely against the windows. It was strange there in the very depths of the town, with ten miles of man's handiwork on every side of us, to feel the iron grip of Nature, and to be conscious that to the huge elemental forces all London was no more than the molehills that dot the fields. I walked to the window and looked out on the deserted street. The occasional lamps gleamed on the expanse of muddy road and shining pavement. A single cab was splashing its way from the Oxford Street end.

'Well, Watson, it's as well we have not to turn out to-night,' said Holmes, laying aside his lens and rolling up the palimpsest. 'I've done enough for one sitting. It is trying work for the eyes. So far as I can make out, it is nothing more exciting than an Abbey's accounts dating from the second half of the fifteenth century. Hullo! hullo! hullo! What's this?'

Amid the droning of the wind there had come the stamping of a horse's hoofs and the long grind of a wheel as it rasped against the kerb. The cab which I had seen had pulled up at our door.

'What can he want?' I ejaculated, as a man stepped out of it.

'Want! He wants us. And we, my poor Watson, want overcoats and cravats and goloshes,* and every aid that man ever invented to fight the weather. Wait a bit, though! There's the cab off again! There's hope yet. He'd have kept it if he had wanted us to come. Run down, my dear fellow, and open the door, for all virtuous folk have been long in bed.'

When the light of the hall lamp fell upon our midnight visitor, I had no difficulty in recognizing him. It was young Stanley Hopkins, a promising detective, in whose career Holmes had several times shown a very practical interest.

'Is he in?' he asked eagerly.

'Come up, my dear sir,' said Holmes's voice from above. 'I hope you have no designs upon us on such a night as this.'

The detective mounted the stairs, and our lamp gleamed upon his shining waterproof. I helped him out of it, while Holmes knocked a blaze out of the logs in the grate.

'Now, my dear Hopkins, draw up and warm your toes,' said he. 'Here's a cigar, and the doctor has a prescription containing hot water and a lemon which is good medicine on a night like this. It must be something important which has brought you out in such a gale.'

'It is indeed, Mr Holmes. I've had a bustling afternoon, I promise you. Did you see anything of the Yoxley case in the latest editions?'

'I've seen nothing later than the fifteenth century to-day.'

'Well, it was only a paragraph, and all wrong at that, so you have not missed anything. I haven't let the grass grow under my feet. It's down in Kent, seven miles from Chatham and three from the railway line.* I was wired for at three-fifteen, reached Yoxley Old Place at five, conducted my investigation, was back at Charing Cross by the last train and straight to you by cab.'

'Which means, I suppose, that you are not quite clear about your case?'

'It means that I can make neither head nor tail of it. So far as I can see, it is just as tangled a business as ever I handled, and yet at first it seemed so simple that one couldn't go wrong. There's no motive, Mr Holmes. That's what bothers me—I can't put my hand on a motive. Here's a man dead—there's no denying that—but, so far as I can see, no reason on earth why anyone should wish him harm.'

Holmes lit his cigar and leaned back in his chair.

'Let us hear about it,' said he.

'I've got my facts pretty clear,' said Stanley Hopkins. 'All I want now is to know what they all mean. The story, so far as I can make it out, is like this. Some years ago this country house, Yoxley Old Place, was taken by an elderly man, who gave the name of Professor Coram.* He was an invalid, keeping his bed half the time, and the other half hobbling round the house with a stick, or being pushed about the grounds by the gardener in a bath-chair. He was well liked by the few neighbours who called upon him, and he has the reputation down there of being a very learned man. His household used to consist of an elderly housekeeper, Mrs Marker, and of a maid, Susan Tarlton. These have both been with him since his arrival, and they seem to be women of excellent character. The professor is writing a learned book, and he found it necessary about a year ago to engage a secretary. The first two that he tried were not successes;

but the third, Mr Willoughby Smith, a very young man straight from the University, seems to have been just what his employer wanted. His work consisted in writing all the morning to the Professor's dictation, and he usually spent the evening in hunting up references and passages which bore upon the next day's work. This Willoughby Smith has nothing against him either as a boy at Uppingham* or as a young man at Cambridge. I have seen his testimonials, and from the first he was a decent, quiet, hard-working fellow, with no weak spot in him at all. And yet this is the lad who has met his death this morning in the Professor's study under circumstances which can point only to murder.'

The wind howled and screamed at the windows. Holmes and I drew closer to the fire while the young inspector slowly and point by point developed his singular narrative.

'If you were to search all England,' said he, 'I don't suppose you could find a household more self-contained or free from outside influences. Whole weeks would pass and not one of them go past the garden gate. The Professor was buried in his work and existed for nothing else. Young Smith knew nobody in the neighbourhood, and lived very much as his employer did. The two women had nothing to take them from the house. Mortimer, the gardener, who wheels the bath-chair, is an Army pensioner—an old Crimean man of excellent character.* He does not live in the house, but in a three-roomed cottage at the other end of the garden. Those are the only people that you would find within the grounds of Yoxley Old Place. At the same time, the gate of the garden is a hundred yards from the main London to Chatham road. It opens with a latch, and there is nothing to prevent anyone from walking in.

'Now I will give you the evidence of Susan Tarlton, who is the only person who can say anything positive about the matter. It was in the forenoon, between eleven and twelve. She was engaged at the moment in hanging some curtains in the upstairs front bedroom. Professor Coram was still in bed, for when the weather is bad he seldom rises before midday. The housekeeper was busied with some work in the back of the house. Willoughby Smith had been in his bedroom, which he uses as a sitting-room; but the maid heard him at that moment pass along the passage and descend to the study immediately below her. She did not see him, but she says that she could not be mistaken in his quick, firm tread. She did not hear the study door close, but a minute or so later there was a dreadful cry in the room below. It was a wild, hoarse scream, so strange and unnatural that it might have come either from a man or a woman. At the same instant there was a heavy thud, which shook the whole house, and then all was silence. The maid stood petrified for a moment, and then, recovering her courage, she ran downstairs. The study door was shut, and she opened it. Inside young Mr Willoughby Smith was stretched upon the floor. At first she could see no injury, but as she tried to raise him she saw that blood was pouring from the under side of his neck. It was pierced by a very small but very deep wound, which had divided the carotid artery.* The instrument with which the injury had been inflicted lay upon the carpet beside him. It was one of those small sealing-wax knives* to be found on old-fashioned writing-tables, with an ivory handle and a stiff blade. It was part of the fittings of the Professor's own desk.

'At first the maid thought that young Smith was already dead, but on pouring some water from the carafe over his forehead, he opened his eyes for an instant. "The Professor," he murmured—"it was she." The maid is prepared to swear that those were the exact words. He tried desperately to say something else, and he held his right hand up in the air. Then he fell back dead.

'In the meantime the housekeeper had also arrived upon the scene, but she was just too late to catch the young man's dying words. Leaving Susan with the body, she hurried to the Professor's room. He was sitting up in bed, horribly agitated, for he had heard enough to convince him that something terrible had occurred. Mrs Marker is prepared to swear that the Professor was still in his night-clothes, and, indeed, it was impossible for him to dress without the help of Mortimer, whose orders were to come at twelve o'clock. The Professor declares that he heard the distant cry, but that he knows nothing more. He can give no explanation of the young man's last words, "The Professor—it was she," but imagines that they were the outcome of delirium. He believes that Willoughby Smith had not an enemy in the world, and can give no reason for the crime. His first action was to send Mortimer, the gardener, for the local police. A little later the chief constable sent for me. Nothing was moved before I got there, and strict orders were given that no one should walk upon the paths leading to the house. It was a splendid chance of putting your theories into practice, Mr Sherlock Holmes. There was really nothing wanting.'

'Except Mr Sherlock Holmes!' said my companion, with a somewhat bitter smile. 'Well, let us hear about it. What sort of job did you make of it?'

'I must ask you first, Mr Holmes, to glance at this rough plan,* which will give you a general idea of the position of the Professor's study and the various points of the case. It will help you in following my investigations.'

He unfolded the rough chart, which I here reproduce, and he laid it across Holmes's knee. I rose, and, standing behind Holmes, I studied it over his shoulder.

'It is very rough, of course, and it only deals with the points which seem to me to be essential. All the rest you will see later for yourself. Now, first of all, presuming that the assassin entered the house, how did he or she come in? Undoubtedly by the garden path and the back door, from which there is direct access to the study. Any other way would have been exceedingly complicated. The escape must also have been made along that line, for of the two other exits from the room one was blocked by Susan as she ran downstairs, and the other leads straight to the Professor's bedroom. I therefore directed my attention at once to the garden path, which was saturated with recent rain and would certainly show any footmarks.

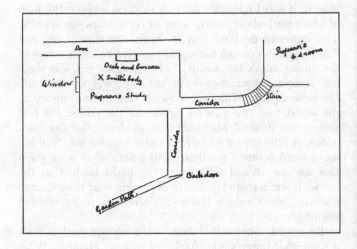

'My examination showed me that I was dealing with a cautious and expert criminal. No footmarks were to be found on the path. There could be no question, however, that someone had passed along the grass border which lines the path, and that he had done so in order to avoid leaving a track. I could not find anything in the nature of a distinct impression, but the grass was trodden down and someone had undoubtedly passed. It could only have been the murderer, since neither the gardener nor anyone else had been there that morning, and the rain had only begun during the night.'

'One moment,' said Holmes. 'Where does this path lead to?'

'To the road.'

'How long is it?'

'A hundred yards or so.'

'At the point where the path passes through the gate you could surely pick up the tracks?'

'Unfortunately the path was tiled at that point.'

'Well, on the road itself?'

224

'No; it was all trodden into mire.'

'Tut! tut! Well, then, these tracks upon the grass, were they coming or going?'

'It was impossible to say. There was never any outline.'

'A large foot or a small?'

'You could not distinguish.'

Holmes gave an ejaculation of impatience. 'It has been pouring rain and blowing a hurricane ever since,' said he. 'It will be harder to read now than that palimpsest. Well, well, it can't be helped. What did you do, Hopkins, after you had made certain that you had made certain of nothing?'

'I think I made certain of a good deal, Mr Holmes. I knew that someone had entered the house cautiously from without. I next examined the corridor. It is lined with coconut matting, and had taken no impression of any kind. This brought me into the study itself. It is a scantily furnished room. The main article is a large writing-table with a fixed bureau. This bureau consists of a double column of drawers with a central small cupboard between them. The drawers were open, the cupboard locked. The drawers, it seems, were always open, and nothing of value was kept in them. There were some papers of importance in the cupboard, but there were no signs that this had been tampered with, and the professor assures me that nothing was missing. It is certain that no robbery had been committed.

'I come now to the body of the young man. It was found near the bureau, and just to the left of it, as marked upon that chart. The stab was on the right side of the neck and from behind forwards, so that it is almost impossible that it could have been self-inflicted.'

'Unless he fell upon the knife,' said Holmes.

'Exactly. The idea crossed my mind. But we found the knife some feet away from the body, so that seems impossible. Then, of course, there are the man's own dying words. And, finally, there was this very important piece of evidence which was found clasped in the dead man's right hand.'

From his pocket Stanley Hopkins drew a small paper packet. He unfolded it, and disclosed a golden pince-nez, with two broken ends of black silk cord dangling from the end of it. 'Willoughby Smith had excellent sight,' he added. 'There can be no question that this was snatched from the face or the person of the assassin.'

Sherlock Holmes took the glasses into his hand and examined them with the utmost attention and interest. He held them on his nose, endeavoured to read through them, went to the window and stared up the street with them, looked at them most minutely in the full light of the lamp, and finally, with a chuckle, seated himself at the table and wrote a few lines upon a sheet of paper, which he tossed across to Stanley Hopkins.

'That's the best I can do for you,' said he. 'It may prove to be of some use.'

The astonished detective read the note aloud. It ran as follows:

Wanted, a woman of good address, attired like a lady. She has a remarkably thick nose, with eyes which are set close upon either side of it. She has a puckered forehead, a peering expression and probably rounded shoulders. There are indications that she has had recourse to an optician at least twice during the last few months. As her glasses are of remarkable strength, and as opticians are not very numerous, there should be no difficulty in tracing her.

Holmes smiled at the astonishment of Hopkins, which must have been reflected upon my features.

'Surely my deductions are simplicity itself,' said he. 'It would be difficult to name any articles which afford a finer field for inference than a pair of glasses, especially so remarkable a pair as these. That they belong to a woman I infer from their delicacy, and also, of course, from the last words of the dying man. As to her being a person of refinement and well dressed, they are, as you perceive, handsomely mounted in solid gold, and it is inconceivable that anyone who wore such glasses could be slatternly in other respects. You will find that the clips are too wide for your nose, showing that the lady's nose was very broad at the base. This sort of nose is usually a short and coarse one, but there are a sufficient number of exceptions to prevent me from being dogmatic or from insisting upon this point in my description. My own face is a narrow one, and yet I find that I cannot get my eyes into the centre, or near the centre, of these glasses. Therefore, the lady's eyes are set very near to the sides of the nose. You will perceive, Watson, that the glasses are concave and of unusual strength.* A lady whose vision has been so extremely contracted all her life is sure to have the physical characteristics of such vision, which are seen in the forehead, the eyelids, and the shoulders.'

'Yes,' I said, 'I can follow each of your arguments. I confess, however, that I am unable to understand how you arrive at the double visit to the optician.'

Holmes took the glasses into his hand.

'You will perceive,' he said, 'that the clips are lined with tiny bands of cork to soften the pressure upon the nose. One of these is discoloured and worn to some slight extent, but the other is new. Evidently one has fallen off and been replaced. I should judge that the older of them has not been there more than a few months. They exactly correspond, so I gather that the lady went back to the same establishment for the second.'

'By George, it's marvellous!' cried Hopkins, in an ecstasy of admiration. 'To think that I had all that evidence in my hand and never knew it! I had intended, however, to go the round of the London opticians.'

'Of course you would. Meanwhile, have you anything more to tell us about the case?'

'Nothing, Mr Holmes. I think that you know as much as I do now—probably more. We have had inquiries made as to any stranger seen on the country roads or at the railway station. We have heard of none. What beats me is the utter want of all object in the crime. Not a ghost of a motive can anyone suggest.'

'Ah! there I am not in a position to help you. But I suppose you want us to come out to-morrow?'

'If it is not asking too much, Mr Holmes. There's a train from Charing Cross to Chatham at six in the morning, and we should be at Yoxley Old Place between eight and nine.'

'Then we shall take it. Your case has certainly some features of great interest, and I shall be delighted to look into it. Well, it's nearly one, and we had best get a few hours' sleep. I dare say you can manage all right on the sofa in front of the fire. I'll light my spirit-lamp and give you a cup of coffee before we start.'

The gale had blown itself out next day, but it was a bitter morning when we started upon our journey. We saw the cold winter sun rise over the dreary marshes of the Thames and the long, sullen reaches of the river, which I shall ever associate with our pursuit of the Andaman Islander* in the earlier days of our career. After a long and weary journey we alighted at a small station some miles from Chatham.* While a horse was being put into a trap at the local inn we snatched a hurried breakfast and so we were all ready for business when we at last arrived at Yoxley Old Place. A constable met us at the garden gate.

'Well, Wilson, any news?'

'No, sir, nothing.'

'No reports of any stranger seen?'

'No, sir. Down at the station they are certain that no stranger either came or went yesterday.'

'Have you had inquiries made at inns and lodgings?'

'Yes, sir; there is no one that we cannot account for.'

'Well, it's only a reasonable walk to Chatham. Anyone might stay there, or take a train without being observed. This is the garden path of which I spoke, Mr Holmes. I'll pledge my word there was no mark on it yesterday.'

'On which side were the marks on the grass?'

'This side, sir. This narrow margin of grass between the path and the flower-bed. I can't see the traces now, but they were clear to me then.'

'Yes, yes; someone has passed along,' said Holmes, stooping over the grass border. 'Our lady must have picked her steps carefully, must she not, since on the one side she would leave a track on the path, and on the other an even clearer one on the soft bed?'

'Yes, sir, she must have been a cool hand.'

I saw an intent look pass over Holmes's face.

'You say that she must have come back this way?'

'Yes, sir; there is no other.'

'On this strip of grass?'

'Certainly, Mr Holmes.'

'Hum! It was a very remarkable performance—very remarkable. Well, I think we have exhausted the path. Let us go farther. This garden door is usually kept open, I suppose? Then this visitor had nothing to do but to walk in. The idea of murder was not in her mind, or she would have provided herself with some sort of weapon, instead of having to pick this knife off the writing-table. She advanced along this corridor, leaving no traces upon the coconut matting. Then she found herself in this study. How long was she there? We have no means of judging.'

'Not more than a few minutes, sir. I forgot to tell you that Mrs Marker, the housekeeper, had been in there tidying not very long before—about a quarter of an hour she says.'

'Well, that gives us a limit. Our lady enters this room, and what does she do? She goes over to the writing-table. What for? Not for anything in the drawers. If there had been anything worth her taking it would surely have been locked up. No; it was for something in that wooden bureau. Hullo! what is that scratch upon the face of it? Just hold a match, Watson. Why did you not tell me of this, Hopkins?'

The mark which he was examining began upon the brass work on the right-hand side of the keyhole, and extended for about four inches, where it had scratched the varnish from the surface.

'I noticed it, Mr Holmes. But you'll always find scratches round a keyhole.'

'This is recent—quite recent. See how the brass shines where it is cut. An old scratch would be the same colour as the surface. Look at it through my lens. There's the varnish, too, like earth on each side of a furrow. Is Mrs Marker there?'

A sad-faced, elderly woman came into the room.

'Did you dust this bureau yesterday morning?'

'Yes, sir.'

'Did you notice this scratch?'

'No, sir, I did not.'

'I am sure you did not, for a duster would have swept away these shreds of varnish. Who has the key of this bureau?'

'The professor keeps it on his watch-chain.'

'Is it a simple key?'

'No, sir; it is a Chubb's key.'*

'Very good. Mrs Marker, you can go. Now we are making a little progress. Our lady enters the room, advances to the bureau, and either opens it or tries to do so. While she is thus engaged young Willoughby Smith enters the room. In her hurry to withdraw the key she makes this scratch upon the door. He seizes her, and she, snatching up the nearest object, which happens to be this knife, strikes at him in order to make him let go his hold. The blow is a fatal one. He falls and she escapes, either with or without the object for which she has come. Is Susan the maid there? Could anyone have got away through that door after the time that you heard the cry, Susan?'

'No, sir; it is impossible. Before I got down the stair I'd have seen anyone in the passage. Besides, the door never opened, for I would have heard it.'

'That settles this exit. Then no doubt the lady went out the way she came. I understand that this other passage leads only to the Professor's room. There is no exit that way?'

'No, sir.'

'We shall go down it and make the acquaintance of the professor. Hullo, Hopkins! this is very important, very important indeed. The professor's corridor is also lined with coconut matting.'

'Well, sir, what of that?'

'Don't you see any bearing upon the case? Well, well, I don't insist upon it. No doubt I am wrong. And yet it seems to me to be suggestive. Come with me and introduce me.'

We passed down the passage, which was of the same length as that which led to the garden. At the end was a short flight of steps ending in a door. Our guide knocked, and then ushered us into the Professor's bedroom.

It was a very large chamber, lined with innumerable volumes, which had overflowed from the shelves and lay in piles in the corners, or were stacked all round at the base of the cases. The bed was in the centre of the room, and in it, propped up with pillows, was the owner of the house. I have seldom seen a more remarkable-looking person. It was a gaunt, aquiline face which was turned towards us, with piercing dark eyes, which lurked in deep hollows under overhung and tufted brows. His hair and beard were white, save that the latter was curiously stained with yellow around his mouth. A cigarette glowed amid the tangle of white hair, and the air of the room was fetid with stale tobacco smoke. As he held out his hand to Holmes I perceived that it also was stained yellow with nicotine.

'A smoker, Mr Holmes?' said he, speaking well-chosen English with a curious little mincing accent. 'Pray take a cigarette. And you, sir? I can recommend them, for I have them especially prepared by Ionides of Alexandria.* He sends me a thousand at a time, and I grieve to say that I have to arrange for a fresh supply every fortnight. Bad, sir, very bad; but an old man has few pleasures. Tobacco and my work—that is all that is left to me.'

Holmes had lit a cigarette, and was shooting little darting glances all over the room.

'Tobacco and my work, but now only tobacco,' the old man exclaimed. 'Alas! what a fatal interruption! Who could have foreseen such a terrible catastrophe? So estimable a young man! I assure you that after a few months' training he was an admirable assistant. What do you think of the matter, Mr Holmes?'

'I have not yet made up my mind.'

'I shall indeed be indebted to you if you can throw a light where all is so dark to us. To a poor bookworm and invalid like myself such a blow is paralysing. I seem to have lost the faculty of thought. But you're a man of action—you are a man of affairs. It is part of the everyday routine of your life. You can preserve your balance in every emergency. We are fortunate indeed in having you at our side.'

Holmes was pacing up and down on one side of the room whilst the old Professor was talking. I observed that he was smoking with extraordinary rapidity. It was evident that he shared our host's liking for the fresh Alexandrian cigarettes.

'Yes, sir, it is a crushing blow,' said the old man. 'That is my *magnum opus**—the pile of papers on the side-table yonder. It is my analysis of the documents found in the Coptic monasteries of Syria and Egypt,* a work which will cut deep at the very foundation of revealed religion.* With my enfeebled health I do not know whether I shall ever be able to complete it now that my assistant has been taken from me. Dear me, Mr Holmes; why, you are even a quicker smoker than I am myself.'

Holmes smiled.

'I am a connoisseur,' said he, taking another cigarette from the box—his fourth—and lighting it from the stub of that which he had finished. 'I will not trouble you with any lengthy cross-examination, Professor Coram, since I gather that you were in bed at the time of the crime and could know nothing about it. I would only ask this—What do you imagine that this poor fellow meant by his last words; "The Professor—it was she"?'

The Professor shook his head.

'Susan is a country girl,' said he, 'and you know the incredible stupidity of that class. I fancy that the poor fellow murmured some incoherent, delirious words, and that she twisted them into this meaningless message.'

'I see. You have no explanation yourself of the tragedy?'

'Possibly an accident; possibly—I only breathe it among ourselves—a suicide. Young men have their hidden troubles—some affair of the heart, perhaps, which we have never known. It is a more probable supposition than murder.'

'But the eye-glasses?'

'Ah! I am only a student—a man of dreams. I cannot explain the practical things of life. But still, we are aware, my friend, that love-gages* may take strange shapes. By all means take another cigarette. It is a pleasure to see anyone appreciate them so. A fan, a glove, glasses—who knows what article may be carried as a token or treasured when a man puts an end to his life? This gentleman speaks of footsteps in the grass; but, after all, it is easy to be mistaken on such a point. As to the knife, it might well be thrown far from the unfortunate man as he fell. It is possible that I speak as a child, but to me it seems that Willoughby Smith has met his fate by his own hand.'

Holmes seemed struck by the theory thus put forward, and he continued to walk up and down for some time, lost in thought and consuming cigarette after cigarette.

'Tell me, Professor Coram,' he said at last, 'what is in that cupboard in the bureau?'

'Nothing that would help a thief. Family papers, letters from my poor wife, diplomas of Universities which have done me honour.* Here is the key. You can look for yourself.'

Holmes picked up the key and looked at it for an instant; then he handed it back.

'No; I hardly think that it would help me,' said he. 'I should prefer to go quietly down to your garden and turn the whole matter over in my head. There is something to be said for the theory of suicide which you have put forward. We must apologize for having intruded upon you, Professor Coram, and I promise that we won't disturb you until after lunch. At two o'clock we will come again and report to you anything which may have happened in the interval.'

Holmes was curiously distrait, and we walked up and down the garden path for some time in silence.

'Have you a clue?' I asked, at last.

'It depends upon those cigarettes that I smoked,' said he. 'It is possible that I am utterly mistaken. The cigarettes will show me.'

'My dear Holmes,' I exclaimed, 'how on earth—'

'Well, well, you may see for yourself. If not, there's no harm done. Of course, we always have the optician clue to fall back upon, but I take a short cut when I can get it. Ah, here is the good Mrs Marker! Let us enjoy five minutes of instructive conversation with her.'

I may have remarked before that Holmes had, when he liked, a peculiarly ingratiating way with women, and that he very readily established terms of confidence with them. In half the time which he had named he had captured the housekeeper's goodwill, and was chatting with her as if he had known her for years.

'Yes, Mr Holmes, it is as you say, sir. He does smoke something terrible. All day and sometimes all night, sir. I've seen that room of a morning—well, sir, you'd have thought it was a London fog. Poor young Mr Smith, he was a smoker also, but not as bad as the Professor. His health—well, I don't know that it's better nor worse for the smoking.'

'Ah,' said Holmes, 'but it kills the appetite.'

'Well, I don't know about that, sir.'

'I suppose the professor eats hardly anything?'

'Well, he is variable. I'll say that for him.'

'I'll wager he took no breakfast this morning, and won't face his lunch after all the cigarettes I saw him consume.'

'Well, you're out there, sir, as it happens, for he ate a remarkable big breakfast this morning. I don't know when I've known him make a better one, and he's ordered a good dish of cutlets for his lunch. I'm surprised myself, for since I came into that room yesterday and saw young Mr Smith lying there on the floor I couldn't bear to look at food. Well, it takes all sorts to make a world, and the Professor hasn't let it take his appetite away.'

We loitered the morning away in the garden. Stanley Hopkins had gone down to the village to look into some rumours of a strange woman who had been seen by some children on the Chatham road the previous morning. As to my friend, all his usual energy seemed to have deserted him. I had never known him handle a case in such a half-hearted fashion. Even the news brought back by Hopkins that he had found the children and that they had undoubtedly seen a woman exactly corresponding with Holmes's description, and wearing either spectacles or eye-glasses, failed to rouse any sign of keen interest. He was more attentive when Susan, who waited upon us at lunch, volunteered the information that she believed Mr Smith had been out for a walk yesterday morning, and that he had only returned half an hour before the tragedy occurred. I could not myself see the bearing of this incident, but I clearly perceived that Holmes was weaving it into the general scheme which he had formed in his brain. Suddenly he sprang from his chair, and glanced at his watch. 'Two o'clock, gentlemen,' said he. 'We must go up and have it out with our friend the Professor.'

The old man had just finished his lunch, and certainly his empty dish bore evidence to the good appetite with which his housekeeper had credited him. He was, indeed, a weird figure as he turned his white mane and his glowing eyes towards us. The eternal cigarette smouldered in his mouth. He had been dressed and was seated in an arm-chair by the fire.

'Well, Mr Holmes, have you solved this mystery yet?' He shoved the large tin of cigarettes which stood on a table beside him towards my companion. Holmes stretched out his hand at the same moment, and between them they tipped the box over the edge. For a minute or two we were all on our knees retrieving stray cigarettes from impossible places. When we rose again I observed that Holmes's eyes were shining and his cheeks tinged with colour. Only at a crisis have I seen those battle-signals flying.

'Yes,' said he, 'I have solved it.'

Stanley Hopkins and I stared in amazement. Something like a sneer quivered over the gaunt features of the old Professor.

'Indeed! In the garden?'

'No, here.'

'Here! When?'

'This instant.'

'You are surely joking, Mr Sherlock Holmes. You compel me to tell you that this is too serious a matter to be treated in such a fashion.'

'I have forged and tested every link of my chain, Professor Coram, and I am sure that it is sound. What your motives are, or what exact part you play in this strange business, I am not yet able to say. In a few minutes I shall probably hear it from your own lips. Meanwhile, I will reconstruct what is past for your benefit, so that you may know the information which I still require.

'A lady yesterday entered your study. She came with the intention of possessing herself of certain documents which were in your bureau. She had a key of her own. I have had an opportunity of examining yours, and I do not find that slight discoloration which the scratch made upon the varnish would have produced. You were not an accessory, therefore, and she came, so far as I can read the evidence, without your knowledge to rob you.'

The Professor blew a cloud from his lips.

'This is most interesting and instructive,' said he. 'Have you no more to add? Surely, having traced this lady so far, you can also say what has become of her.'

'I will endeavour to do so. In the first place, she was seized by your secretary, and stabbed him in order to escape. This catastrophe I am inclined to regard as an unhappy accident, for I am convinced that the lady had no intention of inflicting so grievous an injury. An assassin does not come unarmed. Horrified by what she had done, she rushed wildly away from the scene of the tragedy. Unfortunately for her she had lost her glasses in the scuffle, and as she was extremely short-sighted she was really helpless without them. She ran down a corridor, which she imagined to be that by which she had come—both were lined with coconut matting—and it was only when it was too late that she

understood that she had taken the wrong passage and that
her retreat was cut off behind her. What was she to do? She
could not go back. She could not remain where she was. She
must go on. She went on. She mounted a stair, pushed open
a door, and found herself in your room.'

The old man sat with his mouth open staring wildly at
Holmes. Amazement and fear were stamped upon his expressive features. Now, with an effort, he shrugged his
shoulders and burst into insincere laughter.

'All very fine, Mr Holmes,' said he. 'But there is one little
flaw in a splendid theory. I was myself in my room, and I
never left it during the day.'

'I am aware of that, Professor Coram.'

'And you mean to say that I could lie upon that bed and
not be aware that a woman had entered my room?'

'I never said so. You *were* aware of it. You spoke with her.
You recognized her. You aided her to escape.'

Again the professor burst into high-keyed laughter. He
had risen to his feet, and his eyes glowed like embers.

'You are mad!' he cried. 'You are talking insanely. I
helped her to escape? Where is she now?'

'She is there,' said Holmes, and he pointed to a high
bookcase in the corner of the room.

I saw the old man throw up his arms, a terrible convulsion
passed over his grim face, and he fell back in his chair. At
the same instant the bookcase at which Holmes pointed
swung round upon a hinge, and a woman rushed out into
the room.

'You are right,' she cried, in a strange foreign voice. 'You
are right! I am here.'

She was brown with the dust and draped with the
cobwebs which had come from the walls of her hiding-place.
Her face, too, was streaked with grime, and at the best she
could never have been handsome, for she had the exact
physical characteristics which Holmes had divined, with, in
addition, a long and obstinate chin. What with her natural
blindness, and what with the change from dark to light, she
stood as one dazed, blinking about her to see where and

who we were. And yet, in spite of all these disadvantages, there was a certain nobility in the woman's bearing, a gallantry in the defiant chin and in the upraised head, which compelled something of respect and admiration. Stanley Hopkins had laid his hand upon her arm and claimed her as his prisoner, but she waved him aside gently, and yet with an overmastering dignity which compelled obedience. The old man lay back in his chair, with a twitching face, and stared at her with brooding eyes.

'Yes, sir, I am your prisoner,' she said. 'From where I stood I could hear everything, and I know that you have learned the truth. I confess it all. It was I who killed the young man. But you are right, you who say that it was an accident. I did not even know that it was a knife which I held in my hand, for in my despair I snatched anything from the table and struck at him to make him let me go. It is the truth that I tell.'

'Madame,' said Holmes, 'I am sure that it is the truth. I fear that you are far from well.'

She had turned a dreadful colour, the more ghastly under the dark dust-streaks upon her face. She seated herself on the side of the bed; then she resumed.

'I have only a little time here,' she said, 'but I would have you to know the whole truth. I am this man's wife. He is not an Englishman. He is a Russian. His name I will not tell.'

For the first time the old man stirred. 'God bless you, Anna!' he cried. 'God bless you!'

She cast a look of the deepest disdain in his direction. 'Why should you cling so hard to that wretched life of yours, Sergius?'* said she. 'It has done harm to many and good to none—not even to yourself. However, it is not for me to cause the frail thread to be snapped before God's time. I have enough already upon my soul since I crossed the threshold of this cursed house. But I must speak, or I shall be too late.

'I have said, gentlemen, that I am this man's wife. He was fifty and I a foolish girl of twenty when we married. It was in a city of Russia, a University—I will not name the place.'

238

'God bless you, Anna!' murmured the old man again.

'We were reformers—revolutionists—Nihilists,* you understand. He and I and many more. Then there came a time of trouble,* a police officer was killed,* many were arrested, evidence was wanted, and in order to save his own life and to earn a great reward my husband betrayed his own wife and his companions. Yes; we were all arrested upon his confession. Some of us found our way to the gallows and some to Siberia. I was among these last, but my term was not for life. My husband came to England with his ill-gotten gains, and has lived in quiet ever since, knowing well that if the Brotherhood* knew where he was not a week would pass before justice would be done.'

The old man reached out a trembling hand and helped himself to a cigarette. 'I am in your hands, Anna,' said he. 'You were always good to me.'

'I have not yet told you the height of his villainy!' said she. 'Among our comrades of the Order there was one who was the friend of my heart. He was noble, unselfish, loving—all that my husband was not. He hated violence. We were all guilty—if that is guilt—but he was not. He wrote for ever dissuading me from such a course. These letters would have saved him. So would my diary, in which from day to day I had entered both my feelings towards him and the view which each of us had taken. My husband found and kept both diary and letters. He hid them, and he tried hard to swear away the young man's life. In this he failed, but Alexis was sent a convict to Siberia, where now, at this moment, he works in a salt mine.* Think of that, you villain, you villain; now, now, at this very moment, Alexis, a man whose name you are not worthy to speak, works and lives like a slave, and yet I have your life in my hands and I let you go!'

'You were always a noble woman, Anna,' said the old man, puffing at his cigarette.

She had risen, but she fell back again with a little cry of pain.

'I must finish,' she said. 'When my term was over I set myself to get the diary and letters, which if sent to the

Russian Government, would procure my friend's release. I
knew that my husband had come to England. After months
of searching I discovered where he was. I knew that he still
had the diary, for when I was in Siberia I had a letter from
him once reproaching me and quoting some passages from
its pages. Yet I was sure that with his revengeful nature he
would never give it to me of his own free will. I must get it
for myself. With this object I engaged an agent from a
private detective firm, who entered my husband's house as
secretary—it was your second secretary, Sergius, the one
who left you so hurriedly. He found that papers were kept
in the cupboard, and he got an impression of the key. He
would not go farther. He furnished me with a plan of the
house, and he told me that in the forenoon the study was
always empty, as the secretary was employed up here. So at
last I took my courage in both hands and I came down to
get the papers for myself. I succeeded, but at what a cost!

'I had just taken the papers and was locking the cupboard
when the young man seized me. I had seen him already that
morning. He had met me in the road, and I had asked him
to tell me where Professor Coram lived, not knowing that
he was in his employ.'

'Exactly! exactly!' said Holmes. 'The secretary came back
and told his employer of the woman he had met. Then in
his last breath he tried to send a message that it was
she—the she whom he had just discussed with him.'

'You must let me speak,' said the woman, in an imperative
voice, and her face contracted as if in pain. 'When he had
fallen I rushed from the room, chose the wrong door, and
found myself in my husband's room. He spoke of giving me
up. I showed him that if he did so his life was in my hands.
If he gave me to the law I could give him to the Brotherhood. It was not that I wished to live for my own sake, but
it was that I desired to accomplish my purpose. He knew
that I would do what I said—that his own fate was involved
in mine. For that reason, and for no other, he shielded me.
He thrust me into that dark hiding-place, a relic of old days,
known only to himself. He took his meals in his own room,

and so was able to give me part of his food. It was agreed that when the police left the house I should slip away by night and come back no more. But in some way you have read our plans.' She tore from the bosom of her dress a small packet. 'These are my last words,' said she; 'here is the packet which will save Alexis. I confide it to your honour and to your love of justice. Take it! You will deliver it at the Russian Embassy.* Now I have done my duty, and—'

'Stop her!' cried Holmes. He had bounded across the room and had wrenched a small phial from her hand.

'Too late!' she said, sinking back on the bed. 'Too late! I took the poison before I left my hiding-place. My head swims! I am going! I charge you, sir, to remember the packet.'

'A simple case, and yet in some ways an instructive one,' Holmes remarked as we travelled back to town. 'It hinged from the outset upon the pince-nez. But for the fortunate chance of the dying man having seized these I am not sure that we could ever have reached our solution. It was clear to me from the strength of the glasses that the wearer must have been very blind and helpless when deprived of them. When you asked me to believe that she walked along a narrow strip of grass without once making a false step I remarked, as you may remember, that it was a noteworthy performance. In my mind, I set it down as an impossible performance, save in the unlikely case that she had a second pair of glasses. I was forced, therefore, to seriously consider the hypothesis that she had remained within the house. On perceiving the similarity of the two corridors, it became clear that she might very easily have made such a mistake, and in that case it was evident that she must have entered the Professor's room. I was keenly on the alert, therefore, for whatever would bear out this supposition, and I examined the room narrowly for anything in the shape of a hiding-place. The carpet seemed continuous and firmly nailed, so I dismissed the idea of a trap-door. There might well be a recess behind the books. As you are aware, such devices are common in old libraries. I observed that books were piled on the floor at all other points, but that one bookcase was left clear. This, then, might be the door. I could see no marks to guide me, but the carpet was of a dun colour, which lends itself very well to examination. I therefore smoked a great number of those excellent cigarettes, and I dropped the ash all over the space in front of the suspected bookcase. It was a simple trick, but exceedingly effective. I then went downstairs, and I ascertained in your presence, Watson, without your quite perceiving the drift of my remarks, that Professor Coram's consumption of food had increased—as one would expect when he is supplying a second person. We then ascended to the room again, when, by upsetting the cigarette-box, I obtained a very excellent view of the floor, and was able to see quite clearly, from the traces upon the cigarette ash, that the prisoner had, in our absence, come out from her retreat. Well, Hopkins, here we are at Charing Cross, and I congratulate you on having brought your case to a successful conclusion. You are going to headquarters, no doubt. I think, Watson, you and I will drive together to the Russian Embassy.'

The Missing Three-Quarter

W E were fairly accustomed to receive weird telegrams at Baker Street, but I have a particular recollection of one which reached us on a gloomy February morning some seven or eight years ago, and gave Mr Sherlock Holmes a puzzled quarter of an hour. It was addressed to him, and ran thus:

Please await me. Terrible misfortune. Right wing three-quarter missing. Indispensable to-morrow. OVERTON

'Strand postmark, and dispatched ten thirty-six,'* said Holmes, reading it over and over. 'Mr Overton was evidently considerably excited when he sent it, and somewhat incoherent in consequence. Well, well, he will be here, I dare say, by the time I have looked through *The Times*, and then we shall know all about it. Even the most insignificant problem would be welcome in these stagnant days.'

Things had indeed been very slow with us, and I had learned to dread such periods of inaction, for I knew by experience that my companion's brain was so abnormally active that it was dangerous to leave it without material upon which to work. For years I had gradually weaned him from that drug mania* which had threatened once to check his remarkable career. Now I knew that under ordinary conditions he no longer craved for this artificial stimulus; but I was well aware that the fiend was not dead, but sleeping; and I have known that the sleep was a light one and the waking near when in periods of idleness I have seen the drawn look upon Holmes's ascetic face, and the brooding of his deep-set and inscrutable eyes. Therefore I blessed this Mr Overton, whoever he might be, since he had come with his enigmatic message to break that dangerous calm which brought more peril to my friend than all the storms of his tempestuous life.

As we expected, the telegram was soon followed by its sender, and the card of Mr Cyril Overton, of Trinity College, Cambridge,* announced the arrival of an enormous young man, sixteen stone of solid bone and muscle, who spanned the doorway with his broad shoulders and looked from one of us to the other with a comely face which was haggard with anxiety.

'Mr Sherlock Holmes?'

My companion bowed.

'I've been down to Scotland Yard, Mr Holmes. I saw Inspector Stanley Hopkins. He advised me to come to you. He said the case, so far as he could see, was more in your line than in that of the regular police.'

'Pray sit down and tell me what is the matter.'

'It's awful, Mr Holmes, simply awful! I wonder my hair isn't grey. Godfrey Staunton—you've heard of him, of course? He's simply the hinge that the whole team turns on. I'd rather spare two from the pack and have Godfrey for my three-quarter line.* Whether it's passing, or tackling, or dribbling, there's no one to touch him; and then, he's got the head and can hold us all together. What am I to do? That's what I ask you, Mr Holmes. There's Moorhouse,* first reserve, but he is trained as a half, and he always edges right in on to the scrum instead of keeping out on the touch-line. He's a fine place-kick,* it's true, but, then, he has no judgement, and he can't sprint for nuts. Why, Morton or Johnson, the Oxford fliers, could romp round him. Stevenson is fast enough, but he couldn't drop from the twenty-five line,* and a three-quarter who can't either punt* or drop isn't worth a place for pace alone. No, Mr Holmes, we are done unless you can help me to find Godfrey Staunton.'

My friend had listened with amused surprise to this long speech, which was poured forth with extraordinary vigour and earnestness, every point being driven home by the slapping of a brawny hand upon the speaker's knee. When our visitor was silent Holmes stretched out his hand and took down letter 'S' of his commonplace book. For once he dug in vain into that mine of varied information.

'There is Arthur H. Staunton, the rising young forger,'* said he, 'and there was Henry Staunton, whom I helped to hang, but Godfrey Staunton is a new name to me.'

It was our visitor's turn to look surprised.

'Why, Mr Holmes, I thought you knew things,' said he. 'I suppose, then, if you have never heard of Godfrey Staunton you don't know Cyril Overton either?'

Holmes shook his head good-humouredly.

'Great Scot!'* cried the athlete. 'Why, I was first reserve for England against Wales, and I've skippered the 'Varsity all this year. But that's nothing. I didn't think there was a soul in England who didn't know Godfrey Staunton, the crack three-quarter, Cambridge, Blackheath, and five Internationals. Good Lord! Mr Holmes, where *have* you lived?'

Holmes laughed at the young giant's naïve astonishment.

'You live in a different world to me, Mr Overton, a sweeter and healthier one. My ramifications stretch out into many sections of society, but never, I am happy to say, into amateur sport, which is the best and soundest thing in England. However, your unexpected visit this morning shows me that even in that world of fresh air and fair play there may be work for me to do; so now, my good sir, I beg you to sit down and to tell me slowly and quietly exactly what it is that has occurred, and how you desire that I should help you.'

Young Overton's face assumed the bothered look of the man who is more accustomed to using his muscles than his wits; but by degrees, with many repetitions and obscurities which I may omit from his narrative, he laid his strange story before us.

'It's this way, Mr Holmes. As I have said, I am the skipper of the Rugger team of Cambridge 'Varsity, and Godfrey Staunton is my best man. To-morrow we play Oxford. Yesterday we all came up and we settled at Bentley's private hotel.* At ten o'clock I went round and saw that all the fellows had gone to roost, for I believe in strict training and plenty of sleep to keep a team fit. I had a word or two with

Godfrey before he turned in. He seemed to me to be pale and bothered. I asked him what was the matter. He said he was all right—just a touch of headache. I bade him good-night and left him. Half an hour later the porter tells me that a rough-looking man with a beard called with a note for Godfrey. He had not gone to bed, and the note was taken to his room. Godfrey read it and fell back in a chair as if he had been pole-axed. The porter was so scared that he was going to fetch me, but Godfrey stopped him, had a drink of water, and pulled himself together. Then he went downstairs, said a few words to the man who was waiting in the hall, and the two of them went off together. The last that the porter saw of them, they were almost running down the street in the direction of the Strand.* This morning Godfrey's room was empty, his bed had never been slept in, and his things were all just as I had seen them the night before. He had gone off at a moment's notice with this stranger, and no word has come back from him since. I don't believe he will ever come back. He was a sportsman, was Godfrey, down to his marrow, and he wouldn't have stopped his training and let down his skipper if it were not for some cause that was too strong for him. No; I feel as if he were gone for good and we should never see him again.'

Sherlock Holmes listened with the deepest attention to this singular narrative.

'What did you do?' he asked.

'I wired to Cambridge to learn if anything had been heard of him there. I have had an answer. No one has seen him.'

'Could he have got back to Cambridge?'

'Yes, there is a late train—quarter-past eleven.'

'But so far as you can ascertain, he did not take it?'

'No, he has not been seen.'

'What did you do next?'

'I wired to Lord Mount-James.'*

'Why to Lord Mount-James?'

'Godfrey is an orphan, and Lord Mount-James is his nearest relative—his uncle, I believe.'

THE MISSING THREE-QUARTER ·

'Indeed. This throws new light upon the matter. Lord Mount-James is one of the richest men in England.'

'So I've heard Godfrey say.'

'And your friend was closely related?'

'Yes, he was his heir, and the old boy is nearly eighty— cram full of gout, too. They say he could chalk his billiard-cue with his knuckles. He never allowed Godfrey a shilling in his life, for he is an absolute miser, but it will all come to him right enough.'

'Have you heard from Lord Mount-James?'

'No.'

'What motive could your friend have in going to Lord Mount-James?'

'Well, something was worrying him the night before, and if it was to do with money it is possible that he would make for his nearest relative who had so much of it, though from all I have heard he would not have much chance of getting it. Godfrey was not fond of the old man. He would not go if he could help it.'

'Well, we can soon determine that. If your friend was going to his relative Lord Mount-James, you have then to explain the visit of this rough-looking fellow at so late an hour, and the agitation that was caused by his coming.'

Cyril Overton pressed his hands to his head. 'I can make nothing of it!' said he.

'Well, well, I have a clear day, and I shall be happy to look into the matter,' said Holmes. 'I should strongly recommend you to make your preparations for your match without reference to this young gentleman. It must, as you say, have been an overpowering necessity which tore him away in such a fashion, and the same necessity is likely to hold him away. Let us step round together to this hotel, and see if the porter can throw any fresh light upon the matter.'

Sherlock Holmes was a past master in the art of putting a humble witness at his ease, and very soon, in the privacy of Godfrey Staunton's abandoned room, he had extracted all that the porter had to tell. The visitor of the night before was not a gentleman, neither was he a working man. He was simply what the porter described as a 'medium-looking chap'; a man of fifty, beard grizzled, pale face, quietly dressed. He seemed himself to be agitated. The porter had observed his hand trembling when he had held out the note. Godfrey Staunton had crammed the note into his pocket. Staunton had not shaken hands with the man in the hall. They had exchanged a few sentences, of which the porter had only distinguished the one word 'time'. Then they had hurried off in the manner described. It was just half-past ten by the hall clock.

'Let me see,' said Holmes, seating himself on Staunton's bed. 'You are the day porter, are you not?'

'Yes, sir; I go off duty at eleven.'

'The night porter saw nothing, I suppose?'

'No, sir; one theatre party came in late. No one else.'

'Were you on duty all day yesterday?'

'Yes, sir.'

'Did you take any message to Mr Staunton?'

'Yes, sir; one telegram.'

'Ah! that is interesting. What o'clock was this?'

'About six.'

'Where was Mr Staunton when he received it?'

'Here in his room.'

'Were you present when he opened it?'

'Yes, sir; I waited to see if there was an answer.'

'Well, was there?'

'Yes, sir. He wrote an answer.'

'Did you take it?'

'No; he took it himself.'

'But he wrote it in your presence?'

'Yes, sir. I was standing by the door, and he with his back turned at that table. When he had written it he said, "All right, porter, I will take this myself." '

'What did he write it with?'

'A pen, sir.'

'Was the telegraphic form one of these on the table?'

'Yes, sir; it was the top one.'

Holmes rose. Taking the forms, he carried them over to the window and carefully examined that which was uppermost.

'It is a pity he did not write in pencil,' said he, throwing them down again with a shrug of disappointment. 'As you have no doubt frequently observed, Watson, the impression usually goes through—a fact which has dissolved many a happy marriage. However, I can find no trace here. I rejoice, however, to perceive that he wrote with a broad-pointed quill pen, and I can hardly doubt that we will find some impression upon this blotting pad. Ah, yes, surely this is the very thing!'

He tore off a strip of the blotting-paper and turned towards us the following hieroglyphic:*

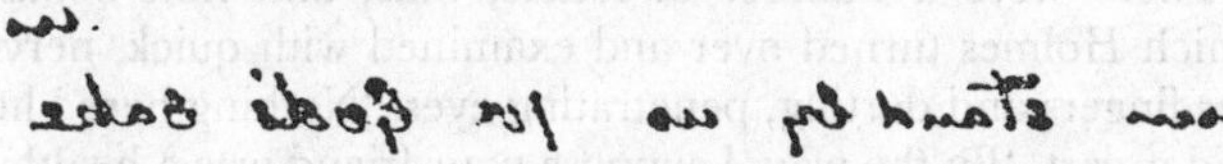

(mirror-image handwriting)

Cyril Overton was much excited. 'Hold it to the glass,' he cried.

'That is unnecessary,' said Holmes. 'The paper is thin, and the reverse will give the message. There it is.' He turned it over, and we read:

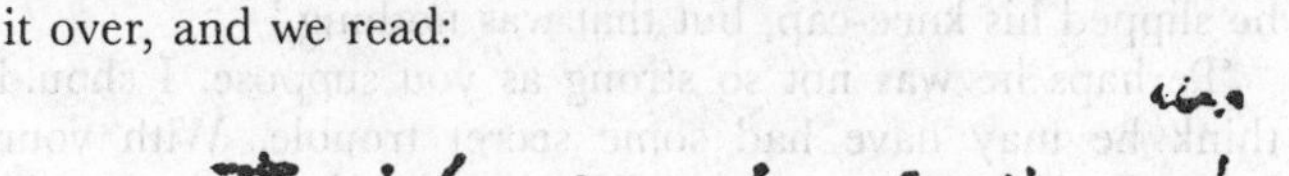

stand by us for God's sake

'So that is the tail end of the telegram which Godfrey Staunton dispatched within a few hours of his disappearance. There are at least six words of the message which have escaped us; but what remains—"Stand by us for God's sake!"—proves that this young man saw a formidable danger which approached him, and from which someone else could protect him. "*Us*", mark you! Another person was involved. Who should it be but the pale-faced, bearded man who seemed himself in so nervous a state? What, then, is the connection between Godfrey Staunton and the bearded man? And what is the third source from which each of them sought for help against pressing danger? Our inquiry has already narrowed down to that.'

'We have only to find to whom that telegram is addressed,' I suggested.

'Exactly, my dear Watson. Your reflection, though profound, had already crossed my mind. But I dare say it may have come to your notice that if you walk into a post-office and demand to see the counterfoil of another man's message there may be some disinclination on the part of the officials to oblige you. There is so much red tape in these matters! However, I have no doubt that with a little delicacy and finesse the end may be attained. Meanwhile, I should like in your presence, Mr Overton, to go through these papers which have been left upon the table.'

There were a number of letters, bills, and note-books, which Holmes turned over and examined with quick, nervous fingers and darting, penetrating eyes. 'Nothing here,' he said at last. 'By the way, I suppose your friend was a healthy young fellow—nothing amiss with him?'

'Sound as a bell.'

'Have you ever known him ill?'

'Not a day. He has been laid up with a hack,* and once he slipped his knee-cap, but that was nothing.'

'Perhaps he was not so strong as you suppose. I should think he may have had some secret trouble. With your assent I will put one or two of these papers in my pocket, in case they should bear upon our future inquiry.'

'One moment, one moment!' cried a querulous voice, and we looked up to find a queer little old man jerking and twitching in the doorway. He was dressed in rusty black, with a very broad-brimmed top-hat and a loose white necktie—the whole effect being that of a very rustic parson or of an undertaker's mute.* Yet, in spite of his shabby and even absurd appearance, his voice had a sharp crackle, and his manner a quick intensity which commanded attention.

'Who are you, sir, and by what right do you touch this gentleman's papers?' he asked.

'I am a private detective, and I am endeavouring to explain his disappearance.'

'Oh, you are, are you? And who instructed you, eh?'

'This gentleman, Mr Staunton's friend, was referred to me by Scotland Yard.'

'Who are you, sir?'

'I am Cyril Overton.'

'Then it is you who sent me a telegram. My name is Lord Mount-James. I came round as quickly as the Bayswater 'bus* would bring me. So you have instructed a detective?'

'Yes, sir.'

'And are you prepared to meet the cost?'

'I have no doubt, sir, that my friend Godfrey, when we find him, will be prepared to do that.'

'But if he is never found, eh? Answer me that!'

'In that case no doubt his family—'

'Nothing of the sort, sir!' screamed the little man. 'Don't look to me for a penny—not a penny! You understand that, Mr Detective! I am all the family that this young man has got, and I tell you that I am not responsible. If he has any expectations it is due to the fact that I have never wasted money, and I do not propose to begin to do so now. As to those papers with which you are making so free, I may tell you that in case there should be anything of any value among them you will be held strictly to account for what you do with them.'

'Very good, sir,' said Sherlock Holmes. 'May I ask in the meanwhile whether you have yourself any theory to account for this young man's disappearance?'

'No, sir, I have not. He is big enough and old enough to look after himself, and if he is so foolish as to lose himself I entirely refuse to accept the responsibility of hunting for him.'

'I quite understand your position,' said Holmes, with a mischievous twinkle in his eyes. 'Perhaps you don't quite understand mine. Godfrey Staunton appears to have been a poor man. If he has been kidnapped it could not have been for anything which he himself possesses. The fame of your wealth has gone abroad, Lord Mount-James, and it is entirely possible that a gang of thieves has secured your nephew in order to gain from him some information as to your house, your habits, and your treasure.'

The face of our unpleasant little visitor turned as white as his neckcloth.

'Good God,* sir, what an idea! I never thought of such villainy! What inhuman rogues there are in the world! But Godfrey is a fine lad—a staunch lad. Nothing would induce him to give his old uncle away. I'll have the plate moved over to the bank this evening. In the meantime spare no pains, Mr Detective. I beg you to leave no stone unturned to bring him safely back. As to money, well, so far as a fiver, or even a tenner, goes, you can always look to me.'

Even in his chastened frame of mind the noble miser could give us no information which could help us, for he knew little of the private life of his nephew. Our only clue lay in the truncated telegram, and with a copy of this in his hand Holmes set forth to find a second link for his chain. We had shaken off Lord Mount-James, and Overton had gone to consult with the other members of his team over the misfortune which had befallen them. There was a telegraph office* at a short distance from the hotel. We halted outside it.

'It's worth trying, Watson,' said Holmes. 'Of course, with a warrant we could demand to see the counterfoils, but we have not reached that stage yet. I don't suppose they remember faces in so busy a place. Let us venture it.'

'I am sorry to trouble you,' said he in his blandest manner to the young woman behind the grating; 'there is some small mistake about a telegram I sent yesterday. I have had no answer, and I very much fear that I must have omitted to put my name at the end. Could you tell me if this was so?'

The young lady turned over a sheaf of counterfoils.

'What o'clock was it?' she asked.

'A little after six.'

'Whom was it to?'

Holmes put his finger to his lips and glanced at me. 'The last words in it were "for God's sake",' he whispered confidentially; 'I am very anxious at getting no answer.'

The young woman separated one of the forms.

'This is it. There is no name,' said she, smoothing it out upon the counter.

'Then that, of course, accounts for my getting no answer,' said Holmes. 'Dear me, how very stupid of me, to be sure! Good morning, miss, and many thanks for having relieved my mind.' He chuckled and rubbed his hands when we found ourselves in the street once more.

'Well?' I asked.

'We progress, my dear Watson, we progress. I had seven different schemes for getting a glimpse of that telegram, but I could hardly hope to succeed the very first time.'

'And what have you gained?'

'A starting-point for our investigation.' He hailed a cab. 'King's Cross Station,'* said he.

'We have a journey, then?'

'Yes, I think we must run down to Cambridge together. All the indications seem to point in that direction.'

'Tell me,' I asked as we rattled up Gray's Inn Road,* 'have you any suspicion yet as to the cause of the disappearance? I don't think that among all our cases I have known one where the motives were more obscure. Surely you don't really imagine that he may be kidnapped in order to give information against his wealthy uncle?'

'I confess, my dear Watson, that that does not appeal to me as a very probable explanation. It struck me, however, as being the one which was most likely to interest that exceedingly unpleasant old person.'

'It certainly did that. But what are your alternatives?'

'I could mention several. You must admit that it is curious and suggestive that this incident should occur on the eve of this important match, and should involve the only man whose presence seems essential to the success of the side. It may, of course, be coincidence, but it is interesting. Amateur sport is free from betting, but a good deal of outside betting goes on among the public, and it is possible that it might be worth someone's while to get at a player as the ruffians of the Turf get at a racehorse. There is one explanation. A second very obvious one is that this young man really is the heir of a great property, however modest his means may be at present, and it is not impossible that a plot to hold him for ransom might be concocted.'

'These theories take no account of the telegram.'

'Quite true, Watson. The telegram still remains the only solid thing with which we have to deal, and we must not permit our attention to wander away from it. It is to gain light upon the purpose of this telegram that we are now upon our way to Cambridge. The path of our investigation is at present obscure, but I shall be very surprised if before evening we have not cleared it up or made a considerable advance along it.'

It was already dark when we reached the old University city. Holmes took a cab at the station, and ordered the man to drive to the house of Dr Leslie Armstrong. A few minutes later we had stopped at a large mansion in the busiest thoroughfare.* We were shown in, and after a long wait were admitted into the consulting-room, where we found the doctor seated behind his table.

It argues the degree in which I had lost touch with my profession that the name of Leslie Armstrong was unknown to me. Now I am aware that he is not only one of the heads of the medical school of the University, but a thinker of European reputation in more than one branch of science. Yet even without knowing his brilliant record one could not fail to be impressed by a mere glance at the man—the square, massive face, the brooding eyes under the thatched brows, and the granite moulding of the inflexible jaw. A man of deep character, a man with an alert mind, grim, ascetic, self-contained, formidable—so I read Dr Leslie Armstrong. He held my friend's card in his hand, and he looked up with no very pleased expression upon his dour features.

'I have heard your name, Mr Sherlock Holmes, and I am aware of your profession, one of which I by no means approve.'

'In that, doctor, you will find yourself in agreement with every criminal in the country,' said my friend quietly.

'So far as your efforts are directed towards the suppression of crime, sir, they must have the support of every reasonable member of the community, though I cannot doubt that the official machinery is amply sufficient for the purpose. Where your calling is more open to criticism is when you pry into the secrets of private individuals, when you rake up family matters which are better hidden, and when you incidentally waste the time of men who are more busy than yourself. At the present moment, for example, I should be writing a treatise instead of conversing with you.'

'No doubt, doctor; and yet the conversation may prove more important than the treatise. Incidentally I may tell you that we are doing the reverse of what you very justly blame, and that we are endeavouring to prevent anything like public exposure of private matters which must necessarily follow when once the case is fairly in the hands of the official police. You may look upon me simply as an irregular pioneer who goes in front of the regular force of the country. I have come to ask you about Mr Godfrey Staunton.'

'What about him?'

'You know him, do you not?'

'He is an intimate friend of mine.'

'You are aware that he has disappeared?'

'Ah, indeed!' There was no change of expression in the rugged features of the doctor.

'He left his hotel last night. He has not been heard of.'

'No doubt he will return.'

'Tomorrow is the 'Varsity football match.'

'I have no sympathy with these childish games. The young man's fate interests me deeply, since I know him and like him. The football match does not come within my horizon at all.'

'I claim your sympathy, then, in my investigation of Mr Staunton's fate. Do you know where he is?'

'Certainly not.'

'You have not seen him since yesterday?'

'No, I have not.'

'Was Mr Staunton a healthy man?'

'Absolutely.'

'Did you ever know him ill?'

'Never.'

Holmes popped a sheet of paper before the doctor's eyes. 'Then perhaps you will explain this receipted bill for thirteen guineas, paid by Mr Godfrey Staunton last month to Dr Leslie Armstrong, of Cambridge. I picked it out from among the papers upon his desk.'

The doctor flushed with anger.

'I do not feel that there is any reason why I should render an explanation to you, Mr Holmes.'

Holmes replaced the bill in his note-book.

'If you prefer a public explanation it must come sooner or later,' said he. 'I have already told you that I can hush up that which others will be bound to publish, and you would really be wiser to take me into your complete confidence.'

'I know nothing about it.'

'Did you hear from Mr Staunton in London?'

'Certainly not.'

'Dear me, dear me!—the post office again!' Holmes sighed wearily. 'A most urgent telegram was dispatched to you from London by Godfrey Staunton at six-fifteen yesterday evening—a telegram which is undoubtedly associated with his disappearance—and yet you have not had it. It is most culpable. I shall certainly go down to the office here and register a complaint.'

Dr Leslie Armstrong sprang up from behind his desk, and his dark face was crimson with fury.

'I'll trouble you to walk out of my house, sir,' said he. 'You can tell your employer, Lord Mount-James, that I do not wish to have anything to do either with him or with his agents. No, sir, not another word!' He rang the bell furiously. 'John, show these gentlemen out.' A pompous butler ushered us severely to the door, and we found ourselves in the street. Holmes burst out laughing.

'Dr Leslie Armstrong is certainly a man of energy and character,' said he. 'I have not seen a man who, if he turned his talents that way, was more calculated to fill the gap left by the illustrious Moriarty. And now, my poor Watson, here we are, stranded and friendless, in this inhospitable town, which we cannot leave without abandoning our case. This little inn just opposite Armstrong's house is singularly adapted to our needs. If you would engage a front room and purchase the necessaries for the night, I may have time to make a few inquiries.'

These few inquiries proved, however, to be a more lengthy proceeding than Holmes had imagined, for he did not return to the inn until nearly nine o'clock. He was pale and dejected, stained with dust, and exhausted with hunger and fatigue. A cold supper was ready upon the table, and when his needs were satisfied and his pipe alight he was ready to take that half-comic and wholly philosophic view which was natural to him when his affairs were going awry. The sound of carriage wheels caused him to rise and glance out of the window. A brougham* and pair of greys under the glare of a gas-lamp stood before the doctor's door.

'It's been out three hours,' said Holmes; 'started at half-past six, and here it is back again. That gives a radius of ten or twelve miles, and he does it once, or sometimes twice, a day.'

'No unusual thing for a doctor in practice.'

'But Armstrong is not really a doctor in practice. He is a lecturer and a consultant, but he does not care for general practice, which distracts him from his literary work. Why, then, does he make these long journeys, which must be exceedingly irksome to him, and who is it that he visits?'

'His coachman—'

'My dear Watson, can you doubt that it was to him that I first applied? I do not know whether it came from his own innate depravity or from the promptings of his master, but he was rude enough to set a dog at me. Neither dog nor man liked the look of my stick, however, and the matter fell through. Relations were strained after that, and further inquiries out of the question. All that I have learned I got from a friendly native in the yard of our own inn. It was he who told me of the doctor's habits and of his daily journey. At that instant, to give point to his words, the carriage came round to the door.'

'Could you not follow it?'

'Excellent, Watson! You are scintillating this evening. The idea did cross my mind. There is, as you may have observed, a bicycle shop next to our inn. Into this I rushed, engaged a bicycle, and was able to get started before the carriage was quite out of sight. I rapidly overtook* it, and then, keeping at a discreet distance of a hundred yards or so, I followed its lights until we were clear of the town. We had got well out on the country road when a somewhat mortifying incident occurred. The carriage stopped, the doctor alighted, walked swiftly back to where I had also halted, and told me in an excellent sardonic fashion that he feared the road was narrow, and that he hoped his carriage did not impede the passage of my bicycle. Nothing could have been more admirable than his way of putting it. I at once rode past the carriage, and, keeping to the main road, I went on for a few miles, and then halted in a convenient place to see if the carriage passed. There was no sign of it, however, and so it became evident that it had turned down one of several side roads which I had observed. I rode back, but again saw nothing of the carriage, and now, as you perceive, it has returned after me. Of course, I had at the outset no particular reason to connect these journeys with the disappearance of Godfrey Staunton, and was only inclined to investigate them on the general grounds that everything which concerns Dr Armstrong is at present of interest to us; but, now that I find he keeps so keen a look-out upon anyone who may follow him on these excursions, the affair appears more important, and I shall not be satisfied until I have made the matter clear.'

'We can follow him to-morrow.'

'Can we? It is not so easy as you seem to think. You are not familiar with Cambridgeshire scenery, are you? It does not lend itself to concealment. All this country that I passed over to-night is as flat and clean as the palm of your hand, and the man we are following is no fool, as he very clearly showed to-night. I have wired to Overton to let us know any fresh London developments at this address, and in the meantime we can only concentrate our attention upon Dr Armstrong, whose name the obliging young lady at the office allowed me to read upon the counterfoil of Staunton's urgent message. He knows where that young man is—to that I'll swear—and if he knows, then it must be our fault if we cannot manage to know also. At present it must be admitted that the odd trick is in his possession, and, as you are aware, Watson, it is not my habit to leave the game in that condition.'

And yet the next day brought us no nearer to the solution of the mystery. A note was handed in after breakfast, which Holmes passed across to me with a smile.

Sir [it ran]—I can assure you that you are wasting your time in dogging my movements. I have, as you discovered last night, a window at the back of my brougham, and if you desire a twenty-mile ride which will lead you to the spot from which you started, you have only to follow me. Meanwhile, I can inform you that no spying upon me can in any way help Mr Godfrey Staunton, and I am convinced that the best service you can do to that gentleman is to return at once to London and to report to your employer that you are unable to trace him. Your time in Cambridge will certainly be wasted.

Yours faithfully,
LESLIE ARMSTRONG.

'An outspoken, honest antagonist is the doctor,' said Holmes. 'Well, well, he excites my curiosity, and I must really know more before I leave him.'

'His carriage is at his door now,' said I. 'There he is stepping into it. I saw him glance up at our window as he did so. Suppose I try my luck upon the bicycle?'

'No, no, my dear Watson! With all respect for your natural acumen, I do not think that you are quite a match for the worthy doctor. I think that possibly I can attain our end by some independent explorations of my own. I am afraid that I must leave you to your own devices, as the appearance of *two* inquiring strangers upon a sleepy countryside might excite more gossip than I care for. No doubt you will find some sights to amuse you in this venerable city, and I hope to bring back a more favourable report to you before evening.'

Once more, however, my friend was destined to be disappointed. He came back at night weary and unsuccessful.

'I have had a blank day, Watson. Having got the doctor's general direction, I spent the day in visiting all the villages upon that side of Cambridge, and comparing notes with publicans and other local news agencies. I have covered some ground: Chesterton, Histon, Waterbeach, and Oakington* have each been explored, and have each proved disappointing. The daily appearance of a brougham and pair could hardly have been overlooked in such Sleepy Hollows.* The doctor has scored once more. Is there a telegram for me?'

'Yes; I opened it. Here it is: "Ask for Pompey* from Jeremy Dixon, Trinity College."* I don't understand it.'

'Oh, it is clear enough. It is from our friend Overton, and is in answer to a question from me. I'll just send round a note to Mr Jeremy Dixon, and then I have no doubt that our luck will turn. By the way, is there any news of the match?'

'Yes, the local evening paper has an excellent account in its last edition. Oxford won by a goal and two tries. The last sentences of the description say: "The defeat of the Light Blues* may be entirely attributed to the unfortunate absence of the crack International, Godfrey Staunton, whose want was felt at every instant of the game. The lack of combination in the three-quarter line and their weakness both in attack and defence more than neutralized the efforts of a heavy and hard-working pack." '

'Then our friend Overton's forebodings have been justified,' said Holmes. 'Personally I am in agreement with Dr
Armstrong, and football does not come within my horizon.
Early to bed tonight, Watson, for I foresee that to-morrow
may be an eventful day.'

I was horrified by my first glimpse of Holmes next morning,
for he sat by the fire holding his tiny hypodermic syringe. I
associated that with the single weakness of his nature, and I
feared the worst when I saw it glittering in his hand. He
laughed at my expression of dismay, and laid it upon the
table.

'No, no, my dear fellow, there is no cause for alarm. It is
not upon this occasion the instrument of evil, but it will
rather prove to be the key which will unlock our mystery.
On this syringe I base all my hopes. I have just returned
from a small scouting expedition, and everything is favourable. Eat a good breakfast, Watson, for I propose to get
upon Dr Armstrong's trail today, and once on it I will not
stop for rest or food until I run him to his burrow.'

'In that case,' said I, 'we had best carry our breakfast with
us, for he is making an early start. His carriage is at the
door.'

'Never mind. Let him go. He will be clever if he can drive
where I cannot follow him. When you have finished come
downstairs with me, and I will introduce you to a detective who is a very eminent specialist in the work that lies
before us.'

When we descended I followed Holmes into the stable-
yard, where he opened the door of a loose-box* and led out
a squat, lop-eared, white-and-tan dog, something between a
beagle and a foxhound.*

'Let me introduce you to Pompey,' said he. 'Pompey is the
pride of the local draghounds,* no very great flier, as his
build will show, but a staunch hound on a scent. Well,
Pompey, you may not be fast, but I expect you will be too
fast for a couple of middle-aged London gentlemen, so I will
take the liberty of fastening this leather leash to your collar.

Now, boy, come along, and show what you can do.' He led him across to the doctor's door. The dog sniffed round for an instant, and then with a shrill whine of excitement started off down the street, tugging at his leash in his efforts to go faster. In half an hour we were clear of the town and hastening down a country road.

'What have you done, Holmes?' I asked.

'A threadbare and venerable device, but useful upon occasion. I walked into the doctor's yard this morning and shot my syringe full of aniseed over the hind wheel. A draghound will follow aniseed from here to John o' Groats,* and our friend Armstrong would have to drive through the Cam* before he would shake Pompey off his trail. Oh, the cunning rascal! This is how he gave me the slip the other night.'

The dog had suddenly turned out of the main road into a grass-grown lane. Half a mile farther this opened into another broad road, and the trail turned hard to the right in the direction of the town, which we had just quitted. The road took a sweep to the south of the town and continued in the opposite direction to that in which we started.

'This *détour* has been entirely for our benefit, then?' said Holmes. 'No wonder that my inquiries among those villages led to nothing. The doctor has certainly played the game for all it is worth, and one would like to know the reason for such elaborate deception. This should be the village of Trumpington* to the right of us. And, by Jove! here is the brougham coming round the corner! Quick, Watson, quick, or we are done!'

He sprang through a gate into a field, dragging the reluctant Pompey after him. We had hardly got under the shelter of the hedge when the carriage rattled past. I caught a glimpse of Dr Armstrong within, his shoulders bowed, his head sunk on his hands, the very image of distress. I could tell by my companion's graver face that he also had seen.

'I fear there is some dark ending to our quest,' said he. 'It cannot be long before we know it. Come, Pompey! Ah, it is the cottage in the field.'

There could be no doubt that we had reached the end of our journey. Pompey ran about and whined eagerly outside the gate where the marks of the brougham's wheels were still to be seen. A footpath led across to the lonely cottage. Holmes tied the dog to the hedge, and we hastened onwards. My friend knocked at the little rustic door, and knocked again without response. And yet the cottage was not deserted, for a low sound came to our ears—a kind of drone of misery and despair, which was indescribably melancholy. Holmes paused irresolute, and then he glanced back at the road which we had just traversed. A brougham was coming down it, and there could be no mistaking those grey horses.

'By Jove, the doctor is coming back!' cried Holmes. 'That settles it. We are bound to see what it means before he comes.'

He opened the door, and we stepped into the hall. The droning sound swelled louder upon our ears, until it became one long, deep wail of distress. It came from upstairs. Holmes darted up, and I followed him. He pushed open a half-closed door, and we both stood appalled at the sight before us.

A woman, young and beautiful, was lying dead upon the bed. Her calm, pale face, with dim, wide-opened blue eyes, looked upwards from amid a great tangle of golden hair. At the foot of the bed, half sitting, half kneeling, his face buried in the clothes, was a young man, whose frame was racked by his sobs. So absorbed was he by his bitter grief that he never looked up until Holmes's hand was on his shoulder.

'Are you Mr Godfrey Staunton?'

'Yes, yes; I am—but you are too late. She is dead.'

The man was so dazed that he could not be made to understand that we were anything but doctors who had been sent to his assistance. Holmes was endeavouring to utter a few words of consolation, and to explain the alarm which had been caused to his friends by his sudden disappearance, when there was a step upon the stairs, and there was the heavy, stern, questioning face of Dr Armstrong at the door.

'So, gentlemen,' said he, 'you have attained your end, and have certainly chosen a particularly delicate moment for your intrusion. I would not brawl in the presence of death, but I can assure you that if I were a younger man your monstrous conduct would not pass with impunity.'

'Excuse me, Dr Armstrong, I think we are a little at cross-purposes,' said my friend with dignity. 'If you could step downstairs with us we may each be able to give some light to the other upon this miserable affair.'

A minute later the grim doctor and ourselves were in the sitting-room below.

'Well, sir?' said he.

'I wish you to understand, in the first place, that I am not employed by Lord Mount-James, and that my sympathies in this matter are entirely against that nobleman. When a man is lost it is my duty to ascertain his fate, but having done so the matter ends so far as I am concerned; and so long as there is nothing criminal, I am much more anxious to hush up private scandals than to give them publicity. If, as I imagine, there is no breach of the law in this matter, you can absolutely depend upon my discretion and my co-operation in keeping the facts out of the papers!'

Dr Armstrong took a quick step forward and wrung Holmes by the hand.

'You are a good fellow,' said he. 'I had misjudged you. I thank Heaven that my compunction at leaving poor Staunton all alone in this plight caused me to turn my carriage back, and so to make your acquaintance. Knowing as much as you do, the situation is very easily explained. A year ago Godfrey Staunton lodged in London for a time, and became passionately attached to his landlady's daughter, whom he married.* She was as good as she was beautiful, and as intelligent as she was good. No man need be ashamed of such a wife. But Godfrey was heir to this crabbed old nobleman, and it was quite certain that the news of his marriage would have been the end of his inheritance. I knew the lad well, and I loved him for his many excellent qualities. I did all I could to help him to keep things straight.

264

We did our very best to keep the thing from everyone, for when once such a whisper gets about it is not long before everyone has heard it. Thanks to this lonely cottage and his own discretion, Godfrey has up to now succeeded. Their secret was known to no one save to me and to one excellent servant who has at present gone for assistance to Trumpington. But at last there came a terrible blow in the shape of dangerous illness to his wife. It was consumption of the most virulent kind. The poor boy was half crazed with grief, and yet he had to go to London to play this match, for he could not get out of it without explanations which would expose the secret. I tried to cheer him up by a wire, and he sent me one in reply imploring me to do all I could. This was the telegram which you appear in some inexplicable way to have seen. I did not tell him how urgent the danger was, for I knew that he could do no good here, but I sent the truth to the girl's father, and he very injudiciously communicated it to Godfrey. The result was that he came straight away in a state bordering on frenzy, and has remained in the same state, kneeling at the end of her bed, until this morning death put an end to her sufferings. That is all, Mr Holmes, and I am sure that I can rely upon your discretion and that of your friend.'

Holmes grasped the doctor's hand.

'Come, Watson,' said he, and we passed from that house of grief into the pale sunlight of the winter day.

The Abbey Grange

IT was on a bitterly cold and frosty morning during the winter of '97* that I was wakened by a tugging at my shoulder. It was Holmes. The candle in his hand shone upon his eager, stooping face, and told me at a glance that something was amiss.

'Come, Watson, come!' he cried. 'The game is afoot.* Not a word! Into your clothes and come!'

Ten minutes later we were both in a cab and rattling through the silent streets on our way to Charing Cross Station. The first faint winter's dawn was beginning to appear, and we could dimly see the occasional figure of an early workman as he passed us, blurred and indistinct in the opalescent London reek. Holmes nestled in silence into his heavy coat, and I was glad to do the same, for the air was most bitter, and neither of us had broken our fast. It was not until we had consumed some hot tea at the station, and taken our places in the Kentish train,* that we were sufficiently thawed, he to speak and I to listen. Holmes drew a note from his pocket and read it aloud:

ABBEY GRANGE, MARSHAM, KENT,* 3.30 am
My dear Mr Holmes—I should be very glad of your immediate assistance in what promises to be a most remarkable case. It is something quite in your line. Except for releasing the lady I will see that everything is kept exactly as I have found it, but I beg you not to lose an instant, as it is difficult to leave Sir Eustace there.
Yours faithfully,
STANLEY HOPKINS.

'Hopkins has called me in seven times, and on each occasion his summons has been entirely justified,' said Holmes. 'I fancy that every one of his cases has found its way into your collection,* and I must admit, Watson, that you have some power of selection which atones for much which I deplore in your narratives. Your fatal habit of looking at everything from the point of view of a story instead of as a scientific exercise has ruined what might have been an instructive and even classical series of demonstrations. You slur over work of the utmost finesse and delicacy in order to dwell upon sensational details which may excite but cannot possibly instruct the reader.'

'Why do you not write them yourself?' I said, with some bitterness.

'I will, my dear Watson, I will. At present I am, as you know, fairly busy, but I propose to devote my declining years to the composition of a textbook which shall focus the whole art of detection* into one volume. Our present research appears to be a case of murder.'

'You think this Sir Eustace is dead, then?'

'I should say so. Hopkins's writing shows considerable agitation, and he is not an emotional man. Yes, I gather there has been violence, and that the body is left for our inspection. A mere suicide would not have caused him to send for me. As to the release of the lady, it would appear that she has been locked in her room during the tragedy. We are moving in high life, Watson—crackling paper, "EB" monogram, coat-of-arms,* picturesque address. I think that friend Hopkins will live up to his reputation, and that we shall have an interesting morning. The crime was committed before twelve last night.'

'How can you possibly tell?'

'By an inspection of the trains and by reckoning the time. The local police had to be called in, they had to communicate with Scotland Yard, Hopkins had to go out, and he in turn had to send for me. All that makes a fair night's work. Well, here we are at Chislehurst Station, and we shall soon set our doubts at rest.'

A drive of a couple of miles through narrow country lanes brought us to a park gate, which was opened for us by an old lodge-keeper, whose haggard face bore the reflection of some great disaster. The avenue ran through a noble park, between lines of ancient elms,* and ended in a low, widespread house, pillared in front after the fashion of Palladio.* The central part was evidently of a great age and shrouded in ivy, but the large windows showed that modern changes had been carried out, and one wing of the house appeared to be entirely new. The youthful figure and alert, eager face of Inspector Stanley Hopkins confronted us in the open doorway.

'I'm very glad you have come, Mr Holmes. And you, too, Dr Watson! But, indeed, if I had my time over again I should not have troubled you, for since the lady has come to herself she has given so clear an account of the affair that there is not much left for us to do. You remember that Lewisham gang of burglars?'

'What, the three Randalls?'*

'Exactly; the father and two sons. It's their work. I have not a doubt of it. They did a job at Sydenham a fortnight ago, and were seen and described. Rather cool to do another so soon and so near; but it is they, beyond all doubt. It's a hanging matter this time.'

'Sir Eustace is dead, then?'

'Yes; his head was knocked in with his own poker.'

'Sir Eustace Brackenstall, the driver tells me.'

'Exactly—one of the richest men in Kent. Lady Brackenstall is in the morning-room. Poor lady, she has had a most dreadful experience. She seemed half dead when I saw her first. I think you had best see her and hear her account of the facts. Then we will examine the dining-room together.'

Lady Brackenstall was no ordinary person. Seldom have I seen so graceful a figure, so womanly a presence, and so beautiful a face. She was a blonde, golden-haired, blue-eyed, and would, no doubt, have had the perfect complexion which goes with such colouring had not her recent experience left her drawn and haggard. Her sufferings were physical as well as mental, for over one eye rose a hideous, plum-coloured swelling, which her maid, a tall, austere woman, was bathing assiduously with vinegar and water. The lady lay back exhausted upon a couch, but her quick, observant gaze as we entered the room, and the alert expression of her beautiful features, showed that neither her wits nor her courage had been shaken by her terrible experience. She was enveloped in a loose dressing-gown of blue and silver, but a black sequin-covered dinner-dress was hung upon the couch beside her.

'I have told you all that happened, Mr Hopkins,' she said wearily; 'could you not repeat it for me? Well, if you think it necessary, I will tell these gentlemen what occurred. Have they been in the dining-room yet?'

'I thought they had better hear your ladyship's story first.'

'I shall be glad when you can arrange matters. It is horrible to me to think of him still lying there.' She shuddered and buried her face for a moment in her hands. As she did so the loose gown fell back from her forearm. Holmes uttered an exclamation.

'You have other injuries, madam! What is this?' Two vivid red spots stood out in one of the white, round limbs. She hastily covered it.

'It is nothing. It has no connection with the hideous business of last night. If you and your friend will sit down I will tell you all I can.

'I am the wife of Sir Eustace Brackenstall. I have been married about a year. I suppose that it is no use my attempting to conceal that our marriage has not been a happy one. I fear that all our neighbours would tell you that, even if I were to attempt to deny it. Perhaps the fault may be partly mine. I was brought up in the freer, less conventional atmosphere of South Australia, and this English life, with its proprieties and its primness, is not congenial to me. But the main reason lies in the one fact which is notorious to everyone, and that is that Sir Eustace was a confirmed drunkard. To be with such a man for an hour is unpleasant. Can you imagine what it means for a sensitive and high-spirited woman to be tied to him for day and night? It is a sacrilege, a crime, a villainy to hold that such a marriage is binding. I say that these monstrous laws of yours* will bring a curse upon the land—Heaven will not let such wickedness endure.' For an instant she sat up, her cheeks flushed, and her eyes blazing from under the terrible mark upon her brow. Then the strong, soothing hand of the austere maid drew her head down on to the cushion, and the wild anger died away into passionate sobbing. At last she continued:

'I will tell you about last night. You are aware, perhaps, that in this house all servants sleep in the modern wing. This central block is made up of the dwelling-rooms, with the kitchen behind and our bedroom above. My maid Theresa sleeps above my room. There is no one else, and no sound could alarm those who are in the farther wing. This must have been well known to the robbers, or they would not have acted as they did.

'Sir Eustace retired about half-past ten. The servants had already gone to their quarters. Only my maid was up, and she had remained in her room at the top of the house until I needed her services. I sat until after eleven in this room, absorbed in a book. Then I walked round to see that all was right before I went upstairs. It was my custom to do this myself, for, as I have explained, Sir Eustace was not always to be trusted. I went into the kitchen, the butler's pantry, the gun-room, the billiard-room, the drawing-room, and finally the dining-room. As I approached the window, which is covered with thick curtains, I suddenly felt the wind blown upon my face, and realized that it was open. I flung the curtain aside, and found myself face to face with a broad-shouldered, elderly man who had just stepped into the room. The window is a long French one, which really forms a door leading to the lawn. I held my bedroom candle lit in my hand, and, by its light, behind the first man I saw two others, who were in the act of entering. I stepped back, but the fellow was on me in an instant. He caught me first by the wrist and then by the throat. I opened my mouth to scream, but he struck me a savage blow with his fist over the eye, and felled me to the ground. I must have been unconscious for a few minutes, for when I came to myself I found that they had torn down the bell-rope and had secured me tightly to the oaken chair which stands at the head of the dining-room table. I was so firmly bound that I could not move, and a handkerchief round my mouth prevented me from uttering any sound. It was at this instant that my unfortunate husband entered the room. He had evidently heard some suspicious sounds, and he came prepared for such a scene as he found. He was dressed in his shirt and trousers, with his favourite blackthorn cudgel in his hand. He rushed at one of the burglars, but another—it was the elderly man*—stooped, picked the poker out of the grate, and struck him a terrible blow as he passed. He fell without a groan, and never moved again. I fainted once more, but again it could only have been a very few minutes during which I was insensible. When I opened my eyes I found that they had collected the silver from the sideboard, and they had drawn a bottle of wine which stood there. Each of them had a glass in his hand. I have already told you, have I not, that one was elderly, with a beard, and the others young, hairless lads. They might have been a father with his two sons. They talked together in whispers. Then they came over and made sure that I was still securely bound. Finally they withdrew, closing the window after them. It was quite a quarter of an hour before I got my mouth free. When I did so my screams brought the maid to my assistance. The other servants were soon alarmed, and we sent for the local police, who instantly communicated with London. That is really all I can tell you, gentlemen, and I trust that it will not be necessary for me to go over so painful a story again.'

'Any questions, Mr Holmes?' said Hopkins.

'I will not impose any further tax upon Lady Brackenstall's patience and time,' said Holmes. 'Before I go into the dining-room I should be glad to hear your experience.' He looked at the maid.

'I saw the men before ever they came into the house,' said she. 'As I sat by my bedroom window I saw three men in the moonlight down by the lodge gate yonder, but I thought nothing of it at the time. It was more than an hour after that I heard my mistress scream, and down I ran, to find her, poor lamb, just as she says, and him on the floor with his blood and brains over the room. It was enough to drive a woman out of her wits, tied there, and her very dress spotted with him; but she never wanted courage, did Miss Mary Fraser of Adelaide, and Lady Brackenstall of Abbey Grange hasn't learned new ways. You've questioned her long enough, you gentlemen, and now she is coming to her own room, just with her old Theresa, to get the rest that she badly needs.'

With a motherly tenderness the gaunt woman put her arm round her mistress and led her from the room.

'She has been with her all her life,' said Hopkins. 'Nursed her as a baby, and came with her to England when they first left Australia eighteen months ago. Theresa Wright* is her name, and the kind of maid you don't pick up nowadays. This way, Mr Holmes, if you please!'

The keen interest had passed out of Holmes's expressive face, and I knew that with the mystery all the charm of the case had departed. There still remained an arrest to be effected, but what were these commonplace rogues that he should soil his hands with them? An abstruse and learned specialist who finds that he has been called in for a case of measles would experience something of the annoyance which I read in my friend's eyes. Yet the scene in the dining-room of the Abbey Grange was sufficiently strange to arrest his attention and to recall his waning interest.

It was a very large and high chamber, with carved oak ceiling, oaken panelling, and a fine array of deers' heads and ancient weapons around the walls. At the farther end from the door was the high French window of which we had heard. Three smaller windows on the right-hand side filled the apartment with cold winter sunshine. On the left was a large, deep fireplace, with a massive over-hanging oak mantelpiece. Beside the fireplace was a heavy oaken chair with arms and cross-bars at the bottom. In and out through the open woodwork was woven a crimson cord, which was secured at each side to the crosspiece below. In releasing the lady the cord had been slipped off her, but the knots with which it had been secured still remained. These details only struck our attention afterwards, for our thoughts were entirely absorbed by the terrible object which lay spread upon the tiger-skin hearthrug in front of the fire.

It was the body of a tall, well-made man, about forty years of age. He lay upon his back, his face upturned, with his white teeth grinning through his short, black beard. His two clenched hands were raised above his head, and a heavy blackthorn stick lay across them. His dark, handsome, aquiline features were convulsed into a spasm of vindictive hatred, which had set his dead face in a terribly fiendish expression. He had evidently been in his bed when the alarm had broken out, for he wore a foppish, embroidered night-shirt, and his bare feet projected from his trousers. His head was horribly injured, and the whole room bore witness to the savage ferocity of the blow which had struck him down. Beside him lay the heavy poker, bent into a curve by the concussion. Holmes examined both it and the indescribable wreck which it had wrought.

'He must be a powerful man, this elder Randall,' he remarked.

'Yes,' said Hopkins. 'I have some record of the fellow, and he is a rough customer.'

'You should have no difficulty in getting him.'

'Not the slightest. We have been on the look-out for him, and there was some idea that he had got away to America. Now we know that the gang are here I don't see how they can escape. We have the news at every seaport already, and a reward will be offered before evening. What beats me is how they could have done so mad a thing, knowing that the lady would describe them, and that we could not fail to recognize the description.'

'Exactly. One would have expected that they would have silenced Lady Brackenstall as well.'

'They may not have realized,' I suggested, 'that she had recovered from her faint.'

'That is likely enough. If she seemed to be senseless they would not take her life. What about this poor fellow,

Hopkins? I seem to have heard some queer stories about him.'

'He was a good-hearted man when he was sober, but a perfect devil* when he was drunk, or rather when he was half drunk, for he seldom really went the whole way. The devil seemed to be in him at such times, and he was capable of anything. From what I hear, in spite of all his wealth and his title, he very nearly came our way once or twice. There was a scandal about his drenching a dog with petroleum and setting it on fire—her ladyship's dog, to make the matter worse—and that was only hushed up with difficulty. Then he threw a decanter at that maid Theresa Wright; there was trouble about that. On the whole, and between ourselves, it will be a brighter house without him. What are you looking at now?'

Holmes was down on his knees examining with great attention the knots upon the red cord with which the lady had been secured. Then he carefully scrutinized the broken and frayed end where it had snapped off when the burglar had dragged it down.

'When this was pulled down the bell in the kitchen must have rung loudly,' he remarked.

'No one could hear it. The kitchen stands right at the back of the house.'

'How did the burglar know no one would hear it? How dare he pull at a bell-rope in that reckless fashion?'

'Exactly, Mr Holmes, exactly. You put the very question which I have asked myself again and again. There can be no doubt that this fellow must have known the house and its habits. He must have perfectly understood that the servants would all be in bed at that comparatively early hour, and that no one could possibly hear a bell ring in the kitchen. Therefore he must have been in close league with one of the servants. Surely that is evident. But there are eight servants, and all of good character.'

'Other things being equal,' said Holmes, 'one would suspect the one at whose head the master threw a decanter. And yet that would involve treachery towards the mistress to whom this woman seems devoted. Well, well, the point is a minor one, and when you have Randall you will probably find no difficulty in securing his accomplices. The lady's story certainly seems to be corroborated, if it needed corroboration, by every detail which we see before us.' He walked to the French window and threw it open. 'There are no signs here, but the ground is iron hard, and one would not expect them. I see that these candles on the mantelpiece have been lighted.'

'Yes, it was by their light and that of the lady's bedroom candle that the burglars saw their way about.'

'And what did they take?'

'Well, they did not take much—only half a dozen articles of plate off the sideboard. Lady Brackenstall thinks that they were themselves so disturbed by the death of Sir Eustace that they did not ransack the house as they would otherwise have done.'

'No doubt that is true. And yet they drank some wine, I understand.'

'To steady their own nerves.'

'Exactly. These three glasses upon the sideboard have been untouched, I suppose?'

'Yes; and the bottle stands as they left it.'

'Let us look at it. Hullo, hullo! what is this?'

The three glasses were grouped together, all of them tinged with wine, and one of them containing some dregs of beeswing.* The bottle stood near them, two-thirds full, and beside it lay a long, deeply stained cork. Its appearance and the dust upon the bottle showed that it was no common vintage which the murderers had enjoyed.

A change had come over Holmes's manner. He had lost his listless expression, and again I saw an alert light of interest in his keen deep-set eyes. He raised the cork and examined it minutely.

'How did they draw it?' he asked.

Hopkins pointed to a half-opened drawer. In it lay some table linen and a large corkscrew.

'Did Lady Brackenstall say that screw was used?'

'No; you remember that she was senseless at the moment when the bottle was opened.'

'Quite so. As a matter of fact, that screw was *not* used. This bottle was opened by a pocket-screw, probably contained in a knife, and not more than an inch and a half long. If you examine the top of the cork you will observe that the screw was driven in three times before the cork was extracted. It has never been transfixed. This long screw would have transfixed it and drawn it with a single pull. When you catch this fellow you will find that he has one of these multiplex knives in his possession.'

'Excellent!' said Hopkins.

'But these glasses do puzzle me, I confess. Lady Brackenstall actually *saw* the three men drinking, did she not?'

'Yes; she was clear about that.'

'Then there is an end of it. What more is to be said? And yet you must admit that the three glasses are very remarkable, Hopkins. What, you see nothing remarkable? Well, well, let it pass. Perhaps when a man has special knowledge and special powers like my own it rather encourages him to seek a complex explanation when a simpler one is at hand. Of course, it must be a mere chance about the glasses. Well, good morning, Hopkins, I don't see that I can be of any use to you, and you appear to have your case very clear. You will let me know when Randall is arrested, and any further developments which may occur. I trust that I shall soon have to congratulate you upon a successful conclusion. Come, Watson, I fancy that we may employ ourselves more profitably at home.'

During our return journey I could see by Holmes's face that he was much puzzled by something which he had observed. Every now and then, by an effort, he would throw off the impression and talk as if the matter were clear, but then his doubts would settle down upon him again, and his knitted brows and abstracted eyes would show that his thoughts had gone back once more to the great dining-room of the Abbey Grange in which this midnight tragedy had been enacted. At last, by a sudden impulse, just as our train was crawling out of a suburban station, he sprang on to the platform and pulled me out after him.

'Excuse me, my dear fellow,' said he, as we watched the rear carriages of our train disappearing round a curve; 'I am sorry to make you the victim of what may seem a mere whim, but on my life, Watson, I simply *can't* leave that case in this condition. Every instinct that I possess cries out against it. It's wrong—it's all wrong—I'll swear that it's wrong. And yet the lady's story was complete, the maid's corroboration was sufficient, the detail was fairly exact. What have I to put against that? Three wine-glasses, that is all. But if I had not taken things for granted, if I had examined everything with the care which I would have shown had we approached the case *de novo** and had no cut-and-dried story to warp my mind, would I not then have found something more definite to go upon? Of course I should. Sit down on this bench, Watson, until a train for Chislehurst arrives, and allow me to lay the evidence before you, imploring you in the first instance to dismiss from your mind the idea that anything which the maid or mistress may have said must necessarily be true. The lady's charming personality must not be permitted to warp our judgement.

'Surely there are details in her story which, if we look at it in cold blood, would excite our suspicion. These burglars made a considerable haul at Sydenham a fortnight ago. Some account of them and their appearance was in the papers, and would naturally occur to anyone who wished to invent a story in which imaginary robbers should play a part. As a matter of fact, burglars who have done a good stroke of business are, as a rule, only too glad to enjoy the proceeds in peace and quiet without embarking on another perilous undertaking. Again, it is unusual for burglars to strike a lady to prevent her screaming, since one would imagine that was the sure way to make her scream; it is unusual for them to commit murder when their numbers are sufficient to overpower one man; it is unusual for them to be content with a limited plunder when there is much more within their reach; and, finally, I should say that it was very unusual for such men to leave a bottle half empty. How do all these unusuals strike you, Watson?'

'Their cumulative effect is certainly considerable, and yet each of them is quite possible in itself. The most unusual thing of all, as it seems to me, is that the lady should be tied to the chair.'

'Well, I am not so sure about that, Watson, for it is evident that they must either kill her or else secure her in such a way that she could not give immediate notice of their escape. But at any rate I have shown, have I not, that there is a certain element of improbability about the lady's story? And now on the top of this comes the incident of the wine-glasses.'

'What about the wine-glasses?'

'Can you see them in your mind's eye?'

'I see them clearly.'

'We are told that three men drank from them. Does that strike you as likely?'

'Why not? There was wine in each glass.'

'Exactly; but there was beeswing only in one glass. You must have noticed that fact. What does that suggest to your mind?'

'The last glass filled would be most likely to contain beeswing.'

'Not at all. The bottle was full of it, and it is inconceivable that the first two glasses were clear and the third heavily charged with it. There are two possible explanations, and only two. One is that after the second glass was filled the bottle was violently agitated, and so the third glass received the beeswing. That does not appear probable. No, no; I am sure that I am right.'

'What, then, do you suppose?'

'That only two glasses were used, and that the dregs of both were poured into a third glass, so as to give the false impression that three people had been there. In that way all the beeswing would be in the last glass, would it not? Yes, I am convinced that this is so. But if I have hit upon the true explanation of this one small phenomenon, then in an instant the case rises from the commonplace to the exceedingly remarkable, for it can only mean that Lady Brackenstall and her maid have deliberately lied to us, that not one word of their story is to be believed, that they have some very strong reason for covering the real criminal, and that we must construct our case for ourselves without any help from them. That is the mission which now lies before us, and here, Watson, is the Chislehurst train.'*

The household of the Abbey Grange were much surprised at our return, but Sherlock Holmes, finding that Stanley Hopkins had gone off to report to headquarters, took possession of the dining-room, locked the door upon the inside and devoted himself for two hours to one of those minute and laborious investigations which formed the solid basis on which his brilliant edifices of deduction were reared. Seated in a corner like an interested student who observes the demonstration of his professor, I followed every step of that remarkable research. The window, the curtains, the carpet, the chair, the rope—each in turn was minutely examined and duly pondered. The body of the unfortunate baronet had been removed, but all else remained as we had seen it in the morning. Then, to my astonishment, Holmes climbed up on to the massive mantelpiece.* Far above his head hung the few inches of red cord which were still attached to the wire. For a long time he gazed upwards at it, and then in an attempt to get nearer to it he rested his knee upon a wooden bracket on the wall. This brought his hand within a few inches of the broken end of the rope; but it was not this so much as the bracket itself which seemed to engage his attention. Finally he sprang down with an ejaculation of satisfaction.

'It's all right, Watson,' said he. 'We have got our case— one of the most remarkable in our collection. But, dear me, how slow-witted I have been, and how nearly I have committed the blunder of my lifetime! Now, I think that with a few missing links my chain is almost complete.'

'You have got your men?'

'Man, Watson, man. Only one, but a very formidable person. Strong as a lion—witness the blow which bent that poker. Six foot three in height, active as a squirrel, dexterous with his fingers; finally, remarkably quick-witted, for this whole ingenious story is of his concoction. Yes, Watson, we have come upon the handiwork of a very remarkable individual. And yet in that bell-rope he has given us a clue which should not have left us a doubt.'

'Where was the clue?'

'Well, if you were to pull down a bell-rope, Watson, where would you expect it to break? Surely at the spot where it is attached to the wire. Why should it break three inches from the top as this one has done?'

'Because it is frayed there?'

'Exactly. This end, which we can examine, is frayed. He was cunning enough to do that with his knife. But the other end is not frayed. You could not observe that from here, but if you were on the mantelpiece you would see that it is cut clean off without any mark of fraying whatever. You can reconstruct what occurred. The man needed the rope. He would not tear it down for fear of giving the alarm by ringing the bell. What did he do? He sprang up on the mantelpiece, could not quite reach it, put his knee on the bracket—you will see the impression in the dust—and got his knife to bear upon the cord. I could not reach the place by at least three inches, from which I infer that he is at least three inches a bigger man than I. Look at that mark upon the seat of the oaken chair! What is it?'

'Blood.'

'Undoubtedly it is blood. This alone puts the lady's story out of court. If she were seated on the chair when the crime was done, how comes that mark? No, no; she was placed in the chair *after* the death of her husband. I'll wager that the black dress shows a corresponding mark to this. We have not yet met our Waterloo, Watson, but this is our Marengo, for it begins in defeat and ends in victory.* I should like now to have a few words with the nurse Theresa. We must be wary for a while, if we are to get the information which we want.'

She was an interesting person, this stern Australian nurse. Taciturn, suspicious, ungracious, it took some time before Holmes's pleasant manner and frank acceptance of all that she said thawed her into a corresponding amiability. She did not attempt to conceal her hatred for her late employer.

'Yes, sir, it is true that he threw the decanter at me. I heard him call my mistress a name, and I told him that he would not dare to speak so if her brother had been there. Then it was that he threw it at me. He might have thrown a dozen if he had but left my bonny bird alone. He was for ever ill-treating her, and she too proud to complain. She will not even tell me all that he has done to her. She never told me of those marks on her arm that you saw this morning, but I know very well that they come from a stab with a hat-pin. The sly devil—God forgive me that I should speak of him so, now that he is dead, but a devil he was* if ever one walked the earth. He was all honey when we first met him, only eighteen months ago, and we both feel as if it were eighteen years. She had only just arrived in London. Yes, it was her first voyage—she had never been from home before. He won her with his title and his money and his false London ways. If she made a mistake she has paid for it, if ever a woman did. What month did we meet him? Well, I tell you it was just after we arrived. We arrived in June, and it was July. They were married in January of last year. Yes, she is down in the morning-room again, and I have no doubt she will see you, but you must not ask too much of her, for she has gone through all that flesh and blood will stand.'

Lady Brackenstall was reclining on the same couch, but looked brighter than before. The maid had entered with us, and began once more to foment the bruise upon her mistress's brow.

'I hope,' said the lady, 'that you have not come to cross-examine me again?'

'No,' Holmes answered, in his gentlest voice, 'I will not cause you any unnecessary trouble, Lady Brackenstall, and my whole desire is to make things easy for you, for I am convinced that you are a much-tried woman. If you will treat me as a friend and trust me, you may find that I will justify your trust.'

'What do you want me to do?'

'To tell me the truth.'

'Mr Holmes!'

'No, no, Lady Brackenstall, it is no use. You may have heard of any little reputation which I possess. I will stake it all on the fact that your story is an absolute fabrication.'

Mistress and maid were both staring at Holmes with pale faces and frightened eyes.

'You are an impudent fellow!' cried Theresa. 'Do you mean to say that my mistress has told a lie?'

Holmes rose from his chair.

'Have you nothing to tell me?'

'I have told you everything.'

'Think once more, Lady Brackenstall. Would it not be better to be frank?'

For an instant there was hestitation in her beautiful face. Then some new strong thought caused it to set like a mask.

'I have told you all I know.'

Holmes took his hat and shrugged his shoulders. 'I am sorry,' he said, and without another word we left the room and the house. There was a pond in the park, and to this my friend led the way. It was frozen over, but a single hole was left for the convenience of a solitary swan. Holmes gazed at it, and then passed on to the lodge gate. There he scribbled a short note for Stanley Hopkins, and left it with the lodge-keeper.

'It may be a hit, or it may be a miss, but we are bound to do something for friend Hopkins, just to justify this second visit,' said he. 'I will not quite take him into my confidence yet. I think our next scene of operations must be the shipping office of the Adelaide–Southampton line, which stands at the end of Pall Mall,* if I remember right. There is a second line of steamers which connect South Australia with England, but we will draw the larger cover first.'*

Holmes's card sent in to the manager ensured instant attention, and he was not long in acquiring all the information which he needed. In June of '95 only one of their line had reached a home port. It was the *Rock of Gibraltar*,* their largest and best boat. A reference to the passenger list showed that Miss Fraser of Adelaide, with her maid, had made the voyage in her. The boat was now on her way to Australia, somewhere to the south of the Suez Canal. Her officers were the same as in '95, with one exception. The first officer, Mr Jack Croker,* had been made a captain, and was to take charge of their new ship, the *Bass Rock*, sailing in two days' time from Southampton. He lived at Sydenham, but he was likely to be in that morning for instructions, if we cared to wait for him.

No; Mr Holmes had no desire to see him, but would be glad to know more about his record and character.

His record was magnificent. There was not an officer in the fleet to touch him. As to his character, he was reliable on duty, but a wild, desperate fellow off the deck of his ship, hot-headed, excitable, but loyal, honest, and kind-hearted. That was the pith of the information with which Holmes left the office of the Adelaide–Southampton Company. Thence he drove to Scotland Yard, but instead of entering he sat in his cab with his brows drawn down, lost in profound thought. Finally he drove round to the Charing Cross telegraph office,* sent off a message, and then, at last, we made for Baker Street once more.

'No, I couldn't do it, Watson,' said he, as we re-entered our room. 'Once that warrant was made out nothing on earth would save him. Once or twice in my career I feel that I have done more real harm by my discovery of the criminal than ever he had done by his crime. I have learned caution now, and I had rather play tricks with the law of England than with my own conscience. Let us know a little more before we act.'

Before evening we had a visit from Inspector Stanley Hopkins. Things were not going very well with him.

'I believe that you are a wizard, Mr Holmes. I really do sometimes think that you have powers that are not human. Now, how on earth could you know that the stolen silver was at the bottom of that pond?'

'I didn't know it.'

'But you told me to examine it.'

'You got it then?'

'Yes, I got it.'

'I am very glad if I have helped you.'

'But you haven't helped me. You have made the affair far more difficult. What sort of burglars are they who steal silver and then throw it into the nearest pond?'

'It was certainly rather eccentric behaviour. I was merely going on the idea that if the silver had been taken by persons who did not want it, who merely took it for a blind, as it were, then they would naturally be anxious to get rid of it.'

'But why should such an idea cross your mind?'

'Well, I thought it was possible. When they came out through the French window there was the pond, with one tempting little hole in the ice right in front of their noses. Could there be a better hiding-place?'

'Ah, a hiding-place—that is better!' cried Stanley Hopkins. 'Yes, yes, I see it all now! It was early, there were folk upon the roads, they were afraid of being seen with the silver, so they sank it in the pond, intending to return for it when the coast was clear. Excellent, Mr Holmes—that is better than your idea of a blind.'

'Quite so; you have got an admirable theory. I have no doubt that my own ideas were quite wild, but you must admit that they have ended in discovering the silver.'

'Yes, sir; yes. It was all your doing. But I have had a bad set-back.'

'A set-back?'

'Yes, Mr Holmes. The Randall gang were arrested in New York this morning.'

'Dear me, Hopkins. That is certainly rather against your theory that they committed a murder in Kent last night.'

'It is fatal, Mr Holmes, absolutely fatal. Still, there are other gangs of three besides the Randalls, or it may be some new gang of which the police have never heard.'

'Quite so; it is perfectly possible. What, are you off?'

'Yes, Mr Holmes; there is no rest for me until I have got to the bottom of the business. I suppose you have no hint to give me?'

'I have given you one.'

'Which?'

'Well, I suggested a blind.'

'But why, Mr Holmes, why?'

'Ah, that's the question, of course. But I commend the idea to your mind. You might possibly find that there was something in it. You won't stop for dinner? Well, good-bye, and let us know how you get on.'

Dinner was over and the table cleared before Holmes alluded to the matter again. He had lit his pipe, and held his slippered feet to the cheerful blaze of the fire. Suddenly he looked at his watch.

'I expect developments, Watson.'

'When?'

'Now—within a few minutes. I dare say you thought I acted rather badly to Stanley Hopkins just now?'

'I trust your judgement.'

'A very sensible reply, Watson. You must look at it this way; what I know is unofficial; what he knows is official. I have the right to private judgment, but he has none. He must disclose all, or he is a traitor to his service. In a doubtful case I would not put him in so painful a position, and so I reserve my information until my own mind is clear upon the matter.'

'But when will that be?'

'The time has come. You will now be present at the last scene of a remarkable little drama.'

There was a sound upon the stairs, and our door was opened to admit as fine a specimen of manhood as ever passed through it. He was a very tall young man, golden-moustached, blue-eyed, with a skin which had been burned

285

by tropical suns, and a springy step which showed that the huge frame was as active as it was strong. He closed the door behind him, and then he stood with clenched hands and heaving breast, choking down some overmastering emotion.

'Sit down, Captain Croker. You got my telegram?'

Our visitor sank into an arm-chair and looked from one to the other of us with questioning eyes.

'I got your telegram, and I came at the hour you said. I heard that you had been down to the office. There was no getting away from you. Let's hear the worst. What are you going to do with me? Arrest me? Speak out, man! You can't sit there and play with me like a cat with a mouse.'

'Give him a cigar,' said Holmes. 'Bite on that, Captain Croker, and don't let your nerves run away with you. I should not sit here smoking with you if I thought that you were a common criminal, you may be sure of that. Be frank with me, and we may do some good. Play tricks with me, and I'll crush you.'

'What do you wish me to do?'

'To give me a true account of all that happened at the Abbey Grange last night—a *true* account, mind you, with nothing added and nothing taken off. I know so much already that if you go one inch off the straight I'll blow this police whistle from my window and the affair goes out of my hands for ever.'

The sailor thought for a little. Then he struck his leg with his great sunburnt hand.

'I'll chance it,' he cried. 'I believe you are a man of your word, and a white man, and I'll tell you the whole story. But one thing I will say first. So far as I am concerned, I regret nothing and I fear nothing, and I would do it all again and be proud of the job. Damn* the beast—if he had as many lives as a cat he would owe them all to me! But it's the lady, Mary—Mary Fraser—for never will I call her by that accursed name. When I think of getting her into trouble, I who would give my life just to bring one smile to her dear face, it's that that turns my soul into water. And yet—and

286

yet—what less could I do? I'll tell you my story, gentlemen, and then I'll ask you as man to man what less could I do.

'I must go back a bit. You seem to know everything, so I expect that you know that I met her when she was a passenger and I was the first officer of the *Rock of Gibraltar*. From the first day I met her she was the only woman to me. Every day of that voyage I loved her more, and many a time since have I kneeled down in the darkness of the night watch and kissed the deck of that ship because I knew her dear feet had trod it. She was never engaged to me. She treated me as fairly as ever a woman treated a man. I have no complaint to make. It was all love on my side, and all good comradeship and friendship on hers. When we parted she was a free woman, but I could never again be a free man.

'Next time I came back from sea I heard of her marriage. Well, why shouldn't she marry whom she liked? Title and money—who could carry them better than she? She was born for all that is beautiful and dainty. I didn't grieve over her marriage. I was not such a selfish hound as that. I just rejoiced that good luck had come her way, and that she had not thrown herself away on a penniless sailor. That's how I loved Mary Fraser.

'Well, I never thought to see her again; but last voyage I was promoted, and the new boat was not yet launched, so I had to wait for a couple of months with my people at Sydenham. One day out in a country lane I met Theresa Wright, her old maid. She told me about her, about him, about everything. I tell you, gentlemen, it nearly drove me mad. This drunken hound, that he should dare to raise his hand to her whose boots he was not worthy to lick! I met Theresa again. Then I met Mary herself—and met her again. Then she would meet me no more. But the other day I had a notice that I was to start on my voyage within a week, and I determined that I would see her once before I left. Theresa was always my friend, for she loved Mary and hated this villain almost as much as I did. From her I learned the ways of the house. Mary used to sit up reading

in her own little room downstairs. I crept round there last
night and scratched at the window. At first she would not
open to me, but in her heart I know that now she loves me,
and she could not leave me in the frosty night. She
whispered to me to come round to the big front window,
and I found it open before me so as to let me into the
dining-room. Again I heard from her own lips things that
made my blood boil, and again I cursed this brute who
mishandled the woman that I loved. Well, gentlemen, I was
standing with her just inside the window, in all innocence,
as God* is my judge, when he rushed like a madman into
the room, called her the vilest name that a man could use
to a woman, and welted* her across the face with the stick
he had in his hand. I had sprung for the poker, and it was
a fair fight between us. See here on my arm where his first
blow fell. Then it was my turn, and I went through him as
if he had been a rotten pumpkin. Do you think I was sorry?
Not I! It was his life or mine; but far more than that—it was
his life or hers, for how could I leave her in the power of
this madman? That was how I killed him. Was I wrong?
Well, then, what would either of you gentlemen have done
if you had been in my position?

'She had screamed when he struck her, and that brought
old Theresa down from the room above. There was a bottle
of wine on the sideboard, and I opened it and poured a little
between Mary's lips, for she was half dead with the shock.
Then I took a drop myself. Theresa was as cool as ice, and
it was her plot as much as mine. We must make it appear
that burglars had done the thing. Theresa kept on repeating
our story to her mistress, while I swarmed up and cut the
rope of the bell. Then I lashed her in her chair, and frayed
out the end of the rope to make it look natural, else they
would wonder how in the world a burglar could have got up
there to cut it. Then I gathered up a few plates and pots of
silver, to carry out the idea of a robbery, and there I left
them, with orders to give the alarm when I had a quarter of
an hour's start. I dropped the silver into the pond and made
off for Sydenham, feeling that for once in my life I had done

a real good night's work. And that's the truth and the whole truth, Mr Holmes, if it costs me my neck.'

Holmes smoked for some time in silence. Then he crossed the room and shook our visitor by the hand.

'That's what I think,' said he. 'I know that every word is true, for you have hardly said a word which I did not know. No one but an acrobat or a sailor could have got up to the bell-rope from the bracket, and no one but a sailor could have made the knots with which the cord was fastened to the chair. Only once had this lady been brought into contact with sailors, and that was on her voyage, and it was someone of her own class of life, since she was trying hard to shield him and so showing that she loved him. You see how easy it was for me to lay my hands upon you when once I had started upon the right trail.'

'I thought the police never could have seen through our dodge.'

'And the police haven't; nor will they, to the best of my belief. Now, look here, Captain Croker, this is a very serious matter, though I am willing to admit that you acted under the most extreme provocation to which any man could be subjected. I am not sure that in defence of your own life your action will not be pronounced legitimate. However, that is for a British jury to decide. Meanwhile I have so much sympathy for you that if you choose to disappear in the next twenty-four hours I will promise you that no one will hinder you.'

'And then it will all come out?'

'Certainly it will come out.'

The sailor flushed with anger.

'What sort of proposal is that to make to a man? I know enough of law to understand that Mary would be had as accomplice. Do you think I would leave her alone to face the music while I slunk away? No, sir; let them do their worst upon me, but for Heaven's sake, Mr Holmes, find some way of keeping my poor Mary out of the courts.'

Holmes for the second time held out his hand to the sailor.

'I was only testing you, and you ring true every time. Well, it is a great responsibility that I take upon myself, but I have given Hopkins an excellent hint, and if he can't avail himself of it I can do no more. See here, Captain Croker, we'll do this in due form of law. You are the prisoner. Watson, you are a British jury, and I never met a man who was more eminently fitted to represent one. I am the judge. Now, gentlemen of the jury, you have heard the evidence. Do you find the prisoner guilty or not guilty?'

'Not guilty, my lord,' said I.

'*Vox populi, vox Dei.** You are acquitted, Captain Croker. So long as the law does not find some other victim, you are safe from me. Come back to this lady in a year, and may her future and yours justify us in the judgment which we have pronounced this night.'*

The Second Stain

I HAD intended 'The Adventure of the Abbey Grange' to be the last of those exploits of my friend, Mr Sherlock Holmes, which I should ever communicate to the public. This resolution of mine was not due to any lack of material, since I have notes of many hundreds of cases to which I have never alluded, nor was it caused by any waning interest on the part of my readers in the singular personality and unique methods of this remarkable man. The real reason lay in the reluctance which Mr Holmes has shown to the continued publication of his experiences. So long as he was in actual professional practice the records of his successes were of some practical value to him; but since he has definitely retired from London and betaken himself to study and bee-farming on the Sussex Downs,* notoriety has become hateful to him, and he has peremptorily requested that his wishes in this matter should be strictly observed. It was only upon my representing to him that I had given a promise* that 'The Adventure of the Second Stain' should be published when the time was ripe, and pointed out to him that it was only appropriate that this long series of episodes should culminate in the most important international case which he has ever been called upon to handle, that I at last succeeded in obtaining his consent that a carefully guarded account of the incident should at last be laid before the public. If in telling the story I seem to be somewhat vague in certain details the public will readily understand that there is an excellent reason for my reticence.

It was, then, in a year, and even in a decade, that shall be nameless, that upon one Tuesday morning in autumn* we found two visitors of European fame within the walls of our humble room in Baker Street. The one, austere, high-nosed, eagle-eyed, and dominant, was none other than the illustrious Lord Bellinger, twice Premier of Britain.* The other, dark, clear-cut, and elegant, hardly yet of middle age, and endowed with every beauty of body and of mind, was the Right Honourable Trelawney Hope, Secretary for European Affairs,* and the most rising statesman in the country. They sat side by side upon our paper-littered settee, and it was easy to see from their worn and anxious faces that it was business of the most pressing importance which had brought them. The Premier's thin, blue-veined hands were clasped tightly over the ivory head of his umbrella, and his gaunt, ascetic face looked gloomily from Holmes to me. The European Secretary pulled nervously at his moustache and fidgeted with the seals of his watch-chain.

'When I discovered my loss, Mr Holmes, which was at eight o'clock this morning, I at once informed the Prime Minister. It was at his suggestion that we have both come to you.'

'Have you informed the police?'

'No, sir,' said the Prime Minister, with the quick, decisive manner for which he was famous. 'We have not done so, nor is it possible that we should do so. To inform the police must, in the long run, mean to inform the public. This is what we particularly desire to avoid.'

'And why, sir?'

'Because the document in question is of such immense importance that its publication might very easily—I might almost say probably—lead to European complications of the utmost moment. It is not too much to say that peace or war may hang upon the issue. Unless its recovery can be attended with the utmost secrecy, then it may as well not be recovered at all, for all that is aimed at by those who have taken it is that its contents should be generally known.'

'I understand. Now, Mr Trelawney Hope, I should be much obliged if you would tell me exactly the circumstances under which this document disappeared.'

'That can be done in a very few words, Mr Holmes. The letter—for it was a letter from a foreign potentate*—was received six days ago. It was of such importance that I have never left it in my safe, but I have taken it across each evening to my house in Whitehall Terrace,* and kept it in my bedroom in a locked dispatch-box. It was there last night. Of that I am certain. I actually opened the box while I was dressing for dinner, and saw the document inside. This morning it was gone. The dispatch-box had stood beside the glass upon my dressing-table all night. I am a light sleeper, and so is my wife. We are both prepared to swear that no one could have entered the room during the night. And yet I repeat that the paper is gone.'

'What time did you dine?'

'Half-past seven.'

'How long was it before you went to bed?'

'My wife had gone to the theatre. I waited up for her. It was half-past eleven before we went to our room.'

'Then for four hours the dispatch-box had lain un-guarded?'

'No one is ever permitted to enter that room save the housemaid in the morning, and my valet, or my wife's maid, during the rest of the day. They are both trusty servants who have been with us for some time. Besides, neither of them could possibly have known that there was anything more valuable than the ordinary departmental papers in my dispatch-box.'

'Who did know of the existence of that letter?'

'No one in the house.'

'Surely your wife knew?'

'No, sir; I had said nothing to my wife until I missed the paper this morning.'

The Premier nodded approvingly.

'I have long known, sir, how high is your sense of public duty,' said he. 'I am convinced that in the case of a secret of this importance it would rise superior to the most intimate domestic ties.'

The European Secretary bowed.

'You do me no more than justice, sir. Until this morning I have never breathed one word to my wife upon this matter.'

'Could she have guessed?'

'No, Mr Holmes, she could not have guessed—nor could anyone have guessed.'

'Have you lost any documents before?'

'No, sir.'

'Who is there in England who did know of the existence of this letter?'

'Each member of the Cabinet was informed of it yesterday; but the pledge of secrecy which attends every Cabinet meeting was increased by the solemn warning which was given by the Prime Minister. Good God,* to think that within a few hours I should myself have lost it!' His handsome face was distorted with a spasm of despair, and his hands tore at his hair. For a moment we caught a glimpse of the natural man—impulsive, ardent, keenly sensitive. The next the aristocratic mask was replaced, and the gentle voice had returned. 'Besides the members of the Cabinet there are two, or possibly three, departmental officials who know of the letter. No one else in England, Mr Holmes, I assure you.'

'But abroad?'

'I believe that no one abroad has seen it save the man who wrote it. I am well convinced that his Ministers—that the usual official channels have not been employed.'

Holmes considered for some little time.*

'Now, sir, I must ask you more particularly what this document is, and why its disappearance should have such momentous consequences?'

The two statesmen exchanged a quick glance, and the Premier's shaggy eyebrows gathered in a frown.

'Mr Holmes, the envelope is a long, thin one of pale blue colour. There is a seal of red wax stamped with a crouching lion.* It is addressed in large, bold handwriting to—'

'I fear,' said Holmes, 'that, interesting and indeed essential as these details are, my inquiries must go more to the root of things. What *was* the letter?'

'That is a State secret of the utmost importance, and I fear that I cannot tell you, nor do I see that it is necessary.

If by the aid of the powers which you are said to possess you can find such an envelope as I describe with its enclosure, you will have deserved well of your country, and earned any reward which it lies in our power to bestow.'

Sherlock Holmes rose with a smile.

'You are two of the most busy men in the country,' said he, 'and in my own small way I have also a good many calls upon me. I regret exceedingly that I cannot help you in this matter, and any continuation of this interview would be a waste of time.'

The Premier sprang to his feet with that quick, fierce gleam of his deep-set eyes before which a Cabinet had cowered. 'I am not accustomed—' he began, but mastered his anger and resumed his seat. For a minute or more we all sat in silence. Then the old statesman shrugged his shoulders.

'We must accept your terms, Mr Holmes. No doubt you are right, and it is unreasonable for us to expect you to act unless we give you our entire confidence.'

'I agree with you, sir,' said the younger statesman.

'Then I will tell you, relying entirely upon your honour and that of your colleague, Dr Watson. I may appeal to your patriotism also, for I could not imagine a greater misfortune for the country than that this affair should come out.'

'You may safely trust us.'

'The letter, then, is from a certain foreign potentate who has been ruffled by some recent Colonial developments of this country. It has been written hurriedly and upon his own responsibility entirely. Inquiries have shown that his Ministers know nothing of the matter. At the same time it is couched in so unfortunate a manner, and certain phrases in it are of so provocative a character, that its publication would undoubtedly lead to a most dangerous state of feeling in this country. There would be such a ferment, sir, that I do not hesitate to say that within a week of the publication of that letter this country would be involved in a great war.'

Holmes wrote a name upon a slip of paper and handed it to the Premier.

'Exactly. It was he. And it is this letter—this letter which may well mean the expenditure of a thousand millions and the lives of a hundred thousand men—which has become lost in this unaccountable fashion.'

'Have you informed the sender?'

'Yes, sir, a cipher telegram has been dispatched*.'

'Perhaps he desires the publication of the letter.'

'No, sir, we have strong reason to believe that he already understands that he has acted in an indiscreet and hot-headed manner. It would be a greater blow to him and to his country than to us if this letter were to come out.'

'If this is so, whose interest is it that the letter should come out? Why should anyone desire to steal it or to publish it?'

'There, Mr Holmes, you take me into regions of high international politics. But if you consider the European situation you will have no difficulty in perceiving the motive. The whole of Europe is an armed camp. There is a double league which makes a fair balance of military power. Great Britain holds the scales. If Britain were driven into war with one confederacy, it would assure the supremacy of the other confederacy, whether they joined in the war or not. Do you follow?'

'Very clearly. It is then the interest of the enemies of this potentate to secure and publish this letter, so as to make a breach between his country and ours?'

'Yes, sir.'

'And to whom would this document be sent if it fell into the hands of an enemy?'

'To any of the great Chancelleries of Europe.* It is probably speeding on its way thither at the present instant as fast as steam can take it.'

Mr Trelawney Hope dropped his head on his chest and groaned aloud. The Premier placed his hand kindly upon his shoulder.

'It is your misfortune, my dear fellow. No one can blame you. There is no precaution which you have neglected. Now, Mr Holmes, you are in full possession of the facts. What course do you recommend?'

Holmes shook his head mournfully.

'You think, sir, that unless this document is recovered there will be war?'

'I think it is very probable.'

'Then, sir, prepare for war.'

'That is a hard saying, Mr Holmes.'

'Consider the facts, sir. It is inconceivable that it was taken after eleven-thirty at night, since I understand that Mr Hope and his wife were both in the room from that hour until the loss was found out. It was taken, then, yesterday evening between seven-thirty and eleven-thirty, probably near the earlier hour, since whoever took it evidently knew that it was there, and would naturally secure it as early as possible. Now, sir, if a document of this importance were taken at that hour, where can it be now? No one has any reason to retain it. It has been passed rapidly on to those who need it. What chance have we now to overtake or even to trace it? It is beyond our reach.'

The Prime Minister rose from the settee.

'What you say is perfectly logical, Mr Holmes. I feel that the matter is indeed out of our hands.'

'Let us presume, for argument's sake, that the document was taken by the maid or by the valet—'

'They are both old tried servants.'

'I understand you to say that your room is on the second floor, that there is no entrance from without, and that from within no one could go up unobserved. It must, then, be somebody in the house who has taken it. To whom would the thief take it? To one of several international spies and secret agents, whose names are tolerably familiar to me. There are three* who may be said to be the heads of their profession. I will begin my research by going round and finding if each of them is at his post. If one is missing—especially if he had disappeared since last night—we will have some indication as to where the document has gone.'

'Why should he be missing?' asked the European Secretary. 'He would take the letter to an Embassy in London, as likely as not.'

'I fancy not. These agents work independently, and their relations with the Embassies are often strained.'

The Prime Minister nodded his acquiescence.

'I believe you are right, Mr Holmes. He would take so valuable a prize to headquarters with his own hands. I think that your course of action is an excellent one. Meanwhile, Hope, we cannot neglect our other duties on account of this one misfortune. Should there be any fresh developments during the day we shall communicate with you, and you will no doubt let us know the results of your own inquiries.'

The two statesmen bowed and walked gravely from the room.

When our illustrious visitors had departed, Holmes lit his pipe in silence, and sat for some time lost in the deepest thought. I had opened the morning paper and was immersed in a sensational crime which had occurred in London the night before, when my friend gave an exclamation, sprang to his feet, and laid his pipe down upon the mantel-piece.

'Yes,' said he, 'there is no better way of approaching it. The situation is desperate, but not hopeless. Even now, if we could be sure which of them has taken it, it is just possible that it has not yet passed out of his hands. After all, it is a question of money with these fellows, and I have the British Treasury* behind me. If it's on the market I'll buy it—if it means another penny on the income tax. It is conceivable that the fellow might hold it back to see what bids come from this side before he tries his luck on the other. There are only those three capable of playing so bold a game; there are Oberstein,* La Rothiere,* and Eduardo Lucas.* I will see each of them.'

I glanced at my morning paper.

'Is that Eduardo Lucas of Godolphin Street?'*

'Yes.'

'You will not see him.'

'Why not?'

'He was murdered in his house last night.'

My friend has so often astonished me in the course of our adventures that it was with a sense of exultation that I realized how completely I had astonished him. He stared in amazement, and then snatched the paper from my hands. This was the paragraph which I had been engaged in reading when he rose from his chair:

MURDER IN WESTMINSTER

A crime of a mysterious character was committed last night at 16, Godolphin Street, one of the old-fashioned and secluded rows of eighteenth-century houses which lie between the river and the Abbey, almost in the shadow of the great tower of the Houses of Parliament.* This small but select mansion has been inhabited for some years by Mr Eduardo Lucas, well known in society circles both on account of his charming personality and because he has the well-deserved reputation of being one of the best amateur tenors in the country. Mr Lucas is an unmarried man, thirty-four years of age, and his establishment consists of Mrs Pringle, an elderly housekeeper, and of Mitton,* his valet. The former retires early and sleeps at the top of the house. The valet was out for the evening, visiting a friend at Hammersmith. From ten o'clock onwards Mr Lucas had the house to himself. What occurred during that time has not yet transpired, but at a quarter to twelve Police-constable Barrett, passing along Godolphin Street, observed that the door of No. 16 was ajar. He knocked, but received no answer. Perceiving a light in the front room he advanced into the house and again knocked, but without reply. He then pushed open the door and entered. The room was in a state of wild disorder, the furniture being all swept to one side, and one chair lying on its back in the centre. Beside this chair, and still grasping one of its legs, lay the unfortunate tenant of the house. He had been stabbed to the heart, and must have died instantly. The knife with which the crime had been committed was a curved Indian dagger, plucked down from a trophy of Oriental arms which adorned one of the walls. Robbery does not appear to have been the motive of the crime, for there had been no attempt to remove the valuable contents of the room. Mr Eduardo Lucas was so well known and popular that his violent and mysterious fate will arouse painful interest and intense sympathy in a widespread circle of friends.

'Well, Watson, what do you make of this?' asked Holmes, after a long pause.

'It is an amazing coincidence.'

'A coincidence! Here is one of three men whom we had named as possible actors in this drama, and he meets a violent death during the very hours when we know that that drama was being enacted. The odds are enormous against its being coincidence. No figures could express them. No, my dear Watson, the two events are connected—*must* be connected. It is for us to find the connection.'

'But now the official police must know all.'

'Not at all. They know all they see at Godolphin Street. They know—and shall know—nothing of Whitehall Terrace. Only *we* know of both events, and can trace the relation between them. There is one obvious point which would, in any case, have turned my suspicions against Lucas. Godolphin Street, Westminster, is only a few minutes' walk from Whitehall Terrace. The other secret agents whom I have named live in the extreme West End.* It was easier, therefore, for Lucas than for the others to establish a connection or receive a message from the European Secretary's household—a small thing, and yet where events are compressed into a few hours it may prove essential. Hullo! what have we here?'

Mrs Hudson had appeared with a lady's card upon her salver. Holmes glanced at it, raised his eyebrows, and handed it over to me.

'Ask Lady Hilda Trelawney Hope if she will be kind enough to step up,' said he.

A moment later our modest apartment, already so distinguished that morning, was further honoured by the entrance of the most lovely woman in London. I had often heard of the beauty of the youngest daughter of the Duke of Belminster,* but no description of it, and no contemplation of colourless photographs, had prepared me for the subtle, delicate charm and the beautiful colouring of that exquisite head. And yet as we saw it that autumn morning it was not its beauty which would be the first thing to impress the observer. The cheek was lovely, but it was paled with emotion; the eyes were bright, but it was the brightness of fever; the sensitive mouth was tight and drawn in an effort after self-command. Terror—not beauty—was what sprang first to the eye as our fair visitor stood framed for an instant in the open door.

'Has my husband been here, Mr Holmes?'

'Yes, madam, he has been here.'

'Mr Holmes, I implore you not to tell him that I came here.'

Holmes bowed coldly and motioned the lady to a chair.

'Your ladyship places me in a very delicate position. I beg that you will sit down and tell me what you desire; but I fear that I cannot make any unconditional promise.'

She swept across the room and seated herself with her back to the window. It was a queenly presence—tall, graceful, and intensely womanly.

'Mr Holmes,' she said—and her white-gloved hands clasped and unclasped as she spoke—'I will speak frankly to you in the hope that it may induce you to speak frankly in return. There is complete confidence between my husband and me on all matters save one. That one is politics. On this his lips are sealed. He tells me nothing. Now, I am aware that there was a most deplorable occurrence in our house last night. I know that a paper has disappeared. But because the matter is political my husband refuses to take me into his complete confidence. Now it is essential—essential, I say—that I should thoroughly understand it. You are the only other person, save these politicians, who knows the true facts. I beg you, then, Mr Holmes, to tell me exactly what has happened and what it will lead to. Tell me all, Mr Holmes. Let no regard for your client's interests keep you silent, for I assure you that his interests, if he would only see it, would be best served by taking me into his complete confidence. What was this paper that was stolen?'

'Madam, what you ask me is really impossible.'

She groaned and sank her face in her hands.

'You must see that this is so, madam. If your husband thinks fit to keep you in the dark over this matter, is it for me, who have only learned the true facts under the pledge of professional secrecy, to tell what he has withheld? It is not fair to ask it. It is him whom you must ask.'

'I have asked him. I come to you as a last resource. But without your telling me anything definite, Mr Holmes, you may do a great service if you would enlighten me on one point.'

'What is it, madam?'

'Is my husband's political career likely to suffer through this incident?'

'Well, madam, unless it is set right it may certainly have a very unfortunate effect.'

'Ah!' She drew in her breath sharply as one whose doubts are resolved.

'One more question, Mr Holmes. From an expression which my husband dropped in the first shock of this disaster I understood that terrible public consequences might arise from the loss of this document.'

'If he said so, I certainly cannot deny it.'

'Of what nature are they?'

'Nay, madam, there again you ask me more than I can possibly answer.'

'Then I will take up no more of your time. I cannot blame you, Mr Holmes, for having refused to speak more freely, and you on your side will not, I am sure, think the worse of me because I desire, even against his will, to share my husband's anxieties. Once more I beg that you will say nothing of my visit.' She looked back at us from the door, and I had a last impression of that beautiful, haunted face, the startled eyes, and the drawn mouth. Then she was gone.

'Now, Watson, the fair sex is your department,'* said Holmes, with a smile, when the dwindling *frou-frou** of skirts had ended in the slam of the door. 'What was the fair lady's game? What did she really want?'

'Surely her own statement is clear and her anxiety very natural.'

'Hum! Think of her appearance, Watson, her manner, her suppressed excitement, her restlessness, her tenacity in

302

asking questions. Remember that she comes of a caste who do not lightly show emotion.'*

'She was certainly much moved.'

'Remember also the curious earnestness with which she assured us that it was best for her husband that she should know all. What did she mean by that? And you must have observed, Watson, how she manoeuvred to have the light at her back. She did not wish us to read her expression.'

'Yes; she chose the one chair in the room.'

'And yet the motives of women are so inscrutable. You remember the woman at Margate* whom I suspected for the same reason. No powder on her nose—that proved to be the correct solution. How can you build on such a quicksand? Their most trivial action may mean volumes, or their most extraordinary conduct may depend upon a hair-pin or a curling-tongs. Good morning, Watson.'

'You are off?'

'Yes; I will while away* the morning at Godolphin Street with our friends of the regular establishment. With Eduardo Lucas lies the solution of our problem, though I must admit that I have not an inkling as to what form it may take. It is a capital mistake to theorize in advance of the facts. Do you stay on guard, my good Watson, and receive any fresh visitors. I'll join you at lunch if I am able.'

All that day and the next and the next Holmes was in a mood which his friends would call taciturn, and others morose. He ran out and ran in, smoked incessantly, played snatches on his violin, sank into reveries, devoured sandwiches at irregular hours, and hardly answered the casual questions which I put to him. It was evident to me that things were not going well with him or his quest. He would say nothing of the case, and it was from the papers that I learned the particulars of the inquest and the arrest with the subsequent release of John Mitton, the valet of the deceased. The corner's jury brought in the obvious 'Wilful murder',* but the parties remained as unknown as ever. No motive was suggested. The room was full of articles of value but none had been taken. The dead man's papers had not been tampered with. They were carefully examined, and showed that he was a keen student of international politics, an indefatigable gossip, a remarkable linguist, and an untiring letter-writer. He had been on intimate terms with the leading politicians of several countries. But nothing sensational was discovered among the documents which filled his drawers. As to his relations with women, they appeared to have been promiscuous but superficial. He had many acquaintances among them, but few friends, and no one whom he loved. His habits were regular, his conduct inoffensive. His death was an absolute mystery, and likely to remain so.

As to the arrest of John Mitton, the valet, it was a counsel of despair as an alternative to absolute inaction. But no case could be sustained against him. He had visited friends in Hammersmith that night. The *alibi* was complete. It is true that he started home at an hour which should have brought him to Westminster before the time when the crime was discovered, but his own explanation that he had walked part of the way seemed probable enough in view of the fineness of the night. He had actually arrived at twelve o'clock, and appeared to be overwhelmed by the unexpected tragedy. He had always been on good terms with his master. Several of the dead man's possessions—notably a small case of razors—had been found in the valet's boxes, but he explained that they had been presents from the deceased, and the housekeeper was able to corroborate the story. Mitton had been in Lucas's employment for three years. It was noticeable that Lucas did not take Mitton on the Continent with him. Sometimes he visited Paris for three months on end, but Mitton was left in charge of the Godolphin Street house. As to the housekeeper, she had heard nothing on the night of the crime. If her master had a visitor, he had himself admitted him.

So for three mornings* the mystery remained, so far as I could follow it in the papers. If Holmes knew more he kept his own counsel, but, as he told me that Inspector Lestrade had taken him into his confidence in the case, I knew that he was in close touch with every development. Upon the fourth day there appeared a long telegram from Paris which seemed to solve the whole question:

A discovery has just been made by the Parisian police [said the *Daily Telegraph*] which raises the veil which hung round the tragic fate of Mr Eduardo Lucas, who met his death by violence last Monday night at Godolphin Street, Westminster. Our readers will remember that the deceased gentleman was found stabbed in his room, and that some suspicion attached to his valet, but that the case broke down on an *alibi*. Yesterday a lady, who has been known as Mme Henri Fournaye,* occupying a small villa in the Rue Austerlitz,* was reported to the authorities by her servants as being insane. An examination showed that she had indeed developed mania of a dangerous and permanent form. On inquiry the police have discovered that Mme Henri Fournaye only returned from a journey to London on Tuesday last, and there is evidence to connect her with the crime at Westminster. A comparison of photographs has proved conclusively that M. Henri Fournaye and Eduardo Lucas were really one and the same person, and that the deceased had for some reason lived a double life in London and Paris. Mme Fournaye, who is of Creole* origin, is of an extremely excitable nature, and has suffered in the past from attacks of jealousy which have amounted to frenzy. It is conjectured that it was in one of these that she committed the terrible crime which has caused such a sensation in London. Her movements upon the Monday night have not yet been traced, but it is undoubted that a woman answering to her description attracted much attention at Charing Cross Station on Tuesday morning by the wildness of her appearance and the violence of her gestures. It is probable, therefore, that the crime was either committed when insane, or that its immediate effect was to drive the unhappy woman out of her mind. At present she is unable to give any coherent account of the past, and the doctors hold out no hopes of the re-establishment of her reason. There is evidence that a woman, who might have been Mme Fournaye, was seen for some hours on Monday night watching the house in Godolphin Street.*

'What do you think of that, Holmes?' I had read the account aloud to him, while he finished his breakfast.

'My dear Watson,' said he, as he rose from the table and paced up and down the room, 'you are most long-suffering, but if I have told you nothing in the last three days it is because there is nothing to tell. Even now this report from Paris does not help us much.'

'Surely it is final as regards the man's death.'

'The man's death is a mere incident—a trivial episode—in comparison with our real task, which is to trace this document and save a European catastrophe. Only one important thing has happened in the last three days, and that is that nothing has happened. I get reports almost hourly from the Government, and it is certain that nowhere in Europe is there any sign of trouble. Now, if this letter were loose—no, it *can't* be loose—but if it isn't loose, where can it be? Who has it? Why is it held back? That's the question that beats in my brain like a hammer. Was it, indeed, a coincidence that Lucas should meet his death on the night when the letter disappeared? Did the letter ever reach him? If so, why is it not among his papers? Did this mad wife of his carry it off with her? If so, is it in her house in Paris? How could I search for it without the French police having their suspicions aroused? It is a case, my dear Watson, where the law is as dangerous to us as the criminals are. Every man's hand is against us, and yet the interests at stake are colossal. Should I bring it to a successful conclusion, it will certainly represent the crowning glory of my career. Ah, here is my latest from the front!' He glanced hurriedly at the note which had been handed in. 'Hullo! Lestrade seems to have observed something of interest. Put on your hat, Watson, and we will stroll down together to Westminster.'

It was my first visit to the scene of the crime—a high, dingy, narrow-chested house, prim, formal, and solid, like the century which gave it birth. Lestrade's bulldog features gazed out at us from the front window, and he greeted us warmly when a big constable had opened the door and let us in. The room into which we were shown was that in which the crime had been committed, but no trace of it now remained, save an ugly, irregular stain upon the carpet.

This carpet was a small square drugget in the centre of the room, surrounded by a broad expanse of beautiful, old-fashioned, wood flooring in square blocks, highly polished. Over the fireplace was a magnificent trophy of weapons, one of which had been used on that tragic night. In the window was a sumptuous writing-desk, and every detail of the apartment, the pictures, the rugs, and the hangings, all pointed to a taste which was luxurious and the verge of effeminacy.

'Seen the Paris news?' asked Lestrade.

Holmes nodded.

'Our French friends seem to have touched the spot this time. No doubt it's just as they say. She knocked at the door—surprise visit, I guess, for he kept his life in water-tight compartments. He let her in—couldn't keep her in the street. She told him how she had traced him, re-proached him, one thing led to another, and then with that dagger so handy the end soon came. It wasn't all done in an instant, though, for these chairs were all swept over yonder, and he had one in his hand as if he had tried to hold her off with it. We've got it all as clear as if we had seen it.'

Holmes raised his eyebrows.

'And yet you have sent for me?'

'Ah, yes, that's another matter—a mere trifle, but the sort of thing you take an interest in—queer, you know, and what you might call freakish. It has nothing to do with the main fact—can't have, on the face of it.'

'What is it, then?'

'Well, you know after a crime of this sort we are very careful to keep things in their position. Nothing has been moved. Officer in charge here day and night. This morning, as the man was buried and the investigation over—so far as this room is concerned—we thought we could tidy up a bit. This carpet. You see, it is not fastened down; only just laid there. We had occasion to raise it. We found—'

'Yes? You found—'

Holmes's face grew tense with anxiety.

'Well, I'm sure you would never guess in a hundred years what we did find. You see that stain on the carpet? Well, a great deal must have soaked through,* must it not?'

'Undoubtedly it must.'

'Well, you will be surprised to hear that there is no stain on the white woodwork to correspond.'

'No stain! But there must—'

'Yes; so you would say. But the fact remains that there isn't.'

He took the corner of the carpet in his hand and, turning it over, he showed that it was indeed as he said.

'But the underside is as stained as the upper. It must have left a mark.'

Lestrade chuckled with delight at having puzzled the famous expert.

'Now I'll show you the explanation. There *is* a second stain, but it does not correspond with the other. See for yourself.' As he spoke he turned over another portion of the carpet, and there, sure enough, was a great crimson spill upon the square white facing of the old-fashioned floor. 'What do you make of that, Mr Holmes?'

'Why, it is simple enough. The two stains did correspond, but the carpet has been turned round. As it was square and unfastened, it was easily done.'

'The official police don't need you, Mr Holmes, to tell them that the carpet must have been turned round. That's clear enough, for the stains lie above each other—if you lay it over this way. But what I want to know is, who shifted the carpet, and why?'

I could see from Holmes's rigid face that he was vibrating with inward excitement.

'Look here, Lestrade!' said he. 'Has that constable in the passage been in charge of the place all the time?'

'Yes, he has.'

'Well, take my advice. Examine him carefully. Don't do it before us. We'll wait here. You take him into the back room. You'll be more likely to get a confession out of him alone. Ask him how he dared to admit people and leave them

alone in this room. Don't ask him if he has done it. Take it
for granted. Tell him you *know* someone has been here. Press
him. Tell him that a full confession is his only chance for
forgiveness. Do exactly what I tell you!'

'By George, if he knows I'll have it out of him!' cried
Lestrade. He darted into the hall, and a few moments later
his bullying voice sounded from the back room.

'Now, Watson, now!' cried Holmes, with frenzied eagerness. All the demoniacal force of the man masked behind
that listless manner burst out in a paroxysm of energy. He
tore the drugget from the floor, and in an instant was down
on his hands and knees clawing at each of the squares of
wood beneath it. One turned sideways as he dug his nails
into the edge of it. It hinged back like the lid of a box. A
small black cavity opened beneath it. Holmes plunged his
eager hand into it, and drew it out with a bitter snarl of
anger and disappointment. It was empty.

'Quick, Watson, quick! Get it back again!' The wooden lid
was replaced, and the drugget* had only just been drawn
straight, when Lestrade's voice was heard in the passage. He
found Holmes leaning languidly against the mantelpiece,
resigned and patient, endeavouring to conceal his irre-
pressible yawns.

'Sorry to keep you waiting, Mr Holmes, I can see that you
are bored to death with the whole affair. Well, he has
confessed all right. Come in here, MacPherson. Let these
gentlemen hear of your most inexcusable conduct.'

The big constable, very hot and penitent, sidled into the
room.

'I meant no harm, sir, I'm sure. The young woman came
to the door last evening—mistook the house, she did. And
then we got talking. It's lonesome, when you're on duty here
all day.'

'Well, what happened then?'

'She wanted to see where the crime was done—had read
about it in the papers, she said. She was a very respectable,
well-spoken young woman, sir, and I saw no harm in letting
her have a peep. When she saw that mark on the carpet,

down she dropped on the floor, and lay as if she were dead. I ran back and got some water, but I could not bring her to. Then I went round the corner to the Ivy Plant* for some brandy, and by the time I had brought it back the young woman had recovered and was off—ashamed of herself, I dare say, and dared not face me.'

'How about moving that drugget?'

'Well, sir, it was a bit rumpled, certainly when I came back. You see, she fell on it, and it lies on a polished floor with nothing to keep it in place. I straightened it out afterwards.'

'It's a lesson to you that you can't deceive me, Constable MacPherson,' said Lestrade, with dignity. 'No doubt you thought that your breach of duty could never be discovered, and yet a mere glance at that drugget was enough to convince me that someone had been admitted to the room. It's lucky for you, my man, that nothing is missing, or you would find yourself in Queer Street.* I'm sorry to have to call you down over such a petty business, Mr Holmes, but I thought the point of the second stain not corresponding with the first would interest you.'

'Certainly it was most interesting. Has this woman only been here once, constable?'

'Yes, sir, only once.'

'Who was she?'

'Don't know the name, sir. Was answering an advertisement about typewriting, and came to the wrong number*—very pleasant, genteel young woman, sir.'

'Tall? Handsome?'

'Yes, sir; she was a well-grown young woman. I suppose you might say she was handsome. Perhaps some would say she was very handsome. "Oh, officer, do let me have a peep!" says she. She had pretty, coaxing ways, as you might say, and I thought there was no harm in letting her just put her head through the door.'

'How was she dressed?'

'Quiet, sir—a long mantle down to her feet.'

'What time was it?'

'It was just growing dusk at the time. They were lighting the lamps as I came back with the brandy.'

'Very good,' said Holmes. 'Come, Watson, I think that we have more important work elsewhere.'

As we left the house Lestrade remained in the front room, while the repentant constable opened the door to let us out. Holmes turned on the step and held up something in his hand. The constable stared intently.

'Good Lord, sir!' he cried, with amazement on his face. Holmes put his finger on his lips, replaced his hand in his breast-pocket, and burst out laughing as we turned down the street. 'Excellent!' said he. 'Come, friend Watson, the curtain rings up for the last act. You will be relieved to hear that there will be no war, that the Right Honourable Trelawney Hope will suffer no set-back in his brilliant career, that the indiscreet Sovereign will receive no punishment for his indiscretion, that the Prime Minister will have no European complication to deal with, and that with a little tact and management upon our part nobody will be a penny the worse for what might have been a very ugly accident.'*

My mind filled with admiration for this extraordinary man.

'You have solved it!' I cried.

'Hardly that, Watson. There are some points which are as dark as ever. But we have so much that it will be our own fault if we cannot get the rest. We will go straight to Whitehall Terrace and bring the matter to a head.'

When we arrived at the residence of the European Secretary it was for Lady Hilda Trelawney Hope that Sherlock Holmes inquired. We were shown into the morning-room.

'Mr Holmes!' said the lady, and her face was pink with indignation, 'this is surely most unfair and ungenerous upon your part. I desired, as I have explained, to keep my visit to you a secret, lest my husband should think that I was intruding into his affairs. And yet you compromise me by coming here, and so showing that there are business relations between us.'

'Unfortunately, madam, I had no possible alternative. I have been commissioned to recover this immensely important paper. I must therefore ask you, madam, to be kind enough to place it in my hands.'

The lady sprang to her feet, with the colour all dashed in an instant from her beautiful face. Her eyes glazed—she tottered—I thought that she would faint. Then with a grand effort she rallied from the shock, and a supreme astonishment and indignation chased every other expression from her features.

'You—you insult me, Mr Holmes.'

'Come, come, madam, it is useless. Give up the letter.'

She darted to the bell.

'The butler shall show you out.'

'Do not ring, Lady Hilda. If you do, then all my earnest efforts to avoid a scandal will be frustrated. Give up the letter, and all will be set right. If you will work with me, I can arrange everything. If you work against me, I must expose you.'

She stood grandly defiant, a queenly figure, her eyes fixed upon his as if she would read his very soul. Her hand was on the bell, but she had forborne to ring it.

'You are trying to frighten me. It is not a very manly thing, Mr Holmes, to come here and browbeat a woman. You say that you know something. What is it that you know?'

'Pray sit down, madam. You will hurt yourself there if you fall. I will not speak until you sit down. Thank you.'

'I give you five minutes, Mr Holmes.'

'One is enough, Lady Hilda. I know of your visit to Eduardo Lucas, and of your giving him this document, of your ingenious return to the room last night, and of the manner in which you took the letter from the hiding-place under the carpet.'

She stared at him with an ashen face, and gulped twice before she could speak.

'You are mad, Mr Holmes—you are mad!' she cried at last.

He drew a small piece of cardboard from his pocket. It was the face of a woman cut out of a portrait.

'I have carried this because I thought it might be useful,' said he. 'The policeman has recognized it.'

She gave a gasp, and her head dropped back in her chair.

'Come, Lady Hilda. You have the letter. The matter may still be adjusted. I have no desire to bring trouble to you. My duty ends when I have returned the lost letter to your husband. Take my advice, and be frank with me; it is your only chance.'

Her courage was admirable. Even now she would not own defeat.

'I tell you again, Mr Holmes, that you are under some absurd illusion.'

Holmes rose from his chair.

'I am sorry for you, Lady Hilda. I have done my best for you; I can see that it is all in vain.'

He rang the bell. The butler entered.

'Is Mr Trelawney Hope at home?'

'He will be home, sir, at a quarter to one.'

Holmes glanced at his watch.

'Still a quarter of an hour,' said he. 'Very good, I shall wait.'

The butler had hardly closed the door behind him when Lady Hilda was down on her knees at Holmes's feet, her hands outstretched, her beautiful face upturned and wet with her tears.

'Oh, spare me, Mr Holmes! Spare me!' she pleaded, in a frenzy of supplication. 'For God's sake* don't tell him! I love him so! I would not bring one shadow on his life, and this I know would break his noble heart.'

Holmes raised the lady. 'I thank God,* madam, that you have come to your senses even at this last moment! There is not an instant to lose. Where is the letter?'

She darted across to a writing-desk, unlocked it, and drew out a long blue envelope.

'Here it is, Mr Holmes. Would to Heaven I had never seen it!'

'How can we return it?' Holmes muttered. 'Quick, quick, we must think of some way! Where is the dispatch-box?'

'Still in his bedroom.'

'What a stroke of luck! Quick, madam, bring it here.'

A moment later she had appeared with a red flat box in her hand.

'How did you open it before? You have a duplicate key? Yes, of course you have. Open it!'

From out of her bosom Lady Hilda had drawn a small key. The box flew open. It was stuffed with papers. Holmes thrust the blue envelope deep down into the heart of them, between the leaves of some other document. The box was shut, locked, and returned to his bedroom.

'Now we are ready for him,' said Holmes; 'we have still ten minutes. I am going far to screen you, Lady Hilda. In return you will spend the time in telling me frankly the real meaning of this extraordinary affair.'

'Mr Holmes, I will tell you everything,' cried the lady. 'Oh, Mr Holmes, I would cut off my right hand before I gave him a moment of sorrow! There is no woman in all London who loves her husband as I do, and yet if he knew how I have acted—how I have been compelled to act—he would never forgive me. For his own honour stands so high that he could not forget or pardon a lapse in another. Help me, Mr Holmes! My happiness, his happiness, our very lives are at stake!'

'Quick, madam, the time grows short!'

'It was a letter of mine, Mr Holmes, an indiscreet letter written before my marriage—a foolish letter, a letter of an impulsive, loving girl. I meant no harm, and yet he would have thought it criminal. Had he read that letter his confidence would have been for ever destroyed. It is years since I wrote it. I had thought that the whole matter was forgotten. Then at last I heard from this man, Lucas, that it had passed into his hands, and that he would lay it before my husband. I implored his mercy. He said that he would return my letter if I would return him a certain document which he described in my husband's dispatch-box. He had

some spy in the office who had told him of its existence.*
He assured me that no harm could come to my husband.
Put yourself in my position, Mr Holmes! What was I to do?'

'Take your husband into your confidence.'

'I could not, Mr Holmes, I could not! On the one side
seemed certain ruin; on the other, terrible as it seemed to
take my husband's papers, still in a matter of politics I could
not understand the consequences, while in a matter of love
and trust they were only too clear to me. I did it, Mr
Holmes! I took an impression of his key; this man Lucas
furnished a duplicate. I opened his dispatch-box, took the
paper, and coveyed it to Godolphin Street.'

'What happened there, madam?'

'I tapped at the door, as agreed. Lucas opened it. I
followed him into his room, leaving the hall door ajar
behind me, for I feared to be alone with the man. I
remember* that there was a woman outside as I entered.
Our business was soon done. He had my letter on his desk;
I handed him the document. He gave me the letter. At this
instant there was a sound at the door. There were steps in
the passage. Lucas quickly turned back the drugget, thrust
the document into some hiding-place there, and covered it
over.

'What happened after that is like some fearful dream. I
have a vision of a dark, frantic face, of a woman's voice,
which screamed in French, "My waiting is not in vain. At
last, at last I have found you with her!" There was a savage
struggle. I saw him with a chair in his hand, a knife gleamed
in hers. I rushed from the horrible scene, ran from the house
and only next morning in the paper did I learn the dreadful
result. That night I was happy, for I had my letter, and I
had not seen yet what the future would bring.

'It was next morning that I realized that I had only
exchanged one trouble for another. My husband's anguish
at the loss of his paper went to my heart. I could hardly
prevent myself from there and then kneeling down at his
feet and telling him what I had done. But that again would
mean a confession of the past. I came to you that morning

in order to understand the full enormity of my offence. From the instant that I grasped it my whole mind turned to the one thought of getting back my husband's paper. It must still be where Lucas had placed it, for it was concealed before this dreadful woman entered the room. If it had not been for her coming, I should not have known where his hiding-place was. How was I to get into the room? For two days I watched the place, but the door was never left open. Last night I made a last attempt. What I did and how I succeeded, you have already learned. I brought the paper back with me, and thought of destroying it, since I could see no way of returning it without confessing my guilt to my husband. Good God,* I hear his step upon the stair!'

The European Secretary burst excitedly into the room.

'Any news, Mr Holmes, any news?' he cried.

'I have some hopes.'

'Ah, thank God!'* His face became radiant. 'The Prime Minister is lunching with me. May he share your hopes? He has nerves of steel, and yet I know that he has hardly slept since this terrible event. Jacobs,* will you ask the Prime Minister to come up? As to you, dear, I fear that this is a matter of politics. We will join you in a few minutes in the dining-room.'

The Prime Minister's manner was subdued, but I could see by the gleam of his eyes and the twitchings of his bony hands that he shared the excitement of his young colleague.

'I understand that you have something to report, Mr Holmes?'

'Purely negative as yet,' my friend answered. 'I have inquired at every point where it might be, and I am sure that there is no danger to be apprehended.'

'But that is not enough, Mr Holmes. We cannot lie for ever on such a volcano. We must have something definite.'

'I am in hopes of getting it. That is why I am here. The more I think of the matter the more convinced I am that the letter has never left this house.'

'Mr Holmes!'

'If it had it would certainly have been public by now.'

'But why should anyone take it in order to keep it in this house?'

'I am not convinced that anyone did take it.'

'Then how could it leave the dispatch-box?'

'I am not convinced that it ever did leave the dispatch-box.'

'Mr Holmes, this joking is very ill-timed. You have my assurance that it left the box.'

'Have you examined the box since Tuesday morning?'

'No; it was not necessary.'

'You may conceivably have overlooked it.'

'Impossible, I say.'

'But I am not convinced of it; I have known such things happen. I presume there are other papers there. Well, it may have got mixed with them.'

'It was on the top.'

'Someone may have shaken the box and displaced it.'

'No, no; I had everything out.'

'Surely it is easily decided, Hope!' said the Premier. 'Let us have the dispatch-box brought in.'

The Secretary rang the bell.

'Jacobs, bring down my dispatch-box. This is a farcical waste of time, but still, if nothing else will satisfy you, it shall be done. Thank you, Jacobs; put it here. I have always had the key on my watch-chain. Here are the papers, you see. Letter from Lord Merrow, report from Sir Charles Hardy, memorandum from Belgrade, note on the Russo-German grain taxes, letter from Madrid, note from Lord Flowers*— good God!* what is this? Lord Bellinger! Lord Bellinger!'

The Premier snatched the blue envelope from his hand.

'Yes, it is it—and the letter intact. Hope, I congratulate you!'

'Thank you! Thank you! What a weight from my heart! But this is inconceivable—impossible! Mr Holmes, you are a wizard, a sorcerer! How did you know it was there?'

'Because I knew it was nowhere else.'

'I cannot believe my eyes!' He ran wildly to the door. 'Where is my wife! I must tell her that all is well. Hilda! Hilda!' we heard his voice on the stairs.

The Premier looked at Holmes with twinkling eyes.

'Come, sir,' said he. 'There is more in this than meets the eye. How came the letter back in the box?'

Holmes turned away smiling from the keen scrutiny of those wonderful eyes.

'We also have our diplomatic secrets,' said he, and picking up his hat he turned to the door.

APPENDIX I

The Field Bazaar

First published in the Bazaar Number of the *Student* (Edinburgh), 11/197 (20 Nov. 1896), 35–6, as 'The Memoirs of Sherlock Holmes. "The Field Bazaar" '. First separate edition, the Athenaeum Press (1934), 2 pp. (100 copies privately printed for A. G. Macdonnell). First American edition, the Pamphlet House (Edgar W. Smith) (Summit, NJ, 1947), 15 pp. (250 numbered copies). MS: present location unknown.

ACD's parody of Sherlock Holmes was written for a special 'Bazaar Number' of the Edinburgh student magazine in connection with a bazaar held in the Music Hall of Edinburgh University between 19 and 21 Nov. 1896 to raise money to build and equip a sports pavilion for a new playing-field. The special number was published on 14 Nov. 1896 (though dated 20 Nov.), and the contributors included Robert Barr, J. M. Barrie, Walter Besant, Professor John Stuart Blackie, S. R. Crockett, Edinburgh University Principal Sir William Muir, Professor Saintsbury, Jessie M. E. Saxby (biographer of Joseph Bell), and Israel Zangwill. The preceding issue (12 Nov. 1896) made specific reference to the Sherlock Holmes parody: 'Dr Conan Doyle . . . has contributed an original story of the "Sherlock Holmes" type. We all remember the indignation aroused by the death of that redoubtable detective, a few years ago. This is the only "Sherlock Holmes" story published since then, and we have to offer our best thanks to the writer for his kindness in thus helping us and the Bazaar.'

It was ACD's first contribution to the *Student*, though the issue for 10 Feb. 1892 (New Series, 6/15, pp. 233–4) had included an article about him, and that for 29 June 1893 (New Series, 7/20, pp. 322–6) had 'an unauthorised adventure of Sherlock Holmes' by 'C', called 'The Mystery of the Spot Ball'. His only other contributions were a letter published on 8 July 1915 (New Series 11, pp. 12–13) and the reprint of a poem called 'The Night Patrol' in May 1920 (16, p. 20).

'The Field Bazaar' created a small stir at the time as it was rumoured that ACD had revived Sherlock Holmes, but it was then quickly forgotten and ACD himself made no mention of it. The rediscovery came after the creation of the Sherlock Holmes Society in London, and was thanks to George J. P. Carruthers who wrote to A. G. Macdonnell (1895–1941, the Honorary Secretary) on 27 Aug. 1934 offering a copy: 'I enclose a copy of the *Student* (the Edinburgh University Magazine) of 20th November 1896 which contains a short Sherlock Holmes sketch by Conan Doyle, and I gladly present it to your Society if the members would care to have it. | As you will notice, this number of the magazine was got up in connection with a bazaar held for the University Field, so your members may not consider it quite fair to decide the University problem from it.'

Macdonnell (otherwise famous as the author of *England Their England* (1933)) had the parody reprinted in an edition of 100 copies which he distributed at the first dinner of the Baker Street Irregulars of New York on 7 Dec. 1934, and at the second dinner of the Sherlock Holmes Society, at Canuto's Restaurant in Baker Street, on 5 June 1935. According to the printed report of the London society, the Honorary Secretary opened the proceedings with an account of his activities: 'From Mr Carruthers (whose dubious part in the affair of "The Solitary Cyclist" it was a little ungrateful to resurrect) he had received a document throwing new and valuable light on Watson's academic career. This document, reprints of which were thoughtfully supplied to members, originally appeared as an article in the Edinburgh University magazine, the *Student* of November 1896, and *pace* Mr [H. W.] Bell, who regards it as a forgery, seems to prove that Watson (but not Holmes) was educated at that University and played in its Cricket XI' (Report of the second meeting of the Sherlock Holmes Society, R. Ivar Gunn (1935), 1).

A hardback edition limited to 250 numbered (and twenty-five unnumbered) copies was published on 1 July 1947 by Edgar W. Smith, of the Baker Street Irregulars, under the imprint of 'The Pamphlet House'.

'I should certainly do it,' said Sherlock Holmes.

I started at the interruption, for my companion had been eating his breakfast with his attention entirely centred upon the paper which was propped up by the coffee pot. Now I looked across at him to find his eyes fastened upon me with the half-amused, half-questioning expression which he usually assumed when he felt that he had made an intellectual point.

'Do what?' I asked.

He smiled as he took his slipper from the mantelpiece and drew from it enough shag tobacco to fill the old clay pipe with which he invariably rounded off his breakfast.

'A most characteristic question of yours, Watson,' said he. 'You will not, I am sure, be offended if I say that any reputation for sharpness which I may possess has been entirely gained by the admirable foil which you have made for me. Have I not heard of débutantes who have insisted upon plainness in their chaperones? There is a certain analogy.'

Our long companionship in the Baker Street rooms had left us on those easy terms of intimacy when much may be said without offence. And yet I acknowledge that I was nettled at his remark.

'I may be very obtuse,' said I, 'but I confess that I am unable to see how you have managed to know that I was ... I was ...'

'Asked to help in the Edinburgh University Bazaar.'

'Precisely. The letter has only just come to hand, and I have not spoken to you since.'

'In spite of that,' said Holmes, leaning back in his chair and putting his finger tips together, 'I would even venture to suggest that the object of the bazaar is to enlarge the University cricket field.'

I looked at him in such bewilderment that he vibrated with silent laughter.

'The fact is, my dear Watson, that you are an excellent subject,' said he. 'You are never *blasé*. You respond instantly to any external stimulus. Your mental processes may be slow but they are never obscure, and I found during breakfast that you were easier reading than the leader in *The Times* in front of me.'

'I should be glad to know how you arrived at your conclusions,' said I.

'I fear that my good nature in giving explanations has seriously compromised my reputation,' said Holmes. 'But in this case the train of reasoning is based upon such obvious facts that no credit can be claimed for it. You entered the room with a thoughtful expression, the expression of a man who is debating some point in his mind. In your hand you held a solitary letter. Now last night you retired in the best of spirits, so it was clear that it was this letter in your hand which had caused the change in you.'

'This is obvious.'

'It is all obvious when it is explained to you. I naturally asked myself what the letter could contain which might have this effect upon you. As you walked you held the flap side of the envelope towards me, and I saw upon it the same shield-shaped device which I have observed upon your old college cricket cap. It was clear, then, that the request came from Edinburgh University—or from some club connected with the University. When you reached the table you laid down the letter beside your plate with the address uppermost, and you walked over to look at the framed photograph upon the left of the mantelpiece.'

It amazed me to see the accuracy with which he had observed my movements. 'What next?' I asked.

'I began by glancing at the address, and I could tell, even at the distance of six feet, that it was an unofficial communication. This I gathered from the use of the word 'Doctor' upon the address, to which, as a Bachelor of Medicine, you have no legal claim. I knew that University officials are pedantic in their correct use of titles, and I was thus enabled to say with certainty that your letter was unofficial. When on your return to the table you turned over your letter and allowed me to perceive that the enclosure was a printed one, the idea of a bazaar first occurred to me. I had already weighed the possibility of its being a political communication, but this seemed improbable in the present stagnant condition of politics.

'When you returned to the table your face still retained its expression, and it was evident that your examination of the photograph had not changed the current of your thoughts. In that case it must itself bear upon the subject in question. I turned my attention to the photograph therefore, and saw at once that it consisted of yourself as a member of the Edinburgh University Eleven, with the pavilion and cricket-field in the background. My small experience of cricket clubs has taught me that next to churches and cavalry ensigns they are the most debt-laden things upon earth. When upon your return to the table I saw you take out your pencil and draw lines upon the envelope, I was convinced that you were endeavouring to realize some projected improvement which was to be brought about by a bazaar. Your face still showed some indecision, so that I was able to break in upon you with my advice that you should assist in so good an object.'

I could not help smiling at the extreme simplicity of his explanation.

'Of course, it was as easy as possible,' said I.

My remark appeared to nettle him.

'I may add,' said he, 'that the particular help which you have been asked to give was that you should write in their album, and that you have already made up your mind that the present incident will be the subject of your article.'

'But how—!' I cried.

'It is as easy as possible,' said he, 'and I leave its solution to your own ingenuity. In the meantime,' he added, raising his paper, 'you will excuse me if I return to this very interesting article upon the trees of Cremona, and the exact reasons for their pre-eminence in the manufacture of violins. It is one of those small outlying problems to which I am sometimes tempted to direct my attention.'

APPENDIX II

How Watson Learned the Trick

First published in *The Book of the Queen's Dolls' House Library*, ed.
E. V. Lucas (London, Methuen, 1924), 92–4 (with a facsimile of the
manuscript on plate 7); reprinted in the *New York Times* (24 Aug.
1924), section 8, 3. First separate edition, Camden House (Chicago,
1947), 5 pp. (sixty copies privately printed for A. J. Bayer and
Vincent Starrett). Present location of MS: the Queen's Dolls'
House, Windsor Castle. The collection of HM The Queen.

The idea for the Queen's Dolls' House was put forward in 1920
and the building was designed by Sir Edwin Lutyens. It was
completed in 1924 and was exhibited at the British Empire
Exhibition at Wembley.

The library is notable for its extensive collection of holograph
works by contemporary authors who were asked to contribute by
Princess Marie Louise (1872–1956), the honorary librarian. She
wrote to ACD from the Ambassadors' Court, St James's Palace, on
29 Aug. 1922:

> Dear Sir Arthur,
>
> You have doubtless heard that a number of artists, authors,
> craftsmen and others have conspired to present to the Queen a
> Doll's [*sic*] House or model residence in miniature, in which
> everything one would find in a King's Palace today is repro-
> duced with minute accuracy so that it will have great historical
> value in the future.
>
> For the Library little books in the autograph of their writers
> are being prepared and will be specially bound.
>
> May I ask if you will be so good as to contribute one of these;
> either something already published which I would ask you to be
> so kind as to copy out, or preferably something original? I
> enclose a small blank book for the purpose.

'How Watson Learned the Trick' was the result, and it provides
a counterpart to 'The Field Bazaar' which was written twenty-six
years earlier. The Royal Archives contain two documents relating
to it. The undated covering note ('With respectful compliments |

from | Arthur Conan Doyle. | Unpublished novelette.'), and a
letter from A. H. Wood (ACD's private secretary) dated 28 May
1923, concerning its future publication: 'In reply to your letter to Sir
Arthur Conan Doyle, who is in America, I have the honour to
inform you that, acting as Attorney for Sir Arthur, I am sure he will
be glad for you to act as you wish with reference to the publication
of his booklet.'

Watson had been watching his companion intently ever
since he had sat down to the breakfast table. Holmes
happened to look up and catch his eye.

'Well, Watson, what are you thinking about?' he asked.

'About you.'

'Me?'

'Yes, Holmes, I was thinking how superficial are those
tricks of yours, and how wonderful it is that the public
should continue to show interest in them.'

'I quite agree,' said Holmes. 'In fact, I have a recollection
that I have myself made a similar remark.'

'Your methods', said Watson severely, 'are really easily
acquired.'

'No doubt,' Holmes answered with a smile. 'Perhaps you
will yourself give an example of this method of reasoning.'

'With pleasure,' said Watson. 'I am able to say that you
were greatly preoccupied when you got up this morning.'

'Excellent!' said Holmes. 'How could you possibly know
that?'

'Because you are usually a very tidy man and yet you have
forgotten to shave.'

'Dear me! How very clever!' said Holmes. 'I had no idea,
Watson, that you were so apt a pupil. Has your eagle eye
detected anything more?'

'Yes, Holmes. You have a client named Barlow, and you
have not been successful in his case.'

'Dear me, how could you know that?'

'I saw the name outside his envelope. When you opened
it you gave a groan and thrust it into your pocket with a
frown on your face.'

'Admirable! You are indeed observant. Any other point?'

'I fear, Holmes, that you have taken to financial speculation.'

'Hou *could* you tell that, Watson?'

'You opened the paper, turned to the financial page, and gave a loud exclamation of interest.'

'Well, that is very clever of you, Watson. Any more?'

'Yes, Holmes, you have put on your black coat, instead of your dressing gown, which proves that you are expecting some important visitor at once.'

'Anything more?'

'I have no doubt that I could find other points, Holmes, but I only give you these few, in order to show you that there are other people in the world who can be as clever as you.'

'And some not so clever,' said Holmes. 'I admit that they are few, but I am afraid, my dear Watson, that I must count you among them.'

'What do you mean, Holmes?'

'Well, my dear fellow, I fear your deductions have not been so happy as I should have wished.'

'You mean that I was mistaken.'

'Just a little that way, I fear. Let us take the points in their order: I did not shave because I have sent my razor to be sharpened. I put on my coat because I have, worse luck, an early meeting with my dentist. His name is Barlow, and the letter was to confirm the appointment. The cricket page is beside the financial one, and I turned to it to find if Surrey was holding its own against Kent. But go on, Watson, go on! It's a very superficial trick, and no doubt you will soon acquire it.'

EXPLANATORY NOTES

ABBREVIATIONS

MS   Manuscript ('originally' denotes that a word or phrase was deleted from the manuscript during composition).

Collier's Weekly   Collier's Weekly Magazine: An Illustrated Journal, published by P. F. Collier and Son, New York (1888–9, as Collier's Once a Week; 1889–95, Once a Week: An Illustrated Weekly Newspaper; 1895–1904, Collier's Weekly: An Illustrated Journal; 1905–57, Collier's: the National Weekly); edited by Norman Hapgood, 1902–12.

Strand   Strand Magazine: An Illustrated Monthly, published by George Newnes, Ltd., London (1891–1950); edited by Herbert Greenhough Smith, 1891–1930.

Newnes (1905)   The Return of Sherlock Holmes, by A. Conan Doyle, illustrated by Sidney Paget (London, George Newnes, Ltd., 1905). The first edition.

Murray (1928)   Sherlock Holmes. His Adventures. Memoirs. Return. His Last Bow & The Case-Book. The Complete Short Stories, by Arthur Conan Doyle (London, John Murray, 1928).

SERIAL PUBLICATION

The stories were serialized in the *Strand Magazine* between Oct. 1903 and Dec. 1904 (with illustrations by Sidney Paget), and in *Collier's Weekly* between 26 Sept. 1903 and 28 Jan. 1905 (with illustrations by Frederic Dorr Steele). The second American serial rights were acquired by the McClure Co. and the series was reprinted between Feb. and May 1905 in the *New York Evening World*, *Philadelphia Evening Bulletin*, *Washington Evening Star*, *Kansas City Star*, *Boston Sunday Post*, *Indianapolis Sunday Star*, *Los Angeles Sunday Times*, *New Orleans Daily Picayune*, *Omaha Illustrated Bee*, *Pittsburg Gazette*, *Cleveland Sunday Plain Dealer*, *San Francisco Sunday Call Magazine*, and in the *Winnipeg Weekly Free Press*.

THE EMPTY HOUSE

First published in the *Strand Magazine*, 26 (Oct. 1903), 363–75, with 7 illustrations by Sidney Paget, and in *Collier's Weekly* 31 (26 Sept. 1903), 12–14, 16, with 7 illustrations (including coloured cover) by Frederic Dorr Steele.

MS: offered by Maggs Brothers, Catalogue 436 (1923), and sold to William K. Bixley; acquired in 1929 by Philip H. and A. S. W. Rosenbach. Present location: Rosenbach Museum and Library, Philadelphia, Penn.

Text: collated with MS and printed texts.

The plot 'was given to me by Jean [Leckie]', according to a letter from ACD to his mother (Carr, 200), and it is based on the facts given in 'The Final Problem' (*Memoirs*).

The empty house may have its origin in ACD's memories of his early escapades in Edinburgh with the local boys at Sciennes Hill Place. It also recalls the empty property in *A Study in Scarlet*, whence the one in the first Raffles story, 'The Ides of March' (*The Amateur Cracksman*, 1899); and Holmes's return has some features similar to the return of Raffles in 'No Sinecure' (*The Black Mask*, 1901): 'I cannot repeat what I said. I have no idea what I did. I only know—I only knew—that it was A. J. Raffles in the flesh.'

The disguise as a bibliophile recalls Poe's description in 'The Murders in the Rue Morgue' of the first meeting of the narrator and Dupin at an obscure library in the Rue Montmartre, 'where the accident of our both being in search of the same very rare and very remarkable volume, brought us into closer communion'.

A further influence may have been an article by Harold Spender (1864–1926) in the *Strand*, 'The End of a Great Mountain Climber' (Jan. 1903), which describes the accident that befell a tourist and three guides at the Dent Blanche and led to the death of Owen Glynne Jones. The opening allusion to the announcement of the deaths by 'Dr Seiler' would have been highly suggestive to ACD in view of the comparable place of 'Peter Steiler' in 'The Final Problem' (*Memoirs*), and the experience of the sole survivor, F. W. Hill, Glynne Jones's fellow-schoolmaster at the City of London School, may have offered inspiration for Holmes's escape.

The story, 'which essays the difficult task of explaining away the alleged death of Holmes, and which also introduces such a villain as Colonel Sebastian Moran', was placed sixth on ACD's list of the twelve best Sherlock Holmes stories ('How I Made My List,' *Strand*,

73 (June 1927), 611–12), and as such was reprinted in the *Grand Magazine*, 52 (Dec. 1927), 444–55.

3 *my adventurous life*: later used as the title of the French edition (Albin-Michel, 1931–2) of ACD's autobiography (*Ma Vie Aventureuse*).

4 *some person or persons unknown*: 'or persons' added in MS. *Some Persons Unknown* (1898) was the title of a collection of short stories by ACD's brother-in-law E. W. Hornung.

The Honourable Ronald Adair: originally 'Robert Adair'; it was corrected to 'Ronald' in the MS, *Strand*, and *Collier's Weekly*, but the error persisted in Newnes (1905) and Murray (1928), suggesting that the correction was made after the typescript had been prepared. The name may have been inspired by the popular song 'Robin Adair', or it could have been taken from Captain Frederick Edward Shafto Adair (1860–1915), the author of *The Big Game of Balistan and Ladakh* (1899) (the title of which resembles the title of the book of Colonel Sebastian Moran). Another namesake would be Sir Robert Adair (1763–1855), the friend of Charles James Fox.

the Earl of Maynooth: perhaps suggested by the Earls of Menteith (the subject of an article in the *Ancestor* for Jan. 1903, the volume which contained a criticism of ACD's heraldry), or from the sixth Earl of Mayo, Richard Southwell Bourke (1822–72), Viceroy and Governor-General of India and MP for Kildare (1847–52), who was assassinated at Port Blair in the Andaman Islands. He shared his name with a governor of New South Wales, Richard Bourke (1777–1855) (though they were not related). Maynooth, in Kildare (near Dublin), is the site of St Patrick's College, the leading Catholic seminary (Maynooth College), and the future Earl of Mayo had supported its state grant but when made Chief Secretary for Ireland (1852) lost his seat at the urging of the local priests.

one of the Australian colonies: until federation in 1901, Australia consisted of six independently governed British colonies.

427 Park Lane: a fashionable road (of forty-four houses) running along the eastern side of Hyde Park.

Miss Edith Woodley, of Carstairs: perhaps suggested by two railway junctions: Woodley Junction near Stockport in Cheshire, and Carstairs Junction near Lanark.

4 *the ... Card Clubs*: the Baldwin was a card club at 79a Pall Mall: 'For a quiet game of whist or bridge with foemen worthy of the best tempered steel, the Baldwin Club is pre-eminently the one to visit', says Henry Leach (G. R. Sims, *Living London*, 1903, iii, 162). The Cavendish Club was at 307 Regent Street in the 1880s, then near Oxford Street, and afterwards on the north side of Piccadilly between Down Street and Park Lane. There was no club called the 'Bagatelle', though clubs for bagatelle (a form of billiards) did exist. A 'mere bagatelle' was a common phrase suggesting a trifling sum of money, and it served as a euphemism for heavy losses at the gaming-tables.

Mr Murray, Sir John Hardy and Colonel Moran: the first name recalls the orderly who saved Dr Watson at the Battle of Maiwand (*A Study in Scarlet*), which may have been suggested by (Sir) John Murray, of the *Challenger* expedition. The second name recalls Sir Thomas Hardy (1769–1839) who was at Nelson's side when he died; and the last may have come from Norbert Louis Moran, a contemporary at Stonyhurst, or from Cardinal Patrick Moran (1830–1911), the controversial Archbishop of Sydney, who wrote scholarly works on the Irish church and saints.

5 *Godfrey Milner and Lord Balmoral*: the first from the High Commissioner for South Africa during the Boer War (Alfred Milner); the second (also used in 'The Noble Bachelor' (*Adventures*) and 'Silver Blaze' (*Memoirs*)) may be a coded reference to the Prince of Wales (by then, King Edward VII), taken from Balmoral Castle, the royal residence near Aberdeen; his involvement in card scandals was notorious.

an expanded revolver bullet: originally 'a bullet of an expanding character'; MS and *Collier's Weekly*, 'an expanding revolver bullet'; a soft-nosed 'dumdum' bullet that expands and inflicts laceration. The bullets were proscribed by the Second Hague Conference in 1899 and ACD denied the claim that they were used by the British Army in South Africa in his pamphlet *The War in South Africa: Its Cause and Conduct* (1902).

6 *him*: in *Strand*, but not in Murray.

an elderly deformed man: originally 'a small deformed man'.

'The Origin of Tree Worship': taken from the sixth volume of the Bibliothèque de Carabas: *The Attis of Caius Valerius Catullus* |

Translated into English Verse by Grant Allen, with Dissertations | On the Myth of Attis, on the Origin of Tree-| Worship, and on the Galliambic Metre | By Grant Allen, B.A., formerly | Postmaster of Merton | College, Oxford (David Nutt, 1892). The argument of the essay (which occupies most of the book) was 'that while all gods were originally ghosts, sacred trees and tree-gods owe their sanctity to having grown in the first place on the tumulus or barrow of the deified ancestor'. Grant Allen (Charles Grant Blairfindie Allen, 1848–99) was born in Canada and his works include *The Woman Who Did* (1895) and *An African Millionaire* (1897). ACD moved to Hindhead at his recommendation, and completed Allen's last novel, *Hilda Wade* (1900), which was running in serial form in the *Strand* at the time of his death. The title of the final instalment, 'The Episode of the Dead Man Who Spoke', may have been in his mind when making another 'dead man' speak.

7 *Church Street*: i.e. Kensington Church Street (which runs north from the High Street, near the home of ACD's brother-in-law E. W. Hornung).

   'British Birds': the title (and half-title) is a common one and there were several recent works to which it could refer, such as *British Birds* (1895), by W. H. Hudson (1841–1922); or possibly a single volume from *A History of British Birds* (6 vols., 1857), by the Revd Frederick Orpen Morris, or the *History of British Birds* (1883–5) by Henry Seebohm.

   Catullus: see above, *The Origin of Tree Worship*.

   'The Holy War': by John Bunyan (1682); or possibly Thomas Fuller's history of the crusades, *The Holy Warre* (1639); a cheap edition of the former would be the most likely.

8 *'you're not a spirit, anyhow'*: as he often was in the parodies and pastiches prior to his return (e.g. John Kendrick Bangs, *The Pursuit of the Houseboat*, 1897).

9 *my cigarette-box and my stick*: as described in 'The Final Problem' (*Memoirs*). The cigarette-case was based on the wedding present ('From Sherlock Holmes') which ACD gave Sidney Paget in 1893.

   'baritsu', or the Japanese system of wrestling: a form of ju-jitsu; correctly 'bartitsu', after the 'new system based on the Japanese style of wrestling' devised by and named after

331

E. W. Barton-Williams. The system was based on 'a sound knowledge of balance and leverage as applied to human anatomy' and was devised 'with the purpose of rendering a person absolutely secure from danger by any method of attack that may arise' ('The New Art of Self Defence', *Pearson's Magazine*, Mar.–Apr. 1899).

10 *land of the living*: Job 28:13.

your picturesque account . . . which I read . . . later: i.e. 'The Final Problem' (*Memoirs*), which was published thirty-one months after his disappearance at the Reichenbach Falls (*Strand*, Dec. 1893).

I might . . . have reversed my boots: by reversing the shoe and tying the foot with the laces, a device favoured by James Fenimore Cooper (1789–1851), R. M. Ballantyne (1825–94), and Thomas Mayne Reid (1818–83), whose stories ACD had read as a boy: 'I had strapped on my mocassins hind-foremost to conceal my tracks', he says in 'My First Book' (*Idler*, Jan. 1893).

11 *ten miles over the mountains*: the route taken by ACD in Aug. 1893 from the Reichenbach Falls to the Baths of Rosenlaui and the ridge of the Great Scheidegg.

I found myself in Florence: as had ACD after his stay at Davos Platz in 1895.

12 *my own most vindictive enemies, at liberty*: this has been denounced as being inconsistent with the implication at the close of 'The Final Problem' that 'the gang' was 'exposed' 'completely'. But it is a presumption in 'The Empty House' that Moran was so exalted an aide to Moriarty as to have left no traces when the gang was otherwise ripe for the taking—save for the unknown other 'most vindictive enemy' who may be Professor Moriarty's brother, also a Colonel (see the opening to 'The Final Problem'); he is in any case dead, imprisoned, or disabled by the date of Adair's murder.

I travelled for two years . . . spending some days with the head Lama: MS 'Thibet' and 'head Llama' (*sic*) added in pencil (the spelling—that of the South American animal—was used in the magazines and early printed texts). 'Thibet' and 'Lhassa' were alternative spellings. The expedition of Colonel Sir Francis Edward Younghusband (1863–1942), which led to to the opening of Tibet, was planned in May 1903. The 'Head

Lama' or 'Grand Lama' in Lhasa was the Dalai Lama (who was a boy in 1892). The confusion over the spelling of 'Lama' was common:

> The Llama of the Pampasses you never should confound
> (In spite of a deceptive similarity of sound)
>   With the Lhama who is Lord of Turkestan.
> For the former is a beautiful and valuable beast,
> But the latter is not lovable nor useful in the least;
> And the Ruminant is preferable surely to the Priest
> Who battens on the woful [*sic*] superstitions of the East,
> The Mongol of the Monastery of Shan.
>
>   (Hilaire Belloc, *More Beasts for Worse Children*, 1897)

the remarkable explorations of . . . Sigerson: based on the Swedish explorer Sven Anders Hedin (1865–1952). The name recalls Dr George Sigerson (1836–1925), author of *Bards of the Gael and Gall* (1897), father of the novelist Dora Sigerson (Mrs Clement K. Shorter), translator of Scandinavian as well as Irish poetry, anthologized alongside ACD.

Persia: modern Iran, which in 1893 was recovering from a severe cholera epidemic, but in 1903 was subjected to the intrigues of the British and Russian governments who were anxious to extend their influence.

Mecca: in Saudi Arabia, the birthplace of Muhammad and thus the holiest city of Islam (visited by Sir Richard Burton in 1853).

the Khalifa at Khartoum: Khartoum (the capital of the Sudan) was razed to the ground in 1885 by the Mahdists, and Caliph Abdullah (Seyyid Abdullah ibn-Seyyid Muhammad) was at Omdurman. He was overthrown by General Kitchener in Sept. 1898. A framed picture of General Charles George Gordon ('Gordon of Khartoum', 1833–85) adorned the walls at 221B Baker Street ('The Cardboard Box', *Memoirs*).

some months . . . at Montpellier, in the south of France: Montpellier was the seat of an ancient university noted for its science faculty and school of pharmacy. Coal-tar is a black, viscous fluid or semi-solid, consisting of hydrocarbons, phenols, and compounds of sulphur and nitrogen. The derivatives include ammonia, creosote, and benzene.

12 *to my satisfaction*: added in MS.

Mycroft had preserved my rooms . . . as they had always been: confirming Holmes's assurance to Watson that 'no great harm was done' even though Moriarty's men 'set fire to our rooms last night' ('The Final Problem', *Memoirs*).

at two o'clock to-day: Holmes says of his enemies who were watching the premises in Baker Street, 'this morning they saw me arrive'. Presumably two hours were required for lunch and to soothe Mrs Hudson after her attack of hysterics.

April evening: originally 'March evening'.

13 *my own sad bereavement*: i.e. the death of Watson's wife, Mary (the Mary Morstan of *The Sign of the Four*).

Work is the best antidote to sorrow: after Thomas Carlyle: 'Work is the grand cure of all maladies and miseries that ever beset mankind' (Inaugural Address, Edinburgh University, 2 Apr. 1866).

half-past nine: originally 'half past ten'.

hansom: a two-wheeled carriage, drawn by one horse, with the driver mounted behind; named after J. A. Hansom (1803–82) who patented the design.

Cavendish Square: at the end of Wigmore Street. The route took them down Wigmore Street, to Manchester Square and Manchester Street; then to Blandford Street, along the mews behind Baker Street into Paddington Street, north along East Street, left into David Street, and down the narrow mews to the back door of Camden House. Bedford House (now the Sherlock Holmes Hotel) extends across the mews to the south of Camden House and prevented them from passing through York Mews South (which was renamed 'Sherlock Mews' in 1937).

14 *hanging in ribbons*: 'A vulgar flaring paper adorned the walls . . . great strips . . . hung down (*A Study in Scarlet*, ch. 3).

Camden House . . . old quarters: originally 'exactly opposite'. A real address. Camden House, at 13 York Place (118 Baker street after 1921), was from 1885 to 1931 the premises of the Camden House School (founded in 1876 in Camden Road). The houses opposite were 30 York Place or 111 Baker Street (the Portman Estate Office), and 29 York Place or 109 Baker Street (a boys' school run by Edwin Thomas Bull).

our little adventures: MS 'your little fairy tales'.

15 *age doth not wither nor custom stale my infinite variety*: 'Age cannot wither her, nor custom stale | Her infinite variety' (*Antony and Cleopatra*, II. ii. 240–1).

Monsieur Oscar Meunier, of Grenoble: from Constantin Emile Meunier (1831–1905), a sculptor, engraver, and painter.

Parker by name, a garrotter by trade: 'by name' added in MS. The garrotter 'approaches his victim from behind, and suddenly throws his arm round his neck, tightening the pressure even to suffocating point, when, strangulation being near, outcry is impossible. Other thieves—one or more—then turn out the pockets of the helpless prisoner' (Arthur Griffiths, *Mysteries of Police and Crime*, 1904).

the jew's harp: a small lyre-shaped musical instrument, played by holding the frame between the teeth and striking the metal tongue. Proficiency on the jew's harp recalls Charlie Peace (Charles Frederick Peace, 1832–79) who was later described by Holmes as a 'violin virtuoso' ('The Illustrious Client', *Case-Book*).

19 *the Molesey Mystery*: from East or West Molesey, near Kingston upon Thames, Surrey; also the name of a character in E. W. Hornung's novel *Denis Dent* (1903).

'You devil . . . clever devil . . . cunning devil': thus in MS; 'fiend' thrice in *Strand* and thereafter.

'journeys end in lovers' meetings', as the old play says: (*Twelfth Night*, II. iii. 44). The date 6 Jan. was chosen as Holmes's 'official birthday' by the Baker Street Irregulars of New York because he quotes twice from the play (here and in 'The Red Circle', *His Last Bow*).

Colonel Sebastian Moran: originally 'Colonel Aloysius Moran' Aloysius was a Christian name of several Stonyhurst contemporaries of ACD, including one Watson.

with his savage eyes . . . like a tiger himself: added in MS.

20 *shikari*: MS 'shikaree'/'shikarri'; from the Hindu, a sportsman or hunter.

merry men: almost certainly an allusion to Robin Hood's outlaws, satirically suggesting the Colonel is a respectable but homicidal authority-figure like the Sheriff of Nottingham.

There could be an echo of the Scots dramatist Joanna Baillie (1762–1851), *Orra*, III. i:

> The wild fire dances on the fen,
> The red star sheds its ray;
> Uprouse ye then, my merrie men!
> It is our op'ning day.

20 *the powerful air-gun*: an airgun walking-cane. 'The butt section is an air reservoir which can be pumped up by means of a small diameter air pump to a pressure of some sixty pounds. A large spring-controlled poppett valve with a projecting steel shank retains the air reservoir', wrote Major Hugh Pollard in the notes for the catalogue of the Sherlock Holmes Exhibition in London (1952).

Von Herder, the blind German mechanic: the name of the German philosopher Johann Gottfried Herder (1744–1803), and of a ship lost at sea in 1882.

21 *Mrs Hudson:* originally 'Mrs Turner' (the name of the house-keeper used in 'A Scandal in Bohemia', *Adventures*).

22 *the mouse-coloured dressing-gown*: the colour of the dressing-gown (described as blue in 'The Man with the Twisted Lip' (*Adventures*)—where Holmes had borrowed it for the evening) has preoccupied Sherlockians since Ronald Knox cast doubt on the authenticity of the story by quoting the imaginary Sau-wosch: 'This is not the first time that a coat of many colours has been as a deception used! But in truth, Sherlock, our modern Joseph, has altogether disappeared, and the evil beast Watson has him devoured' ('Studies in the Literature of Sherlock Holmes', 1912).

Plumb in the middle of the back of the head and smack through the brain: added in MS.

Professor James Moriarty: the Christian name is the same as that of his brother, Colonel James Moriarty, who wrote letters in his defence ('The Final Problem', *Memoirs*).

my index of biographies: from the order of the entries it would appear that Holmes was reading up the page.

Morgan the poisoner: no poisoner of this name is known, but it was the name of the swindler who created the bogus Authors' Alliance in 1887, and of Daniel Morgan (1828–65), the bushranger shot in 1865, who used the name 'Samuel Moran' as an alias.

Merridew of abominable memory: perhaps from John Merridew and his daughter who are characters in *Denis Dent* by E. W. Hornung (1903).

my left canine: one of the four strong pointed teeth between the incisors and molars.

22/3 *Moran, Sebastian, Colonel . . . Bagatelle Card Club*: the 1st Bengalore Pioneers (from Bengal/Bangalore), based on the Madras Pioneers. American texts have 'Bangalore', losing the deliberate ambiguity of the original. The Jowaki Campaign in 1878-9: the pacification of the Pathan tribe of Jowaki Afridis on the North-west Frontier. The 'Afghan Campaign' (or Second Afghan War): the battle at Charasia (*sic*) (6 Oct. 1879), the engagement at Sherpur (23 Dec. 1879), and the occupation of Kabul. *Heavy Game of the Western Himalayas*: originally 'Heavy Game in the Persian—'. Conduit Street connects Regent Street and Bond Street. The clubs are fictitious, though the Tankerville Club (from the Earls of Tankerville) is mentioned in 'The Five Orange Pips' (*Adventures*).

23 *how he crawled down a drain after . . . a tiger*: a field drain or ditch. The story was retold by T. S. Eliot from the standpoint of the other party in his *Old Possum's Book of Practical Cats* (1939) when referring to Gus, the Theatre Cat: 'He once played a Tiger—could do it again— | Which an Indian Colonel pursued down a drain.'

chief of the staff: MS 'Chief of the Staff'.

Mrs Stewart, of Lauder: Lauder, in Berwickshire, south-east of Edinburgh.

I put up the shutters for fear of air-guns: Holmes had flung the shutters together and bolted them securely ('The Final Problem', *Memoirs*).

25 *the Scotland Yard Museum*: the 'Black Museum' (founded 1874), which ACD had visited on 10 Dec. 1892.

THE NORWOOD BUILDER

First published in the *Strand Magazine*, 26 (Nov. 1903), 483-96, with 7 illustrations by Sidney Paget, and in *Collier's Weekly* 32 (31 Oct.

1903), 16–18, 28–31, with 7 illustrations (including coloured cover) by Frederic Dorr Steele.

MS: donated by the author to a Red Cross Charity Sale, London (22 Apr. 1918), £12; David G. Joyce; sold at auction, Anderson Galleries, New York (13 Feb. 1923), $100; and a third time, New York (8 Feb. 1926), $60. Present location: Berg Collection, New York Public Library.

Text: collated with MS and printed texts.

The man who disappears without trace and the man who fakes his own death were already stock devices of the detective story and in many instances were drawn from life. Nathaniel Hawthorne's 'Wakefield' (*Twice-Told Tales*, 1851) was based on the case of a man who was found to have lived under an assumed identity in close proximity to his original home. The endings suggested for *Edwin Drood*, which Dickens left unfinished in 1870, often assume that Edwin Drood has survived, and in *Rodney Stone* (1896) a character (the Earl of Avon) fakes his own death. The Gothic novelists favoured the use of secret passages and concealed chambers, and they were used by Walter Scott in *Woodstock* (a hinged picture), and *Peveril of the Peak* (a sliding panel). His story of *The Black Dwarf* (in which a jilted lover builds his own house and intervenes with drastic effect in the life of the offspring of the former target of his affections) also bears comparison with the present story.

In Fletcher Robinson's 'The Vanished Millionaire' (*Lady's Home Magazine of Fiction*, Dec. 1904; *The Chronicles of Addington Peace*, 1905) Silas Ford disappears leaving a trail of footmarks in the snow. The detective observes that they come to an abrupt halt and infers that the shoes had been worn by somebody else. He then turns his attention to the house and finds the missing man held captive in a priest hole.

Undershaw, at Hindhead, which was built for ACD by J. Henry Ball, a Southsea builder, could also have provided inspiration, as the arrangement of the attics included areas under the eaves which were disguised as cupboards.

ACD was one of the first to use fingerprints in detective fiction and perhaps the first to suggest that the most foolproof system of crime detection (which had been adopted by Scotland Yard in 1901) could be abused. The use of a thumbprint may have been based on a trial in Yorkshire, where (according to an article in *Tit-Bits*, 'Criminals who Convict Themselves', 27 June 1903) a burglar had broken into the house of a clergyman and whiled away a few moments by taking down a book on which he 'left evidence of his taste in the form of a dirty thumb-mark in the book', which led to his arrest.

The button bearing the name of a tailor found in the embers of the woodstack also has parallels in real life. In 'The Race for News' (*Idler*, Nov. 1902) Allen Sangree relates how a reporter investigated a case in which a would-be blackmailer had blown himself up with a bomb. A charred button revealed the name of a Boston clothier and the tailor was able to identify the man.

The fake fire recalls the smoke pellets used to induce Irene Adler to reveal the hiding-place of her papers in 'A Scandal in Bohemia' (*Adventures*).

26 *the death of the late lamented Professor Moriarty*: 'the late lamented' was added in proof. Owen Dudley Edwards suggests (*His Last Bow*, Oxford, 1993) that the phrase was a counterpart to Guy Boothby's 'late lamented Sherlock Holmes' found in the first instalment of *A Prince of Swindlers* (serialized in *Pearson's Magazine* in 1897 alongside ACD's Captain Sharkey stories). Few readers were unaware that the professor had met his death at the Reichenbach Falls ('The Final Problem', *Memoirs*).

the old quarters in Baker Street: originally continued 'as a Junior and insignificant member of the firm'.

Verner: originally 'Crocker'. According to 'The Greek Interpreter' (*Memoirs*), Holmes's grandmother was a sister of the French artist, Horace Vernet (whose 'genius' had inspired Richard Doyle); so Sherlockians suppose that the 'distant relation' was of the same family and that 'Verner' is an anglicized form of 'Vernet'. A more probable source would be Colonel Willoughby Verner to whom ACD refers in *The Great Boer War* (1901). His first name is that of the victim in 'The Golden Pince-Nez'.

27 *ex-President Murillo*: originally 'ex-president'. Presumably Don Juan Murillo, the Tiger of San Pedro in 'Wisteria Lodge' (*His Last Bow*)—a story written in 1908. The name (though not the character) may have been suggested by Manuel Murillo Toro (President of Colombia, 1864–6, 1872–4), or by the painter Bartolomé Murillo.

the Dutch steamship 'Friesland': a ship of this name was owned by the Red Star Line. It was registered in Belgium and launched on 18 Aug. 1889 for service between Antwerp and New York.

27 *the unhappy John Hector McFarlane*: 'the unhappy' added in MS; the name was perhaps based on George James Macfarlane, who received a medal at the siege of Ladysmith and served as Mayor of Pietermaritzburg between 1898 and 1902, or on Harold MacFarlane, the author of several articles on cricket in the *Strand* (including 'Big Hits' in the issue for May 1903).

28 *For God's sake*: 'For Heaven's sake' in *Strand* and subsequent printings.

Jonas Oldacre: originally 'Jonas Cooper', and a 'widower' rather than a bachelor. 'Jonas' is a variant form of the biblical name 'Jonah' (used in the Douai version of the Bible with which ACD would have been familiar). The surname 'Oldacre' was previously used in 'The Croxley Master' (1900).

Lower Norwood: now known as 'West Norwood'; a residential district in the borough of Lambeth with a cemetery and railway station (close to 12 Tennison Road, South Norwood, where ACD lived from June 1891 to Dec. 1894).

entirely: in *Strand* and American texts only.

MYSTERIOUS AFFAIR AT LOWER NORWOOD: originally 'Murder and arson at Lower Norwood'. Possibly the inspiration for Agatha Christie's *Mysterious Affair at Styles* (1920). The headlines were not capitalized in the *Strand* or first British and American book editions, but were later.

London Bridge Station: the terminus for the South-Eastern Railway Co. and the London, Brighton, and South Coast Railway—both of which served Lower Norwood.

29 *Deep Dene House, at the Sydenham end of the road of that name*: originally 'at the end of the road of that name'. Deepdene is a country seat near Dorking and a popular street name (as in 'Deepdene Road' north of Streatham Common). Sydenham is a mile north of Norwood and 6 miles south of London Bridge.

30 *426 Gresham Buildings, EC*: from Gresham House in Old Broad Street (named after the Elizabethan financier Sir Thomas Gresham); a large building containing 265 offices and chambers.

charred remains: originally 'charred animal remains'.

31 *Torrington Lodge, Blackheath*: 'Torrington Lodge' (from the town in Devon or the square in London) added in MS. Blackheath is south of Greenwich and 7 miles south-east of Charing Cross.

32 *an amused expression*: originally 'a most curious expression which certainly seemed to be more threatening than benevolent'.

and witnessed by my clerk: added in MS (a will usually requires two signatures).

33 *'Who opened the door?'* | *'A middle-aged . . . housekeeper'*: twelve lines were deleted from the MS at this point (during the composition): ' "A bad shot that, Mr McFarlane," said Lestrade, with a cynical smile. "Jonas Oldacre is well known as a woman hater, he has no servant except an old Charwoman who comes in for two hours every morning, and he gets all his meals at the Station restaurant. I warn you again that you are only making a bad case worse and that this will all come up against you." | Our unfortunate Client had turned a ghastly colour, and he looked from one to the other of us like a hunted creature. Twice he tried to speak but his dry lips would utter no sound. At last with an effort he was able to continue his statement. | "I am speaking to you, Mr Holmes. You will find out how far I am speaking the truth. I was shown into a sitting room . . ." '

Mr: not in *Strand* or American book texts.

34 *the Anerley Arms*: this may have been based on the Robin Hood Public House at the junction of the Anerley Road and Croydon Road, a mile south-west of Sydenham. Anerley station (1839) took its name from the house which formerly stood there.

four-wheeler: a four-wheeled cab, or 'growler'; a closed carriage for four people, with the driver seated at the front.

35 *clearer*: 'clear' in *Strand* and American book texts.

37 *Blackheath*: originally 'Norwood'; six lines of text were cut from the MS on fo. 16; there was a new fo. 17, and fos. 17–18 were renumbered 18–19. There is no means of knowing why the deletions and additions were made.

38 *the*: 'that' in *Strand* and American book texts.

Thank God: 'Thank Heaven' in *Strand* and subsequently.

39 '*Hyams*': the name of several tailors in London: Montague and Henry Hyam (Fleet Street, High Holborn, and Ludgate Hill), Reuben Hyams (New Broad Street), and Hyam and Co. Ltd. (134–40 Oxford Street). There are payments to Hyams in ACD's account books of the period which suggest it was his own tailor.

somebody or a bundle: 'some body or bundle' in *Strand* and American book texts.

41 *mild-mannered, Sunday-school young man*: perhaps suggested by the famous duet between Bunthorne and Grosvenor in Gilbert and Sullivan's opera *Patience* (1881):

> A most intense young man,
> A soulful-eyed young man,
>   An ultra-poetical,
>   Super-aesthetical,
> Out of the way young man!

or as a contrast to:

> A commonplace young man,
> A matter-of-fact young man,
>   A steady and stolid-y,
>   Jolly Bank-holiday,
> Every-day young man!

Cornelius: a physician in Shakespeare's *Cymbeline* who contrives a deceptive appearance of death; a magician in Fitztraver's song in Scott's *Lay of the Last Minstrel*. Hence a metaphor for contrivance.

42 *inanition*: hunger, emptiness from want of nourishment.

43 *a stain of blood*: originally 'two stains of blood'.

44 *Mrs Lexington*: originally 'Mrs Allington' (though the earlier references were to Mrs Lexington).

THE SOLITARY CYCLIST

First published in the *Strand Magazine*, 27 (Jan. 1904), 3–14, with 7 illustrations by Sidney Paget, and in *Collier's Weekly* 32 (26 Dec. 1903), 16–17, 20–1, with 5 illustrations (including coloured cover) by Frederic Dorr Steele.

MS: First and greater part sold at auction, American Art Galleries, New York (27 Jan. 1922), $120; and again in London (28 Jan. 1925), with the MSS of 'The Priory School' and 'The Dancing Men', £66; and a third time in New York (25 Apr. 1927), $160, to William G. Mennen; presented by him to the Olin Library, Cornell University, Ithaca, NY; private sale (1980). Present location: the collection of Maurice F. Neville, Santa Barbara, Calif. Final two pages given to Pierre Nordon by Adrian Conan Doyle (1966); sold at auction, Sotheby's, London (15 Dec. 1982), £4,000 to Mark J. Hime. Present location: the collection of James D. Pepper, Santa Barbara, Calif.

Text: collated with MS (in part) and printed texts.

The story was written third and is reinstated in this edition in its original position. It was held back to allow 'The Dancing Men' to appear in the *Strand* Christmas Number and the magazine order was retained in the first edition.

The inspiration may have come from *The Complete Cyclist* (1897), the second volume of the 'Isthmian Library' edited by Bertram Fletcher Robinson. Mrs F. Harcourt Williamson (whose surname is used in the story) ends a chapter on 'The Cycle in Society' by saying: 'The beginning of cycling was the end of the chaperon in England, and now women, even young girls, ride alone or attended only by some casual man friend for miles together through deserted country roads. The danger of this is apparent; but parents and guardians will probably only become wise after the event. Given a lonely road, and a tramp desperate with hunger or naturally vicious, and it stands to reason that a girl, or indeed any woman riding alone must be in some considerable peril.'

ACD may also have seen the *Pall Mall Magazine* for May 1903 which contained F. G. Aflalo's 'Symposium of Sport' (alongside the last instalment of E. W. Hornung's novel *No Hero*). 'H. Graves' (to whom a section on 'cycling ladies' is credited) says: 'To women, of course, the bicycle was a gift of heaven, for it relegated the chaperon to the museum of extinct creatures and covered a multitude of unreported dalliances with the other sex.' The writer doubted there would be a 'craze' in the summer of 1903 to match that of 1896, but said that 'On the country house, where it offers unrivalled facilities for easy travel to and from the market town, it will be long in losing its hold.'

ACD had shared the enthusiasm for cycling which gripped the country a decade earlier and had been a keen cyclist. Mention of a Sunday outing (on 21 Nov. 1897) is found in an invitation to Mrs Grant Allen (Hench Collection, University of Minnesota) where

ACD asks if she and her husband would like to join a party of 'ten or twelve of us' who 'are going to Midhurst on cycles'.

His enthusiasm was shared by his sisters, in particular by the youngest, 'Dodo' (Bryan Mary Julia Josephine Doyle, 1877–1927), who in her novel *The Episodes of Marge* (published in 1903 under the pen-name 'H. Ripley Cromarsh') has one chapter entitled 'The Three Cyclists' and another 'The Episode of the Bicycle, and the Man in the Street'. Two of the other sisters, 'Lottie' (Charlotte) and 'Connie' (Mrs Constance Hornung), took part in the 1897 cycling trip, and as both served as governesses in the 1880s it is possible that Miss Violet Smith is based upon one of them, or even perhaps upon the eldest, the musically inclined Annette (who had served as a governess in Portugal before her death in 1890).

ACD's close attachment to Jean Leckie (whom he married after the death of his wife) offers a further possible source of inspiration. Photographs (among the papers of Denis Conan Doyle) taken before her marriage show her cycling with her brothers. She had paid several visits to Undershaw but felt uneasy in the presence of Lady Conan Doyle and preferred to meet away from the house—at London hotels or in the country towns which ACD visited as a member of the MCC. Little is known of their friendship as the numerous letters which passed between them were destroyed after her death, but it is possible that they cycled together near Hindhead, and ACD may have based the 'solitary cyclist' upon himself. His protectiveness towards her and his inability to marry her may be reflected in the relationship between Bob Carruthers and Miss Violet Smith.

A Humber bicycle 'used by Miss Violet Smith' was exhibited in 1951 at the Sherlock Holmes exhibition at Abbey House with a letter from the managing director of Raleigh Industries stating that their files for 1895 and 1896 showed it was the bicycle 'which we delivered to Miss Smith's father at Charlington Hall'. As she was residing at Chiltern Grange and her father was dead, it sounds improbable even by Sherlockian standards.

52 *during those eight years*: originally (and incorrectly) 'seven years' in the MS and *Collier's Weekly*.

the ingenuity and dramatic quality of the solution: the opening paragraphs were revised after the story had been written, to meet the criticism that 'the circumstances did not permit of any striking illustration of those powers for which my friend was famous'. 'Solution' is used in the medical sense of 'termination' or 'crisis' of a disease (the 'resolution').

the solitary cyclist of Charlington: originally 'the solitary man of Charlington Common', showing (as does the title on the first page of the MS, which was originally 'The Adventure of the Solitary Man') that it refers to Bob Carruthers and not Miss Violet Smith.

the curious sequel . . . which culminated in unexpected tragedy: the final paragraphs of the story suggest that the 'sequel' in the common sense was a happy one; 'tragedy' is here defined as 'that branch of dramatic art which deals with sorrowful or terrible events' (*OED*), and the 'unexpected tragedy' refers to the abduction and narrowly averted rape.

Saturday, April 23rd: 23 April 1895 was correctly a Tuesday.

John Vincent Harden: the name recalls John Wesley Hardin who appeared in the Buffalo Bill show. The last name is found—as 'Harden Place'—in 'The Story of Amaroff the Pole' by Fletcher Robinson (*The Chronicles of Addington Peace*, 1905).

53 *the spatulate finger end*: a broad, flattened end (from 'spatula', the instrument used in surgery).

he gently turned it towards the light: 'he' is found in the MS and all the principal texts (rather than the 'she' of corrupt editions).

Farnham, on the borders of Surrey: a market town, on the River Wey, 3 miles south-west of Aldershot, 38 miles south-west of London, served by the London and South-Western Railway.

Archie Stamford, the forger: the MS originally continued, 'Hughes, the poisoner, also came from there'. 'Archie' is a name used in 'The Red-Headed League' (*Adventures*), but may here be taken from Archie Langman, who ran the Field Hospital in South Africa to which ACD was attached in 1900. 'Stamford' is the name of the man who effected the introduction of Holmes and Watson (*A Study in Scarlet*), and recalls the town in Lincolnshire where Harold fought the battle of Stamford Bridge in 1066.

54 *the old Imperial Theatre*: in Tothill Street, opposite Westminster Abbey. Erected 1876 as the Royal Aquarium Theatre, and known as the Imperial Theatre between 1879 and 1889. It reopened as the New Imperial Theatre in 1898 and was

demolished in 1907 to make way for the Wesleyan Central
Hall. ACD's play *Brigadier Gerard* received its first performance
here on 3 Mar. 1906.

54 *Mr Carruthers and Mr Woodley*: the first name recalls that of
Francis Carruthers Gould (1844–1925), the *Westminster Gazette*
cartoonist who was the subject of an 'Illustrated Interview' in
the *Strand* (Jan. 1903). The second (also used in 'The Empty
House') was originally 'Murphy' (which was the name of a
Jesuit preacher at Stonyhurst whom ACD had greatly dis-
liked).

Cyril Morton: the Christian name was that of ACD's brother-
in-law Cyril Angell (1873–1937).

55 *Chiltern Grange, about six miles from Farnham*: an invented place,
from the Chiltern Hills or the parliamentary resignation
device of the Chiltern Hundreds; similar to Whigwell Grange,
the setting of one of the 'Strange Studies from Life' (*Strand*,
1901).

He made odious love to me: in the old sense, 'he made advances'.

56 *Charlington Heath upon one side and . . . Charlington Hall upon the
other*: i.e. Crooksbury Heath, near Farnham. The name possibly suggested by Charlwood south of Reigate, or Charleshill
on the main road from Farnham to Milford. The Hall is
identified with Waverley Abbey, 2 miles south-east of Farnham.

Crooksbury Hill: a wooded eminence on the western border
of Surrey, 3 miles east of Farnham; part of Crooksbury
Heath.

I mentioned it to Mr Carruthers, who seemed interested in what I said:
MS and *Collier's Weekly*, 'I mentioned it to Mr Carruthers
when he came back from London in the evening. He is a very
silent man, but he seemed interested in what I had said.' The
additional lines may have been dropped as the result of a
printer's error, but the *Strand* text is preferred as it does not
raise doubts over the movements of Carruthers (had he
followed Miss Smith in the morning, and then returned to
Chiltern Grange, and afterwards left for London?).

57 *Midland Electric Company, at Coventry*: a real company, though it
was based in Wise Street, Leamington Spa: the Midland
Electric Light and Power Company Limited.

58 *ménage*: the persons who occupy a house, a household (often unconventional), as in 'A Costume Piece' by E. W. Hornung (*The Amateur Cracksman*, 1899) where a prize-fighter was not 'by any means the worst element in the Rosenthall *ménage*'.

60 *a well-known firm in Pall Mall*: such as Davidson and Cross, Estate Agents, of 123 Pall Mall; or Hedger and Winter, of 46a Pall Mall.

Mr Williamson: possibly named after Mrs F. Harcourt Williamson, whose contribution to *The Complete Cyclist* (1897) is quoted above in the introductory note.

62 *I have some proficiency in . . . boxing*: as had ACD, who recalled with pride the scraps he had during his first days on board the Greenland whaler and on arrival in Southsea in 1882.

made some inquiries at a clerical agency: *Crockford*, the compendious clerical directory, would not have provided the information needed.

64 *the duns and drabs and slate-greys of London*: *duns*—dull greyish-browns; *drabs*—dull light browns.

65 *God*: 'Heaven' in *Strand* and later.

66 *a woman's shrill scream*: the scream preceded the placing of the 'handkerchief round her mouth'.

Jingo: possibly derived from a Basque word meaning 'God', and first used as an exclamation in the late 17th century.

glade of greensward: a turfed area between trees.

67 *one arm akimbo*: with one hand on the hip, the elbow turned outwards (usually of both arms).

a short surplice: the cotta, a white linen vesture with short sleeves (frequently tricked out with lace patterns). The wedding was a sham; the priest officiates at a wedding and blesses the union, but it is made before God with the consent of both parties and in the presence of a witness.

68 *Roaring Jack Woodley*: as in 'roaring drunk', or the obsolete 'roaring boy' (meaning a bully, swaggerer, or brawler). Possibly a recollection of 'Roaring Hanna' (the Revd Dr Hugh Hanna) whose preaching was said to have fomented the Belfast religious riots of 1886. 'Roaring Ned Galloway' is the quartermaster of the *Happy Delivery* in 'The Governor of St Kitt's' (*The Green Flag*, 1900).

68 *unfrocked*: defrocked, deposed; 'unfrock'—'to strip (an ecclesiastic) of his frock as a sign of degradation; hence, to deprive of priestly function or office' (OED).

69 *a holy terror from Kimberley to Johannesburg*: a slang expression which means 'a source of whole-hearted fear'. The Jesuit hellfire preacher Murphy, whose name was initially bestowed on Woodley, may have inspired the use of the term. Kimberley, the diamond centre of the Cape Province of South Africa, is 310 miles south-west of the gold-fields at Johannesburg.

'I should call it selfishness': as in 'The Holocaust of Manor Place' (*Strand*, Mar. 1901): 'In the study of criminal psychology, one is forced to the conclusion that the most dangerous of all types of mind is that of the inordinately selfish man.' The source may be 1 Corinthians 13: 4–6: 'Charity suffereth long, and is kind; charity envieth not; charity vaunteth not itself, is not puffed up, doth not behave itself unseemly, seeketh not her own, is not easily provoked, thinketh no evil; rejoiceth not in iniquity, but rejoiceth in the truth.'

cable: overseas telegram.

70 *By God*: 'By Heaven' in *Strand* and subsequently.

71 *cast padre*: an outcast priest; one who is dismissed or rejected, as 'cast soldier'.

THE DANCING MEN

First published in the *Strand Magazine*, 26 (Dec. 1903), 603–17, with 7 illustrations by Sidney Paget, and in *Collier's Weekly*, 32 (5 Dec. 1903), 11–14, with 6 illustrations by Frederic Dorr Steele.

MS: donated by the author to a Red Cross Charity Sale, London (22 Apr. 1918), £10.10s: David G. Joyce; sold at auction, Anderson Galleries, New York (13 Feb. 1923), $100; and again at auction in London (28 Jan. 1925), with the MSS of 'The Solitary Cyclist' (first part) and 'The Priory School', £66. Present location unknown.

Text: collated with printed texts.

The story was the fourth in the series but was published as the third. It was conceived and partly written at the Hill House Hotel, Happisburgh (on the coast of Norfolk). In a letter from the hotel on 14 May 1903, ACD told Herbert Greenhough Smith, the editor of the *Strand*, that he had 'a strong bloody story' which could be placed third so as to separate the two stories which he called 'crimeless' (meaning that the proposed crimes were frustrated).

The 'sight of a child's scribbled drawing gave him the idea of using these little figures as letters in a cryptogram', said the editor in an article after ACD's death ('Some Letters of Conan Doyle', *Strand*, Oct. 1930). The child was G. J. Cubitt, the son of the proprietor of the hotel. He explained in a letter to Cornelis Helling how it came about: 'My girl cousin requested my mother to ask Sir Arthur to write something in her autograph album, in which I previously, at the age of about seven, had written my name and address in the form of dancing men . . . The album gave birth to the idea and he left many drawings about, evidently working out his code' ('The True Story of the Dancing Men', *Baker Street Journal*, 4/3 (July 1954)).

The 'dancing men' cipher resembles 'The Language of the Restless Imps' in the *St Nicholas Magazine* (May–June 1874), though there is no evidence that Cubitt saw it, nor is there evidence that he saw the *Boy's Own Paper* (29 Jan.–5 Feb. 1881) or *The Boy's Own Book* (1888) where it was reprinted as 'The Language of the Restless Fays'. ACD (who contributed to the *Boy's Own Paper* at a later date) called it 'pure coincidence' when the similarity was pointed out to him (see Lyndon Orr, *Bookman* (New York), Apr. 1910).

An article in the *Strand* on 'Human Railway Signals' (Apr. 1903) may have been a further influence, and the flag at the end of a word could have come from the coastguard semaphore (where the alphabet is represented by one or two flags held in seven different positions, with the arms dropped between words and a flag waved when the message is at an end). The field semaphore used by the British and American armies (often shown in manuals as 'stick figures') and a 'tree alphabet' (the 'alphabet of Hermes') also resemble the 'dancing men'.

The cipher which ACD devised is impractical. By using figures without arms it precludes the use of flags for words ending with those letters (though it could be argued that B and V are not common word-endings, and the words which have those endings could be used alone). Also, by using both arms and legs, joints, running and bending figures, upright and upside-down, it offers well over a thousand variations and would be impossible to memorize (though here it could be argued that the complexity of the symbols, the need for a key, and the difficulty of absolute accuracy improve what would otherwise be a simple substitution cipher).

THE DANCING MEN

1. 'AM HERE ABE SLANEY'

Strand

Collier's Weekly

2. 'AT ELRIGES'

Strand

Collier's Weekly

3. 'COME ELSIE'

Strand

Collier's Weekly

4. 'NEVER'

Strand

Collier's Weekly

5. 'ELSIE PREPARE TO MEET THY GOD'
Strand

Collier's Weekly

6. 'COME HERE AT ONCE'
Strand

Collier's Weekly

There are several mistakes in the 'dancing men' characters as reproduced in the magazines and early editions. The *Strand* has the same sign in the fourth and fifth message for V and P [⌐]; and the B and R are confused in the fourth message (so that 'Never' might be read as 'Nepeb'). In *Collier's Weekly* the V and P are confused (first and fourth), but the R was corrected (so that 'Never' read as 'Neper'); M and O and M and C are also confused (the O shown with its right leg bent; the C with a right arm), so that the fifth message could be read as 'Elsie prepare tm meet they Gmd' and the last could read 'Mome here at onme'.

The errors were few in comparison to the strange copy of the cipher published in the New York *Bookman* in Aug. 1903, which appeared thus:

ᚷᛏᛏᚤᚴᛏᛌᛏᛏᛏᚥᛌᛏᚴᚴᛌᛏᛏᛏᚼᚤᚤᛌᚷᛌᚤᚤᛌᛌᛏᛏᛌᛏᚴᛏᛏᛌ

The editors announced that they had heard directly from ACD that four of the new Sherlock Holmes stories (whose titles were given) had been completed. Some of these they had read in manuscript and they promised that they would be discussed in the next issue: 'Meanwhile we wish to call our readers' attention to the above cryptogram, which is the clue to the mystery of one of the four stories whose titles are given. It is a facsimile reproduction of the message which Sherlock Holmes found on the window sill. Sir Arthur expresses himself as considering it very simple. We submit it to our readers, and should be glad to hear what they make of the message.' It was presumably a very hurried impression of the fifth message, but is unintelligble as it stands.

The method of deciphering a cryptogram comes from Edgar Allan Poe's story of 'The Gold-Bug' (a major source for this story) with Holmes offering a simplified version of the analysis provided by William Legrand:

Poe (Legrand)	ACD (Holmes)
'Now, in English, the letter which most frequently occurs is *e* ... E ... predominates so remarkably that an individual sentence of any length is rarely seen, in which it is not the prevailing character.'	'As you are aware, E is the most common letter in the English alphabet and it predominates to so marked an extent that even in a short sentence one would expect to find it most often.'
'... it may well be doubted whether human ingenuity can construct an enigma of the kind which human ingenuity may not, by proper application, resolve.'	'What one man can invent another can discover.'

ACD stayed at Happisburgh when visiting Hornung, who had a country cottage at East Ruston, and he had other reasons beside. His close friend from Edinburgh, David George Thomson, was the head of the County Mental Asylum at Thorpe near Norwich and had persuaded him to join the hospital cricket team, and there were the golf courses at Cromer and Sheringham. He had visited

Cromer in Mar. 1901 with Fletcher Robinson (who gave him the idea for *The Hound of the Baskervilles*), and golf took him to Sheringham later in 1903. ACD probably met the Cubitt family for the first time when staying at the Hill House Hotel and there is no evidence that their friendship outlasted his stay. He did, however, have a psychic experience with 'young Cubitt' during the Great War (that is to say he received a message after Cubitt was killed). He referred to it when lecturing in Norwich in Nov. 1922 and afterwards spoke to the parents who were in the audience, but it was not the Cubitt whose autograph album ACD had seen and who outlived the Second World War.

A photograph of real 'dancing men' was published in the 'Curiosities' section of the *Strand* for Aug. 1904 (p. 236). It was taken in Australia, of miners who adapted the cipher to spell the name of their mine ('Lakeside'), and was sent to ACD who forwarded it to the *Strand*.

The story was placed third on the author's list of the twelve best Sherlock Holmes stories on account of 'the originality of the plot' ('How I Made My List,' *Strand*, June 1927), and as such was reprinted in the *Grand Magazine* (Sept. 1927), and the *Sunday Chronicle*, Manchester (12 Jan. 1930).

73 *South African securities*: or shares in 'South African property', gold-fields. This is partly autobiographical as ACD had the previous year invested in Johannesburg Consols and the Robinson Central Deep mine (which he had visited in 1900), and a decade earlier had purchased 150 shares in the 'Broken Hill property' in Australia. All did badly and the latter were sold at a loss in 1906.
   a professor addressing his class: perhaps a reference to Joseph Bell, the only person whom ACD acknowledged as the 'model' for Sherlock Holmes.

74 *Thurston*: an allusion to Thurston and Co., the billiard-table makers who had showrooms at 16 Catherine Street, near the Strand. The company was founded in 1814 by John Thurston.

   Hilton Cubitt: the surname of the proprietor of the Hill House Hotel and of the Honourable Henry Cubitt, the son of Lord Ashcombe, who shared with ACD the duties of Deputy Lieutenant of Surrey. The Cubitts were an old Norfolk family. The unusual first name (also used in 'The Three Students') may have been suggested by 'Hill House'—in which case ACD would be distinguished from Conrad Hilton: one having used a hotel to make a name, the other having used a name to make a chain of hotels. The conjunction of the two names resembles 'Hinton Blewitt' in Somerset.

74 *Ridling Thorpe Manor, Norfolk*: *Strand*, 'Riding Thorpe Manor'— a misprint, as the later references are to 'Ridling Thorpe Manor'. (American edns. have 'Riding Thorpe Manor' throughout.) The name is a combination of two villages near North Walsham: Ridlington, 4 miles to the east near the coast, and Edingthorpe, 3 ½ miles to the north-east. 'Thorpe' is a common local name: Thorpe Hall, Norwich, was the residence of a member of the Cubitt family; Thorpe Junction is on the route to Cromer; and Thorpe itself was the site of the Country Mental Hospital run by ACD's friend, David George Thomson. Colonel R. G. Cubitt claimed that the house in the story was based on Church House farm, Ridlington (in a letter quoted in the *Sherlock Holmes Journal* 8/1 (winter 1966)), while Shirley Sanderson identified it with Walcott House, 7 miles from North Walsham (*SHJ*, 6/3 (Winter 1963)).

75 *the Jubilee*: Queen Victoria's Diamond Jubilee, which was officially celebrated on 21 June 1897 when the Queen came to London from Windsor and rode in state to Buckingham Palace.

Parker, the vicar of our parish: possibly from Dr Joseph Parker, of the City Temple, the Congregationalist preacher (b. 1830), who died on 28 Nov. 1902. The real vicar of North Walsham was the Revd William M. Hobson.

76 *Elsie Patrick*: the surname is that of David Patrick (1849–1914), the head of the literary staff of W. & R. Chambers, of Edinburgh (and the man who may have accepted ACD's first published story, which appeared in *Chambers's Journal*, 6 Sept. 1879).

If you take me, Hilton: *Collier's Weekly*, 'If you take me, John' (the only time the name is used; presumably a mistake carried over from the MS and typescript).

77 *of that I am sure*: possibly a euphemism for stating that at her marriage she was *virgo intacta*, which would be relevant to the case.

78 *to reach Liverpool Street at one-twenty*: the times given in the story suggest that ACD checked them against Bradshaw's train timetable or recalled the times from his own journeys (though in this instance the train reached the station at 2.20 p.m.).

83 *North Walsham*: a market town, 6 miles east of Happisburgh and 16 miles north of Norwich; served by the Great Eastern Railway (and the Great Northern Joint Railway). The first train from Liverpool Street was at 5.10 a.m.; passengers changed at Thorpe station into the Cromer branch train to reach North Walsham at 9.44 a.m.

84 *the German Ocean*: the North Sea, the alternative name used until the outbreak of the war with Germany in 1914.

86 *at last*: so in all texts, yet it is remotely possible ACD intended 'at least'.

   grey-headed: so in *Strand*, American, and most English texts, but 'grey-bearded' in Murray.

88 *open for a*: followed by 'very' in *Strand*.

90 *Elrige's*: from the Ebridge Mills, North Walsham, owned by Cubitt and Walker; or Elridge, an orderly at the Langman Hospital in Bloemfontein; or from Eridge, in Sussex.

   East Ruston: a village 5½ miles south-east of North Walsham, where E. W. Hornung had his country cottage (East Ruston, Under Stalham).

91 *Abe Slaney*: the American contraction of 'Abraham' (as in Abe Lincoln). The surname, according to a suggestion by Owen Dudley Edwards, could be 'a grafting of the River Slaney, not far from the territory of ACD's Doyle ancestors in Ireland, on the outlaw Joseph Alfred Slade (1824–64), celebrated by Mark Twain in *Roughing It* (1872)'.

92 *that the symbol* 𝑋 *stood for E*: thus in all editions until the most recent Penguin *Return* (1981), which deleted the dancing man and read 'which symbol stood for E'.

   and noted that E was represented by 𝑋 : *Collier's Weekly*, 'and noted 𝑋 as standing for E'.

   [E,] T, A, O, I, N, S, H, R, D and L are the numerical order in which letters occur: *Collier's Weekly* 'is'. This is the order used by compositors, rather than the order given by Poe (E, A, O, I, D, H, N, R, S, T). The *Encyclopaedia Britannica* ('Crypto-

graphy') gives the frequency as E, T, A, O, I, N, R, S, H, D, L.

97 *no one outside the Joint ... dancing men*: 'the Joint'—usually a saloon or a disreputable place associated with approved patrons, thus an alternative for 'gang' or 'secret organization', similar to the 'Lodge' in Freemasonry which is used of both the meeting-place and the organization, (see *The Valley of Fear*). The 'boss of the Joint' was the saloon-keeper (who acts as the head of a gang drawn from the customers of his saloon).

ACD's use of American gangster slang appears well founded in the light of definitions given by Robert Chapman in the *New Dictionary of American Slang* (1986). 'You have the drop on me'—the advantage, literally 'you have surprised me with your gun and that forces me to drop my own' (or here 'to leave it in the holster'); 'on the cross'—dishonest; 'heeled'—armed with a gun; 'pulled off'—fired; 'jay'—'rural', fourth-rate or useless (as in a 'jay town'), so here a 'rustic' or 'simpleton'.

99 *Three-forty is our train ... for dinner*: the train on which ACD had travelled back to London from Cromer. It reached North Walsham at 3.55 and arrived at Liverpool Street at 7 p.m.

THE PRIORY SCHOOL

First published in the *Strand Magazine*, 27 (Feb. 1904), 123–40, with 9 illustrations by Sidney Paget, and in *Collier's Weekly*, 32 (30 Jan. 1904), 18–20, 25, 27–30, with 6 illustrations (including coloured cover) by Frederic Dorr Steele.

MS: sold at auction in New York (26 Jan. 1922), $155; and again in London, (28 Jan. 1925), with the MSS of 'The Solitary Cyclist' (first part) and 'The Dancing Men', £66; collection of Leigh Block, Chicago; sold at Sotheby Parke Bernet, New York (28 Feb. 1974), to Marvin P. Epstein, New Jersey; then by private sale, (1987). Present location: the collection of Glen S. Miranker, San Francisco, Calif.

A facsimile of the original manuscript was published in 1985, with an introduction by Len Deighton (Santa Barbara, Calif., Santa Teresa Press).

Text: collated with MS and printed texts.

The title may have been suggested by Florence Coombe's *Boys of Priory School* (1899), while the conduct of the duke has points in common with the headmaster in 'The Story of the Latin Tutor' (*Strand*, Apr. 1899) who also protects an unacknowledged and degenerate son (even though his character and that of his son are different from those of Holdernesse and Wilder).

The horseshoes 'dug up in the moat of Holdernesse Hall' and designed to counterfeit hoof marks were taken from a photograph published in the 'Curiosities' section of the *Strand* for May 1903 ('To Baffle Pursuit', 25, p. 596): 'These false horseshoes were found in the moat at Birtsmorton Court, near Tewkesbury', says the caption. 'It is supposed that they were used in the time of the Civil Wars, so as to deceive any person tracking the marks. The one on the left is supposed to leave the mark of a cow's hoof, the one on the right that of a child's foot.'

Tyre tracks (and the names of the tyre-makers) appear to have been taken from E. W. Hornung's story 'The Wrong House' (*The Black Mask*, 1901). Raffles insists that he and Bunny should both use Dunlop tyres: 'They seem the most popular brand. I had my eye on the road all the way from Ripley to Cobham, and there were more Dunlop marks than any other kind. Bless you, yes, they all leave their special tracks, and we don't want ours to be extra special; the Dunlop's like a rattlesnake, and the Palmer leaves telegraph-wires, but surely the serpent is more in our line.' This may be compared with the present story in which Watson refers to the tracks running across a bog: 'An impression like a fine bundle of telegraph wires ran down the centre of it. It was the Palmer tyre.'

In the manuscript ACD located the school in a defined area of the Derbyshire Peak District. 'Mackleton' is first described as 'Castleton', and the road running past the school is said to be that between Manchester and Buxton. There is a reference to the boy being found in Liverpool and in Sheffield (afterwards corrected to Liverpool), and ACD describes the road on the north of the moor as 'the Chesterfield high-road'. A glance at a map of the Peak District will show that this is impossible, but there are several incidental points which support the location. To the east of Castleton there is Hallam Moor, and to the north of Buxton there is the Holderness Quarry. Shaw Moor, Blackshaw, Hayes, Thorny Leigh, and even Thorny Croft are found in the vicinity. But the descriptions are not precise (as they were in 'The Dancing Men') and it may be that ACD was using his memories of the moors near his mother's house at Masongill where the Lake District merges into Yorkshire. Derbyshire has 'tors' and 'cloughs', while 'gills' (mountain streams) are found further north, as in 'Masongill' itself, or 'Lowgill' and 'Long Gill' in the Forest of Bowland. For the 'Ragged Shaw' ACD need have looked no further than his back garden where the lawn ran into the 'shaw' or rough heathland, giving the house its name 'Undershaw', while 'ragged' came perhaps from Poe's story 'A Tale of the Ragged Mountains'.

The mention of an Ordnance Survey map implies that ACD made use of one, but in doing so he revealed his ignorance of cartography by including a 'Watershed across moor' on the diagram and making a reference to it in the text. A 'watershed' is the elevated boundary line separating the headstreams which are tributary to different river systems, so it would never appear in marshy ground, or be visible. The error was brought to his attention by the editor of the *Strand* and was changed to 'watercourse' in the text and to a 'Marshy tract across Moor' on the diagram, but it remained unchanged in the American magazine (for which a second copy of the diagram had been drawn).

Holmes's observation about the Dunlop tyre tracks (which were made by James Wilder, the duke's secretary, who must have travelled in both directions as he had to cycle to the school before he could return from it) is untenable: 'The more deeply sunk impression is, of course, the hind wheel, upon which the weight rests. You perceive several places where it has passed across and obliterated the more shallow mark of the front one. It was undoubtedly heading away from the school.' Doubts were first raised in two letters sent to the *Strand Magazine*, and these were forwarded to ACD. He told the editor: 'I don't suppose you take much notice about what Cranks write, but with regard to the two letters from Dublin you sent me—both from the same person by the way—you may be interested to know that I have just been out, tried it on my bike, and got the impressions as in the story, the hind wheel cutting across the line of the front one' (Arthur Conan Doyle Collection, Metropolitan Toronto Library, MSS). He took a photograph of the tracks to prove it, but afterwards realized that it only showed that the front wheel precedes the back one.

In his autobiography he again commented on the problem: 'I had so many remonstrances upon this point, varying from pity to anger, that I took out my bicycle and tried. I had imagined that the observations of the way in which the track of the hind wheel overlaid the track of the front one when the machine was not

running dead straight would show the direction. I found that my
correspondents were right and I was wrong, for this would be the
same whichever way the cycle was moving. On the other hand
the real solution was much simpler, for on an undulating moor the
wheels make a much deeper impression uphill and a more shallow
one downhill, so Holmes was justified of his wisdom after all'
(*Memories and Adventures*, 1924).

A similar observation involving a carriage is found in 'The
Greek Interpreter' (*Memoirs*), but there, if the direction could not
be discovered from the horses' hoofs, it could be inferred from the
tracks as a heavy vehicle impacts the earth behind the wheel.

A later reference to the story is found in 'The Blanched Soldier'
(*Case-Book*) where Holmes refers to it incorrectly as 'the case which
my friend Watson has described as that of the Abbey School, in
which the Duke of Greyminster was so deeply involved'.

The story was placed tenth on the author's list of the twelve best
Sherlock Holmes stories 'if only for the dramatic moment when
Holmes points the finger at the Duke' ('How I Made My List,'
Strand, June 1927), and as such it was reprinted in the *Grand
Magazine* (Apr. 1928).

100 *Dr Thorneycroft Huxtable*: Thorny Croft is in Derbyshire, but
the name was probably suggested by Colonel Thorneycroft
(who commanded the Mounted Infantry during the Boer
War) or by Sir William Hamo Thornycroft (whose statue of
King Alfred in Winchester had received ACD's backing).
Louis R. Huxtable, who graduated MB and CM at Edinburgh at the same time as ACD, would be a possible source
for the second name.

Mackleton, in the North of England: originally 'Castleton, in Derbyshire' (a village 10 miles north-east of Buxton). The invented
name combines Macclesfield and Castleton.

twelve o'clock: originally 'eleven'. This would not have allowed
the client adequate time to reach London from Derbyshire.

101 *this case of the Ferrers Documents*: originally 'the Ferrers deed
case'; an allusion to a famous breach of promise case in 1846
when Lord Ferrers was sued by Mary Smith. The 'documents' were forged letters purporting to come from him and
his brother. A 'Duchess of Ferrers' is mentioned in ACD's
play *The Speckled Band* (1910).

101 *the Abergavenny murder*: from the town in Monmouthshire, or perhaps an allusion to Lady Abergavenny who beat her child to death in 1711.

the Duke of Holdernesse: an invented title, though there were Earls of Holdernesse (Holderness) in three creations, namely John Ramsay, who died without issue; Prince Rupert, who died unmarried; and the Darcy family. The title became extinct on the death of the fourth earl in 1778. Holdernesse is a district of Yorkshire and the name of a parliamentary division.

the late Cabinet Minister: originally 'the Foreign Secretary'.

the 'Globe': originally 'the evening papers'; the *Globe* was a London evening paper founded in 1803, which merged with the *Pall Mall Gazette* in Feb. 1921.

Volume 'H' in his encyclopaedia of reference: the format suggests it was a standard reference work, such as *Kelly's Handbook to the Titled, Landed and Official Classes*.

'Holdernesse, sixth Duke . . . Chief Secretary of State for—': The duke was first described as the 'Lord Lieutenant of Lancashire' (an office then held by the Earl of Derby); his wife was originally the 'daughter of Sir Charles Appleby'; Holdernesse Hall was in Lancashire, and the duke was Secretary of State 'for India' and 'Foreign Secretary'. 'Lord Beverley' was a real title (also used by Fletcher Robinson in *The Chronicles of Addington Peace*, 1905). Carston is an invented name—combining Carstairs and Cranston (ACD's parliamentary agent in Edinburgh in 1900). Hallamshire is a district in the West Riding of Yorkshire. Lord Saltire was a fictitious title used for a very different character in *The Stark Munro Letters* (1895). 'Appledore' is the name of villages in Devon and Kent. ACD was characteristically indifferent to aristocratic niceties and the description should correctly have referred to the 'Sixth Duke of Holdernesse' rather than the 'Sixth Duke'; the father and son should have shared the same titles; the earldom should have preceded the barony; the main seat should have preceded the London address; and 'Lord of the Admiralty' should have read 'a Lord of the Admiralty'.

The duke could be a composite portrait of Lord Salisbury (the Foreign Secretary and Prime Minister—who died on 22 Aug. 1903) and the Duke of Devonshire (whose main seat was at Chatsworth in Derbyshire). Adopting ACD's form, they would appear thus:

> Salisbury, third Marquis, KG, PC ... Viscount Cranborne ... High Steward of Great Yarmouth from 1888 ... Married Georgina Caroline, daughter of Sir E. Hall Alderson, 1857 ... Address: Arlington Street; Hatfield House, Hertfordshire; Manor House, Cranborne, Dorset; Secretary of State for India, Foreign Secretary.

> Devonshire, eighth Duke, KG, PC ... Marquis of Hartington ... Lord Lieutenant of Derbyshire from 1892. Married Countess Louise, daughter of Count von Alten, 1892. Address: Devonshire House; Chatsworth, Derbyshire; Lismore Castle, Ireland. A Lord of the Admiralty, 1863; Secretary of State for India.

The Countess Louise had been the Duke of Devonshire's mistress for many years while married to the Duke of Manchester, thus combining the separate functions which the Duke of Holdernesse divided between two ladies.

102 *a cheque for five thousand pounds*: originally '£10,000'.

'Huxtable's Sidelights on Horace': this was based on the title of one of ACD's talks, 'Sidelights on History'. The Latin poet Quintus Horatius Flaccus (65–8 BC) is quoted in *A Study in Scarlet* and compared to Hafiz in 'A Case of Identity' (*Adventures*). At the time the story was written there had just appeared an edition of the *Odes* (the first volume of George Bell's 'Pocket Book Classics'), a *Horace for English Readers*, and a verse translation of the *Odes* and 'Secular Hymn'.

Lord Leverstoke, the Earl of Blackwater, Sir Cathcart Soames: invented titles. Lord Leverstoke is perhaps from Lord Revelstoke, a director of the Bank of England, or from William Lever, the soap magnate for whose yearbook of 1898 ACD had written 'Burger's Secret' ('The New Catacomb')—thus anticipating his later title 'Lord Leverhulme' (1917). The Earl of Blackwater, from the Blackwater River in Waterford (where ACD's Foley relatives had land); Sir Cathcart Soames, from Cathcart on the borders of Lanarkshire and Renfrewshire, and from the MCC cricketer called Soames.

103 *the South of France*: the Riviera, which was frequented in the

summer by the British aristocracy (including Lord Salisbury, who had a residence at Beaulieu, near Nice).

black Eton jacket: a generic term for a short jacket which reaches only to the waist, as worn at Eton College, from which it takes its name.

Caunter: from Colonel J. E. Caunter, an MCC cricketer.

Heidegger: from the Swiss adventurer Johann Jacob Heidegger (1660–1749), or from Nathaniel Hawthorne's story 'Dr Heidegger's Experiment' (*Twice-Told Tales*, 1851).

107 *two old hounds like Watson and myself*: originally 'one old hound like myself'.

110 *Look at this map*:

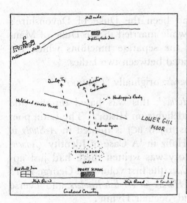 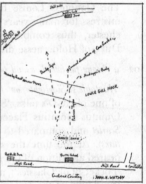

Collier's Weekly   Strand

'Holmes' Map of the Neighborhood of the School' in *Collier's Weekly* is a second copy by ACD of the map used in the *Strand*, and not a facsimile. It retains the reference to the 'Watershed across Moor'. The 'Sketch Map showing the locality' in the *Strand* (also used in the first edition, with 'John H. Watson' deleted), has 'Marshy track' superimposed over 'Watershed'.

the main road: originally 'the main road between Manchester and Buxton'.

112 *the east side*: originally 'the Buxton side'.

362

the Red Bull: perhaps suggested by 'The Red Lion' and 'The Flying Bull', two famous inns near Hindhead.

We will come . . . presently: MS originally continued, 'That unfortunate Dr Huxtable will be seriously ill, I fear. Do you hear him pacing up and down the passage.'

Lower Gill Moor . . . sloping gradually upwards: originally 'to the Black Gill Hills'. Possibly suggested by Lower East Moor near Chatsworth House.

where they rear sheep and cattle: originally 'Here eight miles north is a simple house, Lower Gill House, now untenanted.'

the Chesterfield high-road: originally 'a high road upon the further side at Black Gill Hills'. Chesterfield is a town in Derbyshire, 12 miles south of Sheffield.

113 *with a white chevron on the peak*: a chevron is an inverted V, used on escutcheons and on the arms of uniforms to designate rank. Its position 'on the peak' would be unusual, as crests are usually on the front of the cap.

114 *the master workman who sees his work lies ready before him*: MS continued, 'the artist whose pigments are set out, and who has to blend them into the expression of his own soul'.

cows had left their tracks: originally 'two cows had left their tracks'.

I am familiar with . . . impressions left by tyres: MS continued, 'and their study will certainly repay the student of crime. These are the points which mark the expert . . .'.

a Dunlop . . . outer cover: a Dunlop tyre, named after John Boyd Dunlop (1840–1921), the founder of the Dunlop Tyre Co. The Dunlops were based at Aston in Birmingham and were the 'inventors and largest makers in the world of pneumatic tyres'. In 1903 the tyres came 'with either wired or wireless edges' and could be identified by the trade mark of Dunlop's Head on the inner tube and the outer cover. The patch referred to in the story appears to be a repaired puncture (which would usually be confined to the inner tube and would not be visible).

Aveling: perhaps from Dr Edward Aveling who wrote on Darwin, or from Frederick Aveling, the Boer War critic, or C.

T. Aveling, a cricketer, who died of a heart attack in 1902 when going to the rescue of a drowning lady.

115 *My reasoning*: originally 'My *a priori* reasoning'.

118 *five miles*: originally 'six miles'.

119 *the sign of a game-cock*: possibly an allusion to the 'Cock and Pynot' at Old Whittington, 4 miles from Chesterfield. A stone plaque marks the spot and is inscribed: A.D. 1688 | IN A ROOM WHICH FORMERLY | EXISTED AT THE END OF THIS | COTTAGE (WHAT IS LEFT OF THE | OLD COCK & PYNOT) THE EARL | OF DANBY, THE EARL OF DEVON-SHIRE | AND MR JOHN D'ARCY (ELDEST SON | OF THE EARL OF HOLDERNESS) MET | SOME TIME IN 1688 TO CONCERT | MEASURES WHICH RESULTED IN THE | RE-VOLUTION OF THAT YEAR.

Reuben Hayes: the first name is biblical (Genesis: Reuben was the eldest son of Jacob who arranged for his younger brother Joseph to be put into a pit in Dothan). The second perhaps from Sir George Hayes (1805–69), justice of the Queen's Bench in his final year, and the author of a song called 'The Dog and the Cock'.

120 *Liverpool*: MS 'Sheffield' (here, and below).

corn-chandler: a corn and grain dealer.

121 *he arranged . . . in this fashion*: the arrangement of dots given in the MS and the *Strand* bears no relation to the gait of a horse: and the last two were the same. The correct representation would be: a walk: `:     :     :     : :` ; a canter: `··   ··     ··` ; a gallop: `.     ·     .     .`

123 *It looks like a flight*: originally by both men, 'Two men in the dog cart, so far as I could see. Wilder and Hayes—a curious couple to run together.'

124 *The bicycle . . . tyre*: MS 'The lamp still gleamed from the bicycle. Holmes slipped it off, and turned it towards the machine. I heard him chuckle in the darkness as the narrow tunnel of vivid light fell upon the patch of a Dunlop tyre.'

125 *half an hour's delay*: 'an hour's delay' in American edns.

126 *'The Capital and Counties Bank . . . my agents'*: the bank and branch used by ACD, at 125 Oxford Street. It was amalga-mated with Lloyds Bank in 1918.

129 *with a persistent hatred*: the MS then continued, 'The estates were all entailed and he was aware that even if I wished I could not divert them from the line of succession.'

130 *a led pony*: a pony that was being led.

BLACK PETER

First published in the *Strand Magazine*, 27 (Mar. 1904), 243–55, with 7 illustrations by Sidney Paget, and in *Collier's Weekly*, 32 (27 Feb. 1904), 18–20, 22–5, with 6 illustrations (including coloured cover) by Frederic Dorr Steele.

MS: presented to Robert J. Collier (the son of the publisher P. F. Collier) and remained in the family until 1972; sold at auction, Charles Hamilton Galleries, New York (20 Apr. 1972), $4,700. Present location: the collection of Norman S. Nolan, Middletown, NJ.

Text: collated with MS and printed texts.

There are many literary precedents for the title, including Fielding's 'Black George' in *Tom Jones*, Walter Scott's 'Black Dwarf' in *The Black Dwarf*, Stevenson's 'Black Dog' in *Treasure Island*, 'Black Jack' in 'The Beach of Falesa', and ACD's eponymous 'Black Doctor' (1898).

The background recalls ACD's experience on an Arctic whaler in 1880 when he served on the *Hope* under Captain John Gray. Patrick Cairns may have been based on the hot-blooded chief harpooner Colin Maclean, 'with his six foot of stature, his erect, stalwart figure, and his fierce, red beard, pouring out from beneath the flaps of his sealing-cap'; while Black Peter could have been suggested by the 'swarthy, dark-eyed man, with blue-black-hair and beard' who was rumoured to have fled from the south of England to avoid the law. 'I could believe from his appearance', said ACD, 'that his temper was Satanic, and that the crime for which he was hiding may have been a bloody one' ('Life on a Greenland Whaler,' *Strand*, Jan. 1897).

The central idea is similar to 'The Mystery of the Jade Spear' by Bertram Fletcher Robinson where the victim is transfixed by a spear: 'The force used in throwing the spear was abnormal. Either the murderer must have been a man of remarkable physique, or he must have thrown the spear from a rapidly moving vehicle.' (The story was published in the *Home Magazine of Fiction* in Jan. 1905, and is collected in *The Chronicles of Addington Peace*, 1905.)

The use of identical initials may have been brought to mind by the appearance in *Punch* of articles and poems by the Revd Anthony Charles Deane (1870–1946) signed 'ACD'. Early in the century regular contributors to *Punch* were allowed to use their initials, and soon afterwards Deane recalled, 'I had a letter from Arthur Conan Doyle—whom at that time I had not met—stating that, owing to the identity of our initials, what he described politely as "tributes" to my *Punch* things were being received frequently by him' (*Time Remembered*, 1945).

According to a history of the *The Times* personal column by Stephen Winkworth, the agony column had 'during 1883 a number of so far undeciphered messages in code headed "J.H.N." '; and a few years before there was 'the well-known "C.P.R." series of numerical codes, whose complexity is unparalleled' (*Room for Two More Guns*, 1986). If this is so, then ACD may have been aware of them. However, the recognition of familiar initials had been used before in *The Hound of the Baservilles* (where 'CCH' is identified as the 'Charing Cross Hospital').

ACD dismissed the story as 'carpenter's work' in a letter to the editor of the *Strand*, and he disapproved of the choice of illustrations: 'There is none there to induce anyone to read the story. The story would be better without them. Fancy a picture of "Black Peter" with his beard to the ceiling and a great harpoon driven though him. That's ginger' (Arthur Conan Doyle Collection, Metropolitan Toronto Library).

134   *the sudden death of Cardinal Tosca*: from *La Tosca*, the play by Victorien Sardou (upon which Puccini based his famous opera). It was given three performances by Sarah Bernhardt at the Adelphi Theatre in June 1903. There were cardinals in Irving's *Dante* (which ACD saw at Drury Lane on 30 Apr. 1903), and the conclave of cardinals in Rome met on 20 July 1903 to elect Cardinal Sarto (1835–1914) as Pope (Pius X), but ACD was probably thinking of Cardinal Herbert Vaughan of Westminster who died on 15 June 1903. Vaughan was educated at Stonyhurst (as was his brother Bernard), and as Bishop of Salford (1872–92) had the college in his diocese.

Wilson, the notorious canary-trainer: this may have been inspired by an article in the *Strand* on 'A Phonograph School for Parrots' (Aug. 1903) about a parrot-trainer in Philadelphia who used phonographs to train birds to talk. Owen Dudley

Edwards (*The Quest for Sherlock Holmes*, 58) suggests that the name could have derived from Patrick Wilson (the pock-marked schoolmaster of the Newington Academy in Edinburgh, where ACD was a pupil in 1867–8) taken in conjunction with the Christian name of Black Peter's killer.

Woodman's Lee: from Compton's Lea, Horsham, the home of E. W. Hornung's brother, and from the Woodman family who were friends of ACD in Southsea.

Captain Peter Carey: the name could have been suggested by Claude Currie, whose berth ACD occupied on the *Hope*; or by Captain Carey in William Clark Russell's story 'Brokers' Bay'; Mrs Carey and Jim Carey in *The Episodes of Marge* (1903); Rosa N. Carey, the novelist (1840–1909); or the real Captain Carey (Captain Walter Carey, d. 1932), an expert on torpedoes.

Captain Basil: perhaps named after Captain Basil Hall (1788–1844), the British naval officer and traveller, whose books of travel included *An Account of a Voyage of Discovery to the West Coast of Corea and the Great Loo-choo Island in the Japan Sea* (1818) and *Extracts from a Journal written on the Coasts of Chili, Peru and Mexico in the Years* 1820–21–22 (1824). Or from Captain Basil Hood, the dramatist (Captain Basil Charles Willett Hood, 1864–1917), who wrote the words for Sir Arthur Sullivan's *The Emerald Isle* (completed by Edward Germain), and for Edward Germain's *A Princess of Kensington* (Savoy Theatre, 22 July 1903). The first of these includes a character named 'Black Dan'.

135 *at least five small refuges . . . in which he was able to change his personality* : ACD was perhaps thinking of Raffles who had an artist's studio in the King's Road—'the billycock comes in and the topper goes out, and nobody takes the slightest notice of either' ('A Costume Piece', *The Amateur Cracksman*, 1899).

a huge barb-headed spear. MS, *Strand*, and *Collier's Weekly*, 'barbed-headed'; a harpoon (such as that which ACD kept as a memento of his voyage). By the 1880s these were fired from swivel guns and were hurled only by men 'in the frontispieces of books originating from Paternoster Row' ('The Glamour of the Arctic,' *Idler*, July 1892).

Allardyce's back shop: the name of the second mate in 'The Striped Chest' (*The Green Flag*, 1900); also of Allardyce and Co., Ltd., wholesale stationers, of 136 Southwark Street, near the Sumner Street premises which ACD purchased for the Automatic Sculpture Syndicate (which had a butcher as a sitting tenant).

135 *Stanley Hopkins*: the name is similar to 'Lee Hopkins' ('The Doctors of Hoyland', *Round the Red Lamp*, 1894), and recalls the poet Gerard Manley Hopkins (1844–89), who was resident at the Jesuit house of studies adjoining Stonyhurst in ACD's time and was a friend of his form master, the Revd Cyprian Splaine, SJ.

136 *an old sealer*: a seal and whale fisher.

137 *the steam sealer 'Sea Unicorn', of Dundee*: 'sea unicorn', the popular name for the narwhal (whose tusk resembles that of the fabulous beast), and thus perhaps an allusion to the first steam whaler, the *Narwhal*, of Dundee, built in 1859.

Forest Row, in Sussex: a village, 3 miles south-east of East Grinstead, with a 'wayside station' served by the London Brighton and South Coast Railway.

a strict Puritan: originally a member of the party of English Protestants from the time of Elizabeth I who sought to abolish unscriptural and corrupt ceremonies, hence a person affecting extreme strictness in religion or morals and demanding it of others (especially of his family); a gloomy person.

he always called it 'the cabin': old sailors by tradition hanker for life at sea. The Lords Howe, Hawke, Exmouth, and Rodney all had rooms fitted out as cabins, and Admiral Sir George Tryon (1832–93) converted a summer-house into an exact reproduction of his former cabin ('Ships' Cabins on Dry Land', *Tit-Bits*, 11 Apr. 1903).

138 *a stonemason, named Slater*: a name (previously used in 'The Lost Special', 1898) inspired by the trade, or perhaps taken from Slater's Detective Agency. The story was written nine years before ACD's involvement with the Oscar Slater case.

139 *a lost soul in hell*: 'a lost soul in torment' in *Strand* and subsequently.

brindled: brownish or tawny with streaks of other colour (*OED*).

stock: hasp, handle.

140 *a tantalus*: MS and *Collier's Weekly*, 'a Tantalus'; a rack or stand holding two or three decanters with a folding top that locks

(from Tantalus, the son of Zeus, who was condemned to stand in water which receded when he stooped to drink).

strong ship's tobacco: a general term for a strong, coarse tobacco, favoured by sailors, such as Wilde's Ship Tobacco, 'manufactured by Pensioners from H.M. Navy', which was cut from 'the genuine plug' and could be had in three grades—light, medium, and dark.

San Paulo: the conventional Spanish spelling for São Paulo, Brazil.

141 *Canadian Pacific Railway*: built 1878–86; the company, whose shares were among the strongest of those quoted on the Stock Exchange, had a central London office at 30 Cockspur Street, between Pall Mall and Trafalgar Square, which ACD passed on the way to his club.

in the House . . . brokers: 'The busy, noisy multitude on the floor of the Stock Exchange, or "the House," as it is familiarly called, is composed of innumerable groups or "markets" ' ('A Stock Exchange Transaction', *Strand*, Sept. 1903).

142 a *sheath-knife*: later a 'clasp knife'; the first has a fixed blade within a sheath; the second has a blade which folds into the handle.

that great forest . . . bulwark of Britain: the Ashdown Forest (afterwards used as the setting for *Sir Nigel*).

143 *single-roofed*: 'shingle-roofed' in *Strand*.

144 *He tried . . . a very small penknife*: the MS originally continued, 'He has left half of it, which you would do well to secure, in the slit of the sash of . . .'

ambuscade: here, a party preparing for an ambush.

145 *and for the rustle and whisper of fine rain falling amid the foliage which roofed us in*: added in MS.

Half-past two had chimed: MS and *Collier's Weekly*, 'Three had sounded'.

Norfolk jacket: a loose jacket with waistband.

146 *John Hopley Neligan*: from Joseph William Neligan, who started divorce proceedings against his wife in July 1903, or from C. E. Neligan, an Esher cricketer. The middle name is that of F. J. V. Hopley, a Harrow cricketer, and of Edward William John Hopley (1816–69), the painter; or it could be a variant of

369

'Copley Banks' in the Captain Sharkey stories (*The Green Flag*, 1900)—which recalls another painter, John Singleton Copley (1737–1815). The initials are those of John Henry Newman.

146 *Dawson & Neligan*: the 'West Country Bankers' who 'failed for a million'. Examples of failed banks and commercial fraud were plentiful. The senior partner of Remington, Stephenson and Co. embezzled £70,000, crossed the Bristol Channel in an open boat, and made his escape to Savannah; William Robson of the Crystal Palace Co. crossed to Denmark in 1856 and was captured at Helsingfors; and Jabez Spencer Balfour had been extradited from the Argentine. Closer to home there was E. W. Hornung's father whose business had collapsed leaving unpaid debts which the children were intent on clearing.

147 *He left us a list of the securities he was taking*: added in proof.

148 *a prisoner in your hands*: MS originally continued, 'Such was the story which the unfortunate young man . . .'

Brambletye: from Brambletye House, a ruined Jacobean building, a mile south of East Grinstead. The Brambletye Hotel on the Square in Forest Row was opened in 1866.

149 *Sumner, Shipping Agent, Ratcliff Highway*: from Sumner Street in Southwark, where ACD acquired premises for the Automatic Sculpture Syndicate. The Ratcliff Highway (St Georges Street) ran past the London Docks to Shadwell and was an area of ill repute in the early 19th century.

Lord Street, Brixton: an imaginary London address, found in Liverpool and Greater Birmingham (where there is also Cairns Street, Carey Street, Woodman Road, Lee Street, Dawson Street, and Lancaster Street).

150 *hob-nobbed*: drank, caroused, or held familiar intercourse.

151 *a little ribston-pippin . . . side-whiskers*: the Ribston pippin is a variety of winter apple, originally from Normandy, with a ruddy skin and fluffy centre, named after Ribston Hall in Yorkshire where it was first cultivated.

James Lancaster: possibly an allusion to the English navigator of the same name who led the first trading expedition for the East India Co. in 1600.

Hugh Pattins: from Dr Henry Pattin, Medical Officer of Health for Norwich, a close associate of ACD's friend David Thomson.

Eight pounds a month: MS and *Collier's Weekly*, 'Eight pound a month'; £3 more than the pay of the harpooners on the *Hope* in 1880.

153 *spare harpooner*: correctly the 'loose harpooner'; from the 'spare boat' found on whalers.

the Shetland lights: the lighthouses on the Shetland Isles, at North Unst, Out Skerries, Bressay, and Sumburgh Head.

154 *full of the devil*: 'in a vile temper' (*Strand* and subsequently).

My God!: 'Heavens!' (*Strand* and subsequently).

155 *hempen rope*: a noose.

too large a portion of our carpet: MS and *Collier's Weekly*, 'too large a proportion of our carpet'.

the initials 'P.C.' upon the pouch were a coincidence and not those of Peter Carey: MS and *Collier's Weekly*, 'the P.C. upon the pouch were [was] a coincidence, and not the initials of Peter Carey.'

156 *my address . . . in Norway*: ACD had visited Norway in Aug. 1892 with E. W. Hornung and Jerome K. Jerome (1859–1927).

CHARLES AUGUSTUS MILVERTON

First published in the *Strand Magazine*, 27 (Apr. 1904), 373–83, with 6 illustrations by Sidney Paget, and in *Collier's Weekly*, 32 (26 Mar. 1904), 13–15, 19–20, with 6 illustrations (including coloured cover) by Frederic Dorr Steele.

MS: sold at the American Art Galleries, New York (31 Jan. 1923), $70, to William Randolph Hearst; Scribner Book Store, New York, Sherlock Holmes Catalogue (Nov. 1943), $450; sold to Edgar W. Smith, New Jersey (1944), $300; by private sale after his death to Carl H. Anderson, Philadelphia, (1960). Present location: the collection of Stanfield D. Hill, USA.

Text: collated with MS and printed texts.

The original title, 'The Worst Man in London', was too obviously taken from the play *The Worst Woman in London*, by Walter Melville, which had been revived at the Adelphi Theatre on 7 Mar. 1903, and was therefore changed to the more innocuous 'Charles Augustus Milverton'. The conjunction of the Christian names was not uncommon but two people are suggested as the source: Charles Augustus Howell (1840–90), an Anglo-Portuguese scoundrel and

blackmailer, who was John Ruskin's secretary and a friend of
D. G. Rossetti and Edward Burne-Jones; and Charles Augustus
Bynoe, who was imprisoned for forgery and was the subject of W.
T. Stead's booklet *Wanted a Sherlock Holmes* (*Review of Reviews* Office,
1895). The names were afterwards used by Hilaire Belloc for
'Charles Augustus Fortescue, Who always Did what was Right,
and so Accumulated an Immense Fortune' (*Cautionary Tales for
Children*, 1908). The source of the surname may have been 'Milver-
ton Street', near the Oval Cricket Ground in London.

The plot was influenced by (and was perhaps a conscious parody
of) E. W. Hornung's story 'Wilful Murder' (*The Amateur Cracksman*,
1899): Raffles is threatened with blackmail by his fence and
decides to kill him. He adopts various disguises in order to conceal
his identity and in the process familiarizes himself with the layout
of the grounds. On the fateful night Bunny insists on accompany-
ing him and they make their way to the lonely building, using
corks to cross a high wall covered in spikes. Raffles breaks in, only
to find that the blackmailer is already dead. The killer, who is
known to Raffles, is on the premises and is persuaded to flee the
country.

In the present story a higher law is invoked as justification
and Holmes is a disinterested player, but he uses the methods of
a cracksman. He attempts to take Milverton's pocket-book by
force and afterwards proves himself an experienced safe-breaker.
The amusement with which he considers the danger and the
possibility that he and Watson might share the same cell, recall the
earlier story, as does his suggestion that he and Watson should
wear evening dress, black silk masks, and rubber-soled tennis
shoes.

The engagement to the housemaid may be compared to the
flirtation between Raffles and Amy Werner in 'The Gift of the
Emperor' (*The Amateur Cracksman*, 1899), and with Fletcher Robinson's story 'Mr Taubery's Diamond', where the narrator comes
across 'the amazing spectacle of Addington Peace flirting with a
very pretty nursemaid'. 'I had already noticed that he took pains
to avoid the opposite sex, with that uneasy consciousness of their
presence which marks the bachelor with principles. Yet there he
sat, sharing the same bench and talking earnestly into her ear' (*The
Chronicles of Addington Peace* (1905), 109–10).

Milverton was used again in ACD's play, *The Speckled Band* (1910),
where his attempt to blackmail the Duchess of Ferrers before her

marriage sets the scene at Baker Street. Milverton's address is given as The Firs, Battersea, and Holmes flirts with the cook, but the dialogue is taken from the story.

157 *Appledore Towers, Hampstead*: also called 'Appledore House' in the MS. A name previously found in 'The Priory School'. The house, which recalls stately homes such as Alton and Mentmore Towers, has been identified with Caen Wood Towers on the Highgate side of Hampstead Heath, and with The Logs, the large neo-Gothic structure at the corner of Well Road.

the Zoo: the 'Zoological Gardens' on the north side of Regent's Park, founded in 1826, from which later zoos take their name. It contained 3,000 animals, of which 459 were reptiles. 'If I have cares in my mind,' wrote Thackeray, 'I come to the Zoo, and fancy they don't pass the gate. I recognise my friends, my enemies, in countless cages.'

158 *God*: 'Heaven' (*Strand* and later texts).

He deals with no niggard hand: a mixed metaphor. The cards Milverton dealt so generously were notes from the Bank of England, while the cards he held back until the time was ripe were notes from members of the aristocracy.

159 *the Devil*: 'the Evil One' (*Strand* and later texts).

Lady Eva Brackwell: an echo, perhaps, of Lady Bracknell (in Oscar Wilde's *The Importance of Being Earnest*) who was named after the village in Berkshire. The name appears incorrectly as Lady Eva Blackwell in the Doubleday editions (and those based upon them). The reference to an 'illustrious client' perhaps provided the title for a later story.

the most beautiful débutante of last season: young ladies of good family were presented at court to mark their arrival or *début* on the social scene. The season opened after Easter when the great and good returned to London from their country seats and ended with the race meeting at Goodwood in July.

the Earl of Dovercourt: an invented title, from Dovercourt, near Harwich, and similar to the extinct title the Earl of Dover.

a stately carriage and pair: a 'London carriage', the Victoria, or possibly the Landau (favoured by the aristocracy).

astrakhan: wool resembling fur from young lambs, named after the city of Astrakhan on the Caspian Sea.

something of Mr Pickwick's benevolence: Samuel Pickwick Esq., GCMPC (General Chairman—Member of the Pickwick Club), under whose bald forehead worked a 'gigantic brain' and behind whose circular spectacles there beamed twinkling eyes (Dickens, *The Pickwick Papers*, 1837). Dr Mortimer in *The Hound of the Baskervilles* also has 'keen grey eyes' which sparkle brightly 'from behind a pair of gold-rimmed glasses' giving him 'an air of peering benevolence'.

161 *a coat-of-arms upon the envelope*: other than the Duke of Holder-nesse ('The Priory School'), ACD's youngest son, Adrian, is the only person known to have put a coat of arms on an envelope. ACD means a crest.

Colonel Dorking: from the town of the same name, near Box Hill in Surrey.

the Morning Post: the main society newspaper, which was first published in 1772 and merged with the *Daily Telegraph* in 1937.

boggling: hesitating, demurring; equivocating, haggling.

162 *Milverton had glided as quick as a rat*: originally 'He had sprung'. The emendation was to prevent repetition as Holmes 'sprang from his chair'.

a goatee beard: a chin tuft like a goat. The same disguise sported by Holmes in 'His Last Bow', 'a small goatee beard which gave him a general resemblance to the caricatures of Uncle Sam', save that the beard in 'His Last Bow' is evidently grey (like uncle Sam's) and genuine.

163 *Escott by name*: the name is that of Thomas Hay Sweet Escott (b. 1844), the editor of the *Fortnightly Review* and author of *King Edward VII and his Court* (1903), and is similar to Escot and Escot House, a few miles north of Sidmouth in Devon where ACD stayed on 14–15 August 1903 when playing for the MCC.

164 *For God's sake*: 'For Heaven's sake' (*Strand* and later texts).

'You are not coming': the initial reluctance of Holmes to allow Watson to accompany him is a conscious echo of the exchange between Raffles and Bunny in 'Wilful Murder':

'I'm coming too.'
　'I don't want you.'
　'But I must come!'
An ugly gleam shot from the steel blue eyes.

'To interfere?' said Raffles.

'Not I.'

'You give me your word?'

'I do.'

'Bunny, if you break it . . .'

'You may shoot me, too!'

'I most certainly should,' said Raffles, solemnly. 'So you come at your own peril, my dear man; but, if you are coming . . . well, the sooner the better, for I must stop at my rooms on the way.'

165 *a first class, up-to-date burgling kit . . . adaptable keys*: 'The time has passed,' said an article in *Tit-Bits*, 'when the burglar attacked a safe with a hammer, crowbar, chisel, and a few skeleton keys.' Drills, thermite, blowtorches, and air pumps had taken their place because of the complexity of the locks ('How Scientific Burglars Work', 2 May 1903).

Church Row: an unspoilt street of 18th-century houses in the centre of Hampstead, leading to the parish church of St John.

In Oxford Street . . . hansom: Oxford Street is south of Baker Street while Hampstead is to the north, but it would have been an easier place to find an empty hansom.

166 *These documents are contained in a safe*: originally 'in one of several tin dispatch boxes'.

he is a plethoric sleeper: literally a sleeper having an excess of red corpuscles in the blood (the opposite of anaemic), suggesting 'unhealthy repletion', but here a 'heavy' sleeper. ACD was fond of the word and may have first come across it in William Watson's article on 'Fiction—Plethoric and Anaemic' in the *National Review* (Oct. 1889) which accused George Meredith and Henry James of being 'anaemic', in contrast to their full-blooded, vigorous, virile, and 'plethoric' contemporaries. (ACD wrote an article on Stevenson for the *National Review* in Jan. 1890.)

two of the most truculent figures in London: literally bellicose or aggressive (meaning as pretty a pair of villains as ever walked the London streets).

A sort of tiled veranda: originally a 'stone flagged verandah'.

166 *Holmes removed a circle of glass . . . inside*: this method of gaining an entry was borrowed from Hornung, but ACD omits to explain how the circle of glass was removed. Raffles had 'proceeded to take out a pane with the diamond, a pot of treacle, and a sheet of brown paper' ('Wilful Murder'). It quickly became 'the recognised method in vogue in the burgling industry' (P. G. Wodehouse, 'Jeeves Makes an Omelette').

166/7 *powers, carefully cultivated, of seeing in the dark*: originally 'due to careful cultivation'. Sight cannot be cultivated, but Holmes had good peripheral vision and the ability to use his other senses to create the illusion that he was 'seeing' in the dark.

167 *a portière*: a door hanging, or curtain hung over a doorway.

a marble bust of Athene: Ionic or Attic Greek ('Athena' in Doric), the Goddess of Wisdom; no doubt inspired by one of the busts being copied by ACD's sculpture syndicate.

168 *maw*: stomach, or a craw if a dragon be more bird than beast.

169 *a sharp snick . . . turned on*: 'snick' is a portmanteau word from 'snap' and 'click'. It usually means a small notch or cut.

171 *the Countess d'Albert*: perhaps from Madame Albert (d. 1846), the French actress and 'idol of Paris', who was noted for her grace, beauty, and distinction of manner, or possibly a euphemism for one of Queen Victoria's daughters.

Good God: 'Great heavens' (*Strand* and later).

174 *a middle-sized, strongly built man . . . eyes*: the 'thick neck' was an afterthought. The description of Dr Watson has a double edge as many people would have recognized it as a description of ACD.

'I've got it!' he cried: the MS originally continued, 'Yes, yes. It is she.' The identity of the lady is not revealed.

174/5 *a shop window filled with photographs of the celebrities and beauties of the day*: a reference to the portrait photographer Barraud, of 263 Oxford Street—'A few doors west of the Circus'—founded by William Barraud (b. 1810), the publisher of the portfolio of portraits *Men and Women of the Day* (1899). 'Regent Circus' was the name of the crossing with Regent Street before the construction of the quadrants (1913–28). It is now known as Oxford Circus.

175 *Court dress*: the dress worn by *débutantes* when presented at court. 'A Court dress is worn, as a rule, once only in its full glory. It is a creation over which more thought, time, and labour have been expended than are spent on many a painter's masterpiece. It has cost perhaps a hundred, perhaps a thousand, pounds. It may be studded with diamonds, while in the train alone is enough material to fashion a complete dress' ('From King's to Photographer's Throne', *Pearson's Magazine*, Feb. 1904).

THE SIX NAPOLEONS

First published in the *Strand Magazine*, 27 (May 1904), 483–95, with 7 illustrations by Sidney Paget, and in *Collier's Weekly*, 33 (30 Apr. 1904), 14–15, 28–31, with 6 illustrations by Frederic Dorr Steele.

MS: purchased by Henry E. Huntington (1923). Present location: Henry E. Huntington Library and Art Gallery, San Marino, Calif.

Text: collated with MS and printed texts.

The hiding of a pearl may be compared to E. W. Hornung's story 'The Gift of the Emperor' (*The Amateur Cracksman*, 1899), where a 'pearl of price unparalleled', a 'pearl as large as a filbert—with a pale pink tinge' destined for the King of the Cannibal Islands is stolen by Raffles who conceals it in one of the bullets of his colt revolver: 'in an instant Raffles had found the right one, had bitten out the bullet, and placed the Emperor's pearl with a flourish in the centre of the table.' The story is also similar to 'The Blue Carbuncle' (*Adventures*), in that a jewel is stolen from a London hotel, secreted in an unexpected hiding-place, and tracked down by the thief. It may also be compared to Fletcher Robinson's 'Amaroff the Pole' (published after 'The Six Napoleons') in which bombs are concealed in a bust of Nero. 'With careful packing, they would have got to Paris safe enough,' says Addington Peace: 'The Nero was a known work of art. No one would have suspected it for a moment' (*The Chronicles of Addington Peace*, 1905).

The Raffles stories with Neapolitan settings ('The Fate of Faustina' and 'The Last Laugh') may have provided further inspiration, or at least derive from the same source. ACD and E. W. Hornung had both stayed at Gaiola, the island near Naples owned by Nelson Foley, the husband of ACD's sister Ida. It was while ACD was staying there in 1902 that he first saw the 'meccaneglofo' or sculpture machine of Augusto Bontempi and it so impressed him that he decided to bring it to London. The Automatic Sculpture Syndicate, under the direction of W. G. Jones, opened for business in a shed near the Albert Suspension Bridge in Battersea in the summer of 1903 and was being promoted at the time the story was written (in the *Illustrated London News* for 22 Aug. 1903, *Tit-Bits* for 5 Sept. 1903, and the *Strand* for Nov. 1903). The machine was designed to copy busts and mouldings, but proved an expensive failure as it tended to split the marble and could not provide finished copies.

In drawing on his knowledge of Italian sculptors, ACD is likely to have learned most from Angelo Ballarin, the mechanic who worked the machine in Naples and accompanied it to London, or Colli, the assistant who was promoted after Ballarin returned to Italy.

ACD took an active interest in the business and, as the busts to be copied were cast in plaster by outside contractors, he had a good knowledge of the processes involved. At the time the story was written additional machines were on order and he was on the point of buying new premises at 62 and 64 Sumner Street, Southwark.

176 *police headquarters*: i.e. New Scotland Yard, the headquarters of the Metropolitan Police.

all about it: simply 'about it' in the *Strand*.

Napoleon the First: Napoleon Bonaparte (1769–1821), the great emperor, as distinct from his son, Napoleon II (1811–32), the King of Rome, or his nephew Napoleon III (1808–73), the son of Louis Bonaparte.

177 *Morse Hudson*: possibly from Captain Morse, whose article on 'The Loss of the *Enigma*' was published in the *Strand* at the end of 1903, or from Samuel Morse (1791–1840), the inventor of Morse code. Hudson was the name of a famous soap-maker (whose products were widely advertised). The reference to the parsley in the butter suggests that ACD may have seen a letter in *The Times* from Hudson Brothers (29 Aug. 1903) about inferior butter from Russia and Siberia which was being sold as Danish butter.

hooliganism: wanton acts of vandalism; the earliest recorded use of the word was in 1898 (*OED*).

Dr Barnicot: possibly from the real Dr Barnicot (Joseph Barnicot, of Huddersfield), or a variant of the more common name, 'Barnicoat'.

Lower Brixton Road: the name was added in MS. Brixton Road runs south from Kennington to Brixton Rise. There is no 'Lower' Brixton Road, but the area is sometimes described as 'Lower Brixton' and the prefix is common (as in 'Lower Kennington Lane').

the French sculptor Devine: from Paul de Vigne (1843–1901), a Belgian sculptor who lived in Paris until 1882.

178 *iconoclast*: from the Greek, a 'breaker of images'; originally used of those who took part in the movement of the 8th and 9th centuries against the use of images in religion. It was later the title of a story by ACD ('An Iconoclast', *The Last Galley*, 1911).

179 *French psychologists have called the 'idée fixe'*: literally 'fixed idea', 'an obsession'. It was first used by English and American psychologists in the 1830s and gained a wide currency (as in *Punch*, 12 Aug. 1903, 'Mr Alfred Harmsworth's *idée fixe* is the stage'). 'Monomania' is a form of madness directed against a single object. The most probable 'hereditary family injury' would be syphilis from a camp-follower. ACD wrote his doctoral thesis on syphilis and as an inherited illness it gave him the plot for 'The Third Generation' (*Round the Red Lamp*).

I dare call nothing trivial . . . Abernetty family: this echoes Sergeant Cuff who rebukes Superintendent Seegrave for dismissing a piece of evidence as 'a mere trifle': ' "I made a private inquiry last week, Mr Superintendent," he said. "At one end of the inquiry there was a murder, and at the other end there was a spot of ink on a tablecloth that nobody could account for. In all my experience along the dirtiest ways of this dirty little world, I have never met with such a thing as a trifle yet" ' (Wilkie Collins, *The Moonstone*, 1868). Also 'The Purloined Letter', by Poe, where Dupin tells the story of Abernethy, a doctor, from whom a miser wished to have a free medical opinion; he stated his symptoms as though referring to another person and then asked the doctor what the patient should take. ' "Take!" said Abernethy, "why, take advice, to be sure." '

131 Pitt Street, Kensington: a short road of eighteen houses running parallel to the 'brisk current' of Kensington High

Street, between Campden House Road and Kensington Church Street; 9 Pitt Street was the home of E. W. Hornung.

180 *Horace Harker*: perhaps suggested by John Barker (the department store in Kensington High Street), the Harkers in Bram Stoker's *Dracula* (1897), and Horace G. Hutchinson (Horatio George Hutchinson, 1859–1932), the writer and golfer (with whom ACD was photographed playing golf). Horace Greeley (1811–72) of the New York *Tribune* was the greatest American editor of his time.

the Central Press Syndicate: the Central News Ltd., of 5 New Bridge Street, who supplied 'telegraphic news to newspapers, clubs, and news rooms'. ACD had offered his services as a correspondent at the end of 1898 when war between France and Britain seemed imminent.

181 *Harding Brothers*: i.e. Ponting Brothers, at 123–7 Kensington High Street, next door to the Metropolitan and District Railway Station. *Harding's Art Manuals* may have provided the fictional name.

poor devil: 'poor fellow' (*Strand* and all later texts).

182 *when the stand fell at Doncaster*: a current news story which the *Times Weekly Edition* summarized thus: 'A stand erected on Perth cricket ground, occupied by some hundreds of persons, suddenly collapsed on Saturday, during a match between Perthshire and Forfarshire—a great many of the occupants were injured and twenty-six had to be removed for treatment' (7 Aug. 1903). The change of venue to Doncaster, in Yorkshire, implies that the incident was at the famous racecourse where the St Leger Stakes are run.

183 *he was rattled and hustled*: a mistake in the typescript transformed 'hustled' (the spelling in the MS) into 'bustled' and it was carried through into the serial and book publication. The correct spelling is restored in this edition.

184 *his red lamp*: 'You ask about the Red Lamp,' says the postscript to the preface of the American edition of *Round the Red Lamp* (1894): 'It is the usual sign of the general practitioner in England.'

to docket it: to file it, to endorse a document with a note of the subject or content. A term used by the police of the period who kept separate 'dockets' for each case (as in *Life's Reminiscences of Scotland Yard, in 21 Dockets*, by A. Lansdowne, 1890).

185 *Gelder & Co.*: an invented name, recalling Aart de Gelder, the 17th-century Dutch artist.

    Church Street, Stepney: from Church Street, Kensington; also found in Wapping.

    Beppo: the diminutive form of Giuseppe, and thus the familiar name of Cardinal Sarto who was elected pope on 4 Aug. 1903 (see 'Pope Beppo', *T. P.'s Weekly*, 11 Sept. 1903); also the title of a poem by Byron and the name of a character in two novels by George Meredith. (If ACD named his iconoclast after Pope Pius X, the Pope unwittingly had his revenge when he condemned spiritualism and frustrated the dialogue between the spiritualists and Catholics.)

186 *fashionable London . . . maritime London*: from the headings in *Living London*, vols. 1–3, ed. G. R. Sims (1902–3), which include 'London's Fashionable Amusements', 'Hotel London', 'Artistic London', 'Money London', 'Waterside London'—and also 'Hooligan London' (by Clarence Rook, the author of *The Hooligan Nights*, 1899). The areas listed by ACD are all to the north of the river and would not be on the route from Kennington to Stepney which lies to the south.

188 *'see what the manager . . . has to say to the matter'*: the MS originally continued: 'I may tell you that it is his evidence which I depend upon.'

    Laburnum Lodge, Laburnum Vale, Chiswick: an imaginary address. The name on the gate-post is said to be 'Laburnum Villa'.

    Mr Sandeford, of Lower Grove Road, Reading: various sources suggest themselves, such as Sandiford, a cricketer whom ACD played against at Tavistock (21–2 Aug. 1903); or Woodley and Sandford, the station near Reading. 'Lower Grove' was probably suggested by Chiswick Grove, the large wooded area in the bend of the Thames.

    for I've seldom seen an uglier: originally 'for he looks like the missing link'.

189 *Saffron Hill and the Italian quarter*: 'The Italian Bronze Figure Maker is found chiefly at Saffron Hill and Leather Lane, but there are a few of them in the Italian Quarter in the Peckham Park Road' (Sims, *Living London*).

189 *some Catholic emblem round his neck*: a cross or small medallion (showing the Virgin Mary or a saint such as St Christopher or St Peter—the man's patron saint).

Pietro Venucci, from Naples: originally 'from Florence' (as was Augusto Bontempi who demonstrated his sculpture machine in Florence before being forced to move to Naples). The name combines 'Venice' with Hornung's 'Count Corbucci', from 'The Fate of Faustina' and 'The Last Laugh' (*The Black Mask*, 1901), and is similar to Pietro Vannucci, the real name of the artist 'Perugino' (1446–1523).

the Mafia: a Sicilian secret society, centred on Palermo, with an unwritten code of laws or 'omertá' (manliness), in which the vendetta is used in place of legal redress. As the characters are from Naples, they would more properly have belonged to the Camorra.

190 *the betting is exactly two to one*: originally 'three to one'. The proposed time of departure was also changed from 'not before midnight' to 'not before eleven'.

express messenger: a special messenger who would convey a letter the entire distance, or from the local sorting office, at a pre-paid or partly pre-paid rate of threepence (1¼p) per mile. The Express Delivery Service was established by the Post Office in 1891.

191 *the loaded hunting-crop*: i.e. weighted with lead.

a spot at the other side of Hammersmith Bridge: Chiswick is on the same side of the river as Hammersmith, so they presumably crossed Hammersmith Bridge, drove as far as Barnes, and then returned across the river to Chiswick.

192 *the hall lights flew up, the door opened*: originally 'the hall door opened'.

in shirt and trousers: Josiah Brown was originally 'in a dressing gown'. The 'Burglary Insurance people will have to pay me for my bust,' says a deleted passage, 'so I have nothing to complain of'.

193 *from the shadow of his matted hair*: a late emendation to prevent repetition. He originally glared at them 'like a vicious wild beast', before snapping at Watson's hand 'like a hungry wolf'.

195 *the famous black pearl of the Borgias*: 'The Black Pearl' is the title

of a story by Victorien Sardou. The Borgias were a powerful, scheming, and dissolute family, consisting of Rodrigo Borgia (1431–1503, Pope Alexander VI from 1492), his son Cesare (1476–1507), and daughter Lucrezia (1480–1523) (from whom 'Lucretia Venucci' takes her first name).

196 *Colonna*: perhaps called to mind by 'Cardinal Colonna', a character in *Dante*, the play by Victorien Sardou and Emile Moreau, which Sir Henry Irving produced and starred in, and which ACD saw on the opening night at the Drury Lane Theatre on 30 Apr. 1903. The Colonnas were an ancient Roman family who had provided the leaders for the Ghibelline party in southern Italy. Their feuds convulsed papal politics in the Middle Ages: the action of Sciarra Colonna in striking Pope Boniface VIII at Anagni in 1303 led to the removal of the papacy to Avignon and the Great Schism, and the election of Oddone Colonna (1368–1431) as Pope Martin V in 1417 reunited western Christendom.

Dacre Hotel: possibly an allusion to De Keyser's Hotel at the eastern end of the Victoria Embankment, a popular destination for foreign visitors (though not for royalty who would have stayed at Claridges, Brown's, the Albemarle, the Langham, or the Carlton). Named after Lord Dacre, who appears as a character in ACD's story, 'How the Brigadier Triumphed in England' (*Adventures of Gerard*, 1903).

198 *No, sir, we are damned proud of you*: damned changed to 'very proud' in MS—late—presumably in the light of Newnes's prohibitions. This may be a reference to the article being written by Sir Robert Anderson on 'Sherlock Holmes as seen by Scotland Yard' (*T. P.'s Weekly*, 2 Oct. 1903).

the Conk-Singleton forgery case: possibly an allusion to Singleton Fabian and Co., who acted as chartered acountants for the Automatic Sculpture Syndicate. The large costs involved were already causing ACD concern, and led in time to increasing acrimony and lawsuits between himself and his partner. Messrs Cronk were land agents in Pall Mall whose premises ACD passed on his way to the Reform Club.

THE THREE STUDENTS

First published in the *Strand Magazine*, 27 (June 1904), 603–13, with 7 illustrations by Sidney Paget, and in *Collier's Weekly*, 34 (24 Sept.

1904), 14–15, 27–9, with 9 illustrations (including coloured cover) by Frederic Dorr Steele; the original cover design, showing Holmes against an Oxford background, was not used.

MS: library of David G. Joyce; sold at auction, Anderson Galleries, New York (13 Feb. 1923), to Norton Perkins; and presented by him to Harvard University (11 Nov. 1925). Present location: Houghton Library, Harvard.

Text: collated with MS and printed texts.

ACD obscures the identity of the university, but the description resembles that found in an earlier story, 'Lot 249', which is set in Oxford at 'Old College' with rooms overlooking an 'ancient lichen-tinted court': 'Three young men occupied the sets of rooms which opened on to the separate landings of the old stair. Each set consisted simply of a sitting-room and of a bedroom' (*Round the Red Lamp*, 1894).

The inspiration for the scratched surface may have come from ACD's own experience with cricket shoes, while the way in which the examination is organized and the treatment of the young man found guilty of cheating suggest a school rather than a university.

ACD had worked from home at Edinburgh University and had no experience of college life at Oxford or Cambridge, but his life at Stonyhurst and Feldkirch had points in common. He may have based the description of the examination on memories of the Stonyhurst school examinations, the matriculation papers he sat at London University in June 1875, or those he entered for the bursaries and scholarships offered by Edinburgh University. 'I had a month in which to brush up on my classics and then I went in for these, and was informed a week later that I had won the Grierson Bursary of £40 for two years' (*Memories and Adventures* (1924), 23). He celebrated his good fortune, only to learn that he had been deprived of it.

The unlikely choice of Thucydides also reflects a school memory. Thucydides' unfinished *History of the Peloponnesian War* was normally assigned for upper classes in school and only one book would be used. An 'unseen' would then be taken from one of the other books. Students who were not familiar with the other books would have needed to copy the entire text if they resorted to cheating. The objection that a classical scholar would easily identify the passage, or copy the names to enable the passage to be identified, would not apply to students at school.

ACD refers to the classics in the context of his schooldays in his autobiography: 'To give boys a little slab of Virgil or Homer with no general idea as to what it is all about or what the classical age was like, is surely an absurd way of treating the subject. I am sure than an intelligent boy could learn more by reading a good translation of Homer for a week than by a year's study of the original as it is usually carried out' (*Memories and Adventures*, ch. 20). This suggests that his knowledge of Thucydides was based on a translation and may explain why 'half a chapter' filled three galley proofs. In Richard Crawley's translation of the *History* (1866; reissued by Dent in 1903), the work is given in long chapters. 'What have been hitherto called chapters are,' he said (when issuing the first volume in 1866), 'more properly considered, sections or paragraphs subordinate to these.'

199 *one of our great University towns*: either Oxford or Cambridge (whichever does *not* come most easily to the reader's mind); an imaginary university town on the Oxford and Cambridge model. Cambridge is referred to as 'the university' in 'The Golden Pince-Nez' and provides the setting for 'The Missing Three-Quarter', but here the identity is camouflaged. ACD uses the term 'court-yard' which suggests Cambridge, and 'quad-rangle' which suggests Oxford, but as he used 'court-yard' for an Oxford college in 'Lot 249', nothing can be inferred from it. The same is true of the 'college servant'. This might properly be called a 'gyp' at Cambridge or a 'scout' at Oxford, but the servant acts so oddly that he resembles neither. He is closer to Catholic servants who might be employed at Stonyhurst after their masters had fallen on hard times.

a library . . . laborious researches: either the Bodleian at Oxford, the University Library at Cambridge, or one of several college libraries.

early English charters: written instruments, contracts, or conven-tions by which sales of property or rights and privileges are confirmed and held. Charters were granted by the Crown and the Lords Spiritual and Temporal to boroughs, guilds, reli-gious foundations, and individuals. The study and publication of early English charters was actively pursued at Oxford, with works such as the *Select Charters and Other Illustrations of English Constitutional History* (1870), by Bishop William Stubbs

(1825–1901), or the *Calendar of Charters and Rolls from the Bodleian Library*, by W. H. Turner (1878).

199 *Mr Hilton Soames*: he shares the Christian name with Hilton Cubitt ('The Dancing Men') and the surname with Sir Cathcart Soames ('The Priory School').

the College of St Luke's: from St John's (found at both universities). The Cambridge St John's had ACD's brother-in-law Cyril Angell among its alumni and was used as the setting for the 1923 film of 'The Three Students'; but an equally strong case is made for the Oxford St John's, and for other Oxford colleges, such as University College, which has the correct arrangement of gates and quadrangles. St Luke was the Roman Catholic patron saint of medicine, and St Luke's was the name of an asylum in London.

200 *the Fortescue Scholarship*: an invented name, possibly from George Knottes-Ford Fortescue (1847–1912), Keeper of the British Museum Department of Printed Books who produced its *Subject Index* 1880–1910.

a large passage . . . the candidate has not seen: 'It is never easy to know what candidates have *not* seen, and a chunk of Heliodorus might do, with a bit of the *Cassandra* of Lycophron, and perhaps a corrupt little piece out of Herodas,' said Andrew Lang: 'Probably they are best selected out of things like Plato, his *Laws* or Callimachus, or Polybius, or other authors whom few undergraduates have read exhaustively' ('At the Sign of the Ship', *Longman's Magazine*, July 1904, 269–71).

Thucydides: Greek general and historian (*c*.471–401 BC), author of *The History of the Peloponnesian War*. ACD's revered T. B. Macaulay (1800–59) thought him the greatest historian of all time.

the text must be absolutely correct: ACD illustrated his imperfect grasp of the subject by originally writing 'it must be grammatically correct'.

my servant, Bannister: the name of one of ACD's contemporaries at Edinburgh.

201 *slips*: galley proofs on long narrow sheets of paper.

202 *young Daulat Ras, an Indian student*: a gap was left in the MS both times the name occurs. 'Daulat Ras' was added in pencil

on the first occasion and 'Daulat Rao' on the second (a variant of 'Lal Rao' in *The Sign of the Four*).

205 *Johann Faber*: Johann Lothar von Faber, of Germany (1817–96), the great-grandson of the founder of the lead pencil company, who introduced machinery, acquired exclusive rights to the graphite produced in Siberia, and opened factories across Europe and North America. His widow died in 1903 and the business passed to a granddaughter, Faber-Castell.

207 *Gilchrist*: a joke prevalent in late 1903 concerned a judge who was so out of touch with current events that he asked: 'Who's Connie Gilchrist?' But it is a common Scottish name and could derive from any number of sources. It was also the name of the murder victim at the centre of the Oscar Slater Case which interested ACD eight years later.

got his Blue . . . long jump: anyone who represented either university was commonly referred to as a 'Blue', but Oxford alone had a Blue for long jump. C. B. Fry, who held the record, was an Oxford Blue between 1892 and 1895, and his contemporary, W. J. Oaklet, had caps for hurdles and long jump.

Miles McLaren: possibly named after Archie MacLaren, who captained the English cricket side against Australia in 1901–2 and played with ACD in the MCC team.

210 *three-card trick*: three cards are laid face downwards; one is revealed for an instant then moved rapidly about, and the gullible bystander who has observed an accomplice winning places a bet and invariably fails to identify the card.

211 *the landlady babbled of green peas at seven-thirty*: from the description of Sir John Falstaff's death by Mistress Quickly; he 'babbled of green fields' (*Henry V*, II. iii.).

212 *at least five miles*: the Oxford Iffley Road athletic track was a mile from the centre, and 'Fenners' at Cambridge was closer, so ACD may have been thinking of running-tracks at Edinburgh.

pyramids of black, doughy clay: a special clay invented by the groundsman at Fenners was being used in place of soft earth and sawdust at Cambridge and Oxford, and there was black clay in Edinburgh, but the little pyramids are more likely to have come from cricket shoes than spiked running boots.

Thank God: 'Thank Heaven' in *Strand* and later printings.

214 *it is human to err . . .*: from the Latin, 'errare humanum est' (Polignac, *Anti-Lucretius*, 5.58), which ACD had previously used (as 'Humanum est Errare') in 'The Story of the Latin Tutor' (*Strand*, Apr. 1899). It recalls the famous line in Pope: 'To err is human, to forgive divine.'

215 *several*: followed by 'sharp' in *Strand*.

216 *the fine tan*: sawdust and sand (from the colour); a slang word used to describe the floor of a circus ring or riding-school.

Good God: 'Good heavens' in *Strand* and later.

my sin had found me out: 'be sure your sin will find you out' (Numbers 32: 23).

the Rhodesian Police: the British South African Police, of Southern Rhodesia, which consisted of 40 officers, 400 noncommissioned officers and men, and 550 native police, Rhodesia (which took the name in 1895) was reorganized in 1903.

217 *Mr Gilchrist's tan gloves*: the glove had become an essential element of the detective story since its was first used by Gaboriau, but R. C. Lehmann felt it was inappropriate for a student returning from the running-pits, and highlighted the point in *Punch*, where he described a student returning from the river in a fashionable frock coat and patent leather lace-up boots, and a proclamation by the Chancellor at which the Senior Proctor wore frayed trousers and a Norfolk jacket ('A Way We Have at the "Varsity" ', *Punch*, 15 June 1904). Gloves are a sensible way to avoid chilblains when the body is cooling, as a doctor would know.

until Mr Soames he went for you: the redundant 'he' is found in the MS and all the principal editions.

THE GOLDEN PINCE-NEZ

First published in the *Strand Magazine*, 28 (July 1904), 3–16, with 8 illustrations by Sidney Paget, and in *Collier's Weekly*, 34 (29 Oct. 1904), 15, 18–19, 27–30, with 6 illustrations by Frederic Dorr Steele.

MS: presented to Herbert Greenhough Smith, the editor of the *Strand* (8 Feb. 1916), inscribed 'A Souvenir of 20 years of collaboration'; sold at Sotheby's (18 Apr. 1932), £88, to the Comte de Suzannet; sold again at Sotheby's (26 Mar. 1934), £120, to Permann; sold a third time at Sotheby's (12 July 1967), £900, to El Dieff (Lew David Feldman), New York, and offered in his Catalogue Seventy (1969), $7,500. Present location: Humanities Research Center, University of Texas, Austin, Tex.

Text: collated with MS and printed texts.

The plot may have been suggested by the advice or the appearance of Herbert Greenhough Smith (although 'Thor Bridge' (Case-Book) he declared to be the only ACD story he inspired), and this would explain why ACD gave him this MS. He wore a golden pince-nez, and the name of 'Willoughby Smith' could be a play on his name and on the nickname 'Calamity Smith' (to which ACD referred in a deleted passage of his autobiography).

The story may be compared to Fletcher Robinson's story of 'The Vanished Millionaire' (first published in Dec. 1904), in which Addington Peace finds the entrance to a priest hole by sprinkling flour on the floor (*The Chronicles of Addington Peace*, 1905). The device comes from the Book of Daniel (in the Apocrypha, or Daniel 14: 2–21 in the Douai version of the Bible) where ashes are strewn in the Temple of Bel to prove to the King that the priests (and their wives and children) are consuming the food placed before the idol.

218 *the repulsive story . . . Crosby the banker*: the leech may have been suggested by the 'hairy caterpillar' which kills the rival of Professor Marnac in *The Trail of the Dead* (1904) by B. Fletcher Robinson and J. Malcolm Fraser; while the name may come from the town in Lancashire or from 'Alf Crosby's Wife', a story in *Tit-Bits* (12 Dec. 1903). Leeches are usually olive green or brown in colour but, being bloodsuckers, are associated with the colour red.

the Addleton tragedy . . . the ancient British barrow: the name is similar to 'Addlestone' in Surrey. Barrows are burial mounds (up to 400 feet in length) usually consisting of a stone burial chamber and passageway covered in earth; 'On Ancient British Barrows' was the title of an authoritative account by J. Thurman (*Archaeologia*, 1869).

The famous Smith-Mortimer succession case: implies a contested succession (to a title or estate) between Smith and Mortimer, or between members of the Smith-Mortimer family. Both names recur in the story—Smith as the name of the victim and Mortimer as that of the gardener. ACD had been a student at Stonyhurst when members of its staff were called on to give evidence at the Tichbourne hearings (1871) concerning Sir Roger Tichbourne, whose identity was claimed by Arthur Orton. Tichbourne-Orton has a very faint echo in Smith-Mortimer.

218 *the tracking and arrest of Huret, the Boulevard assassin*: from Jules Huret (1864–1915), a French writer (known in England for his book on Sarah Bernhardt); and from Geomay, the Boulevard St Germain assassin (whose capture was described in the Memoirs of M. Goron, of the Paris Police).

the French President: at the date given in the story it was Jean-Pierre Casimir-Perier (who was elected on 24 June 1894), but ACD was probably thinking of President Loubet who had paid a state visit to London in July 1903.

the Order of the Legion of Honour: the Order instituted by Napoleon in 1802, and presided over by the President (as Grand Master). 'The Legion of Honour seems to have become as much part of the equipment of a well-dressed Frenchman as his hat or his boots', ACD wrote in 1894. 'We sat in the Grand Café of the Louvre, and tried to count the red-ribboned gentlemen as they passed. What can the value of a distinction be which is shared by so many? and what bitterness there must be among the excluded!' ('Paris in 1894: A Superficial Impression', *Speaker*, 9 (21 Apr. 1894), 439).

Yoxley Old Place: from Yoxley Old Hall in Bury St Edmunds, or Yaxley Hall in Suffolk. The building can be identified with Chapter Farm, near Strood, on the London to Chatham road.

a palimpsest: a manuscript, the original writing on which has been effaced to make room for a second (*OED*); 'a half rolled palimpsest' lay on the table in ACD's story of 'The Leather Funnel' (*Strand*, June 1903).

219 *goloshes*: variant of galoshes: overshoes (usually of rubber).

220 *It's down in Kent . . . railway line*: i.e. 7 miles from the great naval dockyard at the mouth of the Medway, 34 miles from Charing Cross, and 3 miles from the South-Eastern and Chatham Railway.

Professor Coram: a name similar to 'Coran' in Fletcher Robinson's story 'Mr Coran's Election' (*The Chronicles of Addington Peace*, 1905); from Thomas Coram (1668–1751) who created the Foundling Hospital and gave his name to Coram Street and Coram Fields in London.

221 *a boy at Uppingham*: a public school in Rutland (founded 1584), at which E. W. Hornung was a student (1880–3) and which provided him with the setting for *Fathers of Men* (1912).

Mortimer, the gardener ... excellent character: a name found in *The Hound of the Baskervilles* and elsewhere, but possibly from J. R. Mortimer whose *magnum opus* on ancient British barrows of east Yorkshire was on the point of publication. A 'Crimean man' was one who fought in the Crimean War (1854–6); a 'bath-chair' is a hand-pushed vehicle with a folding hood and wheels, named after James Heath, of Bath.

222 *the carotid artery*: the main artery which carries blood to the head.

sealing-wax knives: the knives found on desk-stands were intended as paper knives, but some were fitted with handles of ornate design with which to stamp the hot sealing-wax.

223 *this rough plan*: the plan by ACD published in the *Strand* includes the word 'Car'; that in *Collier's Weekly* was redrawn with printed captions; while in the first edition (Newnes, 1905)

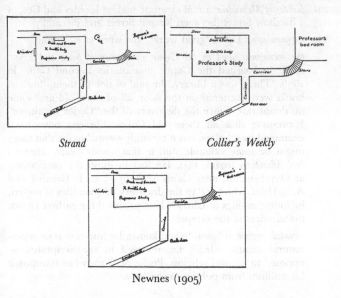

Strand   Collier's Weekly

Newnes (1905)

the original plan is reused, with the 'Car' removed and the line behind the bureau continued to the wall (closing off the 'Door' at the top).

227 *the glasses are concave and of unusual strength*: in the MS and in *Collier's Weekly* this appears as 'convex'. The error in the American magazine was pointed out in a letter to the American *Bookman* (July 1904). ACD had worked at eye hospitals in Southsea and Westminster, studied the eye in Vienna, established himself in Upper Wimpole Street as an eye specialist, and afterwards made great play of his credentials when dealing with the myopia of George Edalji; but the accidental use of antonym is a common error.

228 *our pursuit of the Andaman Islander*: Tonga (*The Sign of the Four*); i.e. the pursuit (down the Thames) of Jonathan Small and the great Agra treasure.

a small station some miles from Chatham: assumed to be Strood; in which case the 'local inn' would be the 'Crispin Crispianus'.

230 *a Chubb's key*: made by the famous locksmith Chubb and Sons (founded in 1818), Lock and Safe Makers to the King and the Bank of England and the inventors of an 'unpickable' lock.

231 *Ionides of Alexandria*: a real cigarette-maker; Ionides and Co., of 3 Swallow Street (between Regent Street and Piccadilly).

232 *magnum opus*: Latin, 'great work', 'the work of a lifetime'.

the documents found in the Coptic monasteries of Syria and Egypt: ACD had visited the Coptic monasteries beyond Cairo in 1896. 'There was a library,' he said of one of them, 'but the books were scattered on the floor, all of them old and some no doubt rare. Since the discovery of the "Codex Sinaiticus" I presume that all these old Coptic libraries have been examined by scholars, but it certainly seemed to me that there might be some valuable stuff in that untidy heap' (*Memories and Adventures* (1924), 134). He had in mind the excavations at Oxyrhynchus, near Cairo (1895–6) by B. P. Grenfell and A. S. Hunt, which led to the discovery of quantities of papyri, including sayings of Christ which predated the earliest known manuscripts of the Gospels.

revealed religion: religion 'made known by inspiration or supernatural means' (*OED*), i.e. revealed in the Scriptures, as opposed to natural religion. Professor Coram has transposed his nihilism from politics to theology.

233 *love-gages*: pledges of love from a lover promising eventual fulfilment, 'love-tokens'.

diplomas of Universities which have done me honour: i.e. granted honorary degrees.

238 *Sergius*: the anglicized form of 'Sergei'.

239 *reformers—revolutionists—Nihilists*: these groups (with the Anarchists) made up the opposition in pre-revolutionary Russia: those who believed in reform, those who agitated for revolution, and those whom Turgenev had called 'nihilists' because of their contempt for the conventions of society. The Nihilists enjoyed their greatest success between 1878 and 1881 when they committed several major terrorist acts with bombs and dynamite, and included among their victims General Trepov (the inspiration for the 'Trepoff Murder' in 'A Scandal in Bohemia' (*Adventures*) and Tsar Alexander II. Their evil reputation and the presence of many exiles in London produced a flood of sensational stories, including ACD's 'A Night among the Nihilists' (1881) and 'An Exciting Christmas Eve' (1883). Trouble had flared again in 1887, but it was the disturbances in the universities in 1901 of which ACD was probably thinking. Reports of the fate of those responsible were reaching England and he would have seen Harry de Windt's article on 'Darkest Siberia and its Political Exiles' which appeared in the *Strand* in Dec. 1902.

a time of trouble: a biblical phrase (as in Job 38: 23; Psalms 9: 9, 27: 5; Jeremiah 2: 27).

a police officer was killed: possibly General Mezentsov, the head of the secret police, who was assassinated by the Nihilists in broad daylight in the streets of St Petersburg, or his successor, General Drenteln, who narrowly avoided the same fate.

the Brotherhood: the word was familiar to readers of the *Strand* from the serialized 'The Brotherhood of the Seven Kings', by L. T. Meade and Robert Eustace (1898). There were 'Brotherhoods' and 'Fraternities' in Freemasonry, chivalry, and the Church, but ACD was probably thinking of the Irish Republican Brotherhood (or Fenian Brotherhood as it was known in the United States). The Nihilists were disparate, despite a belief to the contrary. 'It is an open secret,' said J. E. Preston Muddock in the preface to *Stormlight, or The Nihilist's Doom* (1888) 'that the Russian Nihilists are bound together by a terrible oath, and that death is the penalty of any betrayal of secrets.' Muddock (1843–1943 was the popular detective novelist Dick Donovan, whose eponymous detective had four cases in the *Strand* between the *Adventures* and the *Memoirs*.

239 *Alexis was sent a convict to Siberia . . . salt mine*: the name is the anglicized form of 'Aleksei'; one of the 700 political prisoners who were exiled to Siberia between 1881 and 1888.

241 *the Russian Embassy*: then at Chesham House, Chesham Place, Belgrave Square.

THE MISSING THREE-QUARTER

First published in the *Strand Magazine*, 28 (Aug. 1904), 123–35, with 7 illustrations by Sidney Paget, and in *Collier's Weekly*, 34 (26 Nov. 1904), 15, 18, 27–30, with 6 illustrations (including coloured cover) by Frederic Dorr Steele.

MS: sold at the American Art Galleries, New York (30 Jan. 1923), £130, to William Randolph Hearst; sold after his death to the Scribner Rare Book Department, New York, and offered in their Sherlock Holmes Catalogue (Nov. 1943), £450; sold from their Catalogue 132 (1946) to Vincent Starrett; then by private sale to Rollin Van N. Hadley. Present location: British Library, London.

Text: collated with MS and printed texts.

The story may have been inspired by ACD's memories of the Rugby football matches in which he played at Edinburgh University or by those which he saw as a student (such as the International between England and Scotland played on 19 Mar. 1881, when the English team was short of two players after one had missed a train and another had been detained on business).

The prowess of Godfrey Staunton appears to have been influenced by that of Arthur Budd (1853–99), brother of George Turnavine Budd and 'reckoned by good judges to be about the best forward who ever donned the rose-embroidered jersey of England' (*Memories and Adventures*, 58). Arthur Budd, who was at Pembroke College, Cambridge, played in the 'Varsity match against Oxford and in five Internationals (including the two in Edinburgh which ACD attended). He was also captain of the Blackheath team and president of the Rugby Union. The title of the story may contain an allusion to him, as he was a keen advocate of a three-quarter line with three, instead of four, men. In an essay in the *Rugby Annual* and in 'Past Development in Rugby Football, and the Future of the Game', in *Football: The Rugby Union Game*, ed. F. Marshall (1892, p. 128), he suggested that the fourth three-quarter should be used as an additional forward—and those clubs which adopted this arrangement had a 'missing three-quarter'. (ACD, overawed by George, recalled Arthur as the younger, but *Alumni Cantabrigenses*, Part II, i. 434, records Arthur's admission in Oct. 1872 at the age of 19, while the *British Medical Journal*, 16 Mar. 1889, records George's death at 34.)

Bertram Fletcher Robinson, a graduate of Jesus College, Cambridge, a friend of Arthur Budd, and a Rugby Blue (1891–3), may have influenced ACD's choice of the subject.

The university matches between Oxford and Cambridge were played at the Queen's Club in London in Dec., and if the dates in the story are taken literally then the match would have been played either in 1894, 1895, or 1896. The last would be the most likely as it was the only one of the three won by Oxford.

The theme of a sick person hidden from the world which recurs elsewhere in ACD's work was based on his father's seclusion before he was committed to a lunatic asylum. Dr Bryan Charles Waller, who assisted the family at that time, would be a possible source of inspiration for Dr Armstrong, as might Reginald Ratcliff Hoare, the Birmingham doctor for whom ACD worked in 1877–80. ACD's love-affair with Jean Leckie (his 'wife in hiding'), an occasion when he 'disappeared' to be with her, the consumptive illness of his wife, Touie, and memories of George Budd's elopement with a ward in Chancery are other pieces of the jigsaw.

Blotting-paper as a clue is found in the fictionalized memoirs of the early French detective Vidocq and there were several cases in real life where it had been used, as in the capture of an absconding stockbroker by Detective-Inspector A. Landsowne (*Life's Reminiscences of Scotland Yard*, 1890). However, ACD may have looked no further than the *Strand* for Mar. 1903 which contained a photograph of a message 'written with both hands' with one side in mirror writing ('Curiosities', 359).

243 *ten thirty-six*: originally '9.36' and the client was expected 'by the time that the table is cleared'. The time which the Armstrong carriage spent abroad was changed from 'four' to 'three' hours; and the time which it took Holmes and Watson to reach the outskirts of Cambridge was changed from 'a few minutes' to 'half an hour'.

drug mania: Holmes's recourse to 'a seven-per-cent solution' was no longer felt to be acceptable as several people had suggested that the drug would have an adverse effect on the detective and would—as the MS first said—'destroy his remarkable nature'; however, the 'hypodermic syringe' with which Holmes sprays the wheels of the carriage was originally described as a 'hypodermic needle'.

244 *Mr Cyril Overton, of Trinity College, Cambridge*: originally 'Mr Charles Overton, of Magdalene College, Cambridge'. The surname is that of an MCC cricketer with whom ACD played and who took seven wickets in the match at Bedford on 10 July 1903. The first name recalls 'Cyril Morton' ('The Solitary Cyclist'), whose surname is used for one of the other players.

three-quarter line: a Rugby side usually consists of fifteen players, with eight 'forwards' (who form the 'scrummage'), two 'half-backs', four 'three-quarter backs' (who form a 'line' across the field), and a 'full back'.

Moorhouse: perhaps from Dr Moorhouse, the muscular Bishop of Manchester, with Johnson and Stevenson possibly from Dr Johnson and Robert Louis Stevenson.

a fine place-kick: a kick at goal when the ball is placed on the ground.

couldn't drop from the twenty-five line: couldn't score by dropping the ball and kicking it on the first bounce, from the line on the pitch, 25 yards from the goal.

punt: when the ball is kicked on the drop, before it touches the ground.

245 *Arthur H. Staunton, the rising young forger*: possibly a reference to Louis Staunton who was sentenced to death in 1877 for the murder of his wife by neglect and starvation; or Arthur H. Stanton, the senior curate at St Alban's, Holborn, who was referred to as 'the best man in England' in *V.C.* for 18 June 1903 (the issue of the magazine current at the time of ACD's interview for it by P. G. Wodehouse).

Great Scot: thus in MS, *Strand*, and *Collier's*, the allusion being probably to the 'wizard' Michael Scot (*c*.1175–*c*.1230). Later texts read 'Great Scott'.

Bentley's private hotel: i.e. Morley's Hotel in Trafalgar Square (at which ACD had often stayed). Richard Bentley (1662–1742),

Master of Trinity College, Cambridge, was perhaps the greatest classical scholar of his time. Putting the footballers in a hotel bearing his name is a comic touch.

246 *down the street in the direction of the Strand*: originally 'down Northumberland Avenue in the direction of the Thames Embankment'.

Lord Mount-James: based on a real title (Lord Mount-Charles).

249 *the following hieroglyphic*: the handwriting is that of ACD, who wrote the words backwards and forwards on two pieces of blotting-paper which he fixed to the MS with sealing-wax. One is not therefore the exact mirror image of the other. It was redrawn for the American magazine, thus:

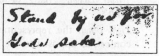

250 *a hack*: a gash or wound on the shin from the toe of a boot.

an undertaker's mute: a hired mourner.

251 *the Bayswater 'bus*: the 'Bayswater' bus of the London and General Omnibus Co. was coloured green and ran from Notting Hill Gate along the Bayswater Road, Oxford Street, Holborn, and Cheapside, to the Bank of England.

252 *Good God*: 'Heavens' (*Strand* and all subsequent texts).

a telegraph office: originally 'two telegraph offices at equal distances from the hotel'. The main office was in Trafalgar Square at the junction with the Strand.

253 *King's Cross Station*: originally 'Fenchurch Street Station'.

we rattled up Gray's Inn Road: MS and *Collier's Weekly*, 'Greys Inn Road'; originally 'we rattled down the Strand'.

254 *the busiest thoroughfare*: either the Trumpington Road or St Andrews Street (the first was the location of the Bull Hotel and the second that of the Castle Inn, either of which could be the inn mentioned in the story).

257 *a brougham*: a closed carriage named after Lord Brougham; favoured by the medical profession.

258 *overtook*: in the old sense, 'caught up with'.

397

260 *Chesterton, Histon, Waterbeach, and Oakington*: villages to the north of Cambridge. Chesterton is on the northern edge of the city; Waterbeach is 5 miles to the north-east, Histon 4½ miles to the north-west, and Oakington 6 miles to the north-west.

Sleepy Hollows: 'quiet backwaters', from Washington Irving's story 'The Legend of Sleepy Hollow' (*The Sketch-Book*, 1820); or indirectly from E. W. Hornung's story 'An Old Flame', where Raffles asks Bunny to find him a quiet retreat: 'Try Ham Common or Roehampton, or some such sleepy hollow a trifle off the line' (*The Black Mask*, 1901).

Pompey: the name recalls the servant of Mistress Overdone in *Measure for Measure*.

Jeremy Dixon, Trinity College: originally 'Jeremy Dixon, St John's.

Light Blues: the representatives of Cambridge in a sporting contest, as opposed to the Dark Blues of Oxford.

261 *a loose-box*: a box or stall in which an animal is free to move about.

a squat, lop-eared . . . foxhound: MS 'a squat little long-haired lop-eared white-and-tan dog, something between a beagle and a spaniel'.

draghounds: the drag is a strong-smelling lure for hounds used instead of a fox; 'draghounds' refers to a club for those pursuing this sport.

262 *John o' Groats*: denotes the northern extremity of the Scottish mainland; the longest distance across Great Britain being from Land's End (in Cornwall) to John o' Groats.

Cam: or Granta, the river from which Cambridge takes its name.

the village of Trumpington: a village 2 miles south of Cambridge. The isolated Vicarage Farm, which lies to the south, is identified as the farm in the story.

264 *whom he married*: ACD's parents were lodger and landlady's daughter.

THE ABBEY GRANGE

First published in the *Strand Magazine*, 28 (Sep. 1904), 243–56, with 8 illustrations by Sidney Paget, and in *Collier's Weekly*, 34 (31 Dec.

1904), 10–12, 23, 25–6, with 6 illustrations (including coloured cover) by Frederic Dorr Steele.

MS: library of David G. Joyce; sold at auction, Anderson Galleries, New York (13 Feb. 1923), $105; Scribner Rare Book Department, New York, Catalogue 126 (62), to James Montgomery, Philadelphia; sold at auction, Parke Bernet Galleries, New York (22 Mar. 1966) (172), $5,400; Rollin van Hadley, Boston. Present location: Fondation Martin Bodmer/Bibliotheca Bodmeriana, Cologny/Geneva.

Text: collated with MS and printed texts.

The story appears to have been partly inspired by the murder of Thomas Bonar and his wife on 31 May 1810 at Camden Place, near Chislehurst. Bonar's head was crushed by a poker and his wife was assaulted and died soon afterwards. No cries were heard by the servants, and before the police arrived next morning Philip Nicolson, the footman, was seen disposing of blood-stained sheets. He then made his escape to London. He was later arrested and went to the gallows in Aug. 1813. There seemed to be no motive. There are a number of common factors, such as the location, the nature of the crime, the fact that Mrs Bonar had asked the footman to close the lawn door before he retired, and the name of the coachman, W. Randall (that of the gang in the story). ACD is said to have stayed nearby at Frognal Place (between Chislehurst and Sidcup) when the story was written, and it is possible that he played golf at Camden Place which had been converted into a golf club in 1894. The house (where Napoleon III died in exile in 1873) has a Palladian front, a driveway through a line of elms, and a neighbouring pond (see Kelvin I. Jones, 'The Mystery of Camden Place', *Camden House Journal*, 4/83).

The attempt to inculpate a gang is found in Poe's 'The Mystery of Marie Rogêt' (1842–3) where the Press received letters which rendered it 'a matter of certainty that the unfortunate Marie Rogêt has become a victim of one of the numerous bands of blackguards which infest the vicinity of the city upon Sunday'. Knots are used by Dupin to deduce that the murder was the work of a sailor. He infers that 'the "hitch" in the bandage, and the "sailor's knot," with which the bonnet-ribbon is tied, point to a seaman', and that his companionship with Marie Rogêt 'designates him above the grade of a common sailor'.

A sham robbery is present in Gaboriau's *L'Affaire Lerouge* (1866) where Tabaret sends three men to drag the river, having correctly inferred that theft was not the true motive. In *Le Crime d'Orcival* (1867) Lecoq deduces that five wine glasses are a blind as the bottles had been emptied beforehand. The murderer, Count Hector de Tremorel, 'did not reflect that his butler would explain about the empty bottles which he put on the table. He thought he was turning wine into the five glasses—it was vinegar, which would prove that no one had drunk out of them.' And there is a common theme of absolution for the killing of a guilty party at the conclusion, although it is the murderer who is absolved here and his executioner in Gaboriau's novel. Lecoq allows the woman who shoots Tremorel to go free: ' "There," said he to himself, "lies a wretch whom I have killed instead of arresting and delivering him up to justice. Have I done my duty? No; but my conscience will not reproach me, because I have acted rightly".' ACD's 'B.24' ('Round the Fire Stories', *Strand* (Mar. 1899)) had turned on a beautiful wife murdering her sadistic husband and deliberately ensuring a burglar would be hanged for her crime.

266 *It was on a bitterly cold and frosty morning during the winter of '97*: the opening lines were changed at the proof stage. The MS and *Collier's Weekly* read: 'It was a bitterly cold and frosty morning towards the end of '97.'

   The game is afoot: 'The game's afoot', Henry V before Harfleur (*Henry V*, III. i. 32; also *1 Henry IV*, I. iii. 276).

   the Kentish train: originally 'the Chislehurst train'.

   ABBEY GRANGE, MARSHAM, KENT: from Abbey Wood, a hamlet near Chislehurst, 11 miles from London. 'Marsham' is an invented place (the name of a village in Norfolk, a Kent cricketer—C. H. B. Marsham—whom ACD played against with the MCC, and a street in London). 'Abbey Grange' could also have been suggested by Abbey Lodge (the villa in Hannover Terrace designed by Decimus Burton and owned by the de Bunsen family until 1903), or by Abbey Street and Grange Walk in Bermondsey. Lewisham is 4 miles south-east of St Paul's, and Sydenham 6 miles south-east of London Bridge.

   I fancy that . . . your collection: originally 'your notes'. Stanley Hopkins appears only in *The Return*.

267 *the whole art of detection*: the textbook had been written by Dr Hans Gross (1847–1915) in 1893, and was later known as the

System der Kriminalistick (*Criminal Investigation*). ACD referred to Holmes's plans for the future in an interview in the *Daily Mail* (8 Oct. 1904): 'You will remember he has always wanted time to write a work on the scientific side of his experience. It is possible that in his retirement he will put his mind on that.'

'EB' monogram, coat-of-arms: originally 'EH'. The name 'Heppenstall' (a Yorkshire name, from Heptonstall) was used through the MS before being changed to the invented name 'Brackenstall'.

lines of ancient elms: originally 'a line of ancient elms'. The avenue was shorter than suggested, as the maid claimed to have seen men at the lodge gate from her room in the house.

268 *Palladio*: Andrea Palladio (1518–80), Italian architect, whose *Quattro Libri dell' Architectura* (1570) influenced and inspired the neoclassical style.

the three Randalls: the name of the coachman in the Chislehurst murder, also of a boxer, Jack Randall (1794–1828), and of a character in R. L. Stevenson's story 'The Beach of Falesa' (Captain Randall).

269 *these monstrous laws of yours*: ACD was expressing his own opinion. His friendship with Sir Francis Jeune (1843–1905), the president of the Probate, Divorce, and Admiralty division (1891–1905); his love-affair with Jean Leckie, and the stigma attached to his mother as the wife of an alcoholic, may explain his interest. He served for ten years as president of the Divorce Law Reform Union (1909–19). Anti-divorce propaganda made much play with theology, so through Lady Brackenstall ACD brings in God on his side.

271 *the elderly man*: originally 'one of the younger ones'.

272 *Theresa Wright*: the surname of Thomas Wright (1810–77) whose *History of Domestic Manners and Sentiments in England in the Middle Ages* (1862) served as a source for ACD's novel *Sir Nigel*.

274 *devil*: 'fiend' (*Strand* and later texts).

275 *beeswing*: the second crust or film in long kept port and old wine. Fine sediment would take the singular possessive; large plentiful sediment, the plural.

277 *de novo*: Latin, 'anew, afresh'.

279 *and here, Watson, is the Chislehurst train*: in the MS and *Collier's Weekly* it reads 'and here, Watson, is the Sydenham train'.

the massive mantelpiece: in the MS and *Collier's Weekly*, 'the massive marble mantelpiece' (contradicting the earlier statement that it was made of wood).

280 *We have not yet met our Waterloo ... victory*: 'Every man meets his Waterloo at last' (Wendell Phillips, 1859). A phrase in common currency, but extended to include Napoleon's victory over the Austrians in Italy on 14 June 1800.

281 *The sly devil ... but a devil he was*: 'The sly fiend—Heaven forgive me that I should speak of him so, now that he is dead, but a fiend he was' (*Strand* and all later printings).

282 *the shipping office ... at the end of Pall Mall*: perhaps an allusion to the Orient Line, which operated the Royal Mail Steamers to Australia, New Zealand, and Tasmania, calling at Gibraltar, Marseilles, Naples, Egypt, and Colombo. The offices were at 16 Cockspur Street at the end of Pall Mall, but the ships sailed from Tilbury, and not Southampton. Other shipping lines with offices in Pall Mall were the Oceanic Steamship Co., the Union Steamship Co. of New Zealand, the Cunard Steamship Co., Ltd., and a passenger agency for several smaller shipping lines.

we will draw the larger cover first: a shooting metaphor, meaning to draw a fox from its covert or temporary lair. When the animal 'breaks cover' the hunt begins.

283 *the Rock of Gibraltar*: ACD's 'Rock Line' follows the convention started by the Donald Currie Co. which named its ships after castles (the 'Castle Line'), and recalls the Japanese battleships of the period which were named after mountains. Bass Rock is at the entrance to the Firth of Forth, where the hero of Stevenson's *Catriona* (*David Balfour* in the US) was marooned. There is no *Rock of Gibraltar* in the Lloyd's Register (though there were ships named *Gibraltar*), but there were two ships called the *Bass Rock*.

Mr Jack Croker: a real Captain Croker was killed in an accident at the Chicago World's Fair in 1893, but Mrs B. M. Croker (1861–1920), the novelist, John Wilson Croker (1780–1857), the editor of Boswell's *Life of Johnson*, Thomas Crofton Croker (1798–1854), a friend of Thomas Moore and collector of Irish fairy stories, and Richard M. Croker (1841–1922) ('Boss Croker of Tammany Hall'), are all potential sources. The name appears in some late, corrupt editions, as 'Crocker'.

Charing Cross telegraph office: originally 'Charing Cross post office'; in Trafalgar Square, at the intersection of the Strand and Charing Cross Road.

286 *Damn*: 'Curse' (*Strand* and later printings).

288 *God*: 'Heaven' (*Strand* and later printings).

welted: raised weals, i.e. beat or flogged.

290 *Vox populi, vox Dei*: 'the voice of the people is the voice of God' (said by Alcuin (735–804) in his Epistle to Charlemagne); popularized by 'F. Anstey' (Thomas Anstey Guthrie) in his series for *Punch* 'Voces Populi' (1890–2).

pronounced this night: echoing the concluding order to Berowne, Longaville, Dumaine, and King Ferdinand to go away for a year before seeking the ladies they love (Shakespeare, *Love's Labours Lost*).

THE SECOND STAIN

First published in the *Strand Magazine*, 28 (Dec. 1904), 603–17, with 8 illustrations by Sidney Paget, and in *Collier's Weekly*, 34 (28 Jan. 1905), 13–15, 28–30, with 6 illustrations (including coloured cover) by Frederic Dorr Steele.

MS: sold at auction, New York (26 Jan. 1922), $170, to William Randolph Hearst; sold after his death to the Scribner Rare Book Department, New York (1940); listed in the Scribner Sherlock Holmes Catalogue (Nov. 1943) as 'sold'; purchased by Christopher Morley (for $450) and presented the same year to Haverford College. Present location: Treasure Room Manuscript Collection, Haverford College Library, Haverford, Penn.

Text: collated with MS and printed versions.

A case of the same name is mentioned in 'The Yellow Face' (*Memoirs*) where it is described as one where the truth was discovered even though Holmes erred: 'I have notes of some half-dozen cases of the kind, of which the affair of the second stain, and that which I am now about to recount are the two which present the strongest features'; and another case with this name is mentioned in 'The Naval Treaty' (*Memoirs*) and is said to deal 'with interests of such importance' and to 'implicate so many of the first families in the kingdom' that 'for many years it will be impossible to make it public'. No case in which Holmes was ever engaged had illustrated the value of his analytical methods so clearly or had impressed those who were associated with him so deeply, says Watson: 'I still retain an almost verbatim report of the interview in which he demonstrated the true facts of the case to Monsieur Dubuque, of the Paris police, and Fritz von Waldbaum, the well-known specialist of Dantzig, both of whom had wasted their energies upon what proved to be side-issues. The new century will have come, however, before the story can be safely told.'

Arthur Bartlett Maurice, the junior editor of the American *Bookman* during a visit to Europe in 1903 asked ACD to provide details of the 'Second Stain' and later claimed to have had 'a very serious conference with Sherlock Holmes and Dr Watson in the rooms in Upper Baker Street' and to have paid a flying visit to Paris 'for the purpose of seeing M. Dubugue [*sic*] of the Paris Secret Police, and learning a little more about those gigantic frauds of Baron Maupertuis, and also of the Adventure of the Second Stain' (*Bookman*, 17 (July 1903), 447).

ACD was fond of this story, which was written at the Golden Cross Hotel with the assistance of his future wife, Jean Leckie, perhaps because of the interweaving of the two letters (as noted by Catherine Belsey in her *Critical Practice*, 116–17). Both are indiscreet, both are frank in a way which is afterwards regretted, both are provocative, and both are 'elusive' in their content.

The 'high diplomacy and intrigue' was given as the reason why ACD placed the story eighth on his list of the twelve best Sherlock Holmes stories in preference to 'The Naval Treaty' ('How I Made My List,' *Strand*, June 1927), and as such was reprinted in the *Grand Magazine*, 52 (Feb. 1928), 698–711.

291 *bee-farming on the Sussex Downs*: the preface to *His Last Bow* (1917) reveals that the farm was 'five miles from Eastbourne', and in 'The Lion's Mane' (*Case-Book*) the villa is said to be 'situated upon the southern slope of the Downs, commanding a great view of the Channel'.

I had given a promise: in 'The Naval Treaty' (*Memoirs*).

one Tuesday morning in autumn: this appears in the MS as 'one Autumn morning'. The autumn date conflicts with the July date given in 'The Yellow Face' (*Memoirs*), as do all the details, leaving readers to conclude that it was one of three separate adventures of the 'Second Stain'.

292 *the illustrious Lord Bellinger, twice Premier of Britain*: D. Martin Dakin (*Sherlock Holmes Commentary*, 1972, 203–4) suggests that the character was inspired by William Ewart Gladstone (1809–98) whom Sidney Paget used as a model for his illustrations. Gladstone was four times Premier of Britain (1868–74, 1880–5, 1886, 1892–4).

the Right Honourable Trelawney Hope, Secretary for European Affairs: originally 'the Honourable', and with interchangeable names, thus 'Mrs Hope Trelawney'. The first name recalls *Trelawney of the Wells* (the play by A. W. Pinero) and Squire Trelawney in *Treasure Island*.

a foreign potentate: perhaps Kaiser Wilhelm II (1859–1941), who ascended the German throne in 1888—in which case the European power interested in sowing discord between Great Britain and Germany would be France or Russia.

293 *Whitehall Terrace*: from Richmond Terrace, Whitehall, opposite Downing Street and the Foreign Office.

294 *Good God*: 'Good heavens' in *Strand*, *Collier's*, and later printings.

Holmes considered for some little time: the MS originally continued, 'Your discovery was made early, sir,' he remarked. | 'Yes, Mr Holmes, before I dressed.' | 'So I gathered from the fact that you have cut yourself twice in shaving.'

the envelope is a long, thin one . . . with a crouching lion: if it were from the German Kaiser the seal would have been a double-headed eagle, but the envelope could have been used to conceal the contents and the seal could have been that of the British Government. However, the story is explicitly a fiction within a fiction so identifiable detail is elided.

296 *a cipher telegram has been dispatched*: diplomatic messages were sent in a 'five figure' cipher based on a code dictionary in which all matters of importance were represented by numbers ('How Diplomatic Despatches are Telegraphed', *Tit-Bits*, 2 Apr. 1904).

the great Chancelleries of Europe: the offices of the chancellors (chief ministers representing a monarch or state), but specifically used of Germany where the office of chancellor was similar to that of the British prime minister.

297 *There are three*: originally 'half a dozen'.

298 *the British Treasury*: the administrative centre for the public revenues, with a building in Whitehall constructed in 1845 to the designs of Kent, Soane, and Barry.

Oberstein: an invented name, recalling 'Rothstein' in 'The Striped Chest' (*The Green Flag*, 1900), and Count Von Beilstein in William Le Queux's *The Great War of 1897* (serialized in 1893). The character is used again in 'The Bruce-Partington Plans' (*His Last Bow*) where the full name and address are given as Hugo Oberstein, 13 Caulfield Gardens, Kensington.

La Rothiere: also found in 'The Bruce-Partington Plans' where the full name and address are given as Louis La Rothiere, of Campden Mansions, Notting Hill. The name recalls La Roncière, who was tried in 1835 on a charge of writing anonymous letters and of wounding a young woman (a case which interested H. B. Irving, one of the early members of the Crimes Club, to which ACD was elected in 1904); and also 'La Rosière' (the Rose Queen), a French equivalent of the May Queen ('La Rosière', *Tit-Bits*, 8 Aug. 1903).

Eduardo Lucas: originally 'Edward Lucas'; from Edward (E. V.) Lucas (1868–1938), whose *Wisdom While You Wait* (with C. L. Graves, 1903) had included several humorous references to Sherlock Holmes, and whose book *Highways and Byways in Sussex* (Feb. 1904) may have commended the county as a suitable place for Holmes's retirement.

Godolphin Street: an invented name, from Sidney Godolphin, first Earl of Godolphin (1645–1712), the statesman who supported the Duke of Marlborough and shared his fall in 1710, or from places named after him, such as the Godolphin School in Hammersmith or Godolphin Avenue in Shepherd's Bush.

299 *the great tower of the Houses of Parliament*: the Victoria Tower, rather than the Clock Tower (containing the bell, 'Big Ben'); 'the Abbey' is Westminster Abbey.

Mitton: from Lady Geraldine Edith Mitton, the author of several volumes in Sir Walter Besant's series 'The Fascination of London' (including that on Hammersmith, Fulham, and Putney, 1903).

300 *the extreme West End*: MS 'west end'. The 'extreme West End' was Kensington and Notting Hill (as these are the addresses of Oberstein and La Rothiere given in 'The Bruce-Partington Plans').

the Duke of Belminster: 'Belminster' is a portmanteau word combining Belgrave and Westminster. The title 'Duke of Westminster' was bestowed on Hugh Lupus Grosvenor (1825–99) in 1874, and he was succeeded by his grandson Hugh Richard Arthur Grosvenor, who married Miss Cornwallis-West in 1901. Viscount Belgrave was one of the Duke's titles.

302 *Now, Watson, the fair sex is your department*: this famous line was added in the MS in place of a nondescript remark, 'Now, Watson, what's the meaning of that?' In *The Sign of the Four* Watson's experience of women was said by him to have extended 'over many nations and three separate continents'.

frou-frou: the rustling sound made by long dresses, and the title of a musical play by Henri Meilhac and Ludovic Halevy which opened at the Adelphi Theatre on 16 June 1903.

303 *a caste who do not lightly show emotion*: 'Her manners had not that repose | which stamps the caste of Vere de Vere' (Tennyson, 'Lady Clara Vere de Vere').

Margate: a seaside resort in Kent, where ACD spent several summer holidays.

while away: 'wile away' in *Strand*.

Wilful murder: premeditated murder; the phrase had been used as the title of the fifth Raffles story in *The Amateur Cracksman* by E. W. Hornung (1899).

304 *three mornings*: originally 'two mornings'; 'the third day' became 'the fourth', and 'the last two days' was altered to 'the last three'.

305 *Mme Henri Fournaye*: her first name appears in the MS as 'Cecile'. The name is a variant of 'Fourneau' used in 'The Last Adventure of the Brigadier' (*Adventures of Gerard*, 1903).

the Rue Austerlitz: a small street in the twelfth *arrondissement* of Paris, near the Gare de Lyon.

Creole: the descendant of a European or Black settler in the West Indies and Mauritius.

There is evidence . . . in Godolphin Street: this was added at the proof stage (and suggests that the *Daily Telegraph* reporter was in possession of evidence which was not known to the police or to Sherlock Holmes).

308 *a great deal must have soaked through*: originally, 'a great deal of blood must have soaked through'.

309 *the drugget*: originally 'carpet'; a drugget is an 'over-carpet or floor-cloth of coarse woollen stuff used for floor or table coverings' (*OED*).

310 *the Ivy Plant*: perhaps suggested by the Vine Tavern in the Mile End Road.

in Queer Street: 'in trouble'; a slang expression (often used of those who have incurred large debts).

Was answering an advertisement . . . number: originally 'Had done some typewriting for Mr Lucas, and that was why she took an interest in the crime'.

311 *accident*: 'incident' in *Strand*.

313 *For God's sake*: 'For Heaven's sake' (*Strand* and later printings).

I thank God: 'I am thankful' (*Strand* and later printings).

315 *He had some spy in the office who had told him of its existence*: added on typescript or at proof.

I remember: thus in *Strand* and American edns. 'I remembered' in later English edns., obviously erroneously.

316 *Good God*: 'Heavens' (*Strand* and later).

Ah, thank God!: 'Ah, thank Heaven' (*Strand* and later).

Jacobs: perhaps from the author W. W. Jacobs (1863–1943), whose work was appearing concurrently in the *Strand*.

317 *Letter from Lord Merrow . . . note from Lord Flowers*: Lord Merrow takes his name from a village near Guildford; Lord Flowers recalls Sir William Henry Flower, the Director of the Natural History Museum (who died in 1899), and Sir Charles Hardy may be an allusion to the admiral of that name (1716–80) who commanded the Channel Fleet.

good God!: thus in MS; 'good heavens!' in *Strand* and all other printings. The final scene in the morning-room shows some features suggesting inspiration from Oscar Wilde's *An Ideal Husband*, act IV.